The Lords of Midnight

The Lords of Midnight

Drew Wagar

Book one of the Midnight Chronicles

based upon the original Lords of Midnight
strategy game by Mike Singleton and the
remakes by Chris Wild

First Published 2018 by Fantastic Books Publishing

Cover design by Jurij Rogelj

ISBN (eBook): 978-1-912053-92-6
ISBN (paperback): 978-1-912053-91-9
ISBH (special edition) 978-1-912053-88-9

Thanks To:

As is typical with my books I have to give a vote of thanks to my immediate family, my lovely wife Anita, sons Mark and Joshua, and also to Abbey. They allow me the time to write these books around my day job and family life – I'm hugely grateful for the chance to write my stories. If they weren't as supportive as they are, these books would not exist.

To Chris Wild, the lore master and 'keeper of the reins' for the landscape of Midnight and beyond. Chris has been working with me on this book since the outset. He's the custodian of the rights pertaining to Midnight, on behalf of the Singleton family – and a great job he does of it too. To him falls the ultimate decision on the lore of the world. It's been a real pleasure to work with him on bringing this story to life. With his help, and through long discussions and reviews, we've striven to make this story contain the essence of the original game of Midnight, to capture in a story Mike Singleton's vision.

To Tom Fahy, without whose tweet this book would never have begun. From small seeds!

To Dave Hughes and John Hoggard, my fellow 'Drinklings', who are creative masters in their own domains. Their encouragement keeps me going when I hit the inevitable bumps in the road – and we had a few in 2017, there's no doubt about that.

To Dan Grubb, my irrepressible publisher, who just makes things happen, usually just in the nick of time, or sometimes just after it.

To Mae, my editor, who always weaves a magic spell over my work and turns it into something everyone thinks is really good. Her direct challenge over the rough drafts dramatically improves them.

All the folks on the Multi-User Midnight forum who welcomed me in when I said I was embarking on this epic quest. I hope I've done you proud in terms of bringing Midnight to life within a book.

To all the fans of the original game all those years ago in the early eighties. I fondly remember discussing strategies and tactics with my school friends in the dilapidated school yards of the era. This game, and others like it, injected some magic into otherwise rather humdrum, grey and overcast school days. I hope I've captured both a bit of nostalgia and written a story that will satisfy your older selves.

But most of all, to Mike Singleton. He created this wonderful ice-bound world within the tiny confines of the ZX Spectrum, peopled with characters that so many remember even to this day. I've trodden as lightly as I can in the snows of Midnight, hoping not to disturb anything, but to capture the essence of what he had in mind. I'd love to know what he would think of what I've done. I hope, as an English teacher, he would be pleased that a young boy of thirteen back in 1984 would have been inspired by his work to write a book about his creation some thirty years later.

Author's Note

Not long after finishing my original Elite Dangerous book 'Reclamation' I, perhaps unwisely, wrote a blog article entitled 'Why Elite is probably the only game I'll ever write a novel for' – or some such. In it I waxed lyrical about the frustrations inherent in writing in someone else's universe, game-world or landscape. I talked about how Elite was unique in that it wasn't 'just another game', but had an almost hermetically sealed and compelling universe that made 'good' books and stories possible, similar in many ways to Star Trek and Star Wars, universes with their own lore and background. I didn't, and still don't at this point, consider any other games worthy of such treatment.

Save one.

I was fortunate that I left myself a small get-out clause. I'd made a solitary exception in the case of one other game; the Lords of Midnight.

Back when I wrote that blog I had no idea that writing a Lords of Midnight story was possible, or even likely. I hadn't played the Lords of Midnight since I last fired up my ancient ZX Spectrum at some point during the early to mid 1990s, more out of curiosity to see if the old thing still worked. It did then, but I no longer have a television I can plug it in to. It now maintains a place of honour, on the wall of my study, alongside a defunct ZX Microdrive, atop a frame that holds the original cassettes (yes – cassettes!) of Elite and the Lords of Midnight.

But, other than Elite, it was the only other game from those days that really captured my imagination. There are many other brilliant ZX Spectrum games, of course, but these are the two, for me, that really count. Perhaps the secret was that both games required you to inject your imagination into them and take part in the story, in fact, they positively encouraged it.

I had fond memories of the Lords of Midnight. I played it for many hours in my teenage years, drawing maps on squared paper, keeping tallies of Lords of Free and Fey with a pencil, finally defeating the forces of darkness and claiming Ushgarak as my own.

The Lords of Midnight is just as deserving a mention as is Elite in the halls of 8-bit gaming fame. Some have suggested it is the best ever game produced for the ZX Spectrum (strictly speaking Elite was a 'port' with the original version coming out on the BBC Micro). The Lords of Midnight featured a novella, it featured novel programming techniques, it was written by a single individual and won many awards in its heyday. Whilst the premise can be considered a pastiche of Lord of the Rings, the game itself turned out to be far better than the contemporary incarnations of Tolkien's work when rendered into 8-bit glory.

The Lords of Midnight garnered a following, a community of players that fondly recalled the way it played, the story it told and the atmosphere it generated. We were fortunate that Mike Singleton was more than a computer programmer. As an English teacher he embodied the game with a sense of grandeur, maturity and significance. I distinctly remember looking up the word 'invigorated' in the dictionary at secondary school in order to find out what it meant. He could have just used the ubiquitous 'Health' or 'Stamina' and a percentage, but he didn't. That sort of thoughtfulness made a difference to the game, the fact that he took himself seriously oozes from every part of his creation.

The game gave you that sense that you were taking part in something that mattered. Failure hurt, great deeds were done, victories celebrated, defeats endured. Even today, people still play it, trying to determine new ways to win, or refine existing strategies.

There was even supposed to be an official novel, way back in the 1980s. For reasons told elsewhere it never happened, but, as a teenager, I recall being very disappointed that it wasn't going to appear. It seemed like it would be a wonderful story to tell and to read – I never thought it would fall to me to be the one to write it! Mike Singleton himself planned to undertake this, but time and events conspired against him.

The genesis of this particular book can be traced to twitter. A chance conversation in April 2016 led to me meet Chris Wild, who now carries the torch for Mike's works. Chris has been responsible for the recreation of both the Lords of Midnight and Doomdark's Revenge for modern computers, tablets and phones – look them up on the various appstores and enjoy the games anew. They are remarkable pieces of work that deserve more recognition. Chris has worked long and hard with me to refine what you are about to read.

We have expanded on the realm of Midnight, both in lore and in detail. Mike had determined some of this, but Chris and I have had to add some paint to the line drawn sketches that were all that were available for parts of the background. We're also conscious that this book is being written in 2018; it's not the 1980s anymore and the book has to stand up against some different literary and social standards, whilst staying as close as possible to the source material. Again, we have tried to be sympathetic in the modifications we've made.

Sadly Mike himself passed away in 2012. I was never fortunate enough to meet him in person, but I have spoken to some who knew him well. The overwhelming impression I get is of a storyteller. I think we would have had much in common. I don't know quite what he would have made of someone else writing up this story in his wonderful world of Midnight, but I trust he would have been glad it was someone who loved his games and wanted to do justice to them. I have tried to be sympathetic to both his game and his own style of writing as evidenced through the novellas he wrote which came with the original game.

So this squares a circle first begun in 1984. It seems that year was the start of many good things. I have approached this project as I did with my Elite book; grateful for the opportunity, conscious of the weight of expectation and hoping I have done it justice. Once again it is written "by a fan, for the fans."

Unlike the Lord of the Rings, an iconic tome which was turned into an 8-bit computer game with limited success in the 1980s, what I've attempted here is the reverse; to take a masterpiece of 1980s programming and turn it into a book, conscious of both the fans, the responsibility of doing justice to Mike Singleton's legacy, and keeping a wary eye (and a respectful distance) from Tolkien's almost overpowering presence in this genre.

Sequels? Yes, the possibility is there. I would hate for this to be the only story that gets told of Mike's wonderful landscape. Whether we get to hear the tales of Shareth, the Icemark and on into the Bloodmarch depends entirely on how this story is received by you and your fellow readers. I am hopeful it will be positive.

You know of the old songs. Night has fallen and the Foul are abroad. The bloody sword of battle is poised to bring death in the domain of Midnight.

Do you want dawn?

Drew Wagar (April, 2018)

Prologue

He stands on the Plains of Blood,
looking south east to the Forest of Thrall.

Cold roused him, numbness in his body replaced by cutting fingers of ice as consciousness returned. For long moments he lay gasping, trying in vain to recall where he was, or even who he was.

The battle.

Snatches of memory came back. Clashing swords, the cries of battle, the dull impacts of blunt weapons. But there was another sound still resonating in his mind, a chill sound that drowned all others.

Dread gripped him, his stomach crushing down inside as vague recall turned to vivid nightmare.

The shrieks. The screams.

His men, brave souls hardened through long practice in the brutal theatre of war, reduced to mindless fools by the terrible weapon of the Witchking.

Doomdark!

He could not form words upon his frost-bitten lips, but the name of that fell evil echoed in his mind nonetheless.

Ice-fear.

A tide that had washed across them as the battle raged, pushing reason aside and shattering their resolve. His men reduced to mindless fools, only for them to be struck down by the swords yet wielded by the Foul. Minds and bodies

1

frozen into shock even as they were brutally hewn by the Witchking's rampaging hordes.

So many men lost. Good men.

Snow was blustering around, the wind howling in his ears. A drift was building up, threatening to bury him where he had fallen. It would be easy to let the cold take him, perhaps it was already too late to escape its grasp. Within short hours he would be entombed in the whiteness, forgotten, just another traveller lost to the everlasting winter of Midnight.

Yet from somewhere within, a gritty determination burnt, yet to be subdued by adversity or injury.

I am Lord Luxor, I will not die unmarked by Free or Fey!

Gasping with the pain he staggered to his knees, using his notched and battered sword as a prop to hoist himself aloft. The wind buffeted him, snow swirling past making it impossible to see. Dim shapes flickered in his vision. He blinked eyes that were stiff with ice, half frozen shut.

The vague outlines of a tall, sombre and forbidding forest loomed ahead.

Thrall.

He staggered toward the trees. Cold and dark the forest would be, but it would afford some shelter from the storm. The forests were home to the Fey. Deep within Luxor knew there to be a village belonging to those strange folk. If he could reach it, there might yet be hope.

He trudged forward, wading through knee deep snow. A hundred yards of painful slog brought him to the forest eaves. Above him the huge branches hung, heavy with ice encrusted over hundreds of moons. He stepped within the wall of trees.

The depth of snowfall was less here, compacted upon a solid layer of ice, making the going easier. The wind faded as he moved deeper within the thickening foliage, fading swiftly to a gentle breeze as if the forest had some strange ability to resist the storm beyond its mere presence. Only an hour of the day remained and Luxor was utterly tired. He had to find some sort of shelter or he would not last the night.

And the Foul may yet be abroad …

He clutched at his side as pain speared his midriff; a wound from the battle. His mail was rent in many places and a sword strike had pierced him. In the warm comfort of a keep or the lofty halls of a citadel, with servants on hand to dress and tend him, the wound would have been of little consideration. Out here, alone and bereft of help, it might well be his undoing. His hand came away slick with blood.

Blood, the battle of Blood … the Plains of Blood. Always there is blood.

He stumbled, falling full length upon the frosted ground. A scattering of ersh, the powder-snow of the new moon, swirled around him, slowly settling in the now still air of the forest, coating his tattered cloak with the finest sparkles of light.

Lord Luxor, of the armies of the Free, who not two days ago stood proud and defiant against the forces of the Witchking, heeded it not.

Murmurs stirred his mind. Snatches of horror, crackles of ice. Amidst the screams and shrieks of his men a terrifying visage rose, dark and sinister. It was cowled, impenetrable, frozen and chill, yet there was malevolence there, deep and brooding. Hatred was piled on hatred that had fed upon itself for many more moons than the lives of men. Within the cowl were the faint outlines of a figure.

Ice white, shockingly devoid of any hint of colour, bleached by cold, evil and obsession. He had been one of the Wise once, but that was long ago. Now there was nothing but pure iniquity, as sharp-edged and brutal as the Frozen Wastes themselves.

The Witchking of Ushgarak.

Luxor recoiled, but the figure pursued him, reaching further into his dreams, defining his nightmares. Cruel laughter resounded about him, causing him to cower still further.

YOU CONSIDER YOU HAVE WON? YOU BELIEVE VICTORY WENT TO THE FREE? YOU HAVE DEFIED ME AND LIVED, THAT I GRANT YOU. I WILL REMEMBER YOU. IN THE FULLNESS OF TIME YOUR SHADE WILL BECOME A TROPHY THAT I WILL TORTURE FOR ALL ETERNITY!

A flare of brightness, a burst of heat; as if an unexpected but welcome sunrise had given a brief glimpse of the summer that legends told had once blessed the realm of Midnight.

Now a cry of anger, revulsion and, yes, there was fear! Fear of the warmth, fear of another power still strong enough to stand against him.

Luxor basked in it, a golden light spreading about him. Beams of welcome sunlight bathed him, warming his skin and easing his fractured thoughts.

Another face, wreathed in brightness, green eyes glowing with colours of a spring he had never seen, blonde hair that shone and sparkled. The cold was forgotten for long moments of bliss.

A Lord of the Free. One who has looked into the heart of winter and survived. He cannot be lost.

A woman's voice, soft and comforting. Luxor had not heard such a sound for many moons. It caressed his ears, relaxing his body. He was helpless, unwilling and unable to resist.

The light faded and his eyes focussed. A hand brushed his cheek and then moved to his forehead. Tenderness and peace salved the frantic fear and horror in his mind. Sanity returned and he looked into the eyes of a woman, crouched above him. She was dressed in forest garb; dark green, a golden broach holding a cloak around her.

4

'Fear not, Luxor, Lord of the Free. I shall tend thee.'

Luxor blinked, swallowing, trying to make his mouth form the words he wished to utter.

'My lady,' he managed to croak.

'I am Aleisha,' she replied, her voice enchanting him even as she spoke. 'And I am Fey. The Witchking's powers cannot touch you here.'

'Fey? But how …'

'Rest now.'

The words were spoken softly, but they echoed in his mind and his body was powerless to resist their impact. Consciousness fled like a mist burning away under a forgotten sun. Her fair face now the centrepiece of a dream more pleasant than any he could remember.

When next he woke, he was elsewhere, a place both warm and comfortable. He looked around him in surprise, seeing the inside of some dwelling, constructed of finely wrought wooden beams in a circular pattern, meeting above him in a series of arches. Before him, in the centre of the room, separated from the rest of the floor, was an iron brazier, in which a fire was burning. A thin, sweet-smelling smoke filled the room.

He was lying in a bower, suspended above the floor by a series of ropes, crafted in an ingenious and ornate manner.

There was another smell too, some kind of broth was bubbling in a pot above the fire, gently simmering.

He tried to sit up, only to find himself almost immobile. Bandages had been wrapped about his chest, legs and arms, his injuries bound tight. A faint moan escaped him.

A creak echoed from nearby, the sound of a chair being moved aside.

'So, you have woken.'

Her voice; the voice that had pierced the icy whiteness with a ray of golden sun.

Luxor looked up and saw her face, no longer wreathed in the vagueness of dreams, but now a pleasurable reality. She was truly fair to his eyes, causing him to catch his breath at her beauty. Blonde hair cascaded around a gentle face with full lips and green eyes. He had never seen such as her before.

'I …'

She smiled and reached out, the back of her hand against his forehead.

'Your strength returns, Lord Luxor of the Free.'

'My men?' Luxor croaked.

'Alas.' Her gaze lowered and she looked away for a moment. 'I found only you.'

'The Witchking …'

A frosty crackle came to his ears and he fancied a faint chill draught swept across him.

'Do not bring him to mind,' she admonished, her voice still soft. 'He cannot reach you here, unless you let him.'

'But I must …'

Her hand was now on his chest, pushing him down. He marvelled at her strength.

'You must do nothing,' she said. 'You have won your battle, such as it is. The Witchking has retreated back to the distant north.'

Luxor allowed himself to relax a little.

'Victory after all.'

She shook her head.

'Victory? No, not a victory, my Lord. A chance to draw breath, nothing more.'

'You say the Witchking will return?'

She nodded. 'As sharp and sudden as winter falls, thus will be his return. Short years from now.'

'Years?' Luxor let out a sigh. 'Years we can plan for.'

'It is little enough time in the reckoning of the Fey.'

She smiled at him, and he forgot his troubles in the radiance that shone from her face.

'Aleisha.'

He felt her hands on his, felt a warmth suffuse him, gently easing the aching weariness from his bones and sinews. She leant closer and he caught her scent, flower blossom, stirring in him feelings he had long put aside for the horrors of war. Softness, gentleness, kindness and gratitude.

And a growing desire.

He felt ashamed for a moment and thought to say something to excuse his errant thoughts.

He felt her finger on his lips, as if she already knew what had run through his mind.

'I have healed you, my Lord Luxor.' Her voice was sultry now. 'Of my powers, much you have shared. I have little time for the rituals my people insist upon. Some things simply are.'

Her breath was on his cheek now, warm and enticing.

'As I have healed you, so you have stirred me. We are as one, you and I.'

The kiss that followed banished all conscious thought.

The Fey are blessed, though some say they are cursed, with a count of years far beyond those ascribed to the people of the Free. How long Lord Luxor and the fair Aleisha remained within the bounds of the Forest of Thrall is not recorded, perhaps it is not even known.

Such a happy meeting must have a counterpoint in sadness, and theirs was no exception. Aleisha knew Luxor had his part to play in a destiny even greater than their love. The Witchking was not defeated, only delayed.

Thus so it was, for the sake of Midnight and all her peoples, that Aleisha put aside her own wants and desires.

She took back all memories of their happiness, wrapping them away in the manner of the Fey and with her heart full of a sadness she could never again reveal, took Luxor to the edge of the domain of Thrall, setting him on a course for his home near the Mountains of Morning.

There she watched him dwindle from sight without a backward glance, her heart broken and gladdened all at once.

Tears streaked her face as she lifted her gaze to the cold wintry sun.

'Go with my greatest blessing, Lord Luxor of the Free. Our love may never be known, yet from it, may spring a hope unlooked for.'

A song, bittersweet, came to her lips. An ancient song. A song of prophecy.

Luxor spurred his steed onwards, the forest eaves flashing past at a dizzying rate. The path twisted and turned before him. Glades came and went, the few flowers that had broken the frosts a faint smudge of colour on the edge of eyesight.

His quarry darted ahead, attempting in vain to elude him; a wild boar. They were plentiful enough in the Forest of Thimrath. With the ease of familiarity and long practice he clenched his thighs against his horse and raised his bow.

The arrow was set to fly when his horse veered aside, almost flinging him from the saddle.

Surprised and alarmed he wrestled the recalcitrant animal about.

'You have cost me my prey and my lunch!' he yelled in frustration. The boar would have gone to ground. He'd have to start all over again.

The horse whinnied and pawed at the ground with its hoof. Used to the ways of horsemanship, Luxor dismounted, patting the horse on the flanks to reassure it.

'Easy boy, easy. What has ailed you?'

He stepped forward along the path.

A faint scent wafted on the breeze. He sniffed, but the smell eluded him.

Sunlight blazed from behind the clouds for a moment, his gaze fell upon a small bundle placed aside the path. Cautiously he approached, drawing his sword and looking to the left and right, fearing an ambush from brigands or other ne'er-do-wells.

Yet there was nothing, not a sound. Even the birds in the trees had grown silent, as if watching events unfold.

The bundle wriggled. Luxor stepped close and prodded the fabrics aside with the tip of his sword.

Within lay a child, a babe, no more than a moon old. It cried with the chill of being exposed to the elements.

Luxor looked about him once more, seeking whoever it was who had abandoned the child, but there was nothing; no sound, no prints, no trace.

Gently, he picked the child up. Its eyes were clenched tight closed as it cried as only babes can, screeching its indignation. Luxor huddled it in his cloak and only then did it calm, snuggling into the warm of his body.

The eyes opened.

Luxor looked into a greenness that took his breath away. For a moment there was flash of gold, a sense of sadness and longing, but somehow infused with hope and joy. It felt as if he should know what it meant.

Then the scent wafted past again. It stirred strange feelings in him, a sense of something just out of reach, a memory of a memory.

Flower blossom!

He had smelt its sweet fragrance before, but never like this. Sunlight flickered around him, almost as if caressing both man and child; a moment of calm and peace amidst the constant demands of Lordship.

But he was alone with the child. There was no one else. The moment passed. The birds sang once more.

Luxor returned to his horse, carefully mounting so as not to disturb the child now asleep in his arms.

'Something tells me this was no chance meeting,' he muttered.

The child stirred and gurgled happily. Luxor looked around as the sunlight faded behind the clouds.

'I shall name you Morkin,' he said to himself. 'It means one unlooked for in the old tongue, or so I recall from my schooling.'

He turned the horse and settled it into a gentle trot, heading for home.

Tears glistened on her cheeks and she stepped forward, her arm outstretched. A gloved hand caught it and gently, but firmly, pulled it back.

'I hate this …' Aleisha whispered.

'It is what it must be,' her companion answered. 'We have done all we can do for the child, for now at least.'

Aleisha turned to look at him. His face was young and fresh, though that meant little to the Fey, all were blessed with such features. Yet there was an age to his eyes, a wisdom that spoke of many moons.

'What will become of him, Corleth?'

Corleth sighed.

'The old songs say that one will be born, half-Fey, half-human, whom the ice-fear cannot touch. Armoured with the laughter and lightness of the Fey and the wild fire of the Free, the ice-fear will roll from him like drops of rain in a summer shower. Perhaps …'

'I would not have him touched by that fell magic,' Aleisha said shaking her head.

'What we wish is rarely what transpires,' Corleth answered. 'Yet, be at peace for now. The boy has a father who will nurture him. In just a short march of moons he will be grown.'

'Without a mother's love …'

Corleth had no answer for her grief.

'Morkin,' Aleisha whispered, amidst fresh tears, 'Morkin. He named him Morkin.'

Chapter One

He stands in the Village of Kor,
looking north to the Forest of Kor.

Dawn broke, overcast and gloomy, above the eaves of the Forest of Kor. The ancient trees stood stark in the faint light, dark and still, coated in many moons of ice and ersh. They were a miracle unremarked by many, yet so essential to life.

A faint mist hung amongst the branches, damp and chilling. The silence was only punctuated by the cry of an occasional eagle, circling high above. Many creatures made the forests of Midnight their home; shelter from the elements, hiding from hunters; knowing they would not be pursued.

Men skirted them, sensing a greater presence within, perhaps taking a fallen tree when they could. Children might scamper inwards as a dare, but would quickly retreat, retracing their steps, intimidated by the silence and the overwhelming majesty of the trees. Others might tell stories of being hit by a branch that swung out unexpectedly, or roots that tripped and coiled about their feet.

The forests did not receive those who did not belong, they were home to others. A people who kept themselves separate and did not welcome visitors.

The Fey ...

Where they came from, the stories did not tell. In all the lives of men that had been recorded, the Fey were always there. Peace loving forest dwellers, yet fierce warriors, they were a mystery to be recounted over fireside talks late in the evening. Old men would recount tales of the past, embellishing their details as they saw fit, but few had seen a living Fey in many moons. Where they were encountered conversations were brief and fleeting, though even now they might be seen occasionally, particularly when the Roads of Light sparkled in the heavens and the Moonstar shone brightly in the midnight sky.

The sky grew brighter, the sun feebly trying to burn through the enveloping greyness. Light spilled to the north, across the desolate Plains of Kor. The legends told that the forest had once stretched across this domain, that the trees had extended all the way to the north east, providing a greenway to the Forest of Dreams, the greatest of all the northern forests of Midnight. Today it was a blasted ruin, scarred and arid, a scorched and empty land that rolled, unrelenting, northwards for league upon league, until it rose up into the twin mountain ranges of Ugrak and Ugrorn, wreathed in clouds that never faded even under the strongest sun.

None went that way, for there lay the heart of winter. The mountains formed an impregnable barrier, the very weather became a fearsome enemy. The Free and the Fey had only a single word for that land.

Despair.

Bearing down across the plains and flanked by the brooding mountains lay the Citadel of Kor, gateway to the lands beyond. The bright snow that coated its exterior did little to conceal the darkness within. The few travellers who crossed the plains did not come close to its sheer walls. By day it seemed still and desolate, yet by night strange glows could sometimes be seen. Some remarked that they were the fires of unearthly forges, others that fell magic was afoot. None dared to find out more.

The entrance rose dozens of feet above the plains. An arch

of stone submerged under centuries of accumulated ice. A portcullis could be seen, likewise frozen in time for years uncounted. About its base, snow lay several feet thick, smooth and undisturbed, sculpted into ornate drifts by the wind. High above, crenelated terraces rose into the swirling clouds, austere against the gloom.

All was still, as it had been for a generation. Nothing moved.

A crack and a heavy groan split the air. Snow shivered, cascading down in gentle streams.

Frosted icicles fell from the arch, splintering and shattering before falling to be buried in the snow below. Now there was a rending sound, as if some heavy machinery, long since unused, was being called back into action against its will.

Ice cracked and sheered, huge sheets and fragments breaking and falling away. The arch was revealed, and the portcullis trembled and began to rise, more ice cracking to reveal ancient iron work.

With an echoing rumble the portcullis rose up, the archway now an entrance to a darkened corridor that led within. There was no light, the darkness complete within a few feet of the threshold. The portcullis shuddered to a halt, only the vicious downward pointing blades of its base now visible, lodged dozens of feet above.

The echoes reverberated around the mountainsides and then faded away. Silence reigned once more.

Then came a breeze, gently sifting the snow drifts that barred the way. Within moments it had risen to a gale, and then a storm, funnelled down from the heights and channelled purposefully to its master's will. The drifts eroded before it, helpless to resist the onslaught. Snow exploded outwards revealing a wide stone-hewn walkway before the entrance. The gale ceased, if as by some unspoken command.

The way to the south was open.

Deep in the Forest of Kor, lights twinkled in the darkness. Fires flickered, both on the ground and in amongst the huge eaves of the trees. In the gloom a complex network of paths and structures could be made out, some hewn from the trees themselves, others blending in amongst them with elegance and sympathy. Faint traceries of smoke rose, spiralling upwards in the chill air. From one such residence voices could be made out, light and carefree.

'It matters not,' said a young Fey, tall and lean. Daerinel was garbed in the bright clothing favoured by the youth of the day. Bold colours; yellows, cyans and magentas, the colours of flowers from a summer few now recalled outside of song and story. 'They would never dare venture into the forests. Our enchantments are deep and the trees care not for the ice-fear.'

'None have heard of the Witchking in over two hundred moons,' said another. 'Perhaps he is no more, finally frozen into oblivion by his own witchcraft.'

That brought a chuckle. A number of young Fey were gathered around a fire that burnt in a brazier in the middle of their room. Over the fire hung a cauldron in which something gently simmered, filling the room with a pleasant aroma.

The room itself served as a hall of sorts, a meeting place for the community. The Fey of Kor were few in number, distant cousins of those to the east in the Forest of Dreams, but eschewing their kindred's faith in stone buildings, preferring to live closer to the trees that both protected and nurtured them.

Today the hall was quiet, but short days from now it would be filled with a throng of people, gathered to mark the height of the Winter Solstice; the dark day. The Fey would gather in solemn reflection, remembering the heart of the winter, and resisting it by lighting fires, candles and torches in a symbolic gesture of defiance. It was a tradition that had its origins in the distant past, ten thousand moons ago or more, a time that few even of the Fey remembered.

'He cannot be so fierce a foe as the stories tell, if mere men were able to put him to flight,' said a third. 'Those so called Lords of the southern lands, with their politics and quarrels. It is said they paid fealty to him in the beginning, called him King.'

'Men are easily led,' Daerinel said. He was a little older than his companions. 'The Witchking promised power; such things will sway their minds with ease. They are a treacherous kind. We are wise to have nothing to do with them.'

The second Fey nodded. Channareth threw a log on to the fire, prompting a crackle of sparks. She watched as the embers grew brighter. 'The battles of Midnight were always those of men. Even the Wise despaired of their arrogance and fool-ishness.'

'The Wise tasked us to watch …' said the third. He was a thinner fellow, with a nervous worried look. Henneth was his name.

Daerinel scoffed. 'The Wise? They holed themselves up in their towers and left Midnight to … him. We have watched for many moons …'

'And we will continue to watch.' Another voice, deep and sonorous broke into their conversation. A figure vaulted into the hall, moving in close to the fire to enjoy the warmth. He was dressed in more subdued colours, deep greens and blues, colours more in keeping with the traditions of the Fey; stealth and a kindred with the winter hues of the forest. A belt was buckled at his waist, and a slim sword fastened there without a scabbard, its metal bright in the flickering firelight.

'My Lord …'

The three young Fey prostrated themselves before the newcomer, but he gestured for them to rise.

'None of that,' he said. 'A warming brew will do far more for me than idle homage. It is cold out there.'

One quickly grabbed a wooden goblet and filled it with broth from the cauldron. The newcomer took it and quaffed it, wiping the back of his hand across his mouth.

'Watching is all we Fey ever do,' he said, looking at them in turn.

'My Lord …?' Channareth asked.

'Just Korinel!' he snapped.

The three young Fey flinched and exchanged a look between themselves. Korinel stepped towards them, the light of the fire casting his visage into sharp relief. His face was aged, but not by many moons; here were the lines of worry and fear, etched on a face that should not have suffered such things. A scar ran the length of one cheek and one eye was half closed.

'Ah … you're too young to remember, none of you were born in those days,' he said. 'The days when the Fey had some honour and did not hide away from the affairs of the lands.'

'We have cut ourselves off from the horrors of the world,' Daerinel began. 'Horrors wrought by men …'

Korinel sneered and shook his head, looking away for a moment before taking another generous gulp from the goblet he held.

'We hide like craven cowards,' he said, looking past the walls of the hall to something they couldn't see. 'We hope that the world will somehow change about us, back to the fair dreams we recall only in empty songs of yestermoon. Fools we have become.'

'Winter will not last forever,' Channareth countered. 'If we're patient, we can outlast it. This is wisdom, not folly …'

Korinel turned upon her. 'No, young one. Winter will not wane. There will be no spring, no summer like those of legend.

Nothing will change unless change is wrought by those who have the power to do so.' He turned away, shaking his head sadly. 'We were that people once. Now only men have wildfire in their hearts.'

'Men?' Channareth exclaimed.

'Yes, men! The people of the Free,' Korinel replied. 'Their days might seem like ersh in the sun to us, but how they live! Every swiftly passing day a gift. I fought alongside them despite the ice-fear of the Witchking, there was true nobility and virtue there. Stood firm they did, against a darkness they could not fully comprehend, but still they fought. We could have ended it there, but we turned away.'

The three youngsters looked at each other.

'Oh, they don't sing songs of that, do they?' Korinel said, turning back to them. 'Not the Fey's finest hour. Near two hundred moons ago, the Witchking was vanquished, his power disrupted. A combined army of the Fey and the Lords of the Free had driven him back across the Plains of Blood. He was weakened, his army shattered. We had suffered sorely, that much is sure, but men had borne the brunt of the attack. Many lost their minds in the crippling onslaught of the ice-fear.'

'We fought alongside men?' Daerinel asked.

'Bravely for the most part,' Korinel said with a nod. 'They knew the battle was yet to be won, they mustered what few armies remained to them, intending to pursue the Witchking and rend his land asunder. They called on us for aid, a final blow to end this curse once and for all. Did we ride with them? Did we venture forth?'

Korinel stopped and drank the last of the broth in the goblet he held.

'No,' he said. 'We did not. We claimed we had done our part; we listened to those we considered wise and faded back into our forest homes, leaving men with a hollow victory, cold and empty. Now our peoples are estranged. We heed them not and they seek us no longer. That is the received wisdom of our leader.'

Korinel tossed the goblet aside. It rolled noisily upon the wooden planks of the hall, spinning in a circle before coming to a halt.

'It will be our undoing.'

The eyesight of the Fey was keen and sharp, but not all seeing. The sun rose higher, but a mist covered the plains to the north, cold and chill. Lake Moon was hidden from sight and even the nearby keeps were hard to make out, their outlines vague and distorted.

The duty guards shifted uncomfortably in their saddles, their horses shuffling their hooves in agitation.

The mist floated amidst the trees, wraith-like, long sinuous strands of moisture sapping the warmth of anything they touched. The guards watched as the mists flowed around the trees. Ice crystalized on the exposed leaves and branches, hoarfrost and icicles growing on them before their eyes as if locking the trees into some ethereal prison, binding them in chains of ice.

'I do not like this,' one muttered. 'I have not seen such mist before. It travels swiftly and not with the wind.'

The other guard nodded, turning his horse about and trotting it forward a pace. 'I have. This is the fell crafts of the Witchking. They say these mists once wrapped themselves about the lands and held fast, locking us all away.'

'The Frozen Wastes …?'

The second guard nodded, but didn't reply. He gazed into the thickening mists for a long moment.

'We should retreat within our boundaries,' he said, after a

moment's consideration. 'The enchantments of the forest should be protection enough from such as this.'

A keening sound echoed out of the mist. It was a lonely call, like the long drawn out howl of a wolf, but far lower. It sent a chill down the spines of the guards.

'What was that?' the first guard asked.

The second guard raised a hand, signalling for silence. Both strained their ears, listening for sounds in the thickening haze. The first guard moved his horse alongside the other, both stood on the boundary of the forest looking north into the mist.

As he did so the arrows struck.

The first guard stared in horror. His comrade fell from his steed with a ghastly gurgle, an arrow through his neck, a spray of red patterning the snow; blood splashed back into the guard's face. His horse reared, almost knocking him from the saddle. Horsemanship and instinct took over. He yanked the horse around and set it back, as it whinnied in fear.

More arrows. Two found their mark. Pain erupted across his chest and shoulder, the blow throwing him backwards to fall upon the snow. He could see the feathered flights; black and roughly hewn in a bloodied haze of vision.

Heavy footsteps, the coarse bark of commands.

A sword being unsheathed.

He drew a shuddering breath, agony burning up his chest. He tried to cry out, but no words came.

A helmet, dark; black against the sky. A cruel chuckle.

More blood.

The faint sound of horns blowing reached the hall. The youngsters did not recognise it, but Korinel turned on his heel, his hand going to the pommel of his sword.

'What does it mean?' one called.

Korinel didn't answer. He strode to the entrance, stepped through and looked out. A narrow ledge framed the outside of the hall, suspended far above the ground and wrapping itself around the huge trunks of the trees.

Below, fires burnt around the perimeter of the village, their flames softened by the strange mist that was blowing through the forest. It was cold, but something other than the coolness of the air was chilling him.

The horns blew again. This time their timbre was unmistakeable. A twin call.

Battle horns!

Korinel raced to the wooden staircases and vaulted down. By the time he reached the ground he could smell smoke upon the air. Flickers of light could be seen from the north. The villagers were awake now, gathering in numbers in the courtyards and streets around him. Cries of fear and worry, punctuated by muted conversation, rose about him. Children cried and parents swarmed around, trying to give them solace. Other warriors quickly assembled. They drew swords and stepped forward, forming a phalanx in front of the frightened village folk. Korinel signalled for silence.

'Remain in the village,' he shouted. 'Doubtless some war band has determined to cause us grief this morn. We will deal with them swiftly. '

Partially reassured the villagers backed away, gathering in groups to watch the departing warriors. Korinel drew his own horn and blew a loud blast upon it.

He marched north, a hundred and twenty five Fey warriors at his side.

To have sounded the horns ... this can be no idle brigands or overzealous caravan of traders. And why haven't the enchantments of the forest prevented them?

Others swiftly joined him, summoned by the call of the horns. The Fey warriors were stationed throughout the Forest of Kor, in detachments like Korinel's, one for each point of the compass. Horses were impracticable in the deeper stretches so the warriors went on foot, lithe and spritely in their familiar surroundings. All were under orders to respond to the call of the horns wherever they might sound. Their meaning was clear. A double blow ...

An attack. But by whom?

Korinel saw his commanders run towards him; he counted only six.

'Where is Kassimer?' he demanded.

The Fey shook their heads and looked north. Firelight was flickering between the trees ahead.

'Assemble,' Korinel called. 'We march now. Be wary.'

The Fey pushed northwards through the trees, drawing up around the familiar clearing where the most northerly detachment of their guard would be stationed. Fires could be seen burning from the ground and in the trees, smoke obscured the view ...

Bodies lay strewn about the clearing.

He could see their Fey companions, their bodies broken and dismembered, lying still on the ground. Slaughtered, disfigured, dishonoured. Some lay hewn by axes and swords, others pierced by many arrows, some even suspended above the ground, strung up by blackened ropes. Many were beheaded, and as the gaze of the warriors at the edge of the clearing rose to take in the horrific view they could see faces they recognised; heads impaled on spears set in the ground, their expressions frozen in agony, flames leaping behind them.

The northern guard ... destroyed. Utterly destroyed.

Gasps of dismay rose about Korinel. Mist swirled, somehow unaffected by the flames and smoke.

The forest ...

Korinel was wise enough to study the dreadful tableaux with enough detachment to see the subtle strangeness of the scene. The trees around the clearing were coated with ice, traceries of frost lay heavy on their branches.

Every root and branch ... frozen! The enchantments are defeated ...

Some of the Fey made to move down into the clearing, but Korinel signalled for them to stay. Nothing moved save the flames. The bodies were still.

'Who would do such a thing?' someone whispered. 'Who could do such a thing ...?'

'Silence!' he called, raising a hand. 'Form ranks! Archers to the front, swords and shields to the flanks!'

A moment's hesitation, but the well-ordered warriors were true to their training, adopting a defensive line. Bows were readied in practiced unison, swords drawn and held ready. The ornate shields of the Fey, marked with the ancient heraldic crest of Korinel, came together in ordered sequence.

A red eagle against a pale sky ...

The mist swirled about them, moving like a live thing amidst the ranks of warriors. Korinel heard the groans and cries as his own heart hammered suddenly in his chest. Sweat chilled on his skin and his sword arm trembled involuntarily.

Ice-fear! No, it cannot be!

Memories of a time long before; another battle far from here. Soot black helmets, soot black swords. The Doomguard, backed by the fell power of the Witchking himself.

But they wouldn't dare enter the forest ... and yet ... What evil does this foretell? We must get word to our cousins ...

'Hold fast!' he cried. A few of the warriors panicked and floundered, but were held and reassured by the stoic courage of their companions.

None have felt that foul taint since ...

Sounds reached them, swords being slowly pulled from scabbards, the screech of metal echoing in unison from all about the forest.

Korinel saw them. It was the eyes he remembered, somehow visible within the blackened helmets they wore. The darkness of their armour was featureless, impenetrable, as if it were wrought from the very depths of night itself, absorbing all light without reflection. They were silhouettes against the flames and the faint light of morning, dozens deep, further than the eye could see.

His jaw dropped open even as his hand went to his sword. 'They've surrounded us! Thousands ...'

Too late. The Witchking must have known we would try to warn the southern Fey, that we might disobey the directive of Lord Dreams. Now the Witchking's perfidy will go unnoticed until he falls upon the southlands unopposed and unexpected ...

Then they advanced. Swords clashed. Screams rent the air.

The villagers trembled as the sounds of battle and screams of the fallen echoed back through the forest. Yet the sounds of battle did not last long. The yells of terror and the clash of weapons faded. Somehow that made the cries of fear from amongst those remaining all the more grim.

Mist wafted through the trees, chill and cold, wrapping itself about folks as they cowered before it. Frosty gusts of wind blustered this way and that, the mist almost solidifying above them. Clouds of vapour swirled about the fires lit around the leafy courtyards and they were smothered, hissing out in moments and plunging the villagers into a darkening gloom. Clouds thickened overhead, cutting off the feeble sunlight. Ice formed about them impossibly quickly, icicles growing before their eyes, a frost carpeting the ground with a faint crackle. The air grew chill and silence fell.

Then came the thump of booted feet, faint at first, but growing swiftly louder. Yet still nothing could be seen.

Daerinel and his companions slowly edged back from the borders of the forest before them, the villagers beside them following their example.

With shocking abruptness strangers emerged from the forest. Tall figures, easily six feet in height, shod in heavy inky black armour. Their shields were a deep crimson, the colour of blood. Their swords were also black, but stained too … with red.

Why have they attacked us? And how?

'The Doomguard …' Channareth gasped. 'Where is Korinel?'

Screams shattered the silence, and folk belatedly tried to run.

The newcomers marched on relentlessly, their pace swift and sure. Swords rose and fell, cutting down any who strayed into the arcs of swinging merciless black metal. Daerinel and Channareth, were swept back by a panicked throng of villagers and then turned to flee themselves.

'The trees!'

They could see some of the villagers climbing the walkways and ladders instinctively fleeing upwards into the only homes they had ever known. Daerinel watched in horror as the dark warriors brought crossbows to bear.

'No …'

Tensioned whipcords released their fury. Folk yelled and fell, cut down as they tried to flee. Torches were set to the wooden buildings on the ground and flames quickly leapt up, consuming everything before them. Arrows parted the smoke, striking down still more hapless villagers.

Daerinel saw some fall prostrate upon their knees before the advancing warriors, begging for mercy. Their heads were hewn from their bodies even as they cried out their surrender.

Channareth was ahead of him, running down the forest track to the south which would ultimately lead out of the forest. The land rose here, the forest covering the foothills of the Gorgrath.

About them a few other villagers were maintaining their pace, running as fast as they could. Others fell behind, and their howls of pain, abruptly cut off, signalled their end.

Channareth was gasping, her breath a cloud of vapour rising up about her. She paused, leaning against one of the huge trunks of the forest. Ice was growing swiftly up it, she pulled her hand away as the ice flowed around the bark of the tree. She stared at it, uncomprehending.

'We cannot stop!' Daerinel said, reaching her. As if to counterpoint his words, arrows whistled past nearby. Another villager fell.

'We must get word to our cousins. To Dreams and Whispers.'

She nodded.

'Strike to the south east, from there we can cut across to the downs and ...'

More arrows.

She paused, a puzzled expression coming across her face. Her gaze found his. She choked, blood pooling in her mouth. She reached out, grabbing his arms as her legs went out from under her. Daerinel watched in horror as her body slid to one side to lie still on the soft snow of the forest floor.

'Channareth...'

He turned. A shadowy figure, a dark sword raised and swinging.

Ice. Blackness.

Few travellers came this far west and none could see it from outside the boundaries of the forest. A product of a time long forgotten and raised by stone-smiths with arts that hadn't been practised for many times the lives of men, it reached higher than even the enormous trees that served as its protection.

Many such structures had been built across the land. Their origins were a mystery to the people of the Free; they were ancient landmarks that most ignored. None could approach them, they were protected by arcane devices, gates with mechanisms that defied understanding, or vegetation that seemed possessed of its own mind. Strong winds might rise up around any who dared to pass too close, forcing them back with the faintest whisper of an angry voice amongst the gale. It was clear that trespassers were not welcome.

The Towers of the Wise.

Long ago, so the stories went in the taverns and inns of the Free, there was a third race. Older and more mysterious, they existed before both Free and Fey, before the Witchking himself, before the onset of the winter. Stories told that they were tasked with the guardianship of Midnight itself, but somehow they had grown weary of their charge and retreated, building their startling edifices and hiding themselves away. No-one knew why they had retreated, no-one knew why they had forsaken the land. The Witchking grew in power unopposed. It seemed the Wise did not care.

Most considered the towers abandoned, thinking that the Wise had perished long ago, leaving their towers as silent witness to a power that might have been turned to good but had been left to falter and wither away. The towers were dark and austere, derelict but not ruinous. Some power, or the vanished craft of their builders, kept them strong against the fiercest winds that might blow from the north. The towers stood across the land of Midnight, strong, indomitable, but utterly still and silent.

Yet, faint lights flickered from this tower, flickering across the forest far below.

CHAPTER ONE

The Forest of Shadows had earned its name from its aspect in the dim light of dawn, the outlines of trees dark on the snow, lengthened by the low angle of the sun. It was a lonely place, a forest that had once played host to far happier times, with the sounds of singing echoing through beautifully tended glades within. Now those glades were lost, overgrown and abandoned. No singing had been heard for a generation. Once a mighty citadel had stood amidst its proud trees, but it had been razed long ago. The Witchking's doing.

Travellers, en route from the Citadel of Gard bound for Shimeril, or traders following the ancient pathways across to the Keep of Blood, paid it little heed, marking it as a waypoint on their map. There was no need to venture into those trees, none lived there that had a choice.

And so, unknown to those who only looked in from its borders, the forest kept its secret. It ringed one of the ancient towers of Midnight.

The Tower of the Moon.

Light flickered again from windows that looked out high above the icy plains that surrounded it, casting a faint glow on the snow below. It was akin to candlelight, but brighter somehow and it slowly moved from window to window as if searching for something.

The light revealed the outline of what most would take to be a man of many years, hunched, leaning upon a staff. The highest room of the tower was an expansive platform, with windows that faced the eight directions of the compass framed by ornate archways wrought with runes and markings indecipherable to those not familiar with ancient writings. The floor was a mosaic of coloured tiles in earthy colours of red, brown and green, with a glorious crescent moon at the centre overlaid with an eye and an eagle.

The man stood at that focal point, his staff clutched in his right hand, a long pepper grey beard reaching almost to his waist. Surrounding him, arranged in a circle, were tables strewn with leather-bound books, scrolls, maps and diagrams. Beside these were notes, written in ornate flowing script, but haphazardly strewn around without obvious semblance of order.

A worried frown creased his forehead. His expression was puzzled, perhaps even alarmed. Fear and uncertainty flickered across his features.

'No. It is too soon.'

The man's voice was rough and coarse, as if unused for a long time.

He straightened, pushing on the staff to pull himself erect, looking east to where the sunlight was growing brighter over the forest. Its light cast shadows through the windows of the tower.

'Not yet two hundred moons, this Solstice? It is too soon! How can he be ready? Has he summoned armies out of the very snow?'

The man stood stock-still for a long moment, eyes closed, his thoughts elsewhere, as if probing the world about him.

His eyes snapped open in alarm.

'To march upon the Forest of Kor already. He seeks to prevent any news of his advance reaching the southlands. The Moonprince must be revealed, Midnight must be roused or all will fail ...'

With haste the man wrote and rolled up a scroll, sealing it with wax. He went to a door and hurried through it, striding up a stone staircase which led to the roof of the tower. A bolted trap door was flung back, allowing him upwards.

He was not fazed by the view, or the height at which he now stood. Wind, cold and sharp, whipped at his cloak, but he ignored it, raising his hands and emitting a strange eerie cry. He repeated it twice more and then stood still, as if listening.

For minutes nothing happened, but then something alerted him and he turned to the north, seeing a shape silhouetted against the sky. Before long the outstretched beating wings of a wyvern could see seen, drawing closer.

It back-flapped as it arrived at the tower, coming to rest before him, bowing its head.

The man drew the tightly bound scroll from his cloak and held it out before him, the wyvern took it in a clawed foot.

'Looking for Corleth the Fey? You must seek the Forest of Thrall!'

With an imperious gesture the man dismissed the reptilian creature. It squawked and dropped from the tower, winging its way to the east, gliding out over the forest.

It was soon lost to sight.

Chapter Two

He stands on the Plains of Rorath,
looking north west to the Keep of Odrark.

The hunting party was returning at a gentle canter, a herald in the lead with a banner fluttering in the morning breeze, a cyan moon and yellow star emblazoned upon a rich magenta backdrop. Behind him rode the Lord whose flag it was, with his entourage in tow and one smaller rider at his side. They were riding north west, the Forest of Thimrath arrayed behind them, with the distant Mountains of Corelay just visible beyond.

Ahead lay the Keep of Odrark, nestled within the Downs of Rorath, backed up against the mountains from which the keep took its name.

It was an old keep and nothing special amidst the greater keeps and citadels of Midnight. Odrark himself had been a minor Lord many years before, slain in battle against the Witchking a generation before in the battle of Blood. With his successors also falling at the battle and his army destroyed, the keep had been abandoned for years before once again being bequeathed to the young Lord Luxor as a mark of honour for his valour in the fight against the Witchking.

For his part Luxor had seen to repairs to the old fortress. He did not have the manpower to defend it in traditional fashion, yet the keep served as a focal point for his subjects and an administrative centre for the villages thereabouts.

Luxor whistled and the herald moved aside and came to a halt, his horse snorting in the cool air, hot breath rising as moisture about its head.

'My Lord?' the herald asked, riding swiftly to Luxor's side. His lord was occasionally short tempered and it would not do to irritate him.

'I see some commotion at my hall,' Luxor said. 'Can you make it out?'

The herald squinted across the bright white crispness of the plains.

'It is still more than a league, sire. Perhaps a little closer …'

'I can see!'

A younger voice came from Luxor's right side. A grin formed on Luxor's face as he turned to regard his young squire.

'Youthful eyes have the sharpness we need no doubt,' Luxor said, with a smile.

The young man trotted his horse, a feisty red-haired mare, alongside his Lord. Morkin had just come of age this last moon; now a man in the eyes of the people and squire to Lord Luxor. Luxor regarded him as he looked, his bright eyes searching out the detail that the older folks could not perceive. His long blonde hair, held in place with a braided band about his head, drifted in the breeze.

He has changed so much in the last few years. Gone is the little boy who chased pheasants in the yard and dreamed of slaying wyverns. Here is now a young man who wishes to make his mark upon the world …

'There are two banners, held aloft by heralds,' Morkin said. 'A company of men accompanies each, perhaps forty strong apiece.'

'Two banners?' Luxor mused. 'Some news then, can you make out their devices?'

'One bears a yellow crescent against red …' Morkin began.

'Lord Brith,' the herald said.

'And the other?'

Morkin adjusted his position in his saddle, straining to get a little more height.

'It is a white crescent against cyan,' Morkin finished, looking around proudly.

'Lord Rorath,' the herald added.

'You have keen eyes indeed, my young squire.' Luxor clapped Morkin on the shoulder. 'What brings my neighbours to my doorstep? Let us find out.'

With a signal, the small hunting company turned about and rode towards the keep, Luxor's banner held high and unfurled.

Luxor rode into the courtyard of the Keep of Odrark and leapt down from his horse, handing its reins to a nearby stablehand. She took it and Morkin's steed, leading the weary horses away.

A servant came to his side.

'Lords Brith and Rorath await your pleasure within, my Lord. They have news, but would discuss it with you in private.'

Luxor nodded and then turned to Morkin. 'See to the kitchens, make sure that boar is turned into a feast!'

'But ...'

'I will let you know what has transpired soon enough. It is likely some tedious administrative affair that would bore you to death. Patience!'

Morkin nodded. Luxor knew the boy would be full of questions later. One lord might visit another on occasion, but to have two at once marked something of import. Already the staff at the keep could be seen talking nervously as they watched the proceedings.

Luxor followed the servant, who hurried up to the heavy doorway to the keep. Luxor stepped within, blinking as his eyes adapted to the contrasting gloom within. His booted feet echoed on the tiled floor.

'The Lords await your pleasure in the great hall, my lord,' the servant said.

Luxor nodded as the servant bowed, opening the doors to the hall.

'Bring us wine and fruit.'

'Immediately, my lord.'

Luxor walked into the hall and heard the doors close behind him. It was sparsely decorated. Luxor's family had little in the way of ancestral trappings. Their history was poorly documented and their line only affirmed by the attestation of some of the other Lords. Rorath and Brith had been amongst those who had wished to see Luxor rewarded for his valour at the battle of Blood all those moons ago. Ratification of his Lordship had seemed a fitting means to that end to them, but the decision had been unpopular with some of the major lords of Midnight in their grand citadels.

For the folks of Odrark, long since bereft of a leader, it had been seen as a boon; Luxor might be short tempered and prone to the odd outburst, particularly if contradicted, but he usually settled down and listened to all sides of an argument once his anger cooled. He had their respect and their loyalty for his work in rebuilding the Keep of Odrark and bringing safety to the lands hereabout.

Lord Brith sat on the left side of the trestle table that ran the length of the hall. He was a thin and pasty looking man, often beset by ill-health. His face bore a thin beard which served to conceal the marks of a pox he had suffered in his youth. He was an uncertain ally, given to unpopular decisions and tolerated rather than liked by his people. His lands were towards the north west of Odrark.

Lord Rorath sat opposite him. A younger man, having taken over from his father who had been slain at the battle of

Blood. He was tall and fit – a practiced warrior, but with little to occupy his time other than the limited affairs of his small estate to the south.

Both rose as Luxor entered and bowed in acknowledgement. 'My Lord.'

Luxor bowed in response.

'My Lords. It is a pleasure unlooked for to see you,' Luxor began. 'But I had no knowledge of your visits. Had you sent messengers ahead I would have been here to greet you when you arrived.'

'We have ridden in some haste,' Rorath began. 'Our apologies for the lack of decorum, it is ...'

Brith interrupted. 'Gard sent me to you. Rorath also received the summons. We were to rendezvous at Odrark.'

Luxor saw Rorath frown, but then he shrugged.

'Lord Gard? How so?' he asked.

Lord Gard was an imposing figure. He was the most powerful Lord west of the Mountains of Corelay, one of four such lords of the southlands. Both Brith and Rorath were his lieges, as was Luxor himself. A host of others also were subservient to him. When Gard spoke, the west took heed.

Brith indicated a rolled parchment that was placed upon the table.

'Come.'

Brith unrolled the parchment and Luxor stepped up beside him. Rorath moved around to join them. Luxor could see it was a map, familiar in its detail; the lands of Midnight.

'Three days ago,' Brith began. 'Lord Gard received a message from Lord Blood. Tidings of woe.'

Brith pointed at a small keep marked just below and to the left of the centre of the map.

'A hunting party that ventured too close to the gap of Valethor failed to return,' Rorath added. 'Blood sent out scouts and found them slaughtered.'

'Slaughtered?'

'Not just slaughtered,' Brith said with a shudder. 'Dismembered, dishonoured in death. They also reported smoke rising from the Citadel of Gorgrath and forces mustering at the Keeps of Valethor.'

Luxor leant forward, placing his hands on the table.

'The Witchking?'

Brith shook his head. 'We do not know. It may be some remnants of the Doomguard making mischief.'

Luxor looked across at Rorath, who nodded.

'Lord Blood is not given to jumping at shadows,' Luxor said.

'Indeed not,' Rorath agreed.

'Lord Blood considers the matter serious enough to request aid,' Brith said. 'Lord Gard received the request and concurs. Even if it is a remnant of the Doomguard, Lord Gard believes it unwise to allow them to build up their strength unhindered.'

'Wise enough,' Luxor said. 'And with the Winter Solstice almost upon us …'

'Exactly,' Rorath said. 'Always this time brings fear to our people. It is the perfect time to make a tactical attack on our domains, to cause maximum disruption.'

'Lord Gard has thus summoned the Lords of the west to march to the Keep of Blood,' Brith said. 'There to make a show of strength visible to any who have the thought to proceed south of the gap of Valethor and, if necessary, march upon and defeat them. Lord Shimeril has also been requested to send his own forces.'

'Quite the assembly,' Luxor acknowledged. 'Such a mustering hasn't been seen since …'

'The war,' Rorath said and took a moment to look at the other two men. Luxor saw Brith shudder, he knew why.

The Ice-fear.

'We march north from my keep in two days,' Brith said. 'I have assembled five hundred riders and three hundred warriors from amongst my folk.'

'And you, my lord Rorath?' Luxor asked.

'Eight hundred and four hundred in the same manner.'

'With Gard, Shimeril and the others we should be not be far short of six thousand,' Luxor mused.

'Indeed,' Rorath said with a chuckle. 'Overkill of course, but none will resist a chance for battle after all these years!'

'Can you muster a force?' Brith asked. 'You are a veteran of wars past; would have you join us.'

'I would turn from no fight, my brothers,' Luxor acknowledged, 'but my people are not fighters. There can hardly be twenty men at arms here and I would need them to defend the keep from brigands.'

'Will you ride with us then?' Rorath asked. 'Lord Gard has instructed us to meet at the Keep of Blood two days after the Winter Solstice.'

Luxor looked at the map. To the west of his old keep lay the Mountains of Odrark. He would have to take the pass through the mountains and then across the valleys into Brith's lands. From there it would be a long march northwards across the dreary Downs of Mitharg until the rolling lands fell away on to the Plains of Blood, bordered on the west side by the mysterious Forest of Shadows.

I haven't been that way for almost two hundred moons, yet a warrior I am.

Luxor looked up.

'A break from the tedium of administration? Is winter everlasting? Yes, I will ride!'

Morkin had done as he was bid. The boar had been sent directly to the kitchens and the servants there were busily at work gutting and prepping it. Satisfied his duty had been done Morkin returned to the courtyard where the men that had accompanied the two Lords waited in two separate groups.

They were distinct. Rorath's men stood to attention in eight rows of five across. Their armour bright and polished, their weapons sheaved. All stood ramrod straight as if on parade, awaiting their Lord's return.

Brith's men were of a different sort, they were slumped down on the flagstones, or leaning carelessly against the walls of the keep, idly chatting amongst themselves. Their armour was tarnished by comparison, tatty and ill-maintained.

Morkin stepped slowly close hoping to overhear their conversation.

'… two days march south for this, no food or wine, and we'll be marching back again with little to show for our efforts. Mark my words.'

'Yeah … and for what? Who is this Luxor anyway? I heard he wasn't much of a Lord.'

Morkin gasped.

'Self-made, so I heard, a few deeds in the last battle, got himself in with the likes of Shimeril and Blood. Has a line so it's said, not that anyone's ever seen it.'

'Reckon he's just another knight, right place at the right time and took advantage of it.'

'Doubt he's even a knight. Coin talks, that's the rumour. Got a fierce temper when provoked too …'

That was too much for Morkin. He spun on his heel, drawing his sword swiftly from its scabbard.

'Dare you speak a word against my Lord!' he called, wishing his voice were deeper. The men looked up in surprise, appraised him for a moment and then laughed.

'And who are you?' one asked.

'I am Morkin, here to defend the honour of Lord Luxor of the Free,' Morkin said, baring his teeth in an attempt to looking grim and fearsome. His sword was now held out in front of him. The tip wavered as he tried to hold it steady.

That made the men laugh even more.

'I will not yield,' Morkin said, furious and blushing. 'Take back what you said about my Lord.'

The larger of the two men moved forward, his arm going to the pommel of his own sword.

'If you want a lesson in swordsmanship boy ...'

The man's sword was in his hand with a quickness that Morkin did not anticipate. The blade came down and he only just parried the blow. With a quick and subtle move Morkin found his own sword twisted from his grasp. It clattered noisily on the icy flagstones.

Morkin stumbled and fell backwards as the man pushed the tip of his own sword towards him.

Metal clashed. The man stepped back as a figure interposed itself between them. Morkin's view was obscured by a thick cloak of midnight blue that billowed out as the newcomer stepped before him.

'Who are you?' said the man who had disarmed him.

'Perhaps it is not too wise to treat Lord Luxor's squire so, especially within the confines of his own keep.'

The newcomer's voice was soft, yet confident and reassuring. It was well spoken too, with educated diction and noble bearing clear to hear.

'His squire?'

'Stand aside, or it will go ill for you.'

Morkin scrambled to get a better view. The two men were already backing away, heads bowed, stumbled words of apology coming from their lips.

The stranger turned, and Morkin caught a glimpse of a shirt of mail, finely wrought like a skin of silver, before the cloak covered it once more. The stranger's arm was out-stretched towards him, a hand proffered. Morkin took it and was firmly hauled to his feet.

'Men of war have short tempers,' the stranger said. 'It is best not to provoke them unnecessarily.'

Morkin picked up his sword and placed it back in its scab-bard. Then he bowed.

'My thanks,' he said.

The stranger acknowledged with a curt nod.

Morkin took a longer look at him. He was tall and thin, with an elegantly erect bearing. His head was covered by a cape, matching the dark blue of his cloak, which was tied by an ornate silver cord at his neck. His head was shadowed, but Morkin could see the faint outline of a surprisingly youthful looking face, lips turned in a half grin.

'I know of you, Morkin,' he said. 'We have met once before, not so far from here.'

Morkin blinked in surprise. 'How so? And what is your name?'

'Questions will have answers in time. My name is Corleth and I must speak urgently to your Lord.'

'He is in council with Lords Rorath and Brith,' Morkin answered.

Corleth nodded and gestured to the gates of the keep. 'They are finished it would seem.'

Morkin followed his gaze and saw that Rorath and Brith had emerged from the keep with Luxor. The two Lords strode across the courtyard, signalling to their men. It was clear they were making preparations to camp. Morkin could see Luxor watching them, his face looked thoughtful.

Bad news?

'Come,' Corleth said. 'You can introduce me.'

Morkin shrugged and walked towards the keep, bowing as he arrived.

'My Lord.'

Luxor turned to regard him. 'Morkin? I trust that feast is prepared ...'

Morkin saw Luxor look up at the figure who stood behind him, taking in the midnight blue cloak. He saw Luxor's eyes narrow.

'My Lord, may I present Corleth, of ...' Morkin belatedly realised he didn't know Corleth's rank or origin. He stammered and looked around.

'I believe Lord Luxor remembers me well enough, young squire,' Corleth said, softly.

Luxor nodded. 'Well enough. What is your business with me, Corleth of the Fey?'

Morkin gasped and stared at Corleth.

A Fey?

Yes, that explained the voice and the features of his face. A Fey! Morkin had met a few of them before, mostly on hunts in the Forest of Thimrath. Lord Thimrath himself was a Fey and presided over lands to the east of Odrark. But the conversations between Free and Fey were few and laced with tension. Even Morkin, despite his youth, could detect some strange aloofness to their dealings. To a rule the Fey kept themselves to themselves, only interacting when required to by duty or by manners. They typically stayed within the boundaries of their beloved woodland realms.

To see one here, at our keep ...

Luxor and Corleth eyed each other for long moments.

'I have a missive for you,' Corleth answered.

'From whom?'

Corleth gestured to the keep. 'Perhaps it would be wiser to discuss it in private,' Corleth said. 'It is a matter of some import.'

Luxor sighed. 'This seems to be a day of bad tidings ...'

Corleth smiled. 'Not bad perhaps, not yet at least. But tidings nonetheless.'

Luxor nodded. 'Morkin, I must ask you to leave us once more …'

'I beg your forgiveness, Lord Luxor,' Corleth said. 'But this concerns both of you. Man and boy.'

Morkin looked up at him in surprise.

Me? How can this Fey be concerned with me? And how does he know me?

Morkin saw Luxor's face cloud with anger.

'I would not bring him into this matter, Corleth.'

'It is not by my wish,' Corleth replied. 'I am only the messenger and this is not my missive. Will you hear me out?'

Morkin looked up at Luxor with a frown. Luxor sighed.

'My Lord?' Morkin asked.

'Join us for supper then,' Luxor said. 'Come within.'

Morkin could see his shoulders were slumped.

Luxor had signalled for wine and food to be brought in to the great hall. Morkin noted that Corleth's place was set with only fruit and vegetables, whilst he and Luxor enjoyed sliced cuts of meat fresh from the kitchen. Corleth had removed cloak and cape, and his mail now sparkled bright in the candlelit hall. It seemed to be light and of no burden to him. Luxor sat at the head of the table, with Morkin to his right side. Corleth sat opposite him. The meal was consumed in silence until the plates were cleaned away by the servants. Morkin saw Luxor dismiss them and the doors to the hall were closed.

Morkin decided to blurt out the question he'd been dying to ask.

'Will you introduce me, my Lord?' he asked. Luxor remained unmoving, so Morkin looked at Corleth. 'Who are you?'

Corleth turned his head to Luxor. Luxor gestured dismissively with his hand, indicating permission, but said nothing.

'I am Corleth of the Fey,' Corleth began. 'My home is in the Forest of Thrall, far to the north and east. I fought alongside your father in the last war against the Witchking, near two hundred moons ago.'

'The Witchking!' Morkin exclaimed. 'Tell me more! Did you slay the Doomguard, did you feel the …?'

'Ice-fear? Of course, it …'

'We do not talk of such things,' Luxor said, his voice a rumble. 'The war was long ago.'

Corleth stopped in mid-sentence and Morkin saw a smile directed his way.

'What brings you to my keep, Corleth?'

'Tidings, Lord Luxor. Tidings from the north and counsel unlooked for.'

'I see the Fey still couch their speech in riddles.'

Morkin looked around at Luxor, puzzled by his gruff speech.

Why is he so unpleasant? What happened all those years ago? Why does no one have a good word to speak of the Fey?

'I will be straightforward then,' Corleth replied, his voice hardening. 'It is no small matter that Lord Gard is calling for soldiers to patrol the Plains of Blood. War bands have been spotted in the gap of Valethor. These are no brigands or soldiers of fortune. There is activity amongst the keeps against the mountains, and from within the Citadel of Gorgrath rises the smoke from many fires.'

Luxor took a deep breath.

'The Doomguard?'

'If not them, who else?'

Luxor leant back. 'Your tidings are already old, Corleth of the Fey. I have heard this already from my own kin. We have been summoned to assist Lord Gard. We march within days. If a remnant of the Doomguard remains we will see it is despatched, there is no need for the Fey to be involved. You can dwell in the depths of your forests, unconcerned for the fates of others, while the Free work to keep Midnight safe.'

Morkin caught the hard-edged tone in Luxor's voice as he finished.

Corleth seemed unfazed.

'Lord Gard knows his duty, I am sure,' Corleth replied. 'But I bring a summons from one greater than he.'

Morkin saw Luxor frown and then his expression broke into a laugh.

'Greater than Lord Gard? The Lord of the entire western realm of Midnight? You must keep exalted company. Who is this great nobleman? Or perhaps it is the Witchking himself! Do you speak for him now? Am I summoned to Ushgarak to bow before him in his frozen desolation?'

Corleth reached inside his cloak and then withdrew something. It was a parchment, rolled into a scroll and finished with a wax seal. The writing on it was peculiar, written by a flowing ornate hand. Morkin stretched across to see it more clearly.

And in gold ink! How is that done?

Luxor eyed the scroll.

'And from whom is this sent?'

Morkin scrutinised the seal. It bore a device. Cyan, with an eagle upon it, wings outstretched. Morkin thought the eagle to be the mark of the Fey. Above it was another symbol though, an eye. It was not one he had seen before.

'An eye?' Morkin asked. 'What does this mean? Who bears such a ...'

'This is some trick,' Luxor said.

Corleth shook his head. 'It is no trick. As I said, I am only the messenger. I do not know what they want of you; only that they see fit to summon you.'

'Who?' Morkin demanded.

Luxor turned to him. 'The eye is an ancient mark, far older

than those of the Free or even the Fey. It is the mark of ... the Wise.'

The Wise! But they are myths, legends! Stories tell that they were once charged with the keeping of Midnight, but they did not foresee the coming of the Witchking. He defeated them and they retreated, hiding forever in their towers as winter took its hold ...

Morkin was dragged out of his reverie by Luxor's next words.

'From whom did you receive this?'

'I myself was summoned in a similar manner,' Corleth said. 'Though my scroll was delivered by a wyvern, tamed by some arcane means, straight to my hand as I walked within my homeland. How it found me I do not know. The instructions bade me journey to the Forest of Shadows and venture within. This I did.'

'Shadows ...' Luxor echoed.

'Those forests have long been impenetrable even to our folk, perhaps save the far north western borders where one of our cousins used to reside. There is a power there, stronger than the Fey. I was bade approach from the south east and the forest opened itself to me as I ventured within.'

Morkin exchanged a glance with Luxor, but neither interrupted the Fey as he continued his story.

'A path presented itself to me of its own accord,' Corleth said. 'I followed it and it closed up behind me. I saw ruins, ruins of a mighty fortress that histories do not record, buried deep within the trunks of that ancient realm. I passed on by and emerged within.'

'Within?'

'The Forest of Shadows encircles a valley,' Corleth said. 'Perhaps a dozen leagues on each side. At its centre stands a tower. The path led me onwards, to its very base.'

Morkin looked at Luxor, seeing his face had gone pale.

'You were truly summoned by the Wise?' Luxor said, his voice barely above a whisper. 'But none have heard from them in many lives of men.'

'It is a great length of time since we have spoken to them,' Corleth said, 'even in the reckoning of the Fey. Though 'spoke' is perhaps giving the description of my encounter rather more grandeur than it deserves.'

'Then what happened?'

'I stood at the base of the tower and knocked upon the door of its threshold. The door was unbolted from within. A scroll was thrust into my hand by an outstretched arm accompanied by words from an aged voice.'

Corleth paused. Luxor raised his eyebrows. Morkin was half out of his seat and leaning across the table.

'Looking for the Lord Luxor and his squire, Morkin? You must seek the Keep of Odrark.'

Morkin gasped and Luxor blinked in surprise.

Who is it of the Wise that knows my name?

'Was that it?' Luxor asked.

'The door was closed and bolted once more,' Corleth replied. 'I knocked upon it, but there was no further answer. The path behind me unfurled once again, it was clear what I was bid to do. And so, here I am.'

Corleth gestured to the scroll on the table.

'And that is the scroll.'

No one moved for a long moment. Morkin looked up at Luxor. Luxor slowly took the scroll up, turning it over in his hands and inspecting the seal. The device was clear; an eye and an eagle. The symbols of the Wise and the Fey.

'I'm surprised you have not opened it yourself.'

Morkin saw Corleth's jaw clench and release.

'I was sorely tempted, but I wager some enchantment lies upon the document to prevent anyone but the rightful recipient to read it. The Wise are not to be trifled with.'

Luxor picked up a knife and was about to work it under the seal. Before he could do so, and upon his touch, the scroll unrolled itself, opening in his hands. Morkin could just make out a wispy and flowing text upon it.

'What does it say?'

Luxor read the text aloud.

Lord Luxor,

I am writing to you in much haste for time is pressing, already great powers work against me. My name is Rorthron and I represent the Council of the Wise. I have sent this message via Corleth of the Fey. Trust him. In these matters the Free and the Fey must work as one.

Long ago the Wise were charged with the custodianship of Midnight, a task we failed in. The council would see that remedied.

I know of your valour on the Plains of Blood two hundred moons ago and I know of what you fight against. I have knowledge and tactics that will be invaluable in your defence of the southern lands.

I am aware you have been summoned by the Lord Gard to rendezvous at the Keep of Blood within the moon, I must insist on a change to your plans.

It is vital that you meet with me at the Tower of the Moon on the eve of the Winter Solstice. The timing is precise; you must arrive before sunset and before the moon rises on that eve. You must also bring your squire, Morkin, with you.

Our business will not take long, you will be able to keep your rendezvous with Lord Gard without further delay. Corleth will ride with you on the road. Tell no other living soul.

Do not delay, Lord Luxor. I look forward to greeting you in person.

As ever,

Rorthron.

Luxor leant back in his chair, pondering the words for a long moment.

'Can it truly be the Wise?' he asked. 'Taking an interest in the affairs of the Free and the Fey after so many moons?'

'Had you suggested this to me scant days ago I would not have believed it either,' Corleth replied. 'Much is new. This council for instance, I have never heard of it.'

'Yet, to have the aid of the Wise in a battle against the Witchking,' Luxor mused. 'We cannot afford to turn down such an offer. But why me? Why not summon Lord Gard himself? I am not the one this Council of the Wise should be treating with.'

'Rorthron seems quite particular,' Corleth said, a faint smile showing on his features.

'What is it you know, Corleth?'

Corleth shrugged. 'Why Rorthron should take an interest in you and your squire I know not. The Wise are older than the Fey and they keep their secrets close. Only on the rarest occasions have they been known to speak to our people and then, only in matters of greatest need or utmost import. All I can say is that there is much more to this than meets the eye. This council have their own reasons for this summons, be of no doubt about that whatsoever!'

'And why me?' Morkin asked.

'Why indeed,' Luxor said, looking over at Corleth. 'That this Rorthron even knows of Morkin alarms me.'

'There is only one way to find out,' Corleth said, getting to his feet. 'I suggest we set out upon the morrow. The Forest of Shadows is many leagues to the north.'

'We're actually going?' Morkin asked, his voice eager.

Luxor sighed, deep and long, but then nodded.

'Break out your travelling gear, young squire,' Luxor said. 'We will seek an answer to these riddles!'

Chapter Three

*He stands at the Keep of Odrark,
looking north west to the Mountains of Odrark.*

Morkin looked out from the top of the keep, looking south across the familiar Downs of Rorath, beyond lay the plains, and, just visible on the horizon, the Forest of Thimrath, half hidden in the pre-dawn mist. A chill wind blustered about him, and he withdrew to stand in the lee of one of the towers, turning about to face northwards, pulling his cloak close about him.

He was dressed in common garb, as were Luxor and Corleth. It was better to travel without an obvious display of rank and privilege, particularly if you didn't want people to note your passing.

Looking out past the crenulations of the keep, the pass through the Mountains of Odrark could just be seen. Beyond was a village in Brith's domain, Morkin knew it would be their destination for the close of the day.

Luxor had briefly spoken to Lords Rorath and Brith, advising them that he would rendezvous with them directly at the Keep of Blood rather than join them on the road. Morkin had sensed they had been rather confused by the change of plan, but had not asked questions with the mysterious Fey alongside.

'We will see you at Blood's table for meat and gravy then,' Brith said. 'Perhaps with a host of willing Fey at your beck and call.'

Brith gave a hollow and humourless laugh. Corleth did not respond.

The two lords rode away with their men, leaving Luxor to make final preparations for their journey north. Morkin could see the horses being made ready, saddled with provisions, camping gear and weapons. Luxor's steed was a pure white stallion, a magnificent beast, but somewhat wayward and headstrong. Morkin's horse was smaller, a red-haired animal reared, so he'd been told, by the Fey of Thimrath. Corleth's horse was somewhere between the two in size, but jet black.

It was time. He ran down the stone stairways to ground level.

Luxor bade goodbye to his retainers, with instructions to the men at arms to guard the keep in his absence.

'I expect a journey of perhaps a moon, no more.'

Corleth had already mounted his steed. Morkin mounted his own horse and trotted up alongside them both. He couldn't wait to start out. Luxor still seemed pensive; the summons seemed to weigh heavily upon him. Corleth remained unmoved, patiently waiting.

'Do not worry about us, my Lord,' came the response. 'All shall be as you left it.'

'I'll hold you to that,' Luxor replied and mounted his own horse. 'Farewell.'

The three trotted out of the gates and down the road that led around the perimeter of the keep. Luxor in the lead, Morkin next and Corleth bringing up the rear.

Through the pass of Odrark they travelled; a cold and lonely road in the midst of winter. Fortune seemed to be with them though, the pass had remained largely clear of snow and the weather remained fine as the day wore on. The world opened out around them as they climbed, affording a glorious view of the mountain peaks and deep valleys.

Few lived in these parts, the mountains of Midnight were prowled here and there by ice trolls who would make short work of the unwary if they were caught, but they saw no sign of them and their progress was unimpeded. They reached the top of the pass before mid-day, stopping for a rest and looking about them. Their home, the keep, could still be seen, now small with the distance, nestling protected in the arms of the mountains.

They did not tarry long, wise to the knowledge that the weather in the mountains could turn within minutes. By late afternoon they had left the mountains behind and turned northwards to the village Morkin remembered from previous trips, pleased to see its welcome light come into view by the close of the day.

They shared a meal and ale at a tavern in the village.

'From here we strike north,' Luxor said, producing a weather-stained map, that he unfurled on a rough wooden table, pointing at various landmarks. 'There are other villages on the route which will see us to the Downs of Mitharg. From there we strike north west until we reach the old Keep of the Moon. From there it is a day's ride to the southern edge of the Forest of Shadows.'

'I came by a similar route on my way to you,' Corleth agreed. 'It is a less travelled road, but safe enough.'

'The Keep of the Moon?' Morkin queried, 'To whom does that belong? There is no Lord Moon.'

Luxor glanced at Corleth.

'You know the history better than I,' he said, 'I care little for the stories of the past.'

'I will tell what little I know.' Corleth nodded and took a generous gulp from his ale. 'Long ago, many lives of men, there was a House of the Moon. Royalty of Midnight they were after a fashion. The stories tell that there was a grand citadel some-where within the borders of the Forest of Shadows. They were mighty indeed, possessed of magic which allowed them to defy the Witchking and order the ways of Free and Fey. It was said they possessed a ring that made this possible, a ring from which they took their name. The Moon Ring.'

'So what happened to them?' Morkin asked.

'They lost it,' Luxor said, with a grim chuckle.

'Lost it? How could they lose something so precious?'

'There was a Moonprince named Rarnor,' Corleth said. 'History has called him "the unlucky". The story goes that he tried to impress a maiden and she stole the ring from him, fleeing south beyond our lands, coming at last to the realm of the Bloodmarch before the way was lost to the ice of the Witchking.'

'And without the ring …'

'Treachery and complacency,' Corleth said with a sigh. 'The Witchking, unable to defeat the forces of Midnight by strength of arms resorted to cunning and guile. Rather than take on all of the Lords he waited until their power had ebbed and then struck at the House of the Moon in a single decisive blow. Without the power of the ring, the Citadel was razed and the House of the Moon destroyed. He con-quered most of the northlands and we have never been able to reclaim them.'

'If only someone could find the ring …'

'The ring is lost,' Luxor said. 'The Witchking himself may even have it, if it ever existed. Do not put your faith in fairy-tales of times long gone, my squire. Moonprinces! As if! Dreams of the idle. Ever since those times it is the Witchking who has controlled all the north of Midnight. He is real enough. All the wars since have been concerned only with keeping the southlands free. We contain the evil of the Witch-king in his own domain. That is our duty.'

'Today few have heard of the ring or the House of the Moon,' Corleth concluded. 'Though the Wise will know far more than I. Perhaps we might ask Rorthron when we arrive at his tower, he should have been there when they were destroyed, after all.'

Morkin blinked. 'Should have been there? What do you mean?'

Luxor chuckled. 'They say the Wise enjoy a length of days beyond even those of the Fey. Rorthron remains the resident of the Tower of the Moon. He would have been consulted by that House; he would have witnessed their fall.' His voice darkened. 'Perhaps he even had a part to play in it.'

'I would not speak ill of …' Corleth began.

'I do not trust the Wise,' Luxor interrupted. 'They have always been self-serving. I put my faith in sharp steel, courage and steadfastness in battle. Something neither the Fey nor the Wise understand.'

Corleth did not talk further, with that the conversation concluded and they took to their rooms in the tavern.

The weather continued to hold for their journey north. Two days saw them pass villages and draw closer to the Downs of Mitharg, a broad series of low hills that blocked their way further north. The group turned to the north west, following a well-used path. A few traders passed in the opposite direction and they acknowledged them with brief pleasantries. It was a common enough road, linking the central keeps with the Citadel of Gard further to the west. As the familiar mountains of home dropped into the southerly mist, another mountain range grew on their western side, sharp and tall. Its jagged and austere appearance in contrast to the ones Morkin was acclimatised too.

'The Mountains of Ishmalay,' Luxor said, seeing his squire squinting into the distance. 'They mark the eastern boundary of Lord Gard's homeland.'

The wind whistled about them, blowing down from the north. Corleth had brought his horse to a stop and was listening intently.

'Do you hear something?' Morkin asked.

'Wolves are abroad,' Corleth replied. 'Perhaps a league away. We should be cautious.'

'Two hours of the day remain,' Luxor answered looking at the westering sun, low over the mountains ahead. 'We won't be able to out distance them. We must make what progress we can. Camping in the open tonight, we will have to set a watch.'

Morkin shivered. It was not from the prospect of sleeping out of doors. He was quite acclimatised to such things, but the wolves gave him pause. The wolves of Midnight were not merely wild animals, despite being organised in packs and with a ferocious temperament. Some held they had a will of their own that was influenced by things unseen. The wolves could often be heard howling, out of sight, under the light of the Moonstar or when the moon itself was full. Their yowlings almost a language, as if they came together at intervals to exchange news of faraway lands and then were dispatched elsewhere with new orders. To encounter wolves at any time was considered bad luck, but to be caught by them under the light of the full moon; that was woe indeed.

'Fear not,' Luxor said, 'they are unlikely to bother us. They recognise a caravan packed with foodstuffs readily enough and Corleth has some skill with the bow as I recall.'

Morkin's fears were not realised. Dawn broke the following day without incident and another day of hard going brought the mountains ever closer. Between the mountains to the west and the downs to the east a narrow valley led between them. They rode down through it.

'Not far now,' Luxor said, bringing his horse to a stop and patting its neck. 'Yonder is the Lith of Odrark, in truth it lies in Brith's domain, I know not why it is named thusly. From here it is but half a day's ride to the Keep of the Moon. We should make it by nightfall.'

Morkin had come across the Liths before. They were some ancient relic of the past, imbued with strange ancient power that kept them free of snow and frost. Two stood not far from home and he had visited them often, wandering around their bases with his friends, playing in their shadows. They were immovable edifices, always old, but never showing any signs of wear. The remnants of a lost religion or monument to events long forgotten perhaps; they remained, but seemed to have no purpose any longer.

'There is a greater line of Liths beyond the mountains in the domain of Gard,' Luxor added as they rode north. 'They stand in an ordered row of five, separated at intervals of a league or so, running north to south.'

'But what are they for?'

Luxor shrugged. 'A creation of the Wise perhaps, or even older. None now know with any certainty. Another question for Rorthron when we arrive.'

The path wound onwards through the valley, angling away from the mountains and cutting deeper into the hills. As twilight began to fan across the sky, a chill mist descended to the ground.

A keep came into view. Morkin could tell at a glance it was unoccupied. No lights shone from its gates, walls or windows. The village about it, what little was left, was merely a ruined collection of collapsed timber-framed buildings, with the faint remnants of livestock pens, stables and liveries. It was clear that no one had lived here for many moons.

'It will afford us a little shelter that's all,' Luxor said, seeing the disappointed expression on Morkin's face. 'Alas, there will be no ale tonight!'

Within the keep the courtyard was in better repair. They found shelter for the horses and Corleth set about making a fire. It was not long before he had a blaze going. Within the walls Morkin found a spring, and after a little effort he freed it from the ice, rewarded with a trickle of water that allowed them to refill water bottles and tend to the horses. Food was next. After an hour had passed the darkness was complete aside from the fire.

'Come, let's take a look around,' Luxor said. 'I have only once before visited this place and then I did not stop. We may never come back this way again.'

Morkin followed him eagerly. Luxor took a brand from the fire and improvised a torch, holding it aloft. He pointed out many of the defensive designs of the keep, explaining how they acted together to repel invaders. Murder holes, sloped floors, unseen passageways. The keep was a remarkable construction. There was much damage in places, but the basic structure remained intact.

'I do not recall hearing that this keep ever fell in battle,' Luxor said, leading Morkin through a narrow passage within. 'Though it certainly saw its share of warfare. It seems it was left behind as history moved on.'

The passageway opened into a wider space. Both of them straightened and took in the view of a large room, its edges faint in the flickering light of the torch.

'This would have been the great hall,' Luxor said, looking about him. 'If the stories of the House of the Moon are to be believed, perhaps this is where they held court.'

Morkin looked around. There was little to see. The floor was covered with broken rubble, here and there dusted with patches of snow that had drifted in from the empty window frames, their glass long missing. There was no furniture or other decoration.

They stepped forward, their footsteps echoing around them.

Morkin could see something on the far wall and stepped towards it.

'My Lord ...'

Luxor stepped alongside, squinting into the gloom.

On the wall, cracked and falling apart, but still visible where the plaster remained was a mural. As they got close they could see it was a painting. They could make out the keep, but here, alongside it were all manner of other buildings. A colonnaded walkway, dressed with flowers, surrounding a courtyard with what looked to be a fountain at its centre. Beyond that was a mighty Citadel, but it wasn't even that grand spectacle that drew a gasp from Morkin.

Green ...!

About the keep and the citadel were great swaths of green and yellow. He could make out the tiny marks of folk. Some moving on well-worn paths, others at work amidst the colour; horses and carts beside them. More people than he had ever seen in a single place. There was a hint of celebration, flags and what might have been tents.

'The long summer,' Luxor said, his voice hushed. 'A dream of long ago. Before the ice.'

'Do you believe Midnight was ever like this?' Morkin whispered.

Luxor paused, looking over the mural in more detail.

'That the Witchking cast our lands into winter is beyond doubt. We have cast all the evils of our world at his doorstep. I do not know if the stories of the long summer are really true but ...'

He straightened and looked around the room.

'... I hope they are. I have the strong feeling that they were.'

'Perhaps one day the Witchking will be defeated and we will see summer again.'

Luxor chuckled. 'It will take a power far greater than any we can wield to defeat the Witchking, my young squire. We had our chance and it was thrown away; the Fey saw to that. The best we can aspire to is to ensure our lands are free from his vile servants. We can be content with that.'

Morkin looked up at Luxor's words.

The Fey again … what did they do that taints them so?

Wind gusted, stirring both the dust and the snow around their feet. Morkin shivered, and saw Luxor pause and reach out, placing his gloved fingers gently on the crumbling mural, tracing the outlines of the Citadel.

'What is it, my Lord?'

'I've seen this before …'

Luxor frowned and then drew back.

'It is nothing. Come, we must rest. Tomorrow we find out whether this quest is worthwhile or a fool's errand.'

He turned on his heel and Morkin followed him back outside.

The day before the Solstice dawned bright and clear, though a stiff breeze was blowing from the north. Before they left the keep, all three walked to the crumbling ramparts, looking northwards.

'There lies our ultimate destination,' Luxor said, pointing north east and bracing himself against the gusts. 'This is the edge of the Plains of Blood, one of the largest open expanses in all Midnight. Lord Blood's keep lies many leagues hence.'

The plain looked dull and uninviting to Morkin's eyes. His gaze was drawn westwards, to where a thick and ominous line of trees could be seen dominating the horizon.

'And that is the Forest of Shadows,' Corleth said from beside him. 'Once the most westerly realm of the Fey.'

'Do the Fey still live there?' Morkin asked.

'I do not know,' Corleth answered. 'If they do they are few

in number and keep themselves well hidden in the depths of the forest. We of Thrall have no trade with them.'

'Hiding, as do all the Fey,' Luxor said, before turning and walking away.

Morkin looked up at Corleth and then looked away, before summoning the courage to ask the question that had been on his mind for days.

'Why does my Lord hate the Fey so?' he asked. 'What is it that you did to him?'

Corleth paused for a long moment before favouring Morkin with a sad look. 'I cannot speak for him,' Corleth answered. 'That you must ask him yourself.'

A road ran north east and south west, a trader's route from the Plains of Blood to the lands of Gard. They arrived at it mid-morning, but saw no travellers upon it. Ahead to the north west lay the mighty timbers of the Forest of Shadows, now spreading out to either side of them, a formidable barrier that seemed impossible to pass.

'From here we must strike our own way,' Corleth said. 'There is no road that runs to the forest, or at least, I never found one.'

The terrain underfoot grew rockier, several times they had to dismount to lead their steeds around treacherous ground. The going was slower, but by noon they had reached the forest edge.

Morkin looked up. As with the Forest of Thimrath near his home, huge drifts of snow had piled up against the outermost fringes. Yet the boundary of this forest was sharp edged; no saplings, the trees simply began, huge, dark and silent, rising out of the plain and barring their way.

Luxor jumped down from his horse and walked to the nearest tree. Its trunk was huge, three or four men placed side by side or more, towering up into the height above. A faint sparkle of ersh drifted down from it, sparkling in the noonday sun, dislodged from far above. Morkin saw him peer into the forest beyond and then try to push his way in. He had not gone more than a handful of paces before he turned back.

'It is impenetrable,' Luxor said. 'None could get far, it is overgrown with barbs and twisted vines as far as I can see. Where is this entrance you spoke of, Corleth?'

'If you cannot see your way ahead, perhaps you should ask for help,' Corleth replied, still sitting in his saddle, clearly amused.

'Ask for help,' Luxor muttered under his breath. He stood tall and yelled into the forest. 'I am Lord Luxor, here at the bidding of Rorthron the Wise. Make way!'

His voice echoed briefly back from the depths, but there was no response. No movement, no sound.

Luxor surveyed the forest for a long moment. 'This truly is a fool's errand,' he said.

He turned and strode towards his horse, only stopping as he felt the ground tremble beneath his feet and saw Morkin's mouth drop open in surprise. As he turned he saw the trees shudder and pull aside, snow showering down about them, leaving a churned and twisted pathway open between their trunks.

'You have a way with words after all,' Corleth said, turning his horse about and directing it towards the path. In a moment he was lost to sight.

'Learn this well, young squire,' Luxor said, looking after the vanished Fey. 'The Wise play games with the lives of men for their amusement and this one would seem to have tricks aplenty. We must be wary indeed.'

Morkin nodded, but couldn't help but feel the thrill of excitement that coursed through him.

The Wise. We are going to meet the Wise!

Morkin watched as Luxor returned to his saddle and gestured for him to go first. The horses plodded on to the new path and ventured into the forest. As they moved forward Morkin heard the trees move once more. Looking behind him he could see the forest close up, sealing off their retreat.

They rode onward through the dreary gloom. Far above they knew the sun to be as high as it would climb in the depths of winter, but no gleam of its rays reached the forest floor, the canopy above was thick with foliage, and that would be covered by a thick blanket of snow.

At ground level the surface was frosted and hard, but clear of snow other than a faint dusting. Ahead the trees continued to make way for them, bending aside and allowing them passage before creaking and groaning their way back into their original posture.

Here and there were boulders, great lumps of stone. Some bore markings and others the distinct sign of having been hewn into shapes and structures. Here was a broken archway, there a series of columns.

'My Lord,' Morkin whispered over his shoulder, 'these are much like those in the mural we saw!'

Luxor nodded and then gestured ahead. The forest was thinning, the last few trees crackling back out of their way. The three travellers eased their horses side by side on a ridge that overlooked a valley entirely encircled by the forest. Before them, perhaps a league away, stood a tower, rising dramatically from the snowy landscape.

Morkin drew in his breath. He had never seen the like before.

'The Tower of the Moon,' Corleth said.

'Let's hope we find some answers there,' Luxor said and spurred his horse down into the valley.

They cautiously rode up to the tower. The closer they came the more remarkable it appeared. Morkin studied it intently. There seemed to be no evidence of wear. Stonework and masonry were straight and true, edges were sharp and firm in the late evening sun. The tower's monstrous shadow stretched out east almost to the edge of the forest they had come from.

Beneath, their horses hooves were now clip-clopping on cobbled stones, a well tended pathway, cleared of snow save for a recent sprinkling, that wound up to the entrance to the tower grounds. They could see stables to their right and cautiously moved across. There was no one in attendance, but three stables were somehow freshly swept and provided with straw, hay and water.

The horses thus attended, the three set out on foot across a courtyard towards the base of the tower.

Luxor drew his sword and held it before him. Morkin followed his example with his own.

'I do not believe that is necessary, or even wise,' Corleth said. 'What do you both intend? To storm this tower yourself?'

Morkin lowered the tip of his sword.

'I will not be taken by surprise,' Luxor returned, coming to a halt and looking up at the indomitable tower.

'Oh I'm afraid it's rather too late for that.'

The voice was deep, but smooth and eloquent, with more than a trace of wry amusement about it. Luxor and Morkin spun around in surprise.

An old man, or what they took to be an old man, stood there directly behind them. Morkin could see his own footprints and those of Luxor and Corleth, but this individual had generated none of his own, the snow about him was undisturbed. He was dressed simply, in a robe of dark mauve, leaning on a metal staff upon which some symbol was fixed. Grey hair and matching thick moustache and beard surrounded a thickly browed face framing a pair of brown eyes that gazed at them. He was tall too, almost as tall as Luxor.

'Rorthron the Wise?' Luxor asked.

'Rorthron of the Wise, to be precise,' the old man responded. 'I would not comment on my own wisdom, such a thing would be presumptuous. And you will not need your sword, Luxor, Lord of the Keep of Odrark.'

'Magic!' Morkin whispered, still looking for the missing footprints.

'Magic?' Rorthron answered with a chuckle, 'You are easily impressed, young Morkin. Silent steps, nothing more.'

'You summoned us …' Luxor began, making a show of sheathing his sword.

'I did indeed,' Rorthron said. 'But long and weary has been your journey. Food and some measure of hospitality awaits within. Come.'

Rorthron was as good as his word. Hot water, welling up from somewhere deep below the tower and housed in frescoed baths within the towers basement, proved a welcome refreshment from the rigours of the journey. Fresh clothing had been laid for all three of them, precisely measured and tailored for size. Salted meats and dried fruits of a kind Morkin had never tasted before were laid upon tables in a room immediately above once they were washed and dried. They made short work of the repast.

'Some measure of hospitality,' Luxor said, not hesitating to avail himself of the food spread around them. 'Our host seems well victualled.'

Corleth nodded. 'The Wise have many means at their disposal.'

'Conjured by magic!' Morkin said. 'It has to be.'

Luxor shook his head in amusement. 'To be young and look upon the world with wonder once again. What you have seen are the parlour tricks of the Wise, the only potent magic left in this world is the fell art of the Witchking, my squire. And that is not something we should dwell upon.'

'On the contrary, the magic of the Witchking is the very reason I have summoned you here.'

Rorthron stood at the entrance to the room, his arrival as unannounced as before.

'It is not considered good manners amongst my people to eavesdrop on conversations without invitation,' Luxor rumbled. 'Rorthron the Wise.'

'I am not of your people, Lord Luxor of Odrark,' Rorthron replied. 'And I will eavesdrop on whomsoever I please within my own domain.'

Luxor stood up, stretching to his full height. Morkin jumped up and placed himself between them.

'My Lord is most curious as to why he has been summoned, oh Rorthron the Wise.'

Morkin looked at Luxor for a brief moment, before turning back to Rorthron.

'Quite the diplomat, your squire,' Rorthron said, a smile growing on his features. 'He is a credit to you.'

'I treat him as if he were my son,' Luxor answered. 'For I have none of my own.' Luxor lowered his voice. 'He enjoys my protection, also.'

'Most appropriate,' Rorthron said with a nod. 'And to answer your question, young squire, I suggest you follow me up to the great hall set atop the very highest level of this tower. We have much to discuss and little enough time to do it in. We must all depart upon the morrow.'

'The Council of the Wise?' Corleth asked.

Rorthron chuckled. 'I suppose you might call it that, yes.'

The Tower of the Moon was arranged around a central flight of stairs contained within a hollow central structure that supported the enormous weight of the building. Off from the stairs were many rooms. Most were sealed by thick wooden doors with ornate and baroque metal fastenings, closed and locked. A few were open, allowing a brief view into lushly decorated libraries, studies and lounges decked out in the manner of the richest Lords and Ladies of the southland. They were far more impressive than the best that the Keep of Odrark could muster.

The staircase spiralled upwards. Morkin quickly lost count of the steps he had taken, it was certainly beyond two hundred when Rorthron paused ahead of him, fumbled in his robes for a moment and then produced a set of heavy locking keys which he used to unlock a door that barred their way.

Thus opened, Rorthron stepped though. Daylight shone about them still, the red glow of sunset warm about them.

Morkin gasped as he looked around. They had reached what must have been the uppermost point of the tower. A wide circular room set with eight huge windows looking out into the whiteness of Midnight. On the floor a massive compass was wrought into the stonework and Morkin could see each window was oriented to provide a view aligned with it. Through the windows he could see the wide expanse of the Forest of the Moon all about them, with a mountain range visible beyond its borders to the north. Above him, the roof of the tower was a crystal dome, refracting light into the room below. Looking out of the windows to the east he fancied he could even make out the distant Keep of Blood beyond the forest, their ultimate destination. He spared a glance to the south, but distant mountains obscured any chance of seeing his home keep.

Within the room were strange metal objects made of brass or bronze propped against the windows, or freestanding in the room. Morkin recognised one of two, they seemed similar to instruments he had seen builders and masons use, but many more of them he did not. Below the windows comfortable leather padded seats faced inwards. A fireplace, nestled between the stone workmanship of the windows, provided warmth.

'Please, make yourself comfortable,' Rorthron said, gesturing to the windows.

Morkin looked about him, seeing Corleth and Luxor doing the same.

'Where are they?' Luxor asked.

'To whom are you referring?' Rorthron asked.

'This council of yours,' Luxor said. 'The Council of the Wise of course!'

'I am guilty of a little deceit, I fear,' Rorthron said, his gaze steady upon Luxor. 'Perhaps I should have said counsel, not council.'

Luxor looked at Corleth. Morkin could see the colour rising in his Lord's face.

Luxor rounded on Rorthron. 'You have brought me here at your whim, for your amusement? Wasting my time whilst the Witchking's foul hordes gather on our northern borders?' His voice rose. 'Sent this Fey lackey to bring me with wishful stories of sage advice to entice me here so you might laugh ...'

'Enough!'

Morkin flinched at the sudden power in Rorthron's voice. It must have been his imagination but he could have sworn the reddening light of sunset flickered outside, as if a veil had momentarily been drawn across it. He trembled. Even Luxor took a step back.

'You speak of what you do not know, Luxor Lord of the Free,' Rorthron said. 'Put aside your pride and listen. Perhaps you will still learn something to your advantage.'

Rorthron took a deep breath and sighed. The sunlight grew back once more and everything was as it had been.

'I have worked for many moons.' Rorthron turned to stare out of the windows of the tower. 'Trying to stir my fellows to action, reminding them of their promises to safeguard this land, a duty we were all sworn to. They call me a fool, young and naïve. Me!' Rorthron chuckled to himself and then a sneer grew on his bearded features. 'They merely wait; wait for better times to come. Well … I have waited some ten thousand moons. I dare say that is long enough.'

'Ten thousand moons …' Morkin whispered.

'Yes little squire,' Rorthron said, turning to look at him. 'I was but a boy like you once. When my eyes were as young as yours I looked out across Midnight, fair and warm, green and lush. The long summer.'

'But …'

'No, it was no legend. I was there. Before the coming of the cold and the imprisonment of Midnight by the foul arts of the Witchking. I saw the Frozen Wastes grow from his enchanted mists, locking our land off and sealing it in cold and sorrow. I saw the fate of so many; the depredation, the starvation and the inevitable conflicts that arose. I watched as only the hardiest survived, and I was powerless to stop it. The land of Midnight itself came to the salvation of the few that remained; the lakes, the hot springs, the forests … without those all would have died.'

Luxor nodded.

'They do say our world wasn't always white, Morkin,' he said softly. 'You've heard the legends of summer when the land was green and teeming with life. Ten thousand moons ago it was, so long that men barely believe such a time ever existed.'

Rorthron turned back to face them. 'Yet the Wise remember. We have scrolls that tell of the first snows falling and the first carpets of ice covering the land. Suddenly, all the lands of Midnight were plunged into this winter of ours. Then came famine, a great famine that ravaged all peoples, and with famine came war.'

'And war we have had ever since,' Luxor said. Morkin heard him take a deep breath and he stepped forward.

Rorthron regarded him.

'I was quick to anger,' Luxor said. 'Allies are unlooked for from beyond our boundaries and new friends are seldom found. Forgive my conduct.'

Luxor held out his hand. Rorthron held his gaze for long moment before taking it.

'It is said amongst the Fey that men are arrogant and unable to recognise their own weaknesses,' Rorthron said, giving Corleth a quick glance. 'I am gratified to find they are wrong.'

Luxor looked across at Corleth, 'The Fey say many things that turn out not to be true.'

'Peace,' Rorthron said. 'The Fey and the Free will have much need of each other in the days to come. The Witchking's greatest weapons are fear, uncertainty and sowing discord. And not necessarily in that order. Do not give him an easy victory.'

'You said you had knowledge and tactics that would aid us against him,' Luxor said.

'Indeed I do. Know you of the House of the Moon?'

Luxor looked at Corleth and Morkin, before turning back to Rorthron.

'We discussed it on our travels,' Luxor said. 'Echoes of the past, a myth of rings, a royal house. Stories for the campfire.'

'Myths you say,' Rorthron said, with faint mirth. 'Myths to men are but yesterday's news to the Wise. You forget where you stand.'

'The Tower of the Moon!' Morkin said, unable to keep the excitement out of his voice.

'Indeed.' Rorthron pointed at Corleth. 'And you were correct in thinking that I did witness those events and even had my part to play in them.'

Morkin noticed that even Corleth looked surprised by this revelation.

'But how did …?' Morkin began.

'I have kept many things secret for many lives of men,' Rorthron said. 'Doubtless I shall continue to do so, but it is time for some at least to be revealed.'

He held out his palm.

Luxor, Morkin and Corleth leant forward.

In Rorthron's palm lay a ring, plain but for an ornate circular bezel on top. It had a curious lustre; for long moments it had the hue of gold, then it seemed festooned with a brighter glow as if aflame. Morkin could see his Lord's face lit by the red glow from the ring as Rorthron held it aloft. Something sparkled in his eyes, something that Morkin had not seen before.

'Rings I have already,' Luxor said, his voice uncertain.

'Not such as this,' Corleth said, his own voice barely a whisper. 'It cannot be …'

'The last of the great War Rings of Midnight?' Rorthron asked. 'The last heirloom of the House of the Moon? The Moon Ring itself? It can be … and it is.'

The ring flickered and flashed before them, mesmerising, but somehow cold and otherworldly.

'But it was lost, was it not?' Corleth asked. 'Long ago …'

Rorthron smiled. 'Rarnor the unlucky? The ring was never stolen away, but that story did allow me to keep it hidden.'

'But none now know how to wield such a ring,' Luxor said. 'Certainly none have the right. The House of the Moon is long gone, destroyed countless moons ago.'

Rorthron nodded. 'You are right in saying that cannot be borne by any who are not of the House of the Moon.'

Luxor frowned. 'Then why offer it ...'

'I would have thought it was patently obvious,' Rorthron returned. 'It is you, Luxor Lord of the Free. You are the last of their line. You ...'

Rorthron gestured with the ring, bringing it close to Luxor's face. The redness grew. Morkin fancied he could see crackles of flame from it, but he could feel no heat.

Rorthron's own visage cracked into a knowing grin.

'You are the Moonprince, the very last one.'

Chapter Four

He stands at the Tower of Doom,
looking north to the Mountains of Death.

Clouds swirled about the Citadel of Ushgarak, funnelled into swirling tempests by the Mountains of Ugrorn and Ugrak. Blizzards blew furiously, enveloping the deserted Plains of Despair in a maelstrom of icy cruelty that refused to relent. The sun was powerless to intervene here in the frozen northland.

About the plains were scattered defensive keeps, austere in the enveloping greyness of the storm, their windows and defensive emplacements backlit by the glow of ruddy furnaces within. Closer, and the sound of hammering could be heard multiplied hundreds of times over, the rough cries of the oppressed and the gruff chants of those who drove them on.

Preparations had been underway for many moons; preparations that neared completion.

Beyond the keeps lay the ragged remnants of a once beautiful forest of the northern realm. Neither the Free or the Fey had records of its original name; it had long been lost to the vagaries of time. Its trees and foliage were now twisted by the dark arts of the Witchking, making a barrier far more formidable than the armies that slowly patrolled the plains to the south.

It had only one name now.

Doom.

Beyond lay another of the towers of Midnight, once as ornately crafted as any others. It had once been the Tower of Gryfallon the Stargazer, one of those who remembered the world before the everlasting winter had fallen upon it, back to the times of the long summer.

A thin veil of dark smoke rose from the tower. Noxious fumes swirled upwards into the heavens as if fed by some broiling fire below.

But there was no flame to be found. Something more arcane drove the billowing gloom above the tower.

Fear.

The interior of the tower was cloaked in darkness, for he that ventured within needed no light with which to conduct his affairs. He had other senses, fortified by fell arts and corrupted sorceries. The blackness merely cloaked a deeper night.

A faint crimson glow crackled, briefly illuminating a corpse like hand shot through with darkened veins starkly contrasting with ice white skin. An arm outstretched within an ebony robe that caught any errant light and despatched it into oblivion.

The crimson glow spluttered briefly, sparking before a face draped in a thick cowl, an eerie red illumination casting a hollow sunken face into sharp relief. Black eyes, set in a bleached face; flesh that seemed frozen upon a skeletal frame.

The dancing crimson sparks swirled and moved in patterns, drawing figures in the air. The outline of a woman's face appeared. She was striking, perhaps even beautiful to the eyes of men, her cheekbones high and distinct, eyes wide, lips voluptuous. Yet her expression was cold, shot through with a fierce and ancient hatred that did not match the youthful vigour of her features.

The robed figure raised its head.

IT IS TIME.

The ice white lips did not move and no sound came from them, but the words were clear nonetheless.

The woman licked her lips, her eyes narrowing as a smile grew across her features. Her expression was bereft of warmth, somehow even colder than the silence that reigned within the Tower of Doom.

'The Solstice!'

Her voice was smooth, silky and enchanting, laced with the sorcery of enticement and manipulation. The Witchking was immune to it, for he had instructed her in its use.

THE ICEMARK?

She pouted and looked aside for a moment.

'The gates of Varenorn are closed, locked and barred. I have sent you as many warriors as I can spare. All is in order. You have enough might to subdue Midnight twice over!'

YOU HAVE DONE WELL. THOSE FEY OF THE NORTH WHO RETAINED THEIR WITS HAVE BEEN SLAIN, THE WRETCHED AND PITIFUL FEY OF THE EAST WILL REMAIN UNDISTURBED FOR NOW. THE SOUTHLANDS WILL BE VANQUISHED BEFORE THEY EVEN BEGIN TO COMPREHEND THE SCALE OF THEIR PLIGHT …

'Now I make my own plans,' the woman replied.

The Witchking raised his head. The question was obvious.

She looked back, her expression challenging, impertinent.

'Can a daughter not have some secrets from her father?'

Shareth was her name, the only thing that the Witchking had ever loved, offspring of some unholy union between him and a nameless forgotten Queen of the Icemark. She was ruler of the frozen Empire far to the north, beyond the icy wastes that defined the borders of Midnight. Those of the Icemark called her Heartstealer, for it was said she had appetites beyond mere lust for power and domination.

The Witchking did not react to her barb, but turned his head slowly to the left. The image of Shareth turned to match. Both stared towards a carved stone pedestal engraved with the words and images of dark sorcery, set in the centre of the darkened tower. What faint illumination was available was concentrated here. A barely discernible glow emanated from an object set reverently on a black velvet cushion atop the pedestal.

With a brief gesture from the Witchking the light brightened, revealing a sparkling object surrounded by faint wisps of mist that swirled gently around it. Impossibly delicate, wrought of the purest crystals of ice in the darkest depths of winter, it was an ornate tiara, a coronet … a diadem.

Shareth's voice was at once lustful and hushed.

'The Ice Crown!'

The Witchking moved towards it. Even he could perceive the utter cold that proceeded from it. Colder even than his heart, this was the purest incarnation of the core of winter; power over the elements.

Incantations passed his lips, long practiced. Ice crackled around the inside of the tower, frost spreading like a live thing across the floor, walls and ceiling. Icicles grew like cruel fingers.

He closed his hand, his skeletal fingers curling into a fist.

The room contracted about him, as if somehow clenched and tense. Ice crackled and shivered about him, bending to his will.

Outside the tower the blizzard stopped, shuddering inwards against itself, clouds rolling and boiling above the tower, concentrating in a thunderstorm that arched upwards into the heavens. Lightning struck the tower once, twice and then a third time. Crackles of light cascaded, bright and actinic, about the room. They coursed through the body of the Witchking himself, but he heeded them not. His arm remained poised, fist clenched towards the Ice Crown, now glowing with a cruel blue-tinged light.

The wind howled, a tornado dropped from the sky, wrapping itself around the tower. The view out was obscured by whirling rain and snow. The windows of the tower shattered under the strain, dashed to oblivion and sucked out into the thunderous gale.

And still the Witchking was unmoved.

Now the tower itself creaked, its ancient stonework straining against the forces that had been summoned from the depths of winter itself. Cracks appeared overhead and underfoot, spidering across the intricately patterns tiles and frescoes that had once been the delight of the Lord of Ushgarak ten thousand moons before.

The Witchking opened his hand.

The storm stopped, as if suspended in a single moment in time, frozen into utter stasis, debris tumbling gently in the air, weightless. The sound was banished and an eerie silence settled over the Plains of Despair. The angry clouds were poised motionless above, awaiting the direction of he who had mastered them.

The briefest curl of his fingers, a gesture towards the hated southlands, was all it took.

The clouds broiled outwards from the Tower of Doom, descending towards the ground, sweeping everything before them in a pallid wall of gloom.

The Witchking turned and watched. The clouds swept outwards in an ever widening circle, undiminished by the distance, winds ripping up more fury as they rode onwards, heading outwards east, west and south.

Behind him the Ice Crown pulsed, adding its own fell counterpoint to the ferocious blast.

He said nothing, but the air around him was rent by laughter, for Shareth the Heartstealer knew what had been unleased.

'Fear, Midnight!' she cried. 'Fear will be your everlasting companion now!'

Darkness had long fallen over the Tower of the Moon, but light still flickered from the windows of its uppermost hall. Figures could be seen moving about in the glow of firelight.

'Gryfallon the Wise was a stargazer, an advisor to Lord Ushgarak himself,' Rorthron said. He had been relating a tale of the woe that had befallen Midnight at the end of the long summer. 'Long ago that citadel was an outpost of men. Ushgarak had prospered as a result, becoming mighty in the reckoning of the Free. Conquest had brought the land under his sway; he was King of Midnight.'

'The Witchking was a man? A King?' Morkin asked.

Rorthron shook his head.

'King Ushgarak's reign was short. Within twelve moons he had been murdered by none other than Gryfallon himself, and the wise counsellor became ruler in his place. None knew of the murder of course, thinking that Ushgarak had succumbed to illness, and Gryfallon was well respected throughout the realm. So he ruled, first through wisdom and cunning, but later via sorcery and slaughter, Gryfallon kept the lands subdued.'

'Gryfallon is the Witchking?' Morkin said, eyes wide. 'The Witchking is one of …'

He faltered, looking crestfallen.

'One of the Wise?' Rorthron asked. 'Alas yes. Who else but we could wield such power?'

'The Lords feared to challenge him,' Corleth said, softly.

'The Fey hid in their forests …' Luxor began.

Rorthron interrupted. 'And the Wise did not interfere. For folly and for shame we stood aside. All the races failed in their duties. Of the Wise, now there are none but myself who will take an interest in the fate of Midnight.'

Luxor chuckled.

'Then at least we can hope for unanimous decisions. Besides, one of you, I'll wager, is worth a score of the rest. We should not be troubled when the hopeless desert us.'

Luxor looked at the Moon Ring, which Rorthron had placed upon an elegant and delicate table nearby.

The House of the Moon. An heir! I can scarce credit it. Would Rorthron lie? To what end? How does one wield this ring? What can it do?

Rorthron seemed somehow aware of the questions in Luxor's mind.

'It is the reason I was very specific in asking you here on the eve of the Solstice,' he said. 'The Witchking's power grows to its most potent in the depths of winter. Long has he been holed up in his northern retreat, biding his time, drawing fell strength from the cold. This very night he will unleash a storm unlike any seen before, all will cower before it.'

'We have faced the ice-fear before,' Luxor said.

Rorthron shook his head. 'Alas, what you faced in your youth was a mere skirmish. The Witchking will drive you all before him, already he is prepared to strike with force of weapons. Yet the ice-fear will be stronger than it has ever been. Even the stoutest warriors will quake before it.'

'If your words are meant to comfort us, they are ill-chosen,' Luxor said.

'This coming war will not be won by force of arms alone,' Rorthron answered.

'This ring must be mighty indeed if it is the source of our victory,' Luxor said.

'The ring will aid you,' Rorthron said, shaking his head. 'But it will not win the war.'

'Then of what use is it?

'It will throw forth the warmth of your mind, a potent sense of your presence and your power. It can mollify the effects of the ice-fear, but it cannot defeat it. It will give you the power of command, the ability to sense the needs and fears of those loyal to you, even see what they see at great distance.'

'Those loyal to me?' Luxor said. 'I am but a vassal of Lord Gard and a poor one at that. There are none who swear allegiance to me. I do not even have a force of warriors!'

Rorthron shook his head. 'Not so. Gard owes his allegiance to you. There is none higher than the Moonprince in the reckoning of the Free.'

Luxor blinked. 'It is an ancient title, long moribund. Gard would likely slay me where I stood for contemplating such arrogance.'

Corleth stepped forward. 'The Fey will follow the Moonprince, where they would not follow Lord Gard.'

Luxor looked at him in surprise.

'The Fey have long suspected that the House of the Moon still survived, 'Corleth said. 'The Wise are not the only guardians of knowledge. I could not be sure until today when Rorthron held forth the Moon Ring, but I have harboured a secret hope that you were the Moonprince.'

'A day of revelations it would seem,' Luxor said, his gaze staying with Corleth for a long moment. 'And how can you be so sure I am an heir of the House of the Moon? My line is weak in the reckoning of the Free. I have no heraldry, no line of any significance ...'

'The ring can only be borne by the Moonprince.' Rorthron said. 'Don it, and you shall see.'

Luxor looked warily at the ring again.

'Do it, my lord!' Morkin said.

Luxor reached out and took it and it seemed for a moment that the ring glittered more sharply in the palm of his hand. The faint glow of morning glimmered in the sky behind him as he held up the ring and inspected it.

He slipped it upon his finger ...

Images rushed before him, snow covered landscapes, mountain ranges, ice swept forests, valleys and here and there, citadels, keeps and villages. All somehow near enough to see yet far enough way that he could perceive them all, as if he were suspended above some fantastic map that stretched out in all directions.

He reeled, panicking, feeling as if he was suspended from the sky. The landscape swung about him, spinning in a nauseating fashion. He felt his stomach lurch and grasped out, only vaguely feeling a nearby pillar for support.

'What is this magic?'

His voice projected around him, echoing back to him in mocking refrain.

Stand firm …

Luxor recognised Rorthron's voice, disembodied and distant, but firm and instructing.

… brace your mind, focus on what you want to see. Look for the Tower!

Luxor tried to calm his racing thoughts, forcing himself to take a deep breath. The horizon straightened out and he could make out familiar features. Those must be the Mountains of Corelay, the forest should be …

He wrestled his view around in his mind and thus he saw.

Yes, that's the way!

He could see the entirety of the Forest of the Moon, a huge ring around the valley and there in the centre was the tower. He moved towards it at an unimaginable speed, stopping just short of the windows, gasping with the effort of staying focussed. Within he could see figures; Rorthron, Corleth, Morkin all standing around … him.

The ring gives the power of farseeing, you can roam Midnight through the eyes of those loyal to you, even command them, urge them to undertake any task they would willingly perform for you …

The vision faded.

Luxor gasped and almost stumbled as his own eyes focussed once more. He was back in the tower, whole and unharmed, yet trembling from head to foot.

'The Moonprince indeed,' Corleth whispered.

'Such a power ...' he muttered. 'Not even the Witchking has such a gift!'

Rorthron shook his head. 'Do not underestimate him. His reach is as great, if not greater. How do you think he commands his Doomguard if not by similar means?'

'But with this ...' Luxor said, thinking through the possibilities. 'It gives us a military advantage! Don't you see? This time, this war, the Moon Ring lends us the power to change our plans at a moment's notice. No longer must we stake all upon a single throw ...'

'True enough,' Rorthron interrupted, his voice hushed. 'Yet to defeat the Witchking you must strike at the source of his power.'

Corleth shook his head.

'No one can approach, even the Fey would not dare.' There was a tremble in his voice. 'Not the Ice Crown. Rorthron, it is not possible ...'

'What is the Ice Crown?' Morkin demanded.

'It is, as its name suggests a crown, fashioned of the purest, coldest crystals of ice,' Rorthron said. 'Forged in the Frozen Wastes on the bleakest of nights by the Witchking himself, the Ice Crown is the source of all his power. It enables him to extract from the heart of the Winter all the bitter forces of cold and bend them to his will. He keeps it secure in the Tower of Doom, north of Ushgarak across the Plains of Despair. None have seen it and lived. Yet all have felt its bitter touch.'

'But with this ring?' Luxor said, excitement growing in his voice. 'Can it be done?'

'And what would happen?' Morkin asked.

'If it were to be destroyed, the Witchking's power would be shattered.' Rorthron said, and then looked at Luxor, shaking his head. 'But it cannot be done by means of the ring. The Witchking would sense your presence before you got within fifty leagues of his icy domain. The same could be said of myself. The Wise know of each other's presence.'

'Then if it is impossible ...'

'It is not impossible,' Rorthron countered, 'One born of Fey and Free, laughter and lightness blended with the wild fire. Such as they could approach the Ice Crown.'

'No ...' Corleth said, his voice barely a whisper. 'You cannot ask that ...'

'And who is this great warrior?' Luxor asked. 'Show him to me.'

'He stands alongside you now, Luxor, Moonprince of Midnight. I asked him to accompany you for this very purpose.'

Rorthron gestured to Morkin.

Luxor straightened. Belatedly Morkin gasped, Rorthron's words so unexpected that they didn't register.

'Me?' Morkin said. "How can it be me? I was but a babe when my Lord Luxor found me. I am no Fey! He gathered me up and took me home and cared for me, as he has cared for me ever since: he has been like a father to me all my life, my own parents lost ...'

'What jest is this?' Luxor demanded. 'Morkin was ...'

'Found in the Forest of Thimrath whilst you were engaged on a hunt,' Corleth said, his voice heavy. 'Do you not remember?'

'Of course I remember, but ... how do you know that?'

Corleth swallowed. 'I placed him there.'

'Placed him?'

'This will explain.'

Corleth held out something between his thumb and first

finger. It was a small amber crystal, glowing like a small sun, soft and soothing.

'A heartstone?' Luxor whispered.

'I have carried this for many years,' Corleth instructed. 'You must both hold it. As its owner would wish.'

Corleth dropped it into Luxor's palm. After a brief exchange of looks with Luxor, Morkin placed his own hand over it. Luxor felt his squire's hand close about his, the warmth of the crystal growing swiftly. He was about to cry out when …

A battle, the foul hordes of the Witchking. Warriors, lost and demented, struggling through treacherous snow. Once such man, collapsed at the edge of a forest.

You came to me Luxor, close to death …

Deep within the forests, a beautiful Feyish woman. Dressing him, nursing him to health.

Aleisha was my name …

The man's strength grew, as did their enchantment with each other. Their love was completed, the days and nights lingered on until she could bear it no longer.

It could not be, Luxor my love, for I am Fey and you are Free …

A child was born of their union, a rare child, of Fey and Free. Delight was speared with pain, but she knew he had been born for a reason beyond her wishes. The Fey journeyed to Rorath on the borders of Corelay.

I left our son with you, Luxor. To be raised as a mortal man …

Upon the path the Fey left the babe, swaddled in warm furs. She dared not linger.

I loved you both, Luxor and Morkin, father and son!

The daydream abruptly stopped. Luxor found himself staring into the tear-streaked eyes of Morkin. He blinked and his own eyes blurred.

'Father?'

'My son,' he whispered. 'Somehow, I knew. Perhaps I have always known …'

'And Aleisha knew,' Corleth whispered. 'I did not believe her at first, but she had faith in the old songs that told one would be born of both Free and Fey. She swore me to silence. I have watched from afar as best I was able. Now it seems, we know why.'

'And my mother, she lives still?' Morkin demanded.

Corleth was silent.

Morkin found his hand clasped by his new-found father even as his expression grew sad.

'She wished to keep you both safe from the knowledge of the Witchking,' Rorthron said. 'With you two, his doom is at hand.'

'His doom?' Luxor asked. 'At our hands? You overreach yourself!'

Rorthron straightened.

'The Solstice is the peak of Doomdark's power. Defeat him now, at the pinnacle of his might, and he will never return, never to blight the lands of Midnight again with his foul schemes. At this moment, he suspects nothing and when the morrow comes, the Solstice itself, he will expect all its glory for himself.'

'He will find his desires thwarted then,' Luxor said.

'Yet beware,' Rorthron said. 'From Ushgarak will issue forth an ice-fear the like of which has never been before, rolling its terror across Midnight like a plague. Tomorrow, at dawn you must don the Moon Ring and send a blaze of hope winging across the land, melting his ice-fear, stabbing him with shock that a warmth still exists that can resist him. It will fill him with doubt, such a thing he has not known since the long Summer.'

'Can this be so?' Luxor whispered.

'Wield the Moon Ring, Luxor. You must challenge Doomdark everywhere; leave one pathway unguarded, one chink open and a flood will pour through. The Moon Ring itself will lend you the power to guide the forces of the Free and under your guidance they will march against Doomdark as one. The Captains of Cold will be blind compared to those whose way is lit by the War Ring of the House of the Moon.'

'And the Ice Crown?'

'Morkin alone can approach it, he ...'

Luxor straightened.

'No.' He shook his head. 'You would send my son, newly found, on a quest to into the heart of darkness, alone and un-aided?'

'It is prophecy,' Rorthron said. 'The old songs ...'

'It is madness!' Luxor roared. 'He is but a boy! You say the Ice Crown lies within the Tower of Doom itself? Thousands upon thousands of Doomguard warriors lie between there and that desolation! None would dare approach Ushgarak! If by some hopeless chance he manages to lay hold of it, what then? Do you even know how to destroy the Ice Crown?'

Rorthron looked uncomfortable.

'You don't?' Luxor said, his mouth hanging open.

'I know of one who does,' Rorthron said. 'Lorgrim the Wise is learned in these matters. Gryfallon was apprenticed to him long ago ...'

'This tale grows ever more extraordinary,' Luxor said. 'I must entrust my son to the Witchking's tutor?'

'You cannot defeat the Witchking any other way,' Rorthron's voice was sharp. 'You are the Moonprince! Morkin is the only one who can approach the Ice Crown. It must be destroyed. There is no alternative.'

'Oh but there is,' Luxor replied, picking up the ring and brandishing it. 'I place my faith in what I know. In the strength of men and the valour of the Free. I will take this ring as a gift and use it as I may. Do not doubt I am grateful for it, Rorthron the Wise, I recognise its power and its worth. But of this mad scheme I will have no part.'

'This is folly, Moonprince,' Rorthron said.

'Look to your own words for folly,' Luxor replied. 'Come, Morkin. We are finished here.'

'Would you give us orders, Moonprince,' Corleth said, his voice soft and calm. 'I was serious when I said that the Fey would follow the Moonprince.'

Luxor turned to regard him.

'If you would truly serve me,' he said, narrowing his eyes, 'then call forth the legions of the Fey and have them rendezvous with us on the Plains of Blood. We will hold back the hordes of the Witchking like we have done before, never doubt it.'

Rorthron sighed deeply.

'If you will not heed my counsel, I will travel on your behalf as well. I can reach the Lords far to the east far more quickly than you can send a messenger.' His voice dropped in pitch. 'You will need their help.'

Luxor's jaw was set.

'Some assistance at last. Ride for Marakith and Kumar then. Ithrorn too if you can. I would see them stand alongside Lord Gard if there is time.'

'It shall be done.'

Luxor nodded peremptorily. 'And you will yet see what men can do.'

'It will be in vain if you do not heed my words, Luxor, Moonprince of Midnight,' Rorthron said. 'I will journey onwards to Lorgrim and seek his counsel. There will come a time when you will be forced to change your mind.'

'You underestimate the valour of the Free,' Luxor returned.

Rorthron looked downcast.

'I wish I did.'

Chapter Five

She stands at the Citadel of Dreams,
looking west to the Forest of Dreams.

Dawn broke clear and bright over the Citadel of Dreams. It was the greatest of the fortresses of the Fey, a gleaming white edifice of marble as bright as the snow that lay thick about its base. They named it Imlath Quiriniel in their tongue, a name that was best rendered as Jewel of Midnight in the common language of the Free. The Fey did not use the hierarchies familiar to men, but Dreams served as something that those of other races would recognise as a capital. Certainly the Fey looked towards the Citadel of Dreams for their guidance.

The great Lord of Dreams himself was deep within, already breaking his fast with a hearty meal. The Fey had long since looked to their forest realms for sustenance, even in the deepest heart of winter their crafts allowed plants to flourish and grow, with just the merest caress of sunlight.

A table, exquisitely carved with artwork that told tales of yore dominated the hall. About it were placed high backed chairs, individually grown and tended as living plants until such time as they were ready to be used. Upon the grandest sat the Lord of Dreams himself, flanked by two courtiers who saw to his needs.

To his right sat his wife, her auburn hair unmarked by the many moons both she and her husband had lived.

Across from her was a girl on the verge of womanhood.

She shared a similar complexion to her mother, but her hair was red, almost to the point of fiery. Her eyes shared the same deep green as her father's.

'Will we take to the forest roads today, father?' the girl asked. She was prodding at the food on her plate, but with little enthusiasm.

The Lord of Dreams didn't answer for a moment. The girl saw her mother give her a fierce look which she returned with an insolent expression. She watched as her father put down his knife on the table with a sharp clunk. He did not turn to her.

'Not today,' he said, his voice barely above a whisper.

'But you said you would. It is the Solstice!'

'Ask me in half a moon,' he grumbled.

'I did and that was half a moon ago,' the girl retorted. 'You promised you'd take me to the forest edge ...'

His fist came down on the table, making the plates and cutlery jump.

'I have said not now, Tarithel!' Dreams roared. 'Do not vex me further on this.'

Tarithel saw her mother gesturing with her hand but ignored her.

Dreams subsided, muttering. 'The forest is no place for a girl at such a time as this.'

'Why not?' Tarithel answered, unfazed.

Dreams shook his head and looked at her, 'Why not?'

'Yes,' Tarithel looked him straight in the eye. 'What is it that you fear so much? Why won't you tell me?'

'You cannot understand.'

'Am I not skilled in horsemanship? Can I not ride and draw a bow?'

Dreams sighed. 'This you can do.'

'Am I not able to defend myself against wolf, troll and skulkrin?' Tarithel continued. 'Am I not learned in forest lore?'

'Enough ...'

'Can I not fight as well as any apprentice warrior?'

'Enough, Tarithel! You will be silent!'

Father and daughter glared at each other.

'I am no skivvy you can order ...'

His tone dropped to a growl. 'Your room, now.'

Tarithel looked across to her mother, whose lips were pursed with disapproval. She gave an exaggerated sigh and got to her feet.

'You can't keep me locked up here forever, father.'

Dreams did not turn as she strode from the hall. The young Fey's shoes clicked on the stone flooring as she strutted out, slamming the wooden door behind her.

'She is right you know,' his wife said.

Dreams sighed and rubbed his brow.

'She is so wilful.'

His wife laughed. 'And where do you think she gets that trait from? She is her father's daughter through and through. You two are so alike ...'

Dreams nodded. 'I would have her kept from the darkness beyond our borders. We are safe here; the affairs of the wider world need not bother us. Our territory reaches for many leagues about us, enough to keep our family busy tending it and nurturing it against the cold.'

'We have much to be grateful for,' his wife said carefully.

Dreams gave her a look, but she said nothing further.

'I believe we are better off as we are. We have a watchful peace. Our arrangement ... remains. We are but half a moon's march from the Witchking's gate and has he bothered us in two hundred moons? No, he has not. We keep to ourselves and he will leave us alone.'

'We once bore arms against him.'

'And where did that get us? Thousands of our finest slaughtered. So many fair Fey that should have seen uncounted moons come and go, and for what? To help the Free? They conveniently forgot that it was they who lauded him as King when he ascended to power, they who fell at his feet drunk with his praise; they that accepted his gifts.'

'The lives of the Free are like ersh in the sun, those alive today are not responsible for the actions of their ancestors …'

'The Free are all the same,' Dreams said. 'Weak, easily led, thinking only of today and never of tomorrow. We do well to leave them to their own petty squabbles. These so called Lords and their gaudy crowns. They are children by any other name.'

Dreams pushed his plate aside and rose to his feet.

'I saw their perfidy. We will not stand with them again. The peace we have forged is what we will keep. The affairs of the Free are not our concern. Times have changed.'

His wife watched him for a moment. 'There is something else we must discuss,' she said, her voice wary.

Dreams sighed.

'We have spoken of this before, this tradition of our house. Must we keep it? She is too young, see how she reacts? Impetuous, impatient! She has too much to learn.'

His wife merely looked at him.

'I cannot change your mind I see,' Dreams replied.

She smiled. 'We are old, Araleth. I am old. Old and hidebound. It is time; you know in your heart that it is so. I cannot stir the forest like I once did.'

He blinked, unused to hearing his own name spoken. Certainly his wife was the only one who dared to use it.

'Lady of the Forest?' he replied. 'A responsibility she is not mature enough to bear. She is not yet even a woman. A mere girl, a child!'

'She is almost of age, a matter of moons, little more. She has the ancient wisdom of the Fey and the touch of empathy for the people. All who live in the citadel love her … adore her even. Yes, she is young, but she has the spark of joy and rapture our people have long since lost. She kindles spirits wherever she goes; her presence brings a lightness and her footfalls a freshness.'

Dreams rubbed his chin.

'Very well,' he said, with a rare but fond smile. 'If it will pacify you, I will see you relinquish your duties as the Lady of the Forest. It is not so often we have cause to celebrate, we will make the most of it. Perhaps this duty will serve to calm Tarithel's waywardness.'

His wife was far too wise to suggest otherwise.

The day dawned bright at the Tower of the Moon. Luxor and Morkin were dressed for travel, their horses laden and ready for the off. Corleth stood nearby, with Rorthron alongside.

'You should consider once again, Moonprince,' Rorthron called. 'Heed my words.'

'My mind is set,' Luxor returned. 'I go to serve Lord Gard, to defend our interests on the Plains of Blood as duty demands.'

'Go then,' Rorthron called. 'I will impart such blessing as I can to speed you on your way, yet do not forget what I have told you. I fear it will not be long before you will be forced to call it to mind.'

Luxor nodded and turned his horse. 'Come, Mor … my son. We ride for Blood, let us hope the wind is at our heels.'

'Don the ring, Moonprince, ere you go. It will aid you and others besides …'

Luxor frowned and muttered under his breath.

'A lackey of the Wise I am become!'

Morkin grabbed his arm. 'I do not believe he means us ill. He did safeguard us, bring us together … Father.'

Luxor looked around, his newfound son's words bringing a tenderness to his face that neither expected. Luxor nodded.

'Perhaps you are right. The wisdom of youth, eh?'

He pulled the ring from an inside pocket and took the glove from his hand. Sunlight smote upon him as he brought the ring out once more. It sparkled and flashed in the light of dawn.

He slipped it on his finger, bracing himself for what was to come.

Tarithel did not return to her room. She climbed the spiralling staircase in the north west tower of the Citadel, reaching the wide open battlements. It was cold here, but the fire in her heart burned brightly enough that she didn't notice the chill. Guards acknowledged her presence and stepped back out of her way, but she did not say a word to them. She walked quickly across to the crenelated defences and looked over, seeing the forest arrayed below her. She stood directly above the western gate. As usual it was open, the sturdy portcullis retracted and the drawbridge lowered across the empty chasm that lay between the land outside and the grounds of the Citadel itself.

She remembered stories she'd been told of how it had once been a moat, filled with water and surrounded by the green of summer. The Citadel retained records of those times, uncounted thousands of moons ago; before the curse, before the everlasting winter.

She watched idly as traders funnelled through the entrance. Carts laden with provisions came and went through the gate. One was loaded with fish, she could smell them clearly even from this vantage point. Fishermen would have been working long at Lake Ithril, some ten or so leagues to the north. Fish miners they were called. She had been there once. The lake had been a wondrous thing, the waters warmed by some strange power deep beneath the earth.

She remembered that journey vividly. Her father had seemed in an unusually good mood at the Summer Solstice. The sun was at its warmest, the snow less than expected, it had been warmer than she had ever known, warm enough that she could wear only light garments outside in the day, something unheard of in recent times.

They had taken a walking trip through the forest, first to see the ancient Lith of Dreams before journeying on the lake. It had the appearance of a vast monument, forged of rock that jutted upwards out of the ground, its sleek sides somehow free of the snow. Tarithel remembered how she had touched the massive edifice, feeling a curious warmth under her fingertips. The Fey did not know much of the Lith, but they tended it, keeping it free of weeds and other unwanted growth, according it much reverence. She remembered learning that theirs was the only forest to contain one of these ancient works, but they were scattered about the land of Midnight ...

A land I will never see, it might was well not exist beyond the edge of the forest as far as I am concerned!

She raised her head and peered west. The forest rolled for uncounted leagues in that direction, right to the limits of her vision, what lay beyond she didn't know.

But one day I will find out. One day I will go there!

Today a mist hung over the forest. She could see it slowly rising in the faint warmth being thrown by the sun. It was little enough comfort.

The shortest day, the heart of winter. The Solstice.

She turned, hearing footsteps behind her. Her eyes widened as she caught sight of her parents. Guards immediately snapped to attention left and right.

'Father! Mother!'

'I thought I told you to return to your room,' her father said. His voice sounded stern, but Tarithel could tell from long experience that there was no real force behind it.

'I …' Tarithel began, and then settled for a pout.

'But it is good we have found you,' Dreams said. 'Your mother has something she wishes to tell you.'

Tarithel blinked in surprise. Her mother hardly ever had much to say to her. Tarithel had tried to take an interest in tapestries and needlework, but she had little talent for either and could never understand her mother's fascination with sitting at a spinning wheel for hours on end. She knew she was her father's daughter; she felt the call of the wild and the forest.

'There is a duty I have,' her mother said. 'A calling my own mother placed upon me long ago. It has not been something I have relished, and I have been derelict in its discharge through disinterest. Our people are poorer for my inaction, I would like to see it remedied.'

Tarithel looked from one to the other. Her father's face gave away no clue.

'I don't understand.'

'Your mother speaks of an ancient tradition of the Fey of our realm,' Dreams said. 'From amongst the womenfolk there is a title given which bestows a certain responsibility upon the bearer.'

'To protect the realm, to nurture the trees and the wildlife that dwells within,' her mother said. 'A counterpoint to the running of the Citadel itself.'

'Whosoever takes this role must be responsible and take their duty seriously,' her father said, his voice gruff once again. 'It is to be taken with reverence. They who take it would have to patrol the forests, learn its ways …'

Patrol the forests!

'What role?' Tarithel demanded.

Her mother smiled. 'I have been, until this day, the Lady of the Forest. Now I am stepping aside, relinquishing the responsibility. It is time for another to take my place.'

Tarithel stepped back.

'Me?'

'You have a love for the trees and for the outside world that far exceeds my own. You were born to this,' her mother said.

Lady of the Forest! They couldn't stop me going out! They'd have to let me go! I could see what lay beyond our borders!

'Or perhaps you don't feel you can rise to the challenge,' her father goaded.

Tarithel looked at him. 'Of course I could! What must I do?'

Her mother smiled.

'Just say yes.'

Tarithel laughed. 'Then yes, yes!'

They shared a rare family embrace. Her mother withdrew after a moment, removing a pendant from her neck.

'Here,' she said, 'it is yours. It will protect you and inspire you.'

Tarithel bowed her head and felt her mother place the pendant around her neck. It felt heavier than she expected. She looked down to see a bright green gem at the end of a silver chain. She stared into its depths, feeling a strange yet comforting warmth emanating from it.

'This jewel is the Heart of the Forest,' her mother said. 'A gem which, it is said, captured the light of the long summer, so many moons ago. The Lady of the Forest has always worn it, since the snow and ice descended upon our lands. It reminds us of what once was and what might ...' she paused. Tarithel looked up. 'And what might yet be. It is hope.'

'I will treasure it!'

'We shall have a celebration to mark the occasion,' Dreams said. 'A banquet in your honour. I dare say there are some things that will need to be learnt. Is that not right?'

Tarithel favoured him with a coquettish look. 'Is that not right, Lady of the Forest?' she replied. 'I might insist on my title being used.'

'You are still my daughter,' Dreams replied. 'I will address you as I see fit.'

'Come now you two,' her mother said, scolding both of them. 'Always vying for the last word.'

'No we're not.' Both Tarithel and Dreams said in unison.

Her mother laughed.

A strong gust of wind blew across the battlements. Tarithel turned, puzzled.

She frowned. At the edge of sight the trees were disappearing. The mist was thickening before her eyes, rolling swiftly across the forest roof. A rolling boiling expanse of cloud was enveloping the forest. She watched in awe as a monstrous wall of grey, reaching up far into the heavens and stretching from north to south before being lost to the limits of vision, swirling inexorably towards the citadel.

'What is this?' her father said from behind her.

She heard the gruff conversations of the guards as they gestured at the forbidding sight.

In eerie silence the bank of cloud continued to close about the forest, Tarithel stepped back as she watched. She felt herself shiver involuntarily.

What is this? Magic? If so, it is not of the Fey.

A stiff breeze rose, blowing snow into flurries that swirled around the battlements. Tarithel blinked to clear her eyes, vaguely hearing faint cries of fear and dismay from somewhere below.

By the time she could see again, the mass of cloud was almost upon them. The courtyards below were obscured. With wide eyes she watched as it finally reached the walls of the citadel.

Chilling mists drenched her clothes in icy condensation, but the cold she felt upon her skin was nothing compared to the chill that cracked into her very heart.

Despair!

Panic gripped her, vertigo threatened to overwhelm her, as if she was poised upon some dreadful precipice and about to fall. Something clutched at her heart, ripping away joy and leaving a ghastly void filled with horrors she didn't want to begin to comprehend. She felt a strange urge, an urge to throw herself from the battlements and dash herself to death on the stones below. She had to brace against it. Dark shapes, death, pain and a terrifying sense of threat. Darkness fell about her, the faint light of the sun extinguished.

Fear!

Vaguely, as if watching from afar, she felt herself fall to her knees. Screams assailed her ears and she recognised them as her own. She clamped her hands over her ears, collapsing into a huddle, her arms wrapped about her knees trying to find some sanctuary from the dread that had descended upon her.

Unreasoning terror!

She drew a shuddering gasp, trying to push against the crazed thoughts that were rising in her mind. Strange words formed, words she had never heard before, spoken by a sepulchral coarse voice that caused her to flinch and twitch. A voice laced with desire, with anger and with lust.

MIDNIGHT.

Somehow Tarithel could feel the enormous will that lay behind the voice, a brooding, clutching presence so dominating that she cowered with even the thought of it. It required her obedience, the denial of her wants and desires, unwitting obedience in all things …

No!

The green gem pulsed at the end of its chain. Tarithel's very nature rose up against the pervading gloom. She was no one's lackey! She gasped in horror at her audacity, but determination flared within her and she pushed back against the fear that clutched at her soul.

Resist! I am the Lady of the Forest!

Her vision returned, snow, ice and whirling mist. She could see the guards writhing on the ground, crying like children under the baleful influence. Her parents were likewise afflicted.

Gasping for breath she staggered to her feet, grabbing at the nearby wall for support.

'Never!'

She yelled into the noxious vapour all about her. Wind gusted and raged about her, twisting her clothes this way and that, almost throwing her to the floor.

DEFIANCE IS DEATH.

Fear hit her like a solid blow. She bent under its force, but she didn't break.

In Luxor's mind, the distant murmur of battle seemed to grow and a warm fire burned in his blood. Suddenly, the horizon expanded and flew away into the distance as into his mind flooded all the hopes and fears of the peoples of the Free. He struggled against it for a moment before relenting to the power of the Moon Ring.

Something rose in him, unbidden. Memories of battles he had never fought, the thoughts and stratagems of Lords he had never known, as if a thousand minds were somehow at his beck and call, all with advice he might draw upon in time of need.

Words echoed in his mind, words that flashed and burnt with power and might. He felt them grow, taking on a life of their own.

Almost against his will he drew his sword from its scabbard and held it aloft, then spurred his white stallion towards the Forest of Shadows. Morkin could scarce keep pace with the fury of his charge.

'Arise, Midnight!" he yelled as he rode, possessed by some arcane wrath of long ago. Words came to him, words he did not know, but somehow seemed intimately familiar. 'Arise the Free! Peril and doom lie at our gates. Waken your valour, arm yourselves with courage! We ride to conquer the Witchking forever! Arise Midnight, arise!'

Tarithel could bear it no longer, the despair clawing and clutching at her mind. She screamed out her indignation, feeling her resolve crumble. No escape from the overwhelming ferocity of the fear that smothered her. She could feel her sanity straining, about to snap into the mesmerising relief of utter madness. She forced her mind to work.

I ... am ... the Lady ... The Lady of ... the Forest!

But then ...

A warmth subsumed her, faint, but tantalising.

Hope blossomed. By sheer force of will she calmed her surging thoughts, focusing on the warmth that she could just sense.

It came from the south, a glow in her mind, counterpointing the green glow of the gem still hanging from her neck.

She staggered to her feet, wiping cold tears from her face and looking over the battlements. She alone stood upright, all others had fallen, crying and weeping at her feet. She looked around her, taking in the scene about and below. Guards collapsed at their posts, traders and farmers screaming and howling at the base of the walls, children crying for their parents, shrieking at the top of their lungs. She ran to her own parents, pulling them to their feet, scared to see the white pallor of their skin.

About her the dour mist lifted, evaporating upwards and retreating whence it had come, boiling and furling its way back to the north and west, silent and windless. Hope edged into the corners of her mind though she almost dared not embrace the feeling lest it might be dashed away.

Yet it grew stronger.

Sunlight broke though the mist with shocking suddenness, despatching the gloom in moments. She blinked, barely able to see, watching the mist boil and writhe away as if in pain. The full dawn broke suddenly over the land.

Sunlight showered the Citadel of Dreams in a blaze of warmth and light. A wave of hope rippled in her heart, bringing a glimmer of gladness unlooked for. It rose within her, reinforcing her thoughts of challenge and resolve. She cried out in glee, throwing her head back and yelling her defiance at the departing gloom. Her cry rang through the forests, carrying across the frozen eaves.

She gasped for breath, her heart pounding in her chest, astonished by the feeling of hope and courage that sang within her. She had felt nothing like it before. Now her tears were of joy.

Words formed on her lips unbidden, she knew not where they came from, nor what they might mean.

'The Moonprince rides!'

'I have guidance for you if you will take it,' Rorthron said, looking across at Corleth. Both were seated on horseback, ready for a trek across Midnight. Behind them the tower was locked and secured.

'You have not led me astray,' Corleth answered. 'But I will not let Luxor down. I would see that rift healed.'

Rorthron nodded. 'That which caused the rift still remains,' he observed. 'Until that changes ...'

'But he is the Moonprince!'

'He is, but he must establish that authority amongst the Free,' Rorthron replied. 'That will not be easy for him. Nonetheless, I advise you to journey north west before you turn east towards the Keep of Blood. Allies you may find.'

'The Fey of this forest?' Corleth asked. 'They remain?'

'They do,' Rorthron said. 'And others besides. All will be needed ere much time has passed.'

Corleth nodded. 'Then I will seek them out. Farewell Rorthron the Wise.'

He turned his horse and rode away, sparing a glance over his shoulder a few moments later. Of both Rorthron and his steed there was no sign.

About the Tower of Doom the storm raged on. Winds ravaged the Plains of Despair, ripping around the keeps and citadels of that desolate domain. Lightning flashed and crackled; thunder echoed back from the mountains.

The wind blew fierce and strong. The Witchking had made it so.

His arm, wrapped in the ice that shrouded everything, still outstretched to the hated south.

A tremble grew in the tower. For long moments it went unnoticed, slowly growing in intensity.

The image of Shareth frowned as she sensed something awry, but before she could call out, her image crackled and flickered before being dashed to oblivion. The Ice Crown vibrated upon its stand, its malevolent blue-white glow pulsing.

The Witchking whirled as the wind about the tower lost its direction, swirling around in chaos and blustering back and forth, heedless to his will.

He gestured imperiously, attempting to regain control of the errant forces he had unleashed, but it was to no avail. The wind turned inwards, mist swept over the mountains about his domain and the faintest flicker of sunlight burst across the desolate Plains of Despair.

A silent howl of pain of indignation was wrenched from the ice-bound figure within the tower, a screech of anger and fury far beyond the hearing of mortal men, yet crushing fear upon the Witchking's minions.

His outstretched arm trembled in disbelief, pointing to the south, disbelief now somehow etched upon the frozen features.

A MOONPRINCE? NO. IT CANNOT BE!

Inexplicable warmth touched him, as painful as a burning brand would be to an unclothed man. Doubt buried into his mind and like a canker, began to grow.

CHAPTER FIVE

THE MOON RING REVEALED? A TALISMAN!
The War of the Solstice had begun.

Chapter Six

They stand in the Forest of Shadows,
looking east to the Plains of Blood.

The trek from the Forest of Shadows eastwards across the Plains of Blood was dreary in the extreme. The forest had parted for them, as expected, and Luxor and Morkin had ridden out into the wilderness.

The chill wind was still blowing from the north, cutting through even their thick travelling cloaks. Hour after hour they slogged on across the plain, their horses snorting and complaining as windswept snow battered at them. The going was slow.

After a few hours they turned north east, following a route highlighted by occasional rock waymarkers sticking out from the snow covered ground. They picked up speed here, the route being a well-used tradeway between the Citadel of Gard to the south and Shimeril to the east.

Morkin could see that the ground underneath had been recently trampled both by the boots of men and the hooves of horses.

'The armies of the southlands,' Luxor called out above the gale. 'A day ahead of us I would say.'

They didn't see the sun that day and night fell about them with little warning, the light fading as they pitched their tents and saw to the horses. Luxor's steed was tired after the long traipse, but Morkin's red-haired mare was still prancing and full of energy.

Perhaps it really is Fey-bred, and that gives it some extra store of strength.

Their supper was meagre, as it proved impossible to get a fire lit, so they ate a quick meal of dried meats and prepared to sleep.

'My Lord ...' Morkin began.

'You had better get used to calling me father,' Luxor said, with a fond grin.

'And I am proud to do so, it just ...' Morkin stopped.

Luxor nodded. 'It is strange, I agree. It will take us a while to adjust. We have learnt many things these last days.'

Morkin nodded, paused and then looked back up. 'Father, why do you hate the Fey so?'

Luxor sighed. 'It is a long story. Another time perhaps, and I do not hate the Fey ... I just ...'

'But if I am half-Fey ...'

Morkin saw his father sigh. 'Not now, Mor ... son.'

Morkin waited, frowning. Luxor turned to look at him and a smile grew on his face.

'I will get no peace until I explain myself, I see. Let's see to the tent first.'

They prepped themselves for sleep, tying down the tent as best they could, trying to ignore the chill gusts of wind that swept about them.

'The Free and the Fey have never had the easiest of relationships,' Luxor began. 'The Fey do not measure things as we do, or think the same way. They value stability and permanence above all. They are most content in their dwellings, and would stay within forever if it were possible. Men require movement and change. Nonetheless, we had lived alongside each other throughout the long winter of Midnight for many years.'

Morkin rolled over, listening carefully.

'They are not natural warriors, not inclined to violence like some of our people. They are a crafty folk, most at home in their forests, tending to such aspects of nature as they see fit. They are few in number overall I think compared to the people of the Free.'

'But they do fight, surely? The Witchking ...'

'They have stood against the Witchking many times. When I was a young man they fought alongside us, not far from this very spot, in defence of the Keep of Blood. Such an army had not been seen for a long time. Free and Fey marched together against the Doomguard. I even called one my friend.'

'Corleth,' Morkin said.

Luxor nodded. 'Corleth. We fought with the hated enemy, he unleashed the ice-fear against us. Free or Fey it smote us down, turning minds to mincemeat. But we threw back the Doomguard. Through valour and swordsmanship we routed his armies. They were in retreat. We might have ended it there.'

'Ended it?'

'The Witchking,' Luxor said, sighing. 'He was weak then, in retreat. The Lords of the Free vowed to pursue him to the gates of his domain, to fight on through to Ushgarak itself, throw down its walls and slay the hated ruler of that domain. I believe it could have been done, but it was not to be.'

'Why not?'

'The Free were led by Lord Gard. You will be presented to him tomorrow at Blood's keep. He is a tough and harsh man, well versed in the art of war and less so in the arts of peace. For their part, the Fey were led by the Lord of Dreams.'

'Dreams? I have not heard of him or his domain.'

'It is far to the north east, beyond the Mountains of Gor-grath.'

'Isn't that the domain of the Witchking?'

'Not quite,' Luxor said. 'Not all the northland belongs to him. The Fey maintain a strong presence in the Forest of

Dreams, and he has yet to oust them from their ancient home. The Citadel of Dreams is a wonder to behold so it is said. The capital of the Fey we would call it.'

'But what happened after the battle?'

'Dreams and Gard disagreed. I know not what the detail was, but the Fey left that very day. Every single one turned aside, leaving the Free alone. Gard reported they refused to fight, that they would not challenge the Witchking further, that we should be content with defending the southlands.'

'And Corleth?'

'He left, obeying his orders without question despite my entreaties. He refused to explain the reasoning of the Fey to me.' Luxor clenched his hands. 'Our friendship failed that day.'

Morkin looked downcast.

'We could have stopped the Witchking!' Luxor said, shaking his head. 'Without the Fey we did not have the might to continue the fight. Their departure was almost the death of me. The remnants of the Doomguard we had defeated mustered against as when they saw the Fey depart. I lost my men and was forced to seek shelter in the forest. It was there ...'

Luxor's expression softened.

'It was there your story begins,' Luxor continued. 'For there it seems I met your mother, Aleisha.'

'I would like to know more of her.'

Luxor sighed, the softness fading away.

'Perhaps that chance will come. I find it hard to trust the Fey. They walked away when we had the one opportunity to rid the lands of this curse. We are likely never to have that chance again. But they also saved my life and have given me a son, thus I must be thankful to them too.'

'I hope I can restore your faith in them,' Morkin said. 'I will be loyal and trustworthy, even though I be half-Fey.'

'I am sorry, my son,' Luxor said. 'Think not on it, never doubt my faith in you.'

'And Corleth has never explained?'

Luxor shook his head. 'We have met seldom in the intervening years, I have sore goaded him as you saw, but he never talks about it. It seems the Fey hold their secrets close. The only sure lesson is that we cannot depend upon them to defeat the Witchking. If he is to be stopped, it will be by the hand of the Free. Now, enough tales of the past. We must look to the future, and a good night's sleep will be essential!'

Morkin settled down to sleep, but his slumber was disturbed by a strange dream. In his mind's eye he saw a girl, standing upon lofty battlements, screaming out in torment as some woe came upon her. He jolted awake, a name upon his lips, yet when he tried to whisper it, it had already gone from his memory.

A fierce and blustery wind blew from the north, whipping around the Keep of Herath. Snow was already piled unseasonably high against the walls, drifting in great dunes in what, long ago, had been green and fertile pastures. They were gone now, remembered only in the ancient annals stored deep in the keep, written by ancient scribes, buried under long moons of ice and snow.

The wind was being funnelled down from the high reaches of the Mountains of Ithril, a jagged barrier that ran half the length of midnight, dividing the northlands from the south all the way from the Citadel of Ithrorn in the far north east, to the Plains of Blood.

Herath toiled across the battlements of his keep, nodding briefly to the guards who stood stoically in the cold, watching over the edge. Conversation was impossible in the howling gale, the wind whipping the banners of the keep back and forth. His motif, a white moon on a green relief, still proudly displayed.

Herath paced around the icy battlements, distracting himself from the thoughts that swirled around his mind.

Talk in the village to the south west had been disquieting of late. No official tidings had reached him from Marakith or Kumar. That in itself was worrying. It was said that the western armies of the Free were marching upon Gorgrath, there to subdue errant forces of the Witchking that had the temerity to wander this far south. Herath had expected to hear tales of gallantry and the swift despatch of the over bold Doomguard.

But nothing, either way.

Herath's keep lay at a well-known strategic point in Midnight's vast expanse. Nestled between the Mountains of Kumar to the south and Ithril to the North, it guarded the only pass through the Mountains of Ithril for many leagues in either direction. It had been built here for precisely that reason, to ensure the mountains remained safe and to give early warning for the citadels of Marakith and Kumar further south.

The canary keep, we've been called. If the Witchking does ever strike again, it is possible he will try this route. If so, we'll be the first to know.

He squinted into the North once more. If the Witchking was moving in Ithril, he could not divine it. Herath had sensed the ice-fear. It had rippled out of the north west, disquieting the warriors he commanded. Many of the older ones had felt it before and told tales of its ghastly impact in battles of the past.

It is the Solstice, the Witchking stirs once more. What is his intent this time?

No answers were forthcoming. Herath gave instructions to double the guard and keep a constant look out. For now, there was nothing else he could do.

The early morning brought Luxor and Morkin to the Keep of Blood. It was a surprisingly ramshackle old fortress. Morkin could see at a glance that it had been rebuilt several times, utilising different types of stone.

'Lord Blood cares little for artistry,' Luxor answered when Morkin pointed it out. 'As long as the walls are up and the gate secured, he's happy.'

Morkin could see hundreds of men at arms arrayed around the keep, with legions of riders on horseback busy organising themselves alongside. Banners were flying from the towers of the keep. Morkin spent a moment identifying them.

Gard, Shimeril, Brith, Rorath, Blood and Mitharg! Such an army must be six thousand strong or more!

Morkin had never seen such a host of men. Most were at work unloading wagons laden with provisions and moving them in towards the keep, others were engaged in preparing weapons, sharpening swords, fetching arrows and bows. Still others were practicing, charging with angry yells or duelling with each other.

'Unfurl our banner,' Luxor instructed. 'It is time we announced our arrival!'

Morkin pulled two long poles from where they were packed against the flanks of his horse and secured them together. Then he unfurled a banner and hoisted it aloft. It fluttered in the wind for a moment before straightening out.

A cyan moon and a golden star against magenta ...

'Say nothing of this Moonprince business,' Luxor said. 'Nor of Rorthron and his machinations. This is not the time.'

Or Corleth?

They rode into the keep and dismounted, handing their horses over to the stablehands nearby. Immediately two Lords came towards them, hands raised in greeting.

'Lord Luxor! You are a sight for sore eyes. I've been putting up with Shimeril's ugly visage all morning. Come to make a pile of Doomguard corpses I trust?'

It had to be Lord Blood, Morkin decided. He was tall, well-built, gruff but somehow friendly and well-disposed. His face was marked with the scars of battle centred around an obviously broken nose. He was dressed in leather armour, with a great broadsword buckled at his hip.

His companion was shorter and stouter. Morkin had met Shimeril before and liked him. The man was rather obese, his flushed face dominated by a huge red moustache, a neatly trimmed beard and a freckled bald head. He seemed to prefer different weapons. Two short swords were in evidence.

'Yes,' Shimeril answered, 'At least with the rotting carcasses of the Witchking's foul hordes on a pyre we might have something to eat that surpasses Blood's culinary expertise.'

Luxor grinned. 'It is good to see you my friends. What news?'

'You're the last to arrive,' Blood said. 'Rorath and Brith arrived just before you. For the most part things are ready. Gard complains as you would expect, nothing is ever done to his satisfaction.'

'No changes from the norm there,' Shimeril said, with a grin.

'He is charged with the defence of the western reaches,' Luxor said. 'It is a serious responsibility.'

'He can afford to be a little more cheerful,' Blood said. 'Battle is afoot once more. We march to splash the Witchking's forces to the winds and smear their entrails across the land! Songs and feasting we shall have upon our victory. What's to be depressed about? This is what we are born for.'

'Tidings from the north do not bode well,' Shimeril said.

'Oh, nonsense,' Blood returned, putting on an affected voice. 'Tidings from the north do not bode well. What of it? Tidings from the north never bode well.'

Shimeril's serious face did not break into a smile as expected. Luxor raised his eyebrows.

'Pour out your tale of woe then,' Blood said, with an expansive gesture.

'I fear,' Shimeril said, glancing to the north, 'that this is no idle remnant of the Doomguard, but that they have newly fortified the Citadels of Gorgrath and the keeps thereabouts. We cannot tell what strength they have assembled, but it would appear to be greater than we suspected from before.'

'An old man's fears,' Blood said. 'The scouts report no such thing ...'

Luxor took a deep breath.

'I have heard that the Witchking stirs once more,' he said. 'Today is the heart of winter, the Solstice itself, the peak of his power ...'

'Come now! We have nothing to fear!' Blood said. 'Look about you, such an army hasn't been mustered in a generation. We will be hard pressed to find enough sport for all these men.'

Shimeril laughed. 'We won't deprive you of your bloodletting, my friend.'

'We had best present ourselves,' Luxor said. 'Come, Morkin.'

'Indeed,' Shimeril said and then looked anxious. 'Be warned, he is not in a good mood.'

Blood coughed. 'When is the good Lord Gard ever in a good mood? He has ... eh ... made himself at home in my hall. You'll find him easily enough.'

'Until later my friends.'

Luxor nodded to the two Lords and made his way towards the inner buildings of the keep, climbing an external stone staircase up the interior wall. Morkin struggled behind him, trying to keep the banner aloft in the stiff breeze.

Two guards at the top snapped to attention and stepped back out of the way. Luxor nodded in acknowledgement and entered the keep. Morkin lowered the standard and followed.

A stone passageway led inside, directly to the main hall. A

small fire was burning within and more guards flanked the entrance. A herald stepped up, looked them over and then turned.

'Lord Luxor of Odrark!'

Luxor and Morkin looked forward to where a man sat at a table, staring down intently at a map that was unfurled on the table, weighted at each end by heavy iron rods. He was balding, his hair wispy, clearly senior in years. He did not acknowledge them, other than to gesture briefly with an outstretched finger, before resuming his scrutiny of the scroll before him.

Luxor walked to the table, Morkin beside him.

'Lord Gard,' Luxor said, 'I come in answer to your summons. I am here with my squire …'

Gard continued to peruse the map, before letting out an exaggerated sigh.

'You're late.'

Finally he looked up.

'Other Lords may appreciate your presence, Lord Luxor of Odrark.' Gard glared at Luxor with a fierce glint in his grey eyes. 'I can only report overwhelming ambivalence. You have no army, no warriors or riders, thus your use is limited. I summoned you only because tradition dictates that I must treat my vassals with equity.'

Luxor stiffened, but didn't say anything. Morkin scowled and then swallowed as Gard looked across at him.

'Your squire does not appreciate my words I see.'

Luxor nudged Morkin with his foot. Gard looked back down at the map, ignoring them for long moments.

'Lord Gard,' Luxor began. 'I have met with one Rorthron the Wise who …'

Morkin looked up at Luxor in surprise.

But you said …

'Yes, I heard about your little deviation. I am glad that you have time to indulge in petty quests and chasing myths. '

'He has given me a gift,' Luxor continued. 'A ring, potent in power, but to use it ...'

'Has he appointed you an army, Lord Luxor?'

'No my Lord ...'

'Is there a host of Fey at your beck and call, Lord Luxor?'

'No my Lord, but ...'

'You of all should remember their perfidy,' Gard said. 'We put our trust in steel and strength of arms.'

'I have said such things myself,' Luxor acknowledged. 'But this was no idle encounter ... the Wise ...'

'Magic and sorcery is what cursed these lands in the first place,' Gard said, anger evident in his voice despite the coolness of his words. 'I will have no part of any such interference from the likes of the Wise. They abrogated their responsibilities moons ago. Do not allow them to addle your mind and twist your thoughts. They are masters of misdirection and to be avoided. Your sword and that of your squire is all I require of you.'

Morkin looked Luxor, awaiting a rebuff. But it did not come. Luxor paused before speaking.

'You have orders, Lord Gard? We are at your disposal.'

'See that you maintain morale about the camp,' Gard replied. 'The troops will appreciate that.'

'Our situation?' Luxor asked.

'Scouts have reported that the twin keeps of Valethor are occupied and passage through the gap of Valethor is therefore being watched. Smoke rises from the Citadel of Gorgrath. It would seem the enemy is preparing some mischief. We march upon the morrow to teach him the error of his ways.'

'Do we know his strength?'

'War bands have been spotted arriving at the Citadel of Gorgrath,' Gard said. 'Perhaps two thousand at most.'

Luxor frowned. 'Are we sure? Rorthron advised that we might face a great force of Doomguard, and that the ice-fear ...'

Gard stopped, took a breath and looked up. 'Yes, we are sure.' His voice rose. 'We have had the Citadel under constant surveillance for many moons, ever since the rumours of wayfarers being ambushed were received. There has been no hint of the ice-fear. I have laboured under its influence in many more battles than you, I'm sure I would recognise it if it were present. It is not.'

Luxor swallowed.

'Any other questions?' Gard sat back in his chair. 'After all, I have all day to indulge you. There are no pressing calls on my time. I am merely organising our attack upon that Citadel, a matter of trivial concern …'

Luxor did not flinch under the cold gaze, but acquiesced.

'No, my Lord Gard.'

'Very well then. See to your duty, Lord Luxor of Odrark. See to it that you do not mention your fairy stories before me again.'

Gard stressed the word 'Odrark', the implication of inferiority was clear.

Luxor turned and strode out, Morkin hurrying to keep pace.

Corleth had quickly reached the forest to the north west of the Tower of the Moon. The valley led in this direction and would, he knew, eventually rise into the twin mountain ranges of Ashimar and Dodrak far to the north. These lands were seldom travelled. Ashimar had once been a fiefdom of the Free, but its keeps were all in ruins. None lived here who had a choice and it was of little use to the Witchking, or so it seemed.

The forest eaves were thinning out as he continued through. Here and there he felt a familiar warmth from the trees about him. He recognised it immediately; the curation and tending of the Fey. It was subtle, men would not have noticed it, but it put in him mind of his home in the distant Forest of Thrall.

So there are Fey here ...

Also subtle, and unmistakable, was the sound of a bow being drawn.

Corleth stopped.

'Raise your hands, stranger,' said a voice.

Corleth did as he was bid, surprised at the swiftness and stealthiness that his captors possessed. He had not heard them until the very last moment.

Almost as if they were but ... Shadows!

A figure appeared in front of him, tall and elegant, dressed in the dark green of traditional Fey apparel, his face hidden by the shadows from the trees about him.

'Speak,' he said, 'and make your words worthwhile. We do not permit strangers to pass.'

Corleth took a breath.

'I am Corleth of the Thrall Fey,' he said. 'I am here upon the bidding of Rorthron the Wise. I seek ...'

The figure stepped out and Corleth saw him clearly now. A grim face, not often given over to humour.

'You seek the Lord of Shadows,' the Fey replied. 'I am he. I know of this Rorthron. He resides in the Tower yonder, to the south. We have spoken on rare occasions, thus I am inclined to hear you out. What business do you have here, Corleth, Fey of Thrall?'

'I come to ask you to join me,' Corleth replied. 'I am loyal to Lord Luxor, the revealed Moonprince of Midnight.'

Whatever Shadows had expected Corleth to say, this was not it; that much was evident upon his face.

'A Moonprince? You jest.'

'I do not.'

Corleth saw Shadows frown as he thought it over.

'And precisely what does this Moonprince ask?'

'That we rally to one banner, Free and Fey alike, to defend our realms from the advance of the Witchking.'

Shadows snorted. 'The Free have never come to my aid in all these long years, why should I come to theirs? I owe them nothing.'

'We are stronger together.'

'I need them not. This forest is a stronghold far more powerful than their Citadels of stone.'

Another Fey ran up to the Lord of Shadows and whispered to him. Corleth tried to catch the conversation but he could not.

'Interesting that you should come to us,' Shadows said, 'as the agents of the Witchking march upon my borders. We will discuss this later. I trust you can wield a sword and a bow, Corleth of Thrall?'

'The Witchking's hordes are here?'

Shadows nodded. 'We have often seen raiding parties travel south through the Mountains of Ashimar, looking for spoils from the territory of Lord Gard to the south. We have done him many a service by dealing with them, scant thanks we have ever received for our troubles. Now it seems they take an interest in us.'

'They are from the Lith of Ashimar, my Lord!' the messenger said. 'An army, many hundreds of them! Our scouts flee back as we speak.'

'This is no raiding party,' Shadows growled.

'The Witchking moves against us all,' Corleth whispered. 'We must unite against him, or all will be lost.'

Shadows gestured for him to be silent and then issued instructions.

'To the western forest edge, quick now!'

Corleth followed as the Fey slipped through the trees at a run. He could see hundreds of warriors flitting between the trunks and branches. Moving within the forest came instinctively to the Fey, but he knew their swift abilities seemed almost miraculous to the people of the Free.

It did not take them long to reach the western boundary of the forest. Shadows called a halt while he surveyed the scene. Corleth could see the Lith in the distance, perhaps two leagues away. Squinting, he could make out a dust plume of snow rising before it, a dark stain at its base.

'An army of the Witchking ...' he gasped. 'Why are they here?'

'Hold here,' Shadows called. 'The wall of the forest remains our defence.'

Corleth saw Shadows look about him, knowing what was going through his mind. They could charge out across the plain, but in so doing would give up their advantage. The armies of the Witchking were well versed in fighting in the open and would be more heavily beweaponed and armoured.

'They are bold indeed,' the messenger said, 'daring to assail us in our own domain.'

Shadows nodded. 'Something has prompted this.' He turned to look at Corleth. 'What do you know, Corleth? What have you not said?'

'I know little more than you, my Lord,' Corleth said. 'Save that Rorthron told me the Witchking's power waxes on the Solstice ...'

'... and today is that very day,' Shadows said.

They watched as the army approached, clearer by the minute. Before long the dark banners and black armour of the Doomguard were visible. They matched ruthlessly forward, their gait brutal and efficient. They made no secret of their approach, but came on with horns sounding.

'How many do you count?' Shadows asked.

The messenger made a quick tally. 'Worse than we thought, perhaps a thousand, my Lord.'

'And armed to the teeth no doubt.' Shadows signalled to his men and bows were strung, arrows notched and swords readied. Corleth prepared himself, likewise.

'We will talk further,' Shadows said, looking at him. 'Assuming we make it out of this alive.'

'I will hold you to that,' Corleth said and was rewarded with the briefest of grins.

The Doomguard warriors were close now, perhaps a hundred yards away.

They stopped advancing, coming to a halt in a sharp line twenty men deep and fifty across. Corleth could just make out their leader, who stepped forward, raising a sword into the air.

'Hold,' Shadows whispered.

At some unspoken and unheard signal, mist coiled out of the ground, writhing up in snake-like filaments, coiling around the legs and arms of the Fey as they crouched by the forest edge. Wherever it touched them, frost grew on their clothes. Yells of confusion and fear resounded through their ranks. Worse though, was the icy chill that struck at them from inside.

Corleth recognised it at once, as did many beside him, but he had not felt it so chill and sharp before, almost as if it had been especially refined, just to be used here.

The ice-fear! The Witchking has learned new foul arts, to direct the fear thus ...

Before they had a chance to recover, arrows swept in about them. Several Fey yelled and fell, slain by the onslaught. The youngest fled, panic overwhelming them as the ice-fear grasped at their souls and promised further terrors. Only the boldest held up, their faces whiter than the snow that lay about them.

'Loose!' Shadows called. 'Loose!'

A scattering of arrows swept back towards the incoming Doomguard, a few finding their targets. Then the battle was joined.

Corleth was assailed by two warriors, clad head to foot in black. His sword rang as he parried the blows before he was able to strike back. Yells and screams reached his ears, but he had no time to pay them heed as more blows fell. Swords rose and fell about him. He despatched the warriors of the enemy, but there were always more to take their place.

'Fall back within the forest!'

Shadows yell reached him and with the other Fey about him they retreated.

Yet the Doomguard advanced on them, unhindered.

Corleth looked about him in surprise and dismay. The enchantments of the Fey lay thick upon the forest. Strangers were discouraged and enemies resisted …

But the trees were unmoved, helpless and useless.

The Witchking can enter our realms with impunity. We are defenceless!

A vision blurred his senses for a moment. The Doomguard running amok through all the forests of the Fey; his own forest set ablaze and burnt to ashes.

No!

He fought back, determination surging in his heart. He struck at the Doomguard before him, making some headway before the icy cold clutched at his heart once more. Never had the ice-fear been so potent.

The Fey were in full retreat now. Backing through the forest as the Doomguard continued to advance, hacking down any stragglers.

Shadows and his people regrouped upon a small rise as the Doomguard swirled about their base. They were outnumbered and surrounded. Corleth looked about him in despair.

It cannot end here, not this way!

'This is no mere skirmish,' Shadows said, breathing heavily. He was injured, his left arm hanging uselessly by his side. 'And how can they penetrate our realm? What power is this?'

'He means to exterminate us,' Corleth replied. 'If he has come in force here, doubtless he has come in force elsewhere. The Free at the Keep of Blood know not that his strength is already greater than we imagined ...'

'Little use that is to us,' Shadows said, looking about him. The Doomguard were readying themselves to assail the cornered Fey.

About them the mist thickened and chilled. Icicles formed on branches and twigs, growing with impossible speed.

The Doomguard stood in silence, as if waiting ...

As one, they marched, swords drawn, a closing ring of black metal, choking off any possibility of escape.

'Fight well,' Shadows called to his people and then looked across at Corleth, muttering under his breath. 'It will be your last.'

Corleth gripped his sword tighter and adjusted his stance.

The ring of metal closed, swords rose, blades clashed. The Fey held their own for a time, before their ranks began to crumble. A mass push by the Doomguard sent them sprawling for grip, almost overwhelmed.

Horns sounded.

But they were not of the Doomguard. These horns were lighter in tone, more melodious. Corleth exchanged a desperate look with Shadows before they wrestled themselves up alongside the remaining Fey.

Arrows whistled out of the mist, cutting down swaths of the Doomguard.

Something attacked from behind them. The Fey answered the horns with their own and the battle was rejoined.

Caught between two flanks the Doomguard were now exposed, trying to turn to meet their new assailants whilst defending themselves against what had, moments before, been their certain prey.

For many long moments Corleth could not see who had come to their aid. The battle raged bloody and brutal about him. He got the faint impression of grey-clad figures, holding knives or short swords, slicing and whirling about the Doomguard. Whoever they were they moved quickly and silently, in a manner of which even the Fey would be proud.

No time to wonder. The Doomguard fought like fury, and twice he was nearly skewered by their blackened swords.

Yet the battle turned. The Fey found themselves advancing on the Doomguard, whose numbers, now depleted, turned and fled. The Fey chased them and the Doomguard ran right into a whirling wall of bright steel that flashed and spun with deadly accuracy.

All fell before it and the Fey paused.

The ground was littered with the bodies of the fallen, Doomguard and Fey alike. Corleth was close to exhaustion, but unharmed. Shadows limped up behind him, suffering from a dozen cuts and now cradling his broken arm.

'Who are these people?'

Corleth shook his head. Before him, line upon line of grey clad figures stood, cloaked from head to foot. They seemed not to be armoured, but each bore a curving silver knife. Most dripped with the dark ruby blood of the slain Doomguard.

One figured stepped forward, indistinguishable from the others save for a more ornate knife, bearing some heraldic crest upon its cross-guard and filigree upon the blade.

Shadows looked at Corleth, who stepped back.

'I would thank you,' Shadows said. 'Such bravery was unlooked for in our time of woe. I would know your name stranger and from whence you come.'

The lead figure stepped forward a pace, securing its knife

at its side and then raising two delicate looking hands to the cowl about its head.

Corleth blinked in surprise as a face was revealed.

The hair was raven black, bound by a silver diadem, almost shining blue in the pale light of the forest. The face was pale, the eyes dark and heavy, the neck adorned by more silver.

The expression was unreadable.

'They call me the Lady of Silence,' the woman said, her voice sharp against the cold air.

Corleth looked at Shadows. Shadows looked around at the Fey behind him and nodded.

As one, the Fey bowed the knee in gratitude.

The armies of the Free marched from the Keep of Blood, banners unfurled in a stiff breeze blowing from the north. Such an army hadn't been seen for generations. Seven lords had gathered together. Four thousand three hundred riders and three thousand three hundred warriors marched across the frozen plain.

Luxor and Morkin had been invited to stand with the army of Lord Blood and rode alongside him. Morkin occupied himself with counting the banners and identifying to whom they belonged. Lord Gard at the lead of course, flanked by Shimeril and Blood on either flank. Lord Blood's army was entirely composed of riders, trained to respond quickly to threats in his domain.

The rest of the army was strung out behind. Morkin could see the banners of Brith and Rorath with which he was already familiar, but there was another. Lord Mitharg likewise counted Gard as his liege.

Sizeable though the army was, it was nothing like as large as the armies of history. Luxor and Blood spoke of the previous war when all the Lords and many of the Fey were present.

'We had thousands of the Fey alongside,' Blood remembered. 'And our own ranks were swelled to bursting. The supply lines were a nightmare to organise, near thirty thousand warriors …'

Morkin looked around him and tried to imagine an army four times the size. He failed, it was impossible. The clash of weapons, shields and armoured horses echoed about him. The sheer noise of an army on the move had come as quite an astonishment to him.

They had been riding all morning but at the slower walking pace that the foot soldiers set. Morkin did not envy them, trudging on weary league after weary league, but those he could see seemed content enough with their lot. They were hardened men, used to the toil of soldiering, thinking little of a ten league march.

Ahead, though the wind blew chill, the twin keeps of Valethor were growing close. The Mountains of Dodrak and Ithril were parted by a narrow valley which the twin keeps overlooked from either side. It was a superb defensive position which had been used to great effect by the Witchking's forces in previous battles.

Morkin looked up at the keeps as the army slowly moved past. They seemed utterly derelict, with no signs of habitation. Scouts had been sent ahead in the early morning reporting that forces of Doomguard had been seen retreating from both of the keeps, heading north towards the Citadel.

'Flushed them out,' Blood said. 'Those keeps are long past defensible. If they plan to resist us, the Citadel will allow them to make the most of what they have.'

Their foe lay further on, three hours march ahead, at the Citadel of Gorgrath.

The army stopped for a brief meal. Morkin overheard the scout reports that indicated some minor fortification of the Citadel had been undertaken. Even from this distance Morkin could see it was badly damaged, but there was definitely something underway. Smoke was rising from within its ramparts.

Lord Gard, astride a huge war-charger, galloped up to them. Luxor, Blood and Morkin bowed in acknowledgement.

'We will arrange ourselves before the Citadel,' Gard called. 'A show of strength. If they relent and retreat to the Citadel of Korkith in good order we will have no further quarrel with them. If they refuse to treat or determine to stay, we shall slay them.'

'How many do we think they are?' Blood asked.

'They number perhaps two thousand at best,' Gard said. 'They would be foolish to attack or even resist us.'

'Are we sure of the reports?' Luxor said. Morkin could see his face was creased with a frown. 'They know where we are and they have seen our armies amass. They must know they stand no …'

'They have holed up in their ruin,' Gard replied. 'A small remnant of the Witchking's cursed progeny. Today we will send a reminder to the Witchking, not to trespass into the lands of the Free.'

He spurred his horse around and galloped away.

'The Witchking plays some trick with us,' Luxor muttered.

'And what of it?' Blood answered. 'We have an army seven thousand strong. Enough to deal with any resurgence of his old might. There is not a hint of the ice-fear my friend, you worry too much.'

Luxor sighed but did not respond as the army got underway once more.

'We struck it hard in the last war,' Blood said, gazing at the Citadel of Gorgrath. 'The Witchking never repaired it. This time we may sack it once and for all.'

The army of the Free had drawn up at the end of the valley. Before them the ancient Citadel stood tall and austere in a grey light of the afternoon. Behind it lay the mountains that shared its name and the shattered ruins of other fortresses that had long ago succumbed to battles forgotten.

The army arrayed itself in a proud and disciplined way. Gard would expect nothing less. Within the ranks ladders, grappling hooks and all manner of other devices of war were being readied. Long experience of siege warfare had taught the armies of the Free the best ways to assault the keeps and citadels of the realm. Archers for the defenders on the walls, ladders reinforced with wrought iron to scale the walls and a concerted attack, timed with precision, bringing all those elements together.

Wars had been fought this way for generations and the techniques required to win were well known and understood by all. Overwhelming numbers remained the greatest key to success, along with soldiers unwearied by a long march prior to the battle. With a rest at Blood, the Free had both of these on their side.

Luxor and Morkin watched as Lord Gard and his heralds rode forward towards the gates, banners aflutter in the breeze. They heard the trumpets announce his arrival before the walls of the citadel. Along with the other Lords, they rode up alongside him, standing perhaps a hundred yards from the walls. The banners of the Free were a glorious sight, raised in a row, signalling the combined might of their force.

Gard looked about him for a moment and then raised his voice.

'To the forces of the Witchking that occupy and hold the citadel. We have seen you pillage our lands and put our people to the sword. This we will not abide. We demand that you give this citadel over to the forces of the Free and retreat northwards to your own domain. We guarantee you safe passage if you will lay down your arms. You have until sundown to comply.'

Silence fell about them, punctuated only by the whistling of the wind through the towers of the citadel. No flags flew, no banners, there was little sign of anything other than a thin plume of smoke to indicate there was anyone within.

Then a lone figure appeared on the battlements. Morkin could make out what he took to be a man, dressed in armour that was black, contrasting sharply with the snow coated walls. The figure stood with one foot propped up on the edge in a jaunty fashion. Morkin saw the horns on his helmet move as he surveyed the army that surrounded him.

The Foul!

It was his first sight of the ancient foe. He tried to remember what he had been taught. Men seduced by the promises and powers of the Witchking as he rose to power, now corrupted beyond any hope of redemption. Fierce and brutal warriors with no thought for mercy or compassion, their hearts frozen by the ice that pervaded the heart of winter from the north.

But no message came. The figure did not speak and seemed to give little heed to the army camped at his gates. Morkin saw him turn and give a brief gesture.

A faint sound, a crunch and a thump. Something came whistling through the air, a projectile aimed at them.

It fell before them, crashing into the snow twenty yards ahead, causing the horses to snort and whinny in alarm.

Morkin stared in horror. It was a corpse, clearly one of their unfortunate scouts judging by the tarnished and soiled clothes. The face bore the marks of torture, the features locked in a frozen grimace of pain. Brands had been applied to arms and legs, a crudely marked crown, the symbol of the Witchking.

'Their answer then,' Gard said. He signalled to men behind him. 'Take our fallen comrade and make preparations to honour him once this business is concluded. We will smite these foul hordes. Leave none alive.'

He wheeled his horse about and rode back to the ranks of warriors. The Lords turned to follow. Morkin looked up to the citadel where the black figure still stood. As he watched it turned and retreated out of sight.

Within minutes orders had been sent around the camp by runners. The respective Lords rode to the head of their armies to govern their men directly. Gard was fully prepared for an assault. Flags were raised in instruction and the army moved forward as one.

From their vantage point on the right flank standing with Lord Blood, Luxor and Morkin could see Gard's warriors marching forward, shields elevated above their heads to defend against arrows shot from the citadel, but none came. Their objective was simple, to reach the great doors and breach them.

Shimeril's warriors advanced on the left side, their aim to scale the walls with ladders and grappling hooks. Blood's warriors were moving in a similar manner on the right flank.

Still there was no response from within the citadel.

'This does not feel right,' Luxor said, shaking his head.

'Will you not say so?' Morkin asked.

'And challenge Lord Gard in the heat of battle? It is not my place, my son, nor the right time …'

Gard's men reached the walls of the citadel. Morkin heard the dull thump of a battering ram slam against the unprotected doors.

Why do the Foul not resist?

Ladders rose in slow motion in an ordered sequence from the ranks of Shimeril and Blood's warriors. Brave souls, clinging on near the top as the ladders were raised, threw out chains with great hooks at the end over the battlements, rapidly pulling back the slack and securing the ladders against the walls. Even before they rested in place men were scaling them. Morkin stared, slack-jawed at the speed at which the assault took place. He knew the warriors of the Free were practiced in the art of war, but he had not expected such prowess. It was one thing to listen to tales about such things, quite another to see them.

More thumps echoed from the front gate and still there was no response from within. By now men had scaled the battlements, swords drawn. Morkin could see them strolling with ease along the battlements, facing no opposition at all.

There's no one there …

It was then that the horns sounded. Deep and sinister.

Morkin heard, but didn't recognise them. He turned around to look; Luxor and Blood doing the same beside him.

Horns from across the valley echoed against the mountainsides. As if in response, a deep blare resonated from the citadel itself.

A thunderous boom and thick black smoke. Morkin jolted in his saddle as a lurid red glow erupted from the citadel. Explosions echoed from the keeps behind them and the ruins either side of the valley. He turned to see smoke billowing into the air.

What …?

Then the cries came. Morkin looked in horror as a black stain spread from the keeps and the ruins. Dark figures, hundreds … no thousands! Thousands of Doomguard warriors emerging from hiding, heading towards them from all sides. Horns blared as the black tide grew.

'Form ranks!' Blood yelled, drawing his sword. 'Form ranks! Archers to the fore!'

Blood's disciplined riders organised themselves quickly, but Morkin could see the rest of the army floundering, unprepared for an attack from the sides or the rear; their quarry had lain before them. Men moved in disarray as they tried to form a defensive line. The armies of the Witchking would be on them in moments.

Then it came.

Mist rose, wraithlike about them. Ice crackled across clothing, penetrating, sharp and severe. Frost grew before their eyes, as if winter had concentrated all its force upon them. Warriors looked about themselves in dismay and bewilderment.

But there was worse to come.

Men screeched in fear as something invisible smote them down. Faces paled. Some fell from their horses and lay quivering upon the snow, tearing at their hair and curling into foetal positions, screaming. A deathly pallor fell across them, freezing their hearts and stealing away their resolve and courage. Despair stalked the men of the Free; they cowered in terror.

No respite. At that moment arrows rained down. The defenders of the citadel had their cue. Morkin raised his shield to protect himself, one arrow penetrating it by a clear inch. He stared at the blackened barb in horror. Atop the citadel he could now see black armoured warriors hacking at the men of the Free in their torment. Men fell from the citadel, crashing to the ground to lie still.

With a groan the doors of the citadel burst asunder to more black smoke and the Witchking's hordes issued forth, beating back Gard's surprised and terrified men.

The blackness swarmed around the beleaguered army of the Free.

Lord Brith caught sight of Lord Rorath bravely fighting through the legions of the enemy towards him. His heralds had deserted him, casting themselves upon the ground even as the enemy hewed them asunder. Brith backed away, his mind shattered into panic by the fear that suffused his being, fear that made his skin contract, his muscles shake and his whole body tremble uncontrollably.

He stared, sword falling from his grasp. Terror etched on his ashen face.

He felt himself pulled from his horse, falling slowly from the creature as it bucked and reared. Mindless terror had him seized, he could only watch, in abject horror as swords descended towards him.

Pain now, but it was brief. Blackness replaced fear. It was a relief to die.

Morkin clenched his mind against the fear that pummelled at him. He had never encountered such a feeling before. Somehow it felt as if deadly cold fingers were grasping at his heart and trying to slow its beat, to freeze his blood within him.

He shivered and found he could cast off the gloom by concentrating. Thoughts of sun and warmth formed his mind; weapons against the ice-fear. He forced back at it and arose victorious. About him men were yelling and cowering in terror, and yet he was able to resist.

He staggered upright, managing to get his eyes to focus. Muffled sounds echoed in his ears, growing clearer every moment.

Screams of fear and pain!

He turned to see Lord Blood's riders fending off a phalanx of Doomguard warriors who had pushed through the ranks of the Free and had threatened to overwhelm them. Only a brave charge from the riders had saved them, battering the dark clad warriors back.

Morkin felt pain, he must have been hit on the head by something …

'Morkin!'

He felt himself lifted up by the collar. It was Luxor, astride one of Blood's horses, streaked in blood. He scrambled into the saddle in front of his father.

'I thought you lost!' he cried. 'That the ice-fear had struck you down and yet ...'

No time to reply. Blades clashed around him, a swinging, clanging tumult of metal. Luxor's horse reared and managed to push past the massed warriors, Blood's own riders forming a protective line around them.

Now they stood on a small premonitory a few hundred yards from the entrance to the Citadel. Around them the battle raged on. Morkin looked about him in horror. Gard's forces brought up the rear having somehow managed to resist the company of Doomguard that had issued from the Citadel. Blood's riders had made good account of themselves upon the flank, likewise Shimeril on the adjacent side ...

But down the length of the valley the armies of the Free had been crushed, caught between the hammer blow of Doomguard armies that had assailed them from either side. There was little but a mass of black. As he watched Morkin saw a lone banner wave haphazardly. He recognised the colours of Lord Mitharg. A few beleaguered men stood defending it. As he watched they were cut down. The banner fell and disappeared from sight.

The few remaining warriors and riders of the Free were in full rout, fleeing before the Doomguard towards the hard pressed armies of Gard, Blood and Shimeril. They were directionless, panicked, overwhelmed by the fear and the ice. Even as they fled they were cut down by the arrows and spears of the enemy. No more than a few hundred reached the safety of the line of riders.

Lord Blood appeared beside them, with Shimeril riding up a moment later.

'The battle does not go well,' Shimeril managed.

'We have lost more than two thirds of our force,' Blood said, tallying up the mayhem and carnage before him.

'Caught off guard,' Luxor said, deadpan. Despite everything, Blood chuckled.

'It would seem our scouts were not as thorough as we might have hoped,' Shimeril added. 'I am dismayed at foretelling the future correctly ...'

'A worthy ploy by our ancient foe,' Luxor said. 'We have grown arrogant and over sure of ourselves ...'

About the promontory the remaining riders and warriors of the Free closed about in a circular formation, facing outwards. At their centre the remaining lords stood, shouting instructions as the enemy circled about.

The battle had reached a natural hiatus. The Doomguard had them surrounded, outnumbered and outflanked. The sudden impact of the ice-fear had destroyed the resolve of the Free, rendering most of the soldiers nothing more than mindless staggering fools to be cut down by the inexorable march of the Doomguard warriors.

Gard staggered up towards them on foot, dragging a wounded leg. With some difficulty he was hoist atop a horse and, grimacing, rode to their sides.

'I will train my scouts better next time,' he muttered. 'If we are fortunate enough to see one.'

The others did not respond. There was nothing to say. Below, the warriors of the Free that remained were those stoutest of heart. Spears, swords and arrows were readied.

The Doomguard stayed where they were perhaps fifty yards back. Waiting ...

'Brace yourselves,' Gard yelled. 'The enemy's fell power of ice and fear will strike once more ...'

Even as he said these words the dreadful oppression smote them once again. Men screamed, dropping their weapons and clutching at their heads. Some ran straight outwards towards the enemy, mindless of the peril and were swiftly cut down. Others fell and cowered upon the ground. Even the Lords flinched under the baleful influence.

Only Morkin was unaffected.

'Father! The Moon Ring! Don it! Don it now!'

Luxor could barely think with the tumult around him. Almost against his will he felt his fingers reach inside the lining of his thick tunic.

It will be in vain if you do not heed my words, Luxor, Moon-prince of Midnight …

A voice echoed in his mind.

Rorthron!

He slipped the Moon Ring upon his finger.

A warmth suffused him, growing from his hand, through his arm, to his body. The ice-fear fell away like snow in the long lost summer sun. A glow of heat, somehow mixed with comradeship, good fortune and stoic bravery emanated from his being.

Heat now, flooding out of him in every direction, as if a furnace of furious hope had been stoked and abruptly opened. Flames flickered in his vision and he feared for a moment that he himself might be consumed. About him he could see hope kindling in the hearts of the warriors and riders. Tiny glows of fire, being fanned to fuller strength.

It will throw forth the warmth of your mind, a potent sense of your presence and your power. It can mollify the effects of the ice-fear, but it cannot defeat it. It will give you the power of command, the ability to sense the needs and fears of those loyal to you, even see what they see at great distance …

Luxor raised his sword. In his mind flashed images of faces. He saw Corleth and an army of the Fey, a woman clad all in grey …

Corleth? Who rides with him? An Army? Is this truth, or a fantasy I see?

137

His voice came to him. He felt the fear and pushed it aside. Men turned towards him. Blood, Shimeril and Gard looked on in astonishment. Luxor's face took on a kingly aspect, lit from within by some arcane power.

'Arise, Midnight!" he yelled. 'Arise men of the Free! The power is ours now!'

He looked and somehow saw a weakness in the massed ranks of the Doomguard. Instinctively he drove towards them, conscious of the men about him forming ranks, riding and marching as one. The armies of the Free drove forward like an arrow head.

Released from the ice-fear the men were emboldened, strong and possessed of a wrath and fury for the treacherous Doomguard. So many of their comrades had been slain, the balance would be paid.

Their weapons cut through the ranks of the Doomguard in a clashing frenzy of metal, hewn limbs and heads cast asunder as they ploughed on through. The Doomguard fell back in disarray, not anticipating that their cornered prey would mount such a furious assault.

Luxor, possessed by a power so fierce he felt it might burst out of him, rode at the head, slicing through the foe, heedless. The Doomguard tried to fall back, but such was their number, they would not move, until they were slain by the flashing weapons of the Free.

But the assault could not last forever, the Doomguard were too many and the Free too few. The momentum of the charge failed and the Doomguard regrouped about them. They had made good account of themselves, but they had not escaped the ring of death that had formed about them.

'It was a bold attempt,' Shimeril said, riding up alongside him. 'What is this talisman you wear? This power you wield?'

'A Moon Ring,' Luxor said.

'A Moon Ring?' Blood asked. 'Some bauble from the past? I counted such things as child's tales.'

'Give it to me,' Gard said, turning his horse in front of Luxor. 'You should not have withheld such a powerful tool. With this we might have saved our men!'

'He didn't!' Morkin shouted, his sense of fairness violated. 'He tried to tell you!'

'Morkin!'

'It cannot be borne by any other than the House of the Moon!' Morkin cried. 'By the Moonprince himself.'

'What nonsense is this?' Gard said, his features gaunt and angry. 'Moonprince? Do as I command, Lord Luxor!'

'I cannot,' Luxor replied. 'Though I would use it under your command.'

'It is perhaps too late for that,' Gard snapped. 'But use it now, drive these foul hordes away and perhaps, should we survive, your conduct will not be judged too harshly.'

Luxor concentrated and the power of the Moon Ring issued forth once more. They all felt it. The Lords, the warriors and the riders. They would not succumb to the power of the Witchking, they would fight on to the bitter end.

Swords and spears were readied one last time. A battle cry erupted from a thousand throats …

Only to be echoed back by faint horns.

The sound repeated again. Horns, bright and cheery, distinct from the dirge-like drone of those belonging to the Doomguard. They were coming from beyond the ranks of the foe, further on down the valley.

'What is this?' Gard muttered, turning his horse around.

'This ring is made of potent stuff,' Shimeril said. 'It has summoned warriors from out of the very ground!'

Luxor shook his head. 'This is not my doing.'

From around the jutting edge of the valley, a series of banners came into view. Dark hued, but flecked with green and blue, a company of riders could be seen rounding the bend in the path. Behind them came dark clad warriors, running on foot, their banners grey.

'I do not know these marks,' Blood said.

Luxor squinted into the distance.

'I do,' he said, a smile growing on his face. 'It truly is Corleth! The Moon Ring, it truly does allow me to see ... And he brings aid to the fight!'

'Corleth?' Blood asked. 'Where in Midnight is the realm of Corleth?'

'Not where!' Morkin said. 'Who! Corleth the Fey!'

'The Fey?' Gard said, his mouth hanging open.

'Sound the horns!' Luxor cried.

The battle was joined. The newcomers, fresh and unwearied from battle, smote upon the Doomguard from the rear, shattering their ranks and driving through. At the same moment, the remaining soldiers of the Free pushed hard towards them.

The Doomguard resisted, knowing that if the two armies were to meet their strength would be increased and the battle lost. The fiercest fighting ensued. The ice-fear battered down against both the Free and the Fey, but Luxor, through the power of the ring, resisted it and turned it back upon itself. Ice and frost crackled across the ground, but was turned to steam by the power of the ring as Luxor rode by.

With a final cry of glee the two armies met, the Doomguard falling between their combined attacks. Luxor saw Corleth in the midst of the Fey warriors and yelled a greeting. Corleth flipped a jaunty wave, despatching Doomguard warriors as he did so and riding towards him.

'Did I not say the Fey would follow the Moonprince?' Corleth cried. 'And that I would call forth our legions in your service?'

'This is a meeting most joyful,' Luxor said, clapping him on the back. 'I had no hope you would come. Let us ride together and cast these foul Doomguard to the four winds!'

The armies joined. Thus emboldened they fell upon their enemies. The tide of the battle was turned, the Doomguard fell back, catastrophically reduced in number. Luxor watched as they retreated towards the Citadel of Gorgrath.

'Hold!' he signalled, wheeling his horse aside. About him men stopped and waited.

'Should we not destroy them?' Shimeril asked, watching the remains of the Doomguard scramble for the relative safety of the Citadel.'

Luxor shook his head. 'We have no longer the strength to assault the place. We must conserve what we have. We have wounded amongst us and a long road back to safety.'

Gard pushed past, placing his horse ahead of Luxor's.

'I say we press on. Form ranks! We will smite these foe in their haven.'

Luxor lowered his sword.

No one moved.

'Do you defy me, Luxor of Odrark? Do I need to remind you that you are my vassal? Do as I say!'

'He is no longer Lord Luxor of Odrark,' Corleth said. 'He is the Moonprince of Midnight. You owe him your loyalty, Lord Gard.'

'Seek not to stand with your betters, Fey!' Gard said. 'We appreciate your assistance today, but one battle does not cover the sins of a generation of betrayal of the Free!'

'Enough!' Luxor said. 'If I am indeed the Moonprince I say we live to fight another day. Who will follow me back to the Keep of Blood?'

'Follow him and I'll have you executed! Executed! Do you hear?' Gard raged.

Blood and Shimeril moved their horses alongside Luxor.

'Luxor is right,' Blood said. 'We have lost too many. A tactical retreat is called for.'

Gard snarled and yelled something incomprehensible. His sword flashed out faster than the eye could see.

But it was not fast enough.

Another blade parried it, turned the edge and sent the sword spinning away. A figure, hooded and dressed in grey stood below, with a knife raised towards Gard.

'Long you have shunned wisdom,' came her voice, and the men around her reacted in surprise and dismay. She lowered her hood. The Lords of the Free looked on in astonishment at a dark-eyed woman. 'You almost led us to our deaths.'

Gard looked down the edge of her knife. She glared, her eyes cold.

'The time of the Moonprince is at hand.'

Chapter Seven

They stand at the Keep of Blood,
looking south east to the Plains of Blood.

Dawn broke, cold and heavy over the old fortifications of the Keep of Blood. Only there could an accurate tally be made, a regroup of warriors and resources. The exhausted troops slumped in largely silent groups, worn out from the battle and the long march back south from Gorgrath. Muscles ached, not only from the weariness of retreat and the weight of the injured they had carried with them, but the silent reproach from the dead they had had to leave behind; only a very few of whom there had been time or energy to bury.

Only then did the true scale of their defeat become plain.

Of the seven Lords of the south that had set out from the Keep of Blood just two days before, only four had returned. Lords Brith, Rorath and Mitharg had fallen, along with the vast majority of their men, under the terrible assault of the Witchking's forces.

Of the seven thousand that had marched north, less than three thousand remained. Those that had escaped were demoralised and broken, seeing their comrades slain and forced to leave their bodies left behind to be disgraced and dishonoured by the Foul.

Had it not been for the intervention of the Lord of Shadows and the mysterious woman, all might have been lost.

Many had considered that the keep would be a sanctuary,

but the growing light of dawn brought news that legions of the Witchking's forces were gathering on the plains to the north. Not only had they prepared a trap, they were prepared for the aftermath too.

'He has long rehearsed his strategy,' Blood said, looking northwards from the keep. 'This was no idle skirmish, this is the vanguard of his entire plan! He intends to vanquish us completely.'

'Riders have been sent with warnings for Marakith, Kumar, Dawn and faraway Xajorkith,' Shimeril added. 'Calling for them to prepare for open war.'

Luxor nodded.

'We must deal with our own problems first,' he said.

He felt Morkin nudge him and turned to see the strange woman approaching. She was flanked by many of her warriors. They were all women too; a sight Luxor had never seen before. He did not doubt their prowess, he had seen how they had cut through the hordes of the Doomguard.

I saw her, via the Moon Ring. She was alongside Corleth …

'I would have your name, my Lady,' Luxor said. 'We owe you a debt of gratitude.'

The woman responded with a formal curtsey.

'I am Silence, a vassal of Lord Gard, though doubtless he has never mentioned me or my kindred.'

Luxor shook his head. 'He has not, yet I would know more.'

'Long we have guarded the far western borders of the Free, from Ashimar to Dodrak and beyond, smiting the Doomguard wherever they might be found.'

'Ashimar?' Luxor said. 'Yet lore tells me that those lands are barren and empty.'

The woman visibly bristled.

'They are kept free and clear by the actions of my folk,' she snapped. 'And little credit do we receive for our pains.'

'I have not heard your name mentioned before,' Luxor said. 'But your valour is recognised now.'

'My father's domain was usurped by Gard's ancestors long ago. He calls his home the Citadel of Gard, but it was not always thus. Now he tolerates our presence, demanding taxes and tithes which we honour as we promised we would.'

'And your father …?'

'My father died in the last war and left no male heir, yet I am his sole descendent. I refused to see our family name lost to history. Lord Gard wished us to submit to him and become part of his domain.'

'And …?'

'I refused.'

Luxor paused, considering for a moment, before a smile crept across his face. 'In that case, Lady of Silence, you and I have much in common.'

Her lips turned upwards slightly, in what Luxor took to be a smile.

'Just Silence is fine,' she said. 'Address me as you would the other Lords. I will answer. I am not overly fond of rank or titles.'

Luxor nodded. 'Silence it will be.'

She stepped forward before he had a chance to move away.

'You are truly the Moonprince, are you not?'

Luxor frowned, dropping his voice. 'In truth I do not know. A week ago, I was but a lower ranked Lord, a vassal much as yourself. Since then I have been told I am a descendent of the legendary House of the Moon, and have been entrusted with a talisman of the Wise …'

'My father spoke of the Moonprince when I was but a child,' she said. Her face portrayed earnestness and expectation. 'Only he can save Midnight from the darkness.'

'I know not whether I am he,' Luxor replied.

She fixed him with a stare. 'If you are not, our doom is at hand.'

She bowed her head and walked away, her warriors accompanying her. Luxor, Blood and Shimeril watched her go.

'This … er … Moonprince business,' Blood asked. 'Would you care to enlighten us?'

'I have heard tell of it,' Shimeril said. 'Yet the House of the Moon was destroyed hundreds of moons ago by the Witchking himself, nothing remains of it, or so I thought.'

Luxor shrugged. 'So I thought too. I was summoned by one Rorthron the Wise …'

'The Wise?'

Luxor recounted his tale prior to arriving at the Keep of Blood whilst the other two lords listened attentively.

'And this ring is actually the Moon Ring?' Blood exclaimed. 'One of the War Rings of Midnight? Why with such a power we should rout the Foul, not flee from them!'

'If memory serves it gives the power of command and vision,' Shimeril said. 'It is not a weapon, nor can it replace the might of an army.'

'But still …'

'Yet its potency is not in doubt,' Luxor said. 'I saw Corleth, Shadows and Silence prior to their arrival. With practice I will hope to hone its use. But some will not recognise its authority.'

'Gard almost led us to destruction,' Blood said. 'If it were not for you and the intervention of these others then …'

Shimeril could see the doubt on Luxor's face. 'Gard is no King, Luxor. There is no treason against him. If you are indeed the Moonprince, then you are royalty. Your rank exceeds his. Take it. We will follow.'

Luxor looked from one to the other and then nodded.

'Come then.'

Far to the north the wind blew crisp and sharp. The sky was clear, the cold sharper than the finest sword-blade's edge, for here was the source of that cold. Traceries of ice crystals swirled above a grim and forsaken Citadel, curling in a bitter and arctic beauty.

Long ago, Ushgarak had been the capital of Midnight, a city of wealth and power, holding court and dominion over lush and verdant lands. Midnight itself, luxuriating in the long summer, had caused great wealth to flow into the city. But the zenith of its power had been short lived. Lord Ushgarak had been seduced by the promise of more power, more dominion. Briefly he claimed to be King of Midnight, but he was subverted and murdered by his own advisor, Gryfallon the Stargazer.

Ten thousand moons had since passed and that advisor now ruled the frozen north in his place. Gryfallon no longer had a heart for the stars; he no longer gazed fondly upon the sparkling moonstar, the moon itself or even the faint traceries of the Roads of Light in the heavens. His gaze was earth-bound, his will implacable, his desires and thoughts bent on a single objective.

The halls of the citadel had been left much as they were in Lord Ushgarak's time. Tapestries and carpets still draped the rooms and halls, tables were lined with cutlery and place settings, beds were made with linen and fine hangings, candles stood in holders and candelabras, but unlit. Nothing had been disturbed, much less used, in all that time. Frozen, locked in time. None but the Witchking were permitted within the inner courts of the Citadel, though the Doomguard patrolled the walls. Ushgarak was the Witchking's lone sanctuary.

Cold, with no hint of warmth, ice cracking into splinters around it – a sepulchral arm moved forward. Frozen fingers gestured southwards, ice tinkling in the air about them.

The fingers clenched, vibrating for a moment before curling into a fist.

THE FREE WERE NOT DESPATCHED?

The anger was beyond chilling. In a man it would have been a yell of frustration and vindictive torment, here it was inaudible, but the very air rang with its fury.

The Citadel of Ushgarak shuddered from the force of that vehemence.

SO. THIS YOUNG MOONPRINCE SEEKS TO CHALLENGE ME? HE WILL SOON DISCOVER THE FOLLY OF HIS WAYS.

The Witchking cast his own vision out, sensing the warmth emanating from the southern lands. The location of the Moonprince was clear enough, not far south of the Citadel of Gorgrath. He turned his vision aside as the hated balm of the Moonprince's presence threatened to thaw the chill he had extended.

YOU WILL NOT KINDLE HOPE IN THEIR HEARTS. I WILL SEE TO THAT. NO INTERFERENCE WITH MY PLANS CAN BE TOLERATED. THAT WHICH WAS TORN ASUNDER MUST BE REUNITED. I WILL SEE IT DONE!

Instructions were sent to his hordes, his captains, their hearts chilled far past any possible compassion or empathy for men they might have once called brothers. His forces rallied despite the unexpected set back. Their strength redoubled, their lust for war wreathed in the joy of causing pain and rendering fear.

NOW, STRIKE HARD AND STRIKE FAST. WE VANQUISH THIS UPSTART MOONPRINCE BEFORE HE HAS A CHANCE TO RISE!

From the citadels and keeps his loyal legions issued forth, striding with implacable inevitability from their hideouts and lairs. The plains of the southlands opened before them, defenceless before their irresistible might.

Gard looked up as Luxor, Blood and Shimeril entered the makeshift tent where their erstwhile commander was stationed. Two guards flanked him.

'Come to make reparations for your conduct, Luxor of Odrark?' Gard said. 'We are fortunate indeed that we survive to see your crimes articulated and your insolence punished. What have you to say for yourself?'

'I tried to tell you of the tidings I had received,' Luxor replied. 'You had no time for me. It is a legacy beyond my understanding too ...'

'If such powers are beyond you then give them to one who is prepared!' Gard roared, stomping across to Luxor. 'This ring, give it to me!'

He caught Luxor's hand and his fingers closed about the ring.

A flicker, as if a pall of gloom had closed about the tent. A restless breeze shifted the canvas and a disembodied voice arose about them.

Assail not the Moonprince, Lord of Gard.

Gard stared about him in abject shock, seeking the source of the echoing voice.

'Who ... who are you?' Gard demanded, shrinking back

The breeze stiffened into a wind, flapping the fabric of the tent and canting it over on its poles. Shouts of alarm came from without.

Long have we watched over the affairs of the Free and the Fey. Now we deem it time to reveal our plans. We are the Wise. Seeking the Witchking's demise? You must pledge your loyalty to Luxor. Luxor, the Moonprince.

'The Wise!' spluttered Gard. 'What trick is this ...?'

Unbidden, Luxor gestured with the Moon Ring. The warmth of his mind spread around those present in the tent.

I know not how it has come to this, only that I can command its power! The Moon Ring allows me to see through the eyes of those whose loyalty I enjoy. It can resist the ice-fear. It is our best hope to prevail in this fight. The Free and the Fey, all those who can resist the Witchking, we must band together or we will die in isolation. I ask for your oaths, Free and Fey alike!

The warmth passed, the breeze faded away. Not a word was spoken. Gard stared at Luxor, who returned the look without flinching.

'You have my service,' Blood said, kneeling before Luxor.

'And mine,' Shimeril said, doing likewise beside him.

Luxor turned to see Silence appear at the entrance of the tent.

'I have already given my service to you,' she said softly, 'but I will demonstrate it once more.'

She knelt alongside Blood and Shimeril, her head bowed.

Gard stood resolute, his mouth working, his jaw clenching and unclenching.

'It seems I have a choice,' he said. 'Between continuing alone or becoming a pawn in the games of the Wise.'

'I do not fully trust the Wise myself,' Luxor said. 'Yet the words of Rorthron have proved true, dependable and reliable. This Moon Ring may be our salvation and if my ancestry alone is what allows us to use it, then use it we must. I would have your counsel and guidance still Lord Gard. We need all to combat this darkness.'

Luxor stretched out his hand.

Gard did not move. His eyes narrowed.

'Very well, Luxor – so called Moonprince of Midnight,' he said. 'I will not defy the will of the Wise.'

He reached out himself and took Luxor's hand, shaking it firmly.

'I hope we place our trust in them well.'

'As do I,' Luxor replied.

The sound of footsteps came from beyond the tent. All turned to see Corleth at the entrance.

'My Lord Luxor, come quickly …'

Luxor looked around him at those assembled and then followed Corleth out.

Corleth led him across the courtyard and into another tent. A Fey lay there. Luxor could tell at once that he suffered from grievous wounds. It was the Lord of Shadows.

'He is here,' Corleth announced. Luxor went to Shadow's side.

'My Lord,' he said, grabbing Shadow's right hand in his, for his left was broken and bound in a splint. Shadow's grip was weak.

'My folk, they fought well?' Shadow's voice was faint.

'You saved the morrow,' Luxor said. 'Without your help we would have all be slain.'

Shadows swallowed and nodded. 'That is sweet news. Moonprince. I …'

Luxor moved closer, struggling to hear the fading voice.

'Yes, my Lord Shadows …'

'It is vital that the Free and the Fey are united in the struggle against the Witchking. Our peoples are proud and independent, but this must be overcome. Our differences are fewer than that which we hold in common …'

'I have been guilty of pride myself,' Luxor said.

'Not all the Fey stand aloof from the troubles of the Free,' Shadows managed to say. 'They will follow the Moonprince. You must reach out to them …'

'I will take your words with me,' Luxor said. 'Your valour has restored my faith that honour remains in the Fey.'

'Corleth …' Shadows said. 'Take my men, fight for the purposes of the Moonprince. See we do not flinch from the task ahead.'

'I will see it done,' Corleth answered.

Shadows took Luxor's hand and moved it across, briefly releasing it as he grabbed Corleth's hand and brought both together.

'The Free and the Fey. If you do not act as one, you will be lost. The Wise knew this … even the Fey knew this … be the Moonprince, Lord Luxor … be …'

The words failed. Shadow's grip went slack in their grasp. For long moments neither Luxor nor Corleth moved, gazing upon the still body of their fallen comrade.

Luxor looked across at Corleth.

'Know you why the Fey would not march on the Doomguard in the last war?' he asked softly.

Corleth swallowed. 'Yes, Moonprince. I do.'

Luxor inclined his head.

'And?'

'We feared the victory more than the defeat,' Corleth said. 'The Wise counselled that the end of the Witchking at that time would lead to the crowning of a new King, a King of the Free. King Gard of Midnight.'

Luxor sighed and lowered his head.

'Yet that power, however well intentioned, would turn to ill. We feared the rise of another tyrant. Better that a known evil be kept at bay than transformed into another frightening form and Midnight be plunged into war everlasting. So we would not march on the Witchking only to see him replaced by worse.'

'And now?' Luxor whispered.

'The Wise have restored the House of the Moon,' Corleth said. 'It is your right to govern and your duty to govern well. The Wise have ordained it to be you … and only you. We would see that done. I will take that message to my folk and seek to convince them.'

Luxor thought about that for a long moment.

'It would seem the Fey followed wisdom where the Free fell into folly,' he said. 'I have done you a great disservice, Corleth of the Fey. I would make amends for that.'

'A friendship restored would be adequate compensation.'

Luxor looked across at him gratefully. 'Then let us work as one, from this moment forwards.'

'I am at your service, Luxor, Moonprince of the Free and the Fey!'

There was little time for thought or plan. The Doomguard could be seen issuing from the gap of Valethor and it was clear that a pursuit was underway. Luxor instructed the Lords to rally their forces, make as much preparation for the fallen as could be managed and to gather up food and provisions.

He had spoken at length to Corleth, and their plan was to swiftly march to the Citadel of Shimeril, there to rendezvous with the forces of the Free in the east. Upon the road, Corleth would go with what remained of the Shadow Fey and seek assistance from the Fey of the Forest of Thrall. The rest would make what pace they could to Shimeril's domain, its walls would be easier to defend than Blood's keep.

'We cannot hope to keep the Plains of Blood, nor any part of the west,' Luxor said, his face a mask of frustration.

'Think not of it,' Lord Blood replied. 'The Free have seldom held this approach to the north for long in the face of massive force. A retreat is in order. We shall rally and drive the Foul back in time. Fear not for this old keep! It has changed hands many times in the past. It will still be here upon my return ...'

Shimeril was less enthusiastic.

'My citadel is ill prepared for a long siege,' he told Luxor. 'We did not see an invasion as an outcome of this battle. Provisions are not in place. Only five hundred men guard my home and there are few we can recruit to bolster it.'

'Word has been sent to Marakith, Kumar and others besides,' Luxor assured him. 'Help is coming.'

'It will not be enough.'

'What do you suggest?'

Shimeril sighed. 'We have time to summon our forces further south and east. Guarded by the mountains behind it, I would say the Citadel of Dawn should be our rally point.'

Luxor looked at Blood.

'It is perilously close to Xajorkith to mount a defence, but it is very much defensible. It pains me to admit it, but I fear we cannot resist the Foul without further support. Our hope may yet lie in reaching Dawn.'

'It is a three day march onward from Shimeril,' Blood noted.

Luxor looked at Gard, who gave a brief nod. 'It is a sound strategy.'

'Very well,' Luxor said. 'So be it. We will rendezvous at the Citadel of Dawn as fast as we are able. Send word to the Citadel of Shimeril to strip it of all provisions and weapons. It must be evacuated as soon as possible before the armies of the Foul prey upon the innocent.'

Luxor signalled to Corleth, who rode up alongside him. 'You journey to Thrall?'

'As instructed,' Corleth replied.

'We ride for Dawn. We cannot tarry at Shimeril, we do not have the means. In four days we will arrive.'

Corleth nodded thoughtfully. 'It will give me a chance to rally the Fey of Thrall to our cause and send messengers further on.'

Luxor took a deep breath.

'I would have you take Morkin with you,' Luxor said.

Corleth frowned. 'He will want to stay at your side.'

Luxor sighed. 'I know, but the Foul will now pursue us,

night and day. The Fey can protect him better than I and he has not the long years of swordsmanship that goes with being a warrior.'

'I think you underestimate him,' Corleth said. 'He will not thank you for this.'

'You know what lies before me, Corleth,' Luxor rumbled. 'We flee before an army greater than we have ever known. The path ahead is strewn with blood, death and fear. I do not see how we can turn this tide.'

'We may yet prevail.'

'Perhaps, but a father will always seek to protect his son. Besides, he is half-Fey, he has a chance to ...' Luxor looked up at the distant Forest of Thrall, just visible to the east. '... learn of his mother and his heritage.'

Corleth smiled. 'So you place a little value on the lore of the Fey, eh?'

'I would see him safe. Deep in your forests is as safe as can be had.'

'Luxor, the forests will not stand against the might of the Witchking for long, Shadows was breached ...'

'He must stay in Thrall,' Luxor said, firmly.

Corleth sighed.

'I will take him,' he said. 'If he will come. But you must tell him so yourself.'

The armies left as soon as they were able, striking east across the barren Plains of Blood, still carrying the weapons and paraphernalia of war. The going was slow, but they dared not leave too much behind, it would be required in defence of Dawn.

Nightfall saw the armies encamped around Lake Blood, some five leagues east of the keep. The waters, warmed from far below, were free from ice and they were able to supplement their supplies with freshly caught fish. Fishing remained one of the few trades virtually untouched by the winter of Midnight. Many of the lakes were farmed especially to cater for the needs of the people.

It was a cloudless night, the temperature falling precipitately. Luxor forbade any fires and set strict watches upon the borders. No moon lit the sky, and only the Moonstar sparkled faintly low on the horizon. He knew, as all of the warriors did, that the Foul moved as easily through the darkness as the Free did within the day.

'They will position themselves to ambush us somehow,' Gard muttered, staring out into the darkness. Faint flickers of red could be seen far away in the west.

'There is little cover for us here on the plain,' Luxor said with a nod. 'We must make Shimeril tomorrow, or we will be lost.'

The red light grew in intensity and a spout of flame could be seen rising into the heavens, thick smoke billowing above it, blotting out the stars.

Lord Blood stared at it, his face set in anger.

'We will rebuild it upon our victory,' Shimeril told him. 'I have stone-smiths who will undo whatever damage the Foul inflict.'

Blood nodded. 'The bloody sword of battle brings death on the Plains of Blood once more. Let us see what dawn brings.'

'Do you want dawn?' Gard asked, grimly. The rhetorical question hung in the air.

Luxor decided to answer it.

'Dawn will come, whether we want it or not.'

Dawn did come and with it a change in the weather. Clouds had gathered to the north, a thick rolling pall of fog, seeping over the Mountains of Ithril and creeping southwards as they watched. More threatening were the armies of the Witchking, easily visible across the Plains of Blood, making no attempt to disguise their progress.

Behind them they could see the Keep of Blood, just short of the horizon. Its sides were blackened, testament to the fire that had raged within. Smoke still wafted from it, yet its stern walls had not collapsed.

Blood took a long look and then turned about.

'Are we riding for Dawn or not?'

Luxor nodded, issuing instructions. The armies of the Free made ready to move on. He was about to mount his own stallion when a voice interrupted him.

'They will harry us on our right flank, force us to fight in the open.'

It was Silence. She had been watching the movements of the Doomguard with a practiced eye, standing atop a nearby hillock since the sun had risen.

Luxor looked at her. 'I do not disagree, but I see little we can do about it. They must know where we are bound.'

'They will overrun us before we reach Dawn,' Silence said. 'If that occurs, we are all lost.'

'Then we must flee before them.'

'We could take the initiative,' Silence said. 'Force them to reconsider.'

Luxor took a breath. 'What do you have in mind?'

'Give me horses,' Silence said. 'My warriors will outflank them to the north and to the south. We will attack stealthily and as they respond we will retreat and hide. It will cause disarray amongst them and slow them down.'

Luxor thought about it. 'The risk … if you miscalculate, we could not come to your aid.'

Silence's face portrayed a rare smile.

'This is how I have fought my whole life, Moonprince. Knowing when to pick fights, how to hide, when to run. Always I have been outnumbered, but never beaten. Trust me, it will work.'

'I do not like it.'

Silence made to protest, but Luxor held up a hand.

'But I do not doubt your prowess in such things. Go with my blessing. I will be able to follow your progress via the Moon Ring.'

The arrangements were swiftly made. Many warriors were less than pleased to lose their steeds, but the orders were firmly given. The grey clad women of Silence rode out behind their mistress, the pale sun behind them, heading into the west.

Corleth watched them go and then rode up alongside Luxor.

'That one has a measure of courage and fortitude that most of us can only aspire to,' he said.

Luxor nodded.

'Songs should be sung about her conduct. I only hope she lives long enough for them to be written.'

Luxor could see Morkin riding up the nearest flank and signalled to him. The young man swung his horse about and galloped towards them.

'Corleth rides for Thrall, there to begin the task of rallying the Fey,' Luxor announced.

Morkin looked east. 'I feel sure that he will rouse a mighty hoist for us! A fearsome band of Fey like the stories of old. Even if I take my leave of him now ...'

'You will not be taking your leave of Corleth,' Luxor said. 'You will be riding with him.'

Luxor saw the look of crushing disappointment gather on his son's features. 'But father, no! I will fight ...'

'It is too dangerous ...'

'I have seen the battle we fought,' Morkin replied. 'Did I not fight well? Was I not unaffected by the ice-fear?'

'You fought bravely, none can say otherwise,' Luxor said. 'And your immunity from the fear both delights and scares me ...'

'Then ...?'

'Morkin, there are greater horrors in warfare, horrors the like of which you have not seen.' Luxor continued. 'I do not wish you to know of such things. And you do not yet have all the skills of a warrior ...'

'But ...'

'It is decided!' Luxor said. 'Do not defy me in this.'

Morkin's face was set in anger. He raised his chin, but did not retort.

'You will go to Thrall and stay there with the Fey until this matter is ended,' Luxor instructed. 'Corleth will take you there with his company.'

Luxor watched as Morkin tried to formulate some words, his breath floating up before him in the frigid air.

'Yes, father,' was all he managed.

'It will give you a chance to learn more of your past ...'

'... but I want to fight!'

'... and of your mother.'

'My ... mother?' Morkin now showed some curiosity.

'Aleisha,' Corleth said softly, deciding to join the conversation. 'The Forest of Thrall was her home.'

Luxor reached over to grab his son's shoulder, pulling him into an embrace.

'Your time will come, son,' he said, 'but it is not now. You are to go to Thrall and stay there, the words of the Wise be damned. Stay there and stay safe. The hordes of the Foul cannot reach you there. It will do me no end of good to know you are safe. I will fight all the harder.'

Morkin swallowed and nodded. 'I will do this for you, father.'

He looked away, pulled back and rode off, his distinctive red-haired mare cantering down the line of warriors still marching forward.

'Keep an eye on him.'

'I will do my best,' Corleth said. 'He has a great spirit though, I would not dare to say what he might do.'

Luxor was about to comment further, but Corleth finished the sentence for him. '... he seems alike unto his father to me.'

The day's trudge wore on, weary league after weary league. They passed another keep, set aside from the road they were travelling, already being emptied of its guards to bolster their forces. It was little more than a waymarker on their journey south, too small to be of any use against the pursuing hordes. The people of the villages nearby had long since fled. Rounding a bend in the path, they topped a faint rise in the land.

Beyond a welcome sight greeted them. The Citadel of Shimeril lay at the edge of a rising length of hills, the far side of the Downs of Mitharg. The going became easier as they left the Plains of Blood and reached Shimeril's domain, the land of Iserath. As they stopped for a brief rest and a meal, their destination lay but three leagues to the south. Spirits had risen.

Luxor was about to dismount when the Moon Ring pulsed. His eyes took on a glazed look.

'Father?'

Morkin had ridden up alongside him, pulling at his arm. 'Father!'

Morkin saw Luxor blink and then focus on his surroundings.

'I am sorry my son.' Luxor blinked and rubbed his forehead with the back of his hand. 'This ring, it wearies my mind to concentrate so. Silence has crossed swords with the enemy. She has fled to the west once more.'

'Is she safe?'

Luxor shook his head. 'No. They pursue her in a fury, but her plan seems to be working. We must not tarry long. She is buying us time at great risk!'

'Are you all right, father?'

Luxor sighed. The pulse of the Moon Ring was not so much unpleasant as it was draining. He felt almost as if it were using him as a source of power. He could sense the ice-fear about him, a constant lethargy in the air, a pall of gloom that threatened to cast a dampness on hope and joy. He could feel the Moon Ring funnel his own warmth outwards, challenging the ice-fear and wrestling with it, but at the cost of his own invigoration.

'It is nothing, my son,' Luxor replied. 'Much has transpired and I must get to grips with it all!'

Shadows were lengthening as the company approached the walls of the Citadel of Shimeril. Morkin stared up at it as they approached, awed by the spectacle. Unlike the desolate foreboding mass of the Citadel of Gorgrath, here there was light and life. The Citadel showed evidence of being well tended, guards could be seen patrolling the walls, stonework was well maintained and everything was neat and tidily kept. As he watched the great gates swung outwards and trumpets blew to announce their arrival.

Morkin looked about him as he rode into the courtyards within. He missed the comforting firelights that would have been in the alcoves. Now they were cold and dark, their owners having fled the day before. The courtyards were conspicuously empty of children, the bustling market was empty, no traders hawked their wares. Warriors ran around hustling the remaining folk into hastily prepared carts and wagons packed with provisions. They were organised into caravans

161

and sent out into the wilderness, guarded by the few warriors that could be spared for the task. The sense of barely concealed panic permeated the place.

The welcome scent of roasting meat was upon the air though, making his stomach rumble in protest.

Luxor must have felt equally famished, but none of the Lords would have any part of feasting until the needs of their men were met. Morkin followed their example, sensing a certain nobility in the practise. Even Lord Gard, who Morkin thought might not honour such a tradition was seen to be walking about his men, ensuring they had sufficient food, drink and clothing.

'There is a saying,' Shimeril told him. 'A tradition in times of war, young lad. No Lord may feast, or rest or sleep, 'til he sees to those who defend his keep.'

'I will remember it,' Morkin replied.

Shimeril nodded. 'Perhaps one day you will be a Lord. How you treat your people determines how great a Lord you will be.'

Food did eventually come Morkin's way, but he ate quickly without much zeal. Luxor himself had eaten with little appetite and was standing atop the battlements, looking out to the north and west. Morkin could see the other Lords were joining him. Below frantic preparations for the evacuation continued, but Morkin could see that the battlements were manned and the Citadel was close to a state of readiness.

Many caravans had already left, with the bulk of the civilian population already a day's march to the south east. The army of the Free would rest only overnight in order to replenish their strength and rest. A three day march lay ahead of them, with the forces of the Doomguard not far away.

Luxor nodded to Corleth and Morkin.

'You leave upon the morrow. Thrall is an easy ride now, the Foul cannot reach you there. They should not notice your departure.'

As plans went it had come off rather well. The Doomguard had clearly not expected any resistance from the fleeing armies of the Free.

With little warning of what was about to happen to them, Silence and her warriors quickly despatched the scouts that rode ahead of the army, ensuring that no word of their presence returned.

Silence had broken her warriors into two groups, putting her second in command in charge of the second group and sending them to the opposite flank of the ranks of marching Doomguard. Their stealth paid off, the Doomguard did not react, unaware they were being stalked.

Silence withdrew a pendant that hung on a long chain around her neck and held it up. She angled it against the sun, catching its rays and directing them across the featureless plains. A faint sparkle came from far away. A signal.

Ready ...

No battle cries, no shouts of rage or intimidation. They rode in near silence, even the horses were fleet of foot, their hooves whispering softly in the thin snow that pervaded the plains. Arrows flew, swift and sure, striking down the Doomguard, who fell in alarm, breaking out of their positions in rank and file looking for the source of their attackers.

But the warriors of Silence had already retreated. Their arrows launched at a high angle, raining down upon the Doomguard several seconds later. Silence had surveyed the land well, the hillocks and rises in the plain were slight, but she instinctively knew how to use them. Years of fighting in this manner had honed her art.

The other company achieved something similar. Dozens

of the Doomguard lay dead and the centre of the column of warriors was in disarray.

Silence smiled.

We have only just begun.

Another sparkle from her pendant. Her warriors roused their horses and galloped, rendezvousing with their companions half a league ahead of the now halted Doomguard. The warriors of Silence arrayed themselves in a line, just one rider deep, their entire strength spread wide across the plain.

Then came the charge.

This time they did holler, horns sounded. High pitched shrieks of anger and doom. Arrows flew as they closed.

The front ranks of the Doomguard were foot soldiers, who saw the charge with terrified eyes. With the churning snow around them it seemed they were beset by a vast army, bearing down on them at speed. Some dug in halberds into the frosty surface, but many panicked, stumbling back against their companions. Arrows, slicing into them in a ferocious barrage, added to the pandemonium.

Just as they bore down on the vanguard of the foe, the warriors of Silence split down the middle and formed two parallel lines, running either side of the ranks of Doomguard. Bewildered, the forward warriors watched as the attacking riders ran down their flanks, bright blades flashing, cutting down those unprepared.

Cries of warning went up. Arrows began to be returned, if sporadically. Deep horns sounded.

At those notes, the warriors of Silence abruptly turned and retreated, galloping tangentially out across the plains and disappearing into the snowy wasteland.

Corleth, Morkin and the remaining Fey of Shadows departed at first light.

'Farewell, my son,' Luxor said. 'Always look to the dawn, keep your hope alive.'

'Farewell father,' Morkin said, still downcast.

'We will defeat the hordes of the Foul when we make our stand at Dawn,' Luxor said. 'The Witchking can no longer surprise us with his scheming, and we have the Moon Ring to fend off the ice-fear and stay in contact. Be of bold heart. We will prevail. I will soon be back with you to drink a cup of homecoming.'

'I will see him safe to the Village of Thrall,' Corleth said. 'From there I will venture on and summon what Fey I may to join your cause.'

Luxor nodded, clasped Corleth's hand and then released it, pulling Morkin into a close hug.

'Now go!' Luxor called, stepping back.

The company rode out from the Citadel of Shimeril, heading north west towards the ice boughs of the Forest of Thrall. Luxor watched them until they were out of sight.

'Farewell, my son.'

The army of the Free had been marching all through the day, following a well-worn track to the south east. The road to the Citadel of Dawn was well travelled, a major trade route to and from the southlands. The sun was low as evening came on once more, the snow lit a lurid red and grey with the lengthening shadows.

The end of the first day of their march brought the army to a village built alongside Lake Shimeril, on the east of that domain. The Citadel itself, now abandoned, was silhouetted in the evening light, stark against the horizon.

'It is a hard thing to abandon one's home without a fight,' Blood said, as he saw Shimeril looking back towards it.

'Aye,' Shimeril replied. 'But I hope the Doomguard will demolish the west wall, I've been meaning to see that repaired for many moons.'

Blood chuckled. 'And that tower room I slept in before, why there was a crack the full length of the wall! My bones still creak with the cold draught ...'

They shared a moment of laughter.

'What think you of our chances?' Blood said after a moment.

Shimeril rubbed his chin. 'I think our strategy is right, yet our means is insufficient. If Kumar and Marakith make it to Dawn ahead of the Doomguard, perhaps we have a chance, but a slim one I fear. That hammer blow at Valethor ... the ice-fear ...'

'We have our Moonprince ...'

'And I have confidence in our young Lord,' Shimeril said. 'More perhaps than he has in himself.'

'Legends out of the past become real,' Blood said. 'The Witchking's power waxes, even the Wise take an interest in our affairs. We may yet live to see the Fey fight once more. Strange times indeed for Midnight.'

'One way or another our doom approaches,' Shimeril replied. 'This time there will be no stalemate, no uneasy tension to last for moons. This time we win, or we lose.'

The march continued without incident. The Army trudged onwards south east until the rising line of the Mountains of Morning rose up before them and the road turned eastwards. They came across villages, already hastily abandoned having received word of the approaching armies of the Foul.

As the third day of their march dawned, the Citadel that took its name from the rising sun could be seen grey against the bright sky. The army picked up pace, knowing that their destination was close at hand.

The Citadel of Dawn nestled in a natural valley within the Mountains of Dawn. The only access for an invader was from the north or the south west, and the way to the south west was guarded by a supplementary keep. From there it was but two days ride to the southern Citadel of Xajorkith and reinforcements would come from that way if necessary.

To the north the Citadel blocked the way, and would force an enemy to assail it directly. To move further south, any potential conqueror would have little alternative than to strike through the Mountains of Dawn. That was sheer folly, attempting a passage through the mountains away from the passes was nigh on impossible, and even if it was, it would leave an army too exhausted to fight on arrival at its destination.

The Citadel of Dawn was a staging point where the force that held it could dominate the southland. And the Lords of the Free knew this well.

Luxor and the other Lords moved to the front of the column of warriors as it moved towards the Citadel. Flags were raised and answering trumpets sounded from the towers.

'At least we are expected,' Luxor said.

'Dawn will not be happy about it,' Shimeril said.

'It will be the making of the man,' Blood chuckled.

'It had better be,' Gard said, with a faint sneer.

Luxor had only met Dawn once before. He was a popular figure with his people and a capable administrator, but he was not an enthusiastic warrior. He had seldom been seen on the field of battle.

As they rode up the wide cobbled approach to the Citadel, the Lord of Dawn rode out to meet them.

He clearly was confused. Luxor rode at the fore of the group, flanked by Shimeril, Gard and Blood, with the other Lords behind.

'My Lord Luxor?' he queried.

'Luxor the Moonprince,' Blood said, with a deep voice.

'Moonprince ...' Dawn echoed. 'I received your summons as if it were a dream, but truth be told, did not understand it.'

'We can explain later,' Luxor said. 'For now, we have much in the way of preparations. Is your Citadel prepared for a siege? The forces of the Doomguard march upon our tails!'

'We received messages telling us to prepare for war, and such provision as can be made has been made,' Dawn replied. 'Lord Morning arrived today with a force of warriors and riders. But the Doomguard, here in the south? Say it is not so.'

'It is so,' Shimeril said. 'What you see is all that remains of the armies of the west.'

They saw Dawn swallow and gulp, casting his eyes across the warriors arrayed behind them.

'So few ...' he muttered. 'Come within then, much must be said and done.'

'No news of Silence?' Blood asked much later.

Preparations within the Citadel of Dawn had consumed the rest of the day. Dawn had been as good as his word. The Citadel was well stocked and its defences in good order. His own army was fresh and ready for the fight to come. Whilst the Citadel was now crowded, the commoners there had welcomed in the refugees from Shimeril and had accommodated them as well as they could.

Evening had fallen and the Lords stood atop the defences, looking north across the plains.

Luxor shook his head. 'I cannot sense her yet ...'

He stretched out his arm. Upon his finger the Moon Ring flickered and glowed. Luxor's eyes were closed, the strain evident on his face.

The Lords waited about him, muttering under their breath. They felt the nagging doubt of the ice-fear retreat as the Moon Ring pushed forth its own strange ethereal influence.

'She is close …'

Then, in the gathering gloom they could hear the faint sound of drumming. Firelight flashed across the plain, small blazes spread around before them. The Doomguard was not far from the gates of the Citadel.

'Where is she?' Shimeril asked.

The light began to move, closing together and moving towards the Citadel.

'Have guards make ready to close and bar the gates,' Dawn ordered.

'But she's still out there!' Shimeril protested.

Blood took him by the arm. 'If she does not make it by nightfall, she will not make it at all.'

Luxor gasped and then sucked in deep lungfuls of breath.

'She is there!' he pointed, 'They ride just ahead of a host of Doomguard, baying at their heels. They are being ridden down. See the flames, they are just ahead!'

'What can we do?' Shimeril demanded.

'Archers!' Luxor cried. 'Assemble archers! We must give them cover!'

Safely concealed, the warriors of Silence regrouped and found a vantage point to observe their enemies on the Plains of Iserath. None had fallen in the previous days' daring attack, and they had slain a goodly count of the foe. Silence smiled as she watched. The Doomguard army had been slowed, clearly under the impression that they were under attack by a larger force.

Faint shouts, orders being bellowed, reached their ears. Dark flags were raised and calm slowly descended upon the army. After an hour it was on the march again, relentlessly pressing onwards across the Plains of Iserath.

To her surprise they had ignored the Citadel of Shimeril other than to assess it had been abandoned. The army had moved on almost straightaway. Silence and her warriors had stealthily followed the Doomguard as they rode onwards towards Dawn.

'What next, my Lady?' asked her second.

Silence watched for a few more moments.

'We have bought time for our friends, but we must buy more. They have posted more scouts ahead and to the sides. We ride around and harry them from the rear. But be warned, we will not catch them so unprepared next time.'

None disagreed with her assessment. Swiftly they rode; their passing unnoticed by the marching Doomguard until they were positioned behind the army. Here the snow was compacted by the passage of many booted feet. The army remained vast, thousands of warriors and riders, more than a match for the shattered forces of the Free.

The sun was low now, casting long eerie shadows across the plain as they looked out across the landscape. Less than two hours of the day remained, but the troop remained invigorated, knowing their success might prove the difference between life and death for those fleeing to the safety of the citadel.

'Once more,' Silence announced. 'A combined assault on their rear flank, we engage for a minute and then turn and flee to the south.'

Nods from around her signalled assent. She spurred her horse and galloped off. Her warriors forming into a V-shaped phalanx at her hand signal. Bows were readied, swords and knives head fast. The rear formation of the Doomguard came into view as they topped a rise, marching away from them, unaware of the approaching riders of Silence.

Silence signalled to hold as they rode down upon the foe. The closer they could get before they were seen, the more impact they would have.

Two hundred yards was all that was left when a Doomguard turned and yelled. At this, Silence's folk unleashed their arrows, striking down a dozen of the enemy.

One hundred yards and swords flashed in the light of the sun blazing behind them. They had the advantage, hard to see against the brightness of the sky, the Doomguard blinded by the sunlight.

A deep horn sounded once, drawn out and long.

Silence watched in horror as the rear Doomguard spun around, halberds planted in a fierce impenetrable forest of blackened steel. Another horn blew, off to the right. Arrows sprung out and this time, some found their targets.

With screeches of pain, warriors of Silence fell from their steeds.

Silence raised her hand and turned her horse about, cutting down two Doomguard warriors who attempted to grab hold and pull her down.

'Flee, to the south!' she cried, making the hand gesture to indicate retreat.

They have anticipated this! Reactions far quicker than any they have shown before!

The warriors of Silence disengaged, but it was too late for some. Unable to turn about in time, a few were forced into the line of halberds, their horses slain and their bodies cast into the mass of Doomguard. Faint shrieks, quickly cut off, marked their demise. Others were slain even as they fled, the arrows of the Doomguard finding targets.

Then the thunder of other hooves reached their ears. Bright torches spread firelight along the flanks of the Doomguard army and a column of riders could be seen racing towards them.

'Flee!' Silence called. 'We have done all we can, flee to the Citadel of Dawn!'

Her warriors, the three quarters that were left, rode south and then turned east, racing across the plains. But their horses were tiring, having ridden long and hard throughout the day. Those of the Doomguard were fresh and well rested.

Silence signalled to her second to take the lead and dropped back through the ranks of her folk to get a better view. A detachment of the Doomguard rode upon their heels, torches streaming sparks as they were held aloft.

She gasped as she saw them clearly. They had an easier time of it now, the fleeing warriors of Silence could easily be seen in the glowing light of sunset.

Five hundred riders, perhaps more!

No way they could turn and fight. She spurred her horse around and fled before them.

Atop the Citadel the watchers could only gasp in horror as the scene unfold beneath them. Half a league away a mass of dark clad Doomguard were riding down the warriors of Silence, swiftly gaining on them.

They reached the range of their own arrows and a barrage was unleashed.

Luxor watched as the rear ranks of Silence's diminished force crumpled and fell beneath the onslaught.

He looked desperately across at Dawn, who shook his head.

Not in range … not yet!

Dawn had his arm held aloft, poised and ready. He knew his archers and knew the lands hereabouts. He would know when …

His arm dropped. The archers loosed their weapons. Fire

tipped arrows surged into the gloom, arching high into the sky before dropping upon those below.

Dawn had timed it to perfection. The arrows thudded down just as the beleaguered riders of Silence charged past, the arrows cutting down merciless into the Doomguard galloping up close behind them. Dozens were slain and the Doomguard warriors came about, realising their peril in close proximity to the defences of the Citadel.

As they watched from the battlements, the fires of the Doomguard were extinguished and the warriors faded away in the gloom, riding northwards.

Luxor leapt from the battlements as the troop rode in. It was clear to see they were exhausted. Silence was already dismounted and seeing to her folk. Many were wounded and still more had been left behind.

'Close the gates!' Dawn yelled.

The heavy gates of the Citadel swung back, their huge mechanisms rumbling as they wrenched the mighty barricades into place. They shut as the last of the warriors of Silence rode through.

Silence turned as Luxor approached.

'The Citadel, is safe?'

Luxor nodded. 'All are safe within and we are prepared for a siege. Our thanks, my lady. We would have been overtaken if you had not diverted them.'

'I have paid a heavy price,' Silence replied. 'The Doomguard anticipated our second attack, a sense of preparation I have not found before.'

Luxor frowned. 'Doubtless the vision of the Witchking lies upon us now. He will be directing his armies by his foul enchantments.'

He raised his voice.

'Let none doubt the valour of Silence and her people,' he cried. 'They have saved our lives twice in quick succession, deeds that will be long remembered. Make no mistake, times of war are upon us once again and we must rise to defeat the foe.'

Cheers greeted his speech but he could sense the fear and trepidation around him. For all their efforts, the folk of Silence had only bought them time enough to prepare a defence. An army, bent on their destruction and still far bigger than their own forces lay but a day's march away.

And less than half of the warriors who had set out three morns before with Silence had returned.

Chapter Eight

They stand in the Village of Thrall,
looking east to Lake Thrall.

The Forest of Thrall was unlike any forest Morkin had ever
been within before. As was typical for the borders, snow had
piled up in deep drifts around its edge, but a vaulted arch of
ice had been carved amidst the trees, cunningly concealed by
the lee of the land, decorated in the manner of the Fey. Morkin
admired it as they approached. Behind them, the warriors of
Shadows followed in a line.

'There are many entrances to the forests,' Corleth said, 'but
they evade the eyes of those who do not revere the trees.'

'Fey magic,' Morkin whispered.

Corleth shrugged. 'Magic is not a word the Fey would use;
it is how men describe our craft. We seek only to protect and
nourish the forests. In return, they protect and nourish us.'

The pair rode their horses under the arch. A pathway un-
folded before them leading deeper into the dark interior of
the forest.

Beneath their feet the snow thinned abruptly. Here and
there Morkin could see greenery to the side of the path, somehow untouched by the frosts and the cold.

Corleth saw the puzzled looked upon his face and chuckled.

'Even in the depths of winter, Midnight has a hidden heat.'

'A hidden heat?'

Corleth nodded. 'How do you suppose the lakes do not freeze?'

Morkin considered the point. 'I always thought … well, now you mention it I have no idea. Why don't they freeze?'

'I do not know if it is true, but I see no reason why it should not be so,' Corleth began. 'It is said there is a source of heat far below, deep in the rocks that underpin our realms, untouched by the winter frosts. Sometimes that heat is nearer the surface, sometimes further below. Where it rises close it has the potency to melt the ice that binds Midnight and we see lakes and greenery, free from the ice. It is a blessing, without it there would be no fish, no farming, no crops and no life!'

'If it can defy the will of the Witchking, it is powerful indeed!'

'There are things more ancient and potent in the world than even the Witchking, my young friend,' Corleth said. 'There is much in Midnight that bides its time, waiting for his passing.'

The conversation lapsed as they continued on. Hours passed and the sun rose a little higher in the sky, casting a faint flickering illumination through the branches of the great trees. The ground beneath them began to rise and the trees thinned, until they were standing upon a rise of gentle hills that rolled ahead of them.

'Beyond lies the Village of Thrall,' Corleth said, gesturing to the north east. 'We will arrive before sundown.'

The sun had settled behind the eaves by the time they made their approach. The village of the Fey was nothing like the villages of men. Those had been rough but comely affairs, constructed of timber hewn from trees with a main street which all trade and passers-by traversed. One could always find the local alehouse and blacksmith, nestled alongside shops and outfitters catering for visitors.

But the village of the Fey had none of these, at least as far as Morkin could see. There was no main street. The Fey were not so fond of straight lines and the buildings that were present seemed to have grown rather than been placed and planned. Some were intertwined with the trees, others half buried in the hills. Even ice had been used in their construction, somehow wrought into smooth organic curves, huge buttresses that supported the pathway into the village, forming a bridge that rose into defensive ramparts also made of ice.

Lights shone from the village, some were firelights, flickering with a comforting yellow, but others were bright white, almost star-like in their brilliance, shining steadily. Morkin wondered what they were.

A pair of guards, dressed in thin but brightly polished armour that framed tunics and garments of green and blue, stood before them at the threshold of the bridge.

'Corleth,' the first guard said, immediately recognising him. 'It is good to see you once more and know of your safe return. Lord Thrall has been exceedingly worried by your long absence. These warriors you bring ...'

Corleth nodded. 'The Fey of Shadows. I have news enough for Lord Thrall. For now we require shelter after a long road.'

'It will be arranged. Your companion?'

'This is Squire Morkin,' Corleth said, with a mischievous smile. 'Son, it is now revealed, of Lord Luxor.'

'Luxor ...?'

'Much must be told, but I must reveal it to Lord Thrall first,' Corleth said. 'We are in some haste.'

The guard nodded to his companion.

'I will take you to him myself.'

The warriors of Shadows departed, glad of the chance to rest. Corleth and Morkin were led across the bridge into the heart of the village. Everywhere a smooth curve, as if edges were not to be tolerated unless absolutely necessary.

Stablehands relieved them of their horses and promised their gear would be stowed and made available when required. Thus relieved they were taken to a grand hall that occupied a rise within the village. It was a two storey building, commanding a view out across the landscape from its higher floor. More guards stood at the doors, which opened as they approached.

'Welcome Corleth of the Fey and Morkin of the Free!'

Morkin did not see the herald, nor could he see much else due to the dazzling brightness of the interior. His overwhelming impression was of lights in every direction he looked, as if the stars themselves had been taken from the heavens and peppered throughout the interior. He blinked, trying to see clearly.

He heard the door close behind him and his eyes began adjusting. A warmth suffused him, though he could see no fires lit. Figures moved before him and then his vision cleared and he was looking up into an imposing drawn and severe face. This was no common Fey, but a Lord of their race. Morkin could sense the grandeur, the responsibility, the nobility and the concern of the Fey before him, even as he looked into his face.

The Lord of Thrall!

Beside him, Corleth bowed and Morkin copied the movement.

'Long you have tarried beyond our borders, Corleth,' Thrall intoned. His voice had a deep and measured timbre. 'Have you news of the errand upon which the Wise called you forth? We have heard only rumours of evil since.'

'Much has transpired my Lord,' Corleth replied.

'I would hear it,' Thrall answered. 'We have heard little from the west, but what we have heard from the north is disturbing.' His attention turned to Morkin. Morkin returned the look without flinching, even though Thrall frowned momentarily as he studied him.

'Squire Morkin of the Free,' Corleth explained. 'Son of Lord Luxor.'

'It is rare that we entertain the sons of men within our realm,' Thrall said.

Morkin bowed once more. 'I am most humbly honoured to be here in your presence, my Lord.'

'And rarer still to meet one of the Free with soft words and grace,' Thrall said.

Corleth coughed. 'Morkin has his own story, my Lord.'

'So I see. Come. Sit and dine with me.'

The guards upon the high walls of the Citadel of Dreams kept a wary watch on the distant horizon. No change from the west. No explanation of the frightening wall of cloud had been given. Folk muttered about it, but continued about their business.

Tarithel had asked and been refused an explanation.

'There is much beyond our borders,' her father had said. 'Much that is evil. Some wrought by the hands of men, and fouler things beside. Do not think upon it, we have withstood it. Consider it a warning not to meddle in the affairs of the Witchking.'

Tarithel wasn't convinced that it was any power of the Fey that had turned aside the malevolent storm, but she was wise enough not to contradict her father directly. She determined to walk around the citadel, eavesdropping on any and all conversations she could.

She had picked up tantalising hints, fragments of history, lore and stories. Some spoke of the evil Witchking far to the west; some of the folly of the Free. Most of the storytellers looked grim and subdued, but she saw faint glimmers of hope in the eyes of some. There was vague talk of an end to winter and the return of summer rains. Mention of old songs and a word, a word that resonated with her own memory of the strange rolling cloud.

Moonprince!

Who was this Moonprince? Was he an adversary of the Witchking come to defeat him?

My father will not tell me, I must answer this riddle myself.

Lord Dreams had summoned leading nobles to his court, held within the great hall of the citadel. Tarithel had not been invited, but she didn't intend to let a little thing like that stop her.

She had been a resident of the citadel for all her short life, and, being an inquisitive young Fey-girl, she had found all manner of hiding holes, concealed places and forgotten passageways. The games of hideaway she had played as a child came very usefully to mind when she needed to discover something best kept secret.

And, surely, if I am the Lady of the Forest and sworn to protect it, I must know what could threaten it, no?

The great hall had once been served by a series of bells driven by a complex mechanism of cogs and wheels. Tarithel had found it long since rusted into place, its movement no longer understood. It had been some gift of men in a time long past so it seemed, now forgotten by all but her.

The mechanism was housed into a room immediately above the hall. It was dusty and dirty, but in the midst of the mechanism was a grating from which it was possible to see all who moved below. Reaching the grate was tricky. Tarithel had to wriggle herself into position between the huge circular cogs and workings and then stay very still in the confined space. There was a danger of making too much noise. Thus she made sure she arrived beforehand and only left once all below had gone.

Thus she knew secrets far beyond those told to her direct.

Today she had made her way there well in advance, taking

with her a drink, some food and wraps of linen, partly to prevent dirtying her clothes, and partly for warmth, the room was unheated and was sorely cold.

But she could hear everything that was said.

Her father was speaking to the captains of the guard, grim Fey who journeyed throughout the Forest of Dreams, tasked with keeping their borders secure.

'There is no immediate threat to our borders, sire,' one captain reported. 'We saw the foul armies of the Doomguard moving south across the Plains of Kor, but they bother us not.'

'And they will not bother us,' Dreams replied. 'The agreement we reached at the end of the last war remains. We will not take up arms against the Witchking.'

The guard shifted uncomfortably from one foot to the other. 'My Lord, rumours are that the Witchking makes war upon the lords of the south.'

'If they have angered him, it is their problem to contend with,' Lord Dreams replied. 'And Korinel, what of him?'

The captain sighed. 'It is as we feared, my Lord.'

Lord Dreams cursed, a foul profanity that made Tarithel gasp and then clamp her hand over her mouth. She had never heard her father utter such a word before.

She watched her father pace about for a long while before turning back to the captain.

'Do we know what Korinel did to anger the Witchking?'

The captain shook his head. 'Perhaps he prevented the armies of the Witchking heading south …'

'He was always a warmonger,' Dreams said. 'No word of this is to leave this room, is this understood?'

'Yes, my Lord.'

'If people hear this there will be panic, demands for action that we can ill afford, unrest and discord. Send word to Whispers with notice of warning. He should also be aware. My order stands, the Fey are not to defy the Witchking.'

'It will be done, my Lord.'

'I want constant patrols on the borders, nothing else is to get in, or out. Is that clear?'

'Yes, my Lord.'

'Quickly now, dismissed.'

Tarithel watched as the captains marched out of the hall. She waited, frustrated, as her father continued to pace about below for several minutes.

'We had a pact, he would not bother us and we would not bother him. A promise he gave me! True enough this attack has not been raised against my realm but… Korinel, you fool!'

She heard him mutter just before he strode out.

'I will not have this, not have this happen in my days!'

Then he was gone. Tarithel waited another minute to be sure and then began the laborious process of extracting herself from the insides of the ancient mechanism.

Something bad has happened, but what is it? Father keeps secrets from his family and from the people. A pact with whom? Not the Witchking himself? How could we be allied with evil? Trouble beyond our borders for sure, the Witchking's doing? And what of this Moonprince? Who is he? What has happened to Korinel?

She racked her brains for a moment before it came to her. Korinel was the leader of a band of Fey that lived in the shadow of the Witchking's realm, the Forest of Kor, but three days march from the hated realm of Despair.

A thought came into her mind. It scared and terrified her all at once.

I'm going to find out. The Lady of the Forest indeed!

She'd have to be quick. The Captains would be sending messengers to close the borders. They would be ready to depart within minutes. If she was going to do anything she would have to go now.

Her mind made up, she wrestled herself free, dumped the

linen garments and made her way out of the hidden machinery loft. In her haste, she omitted to see that the linen had fallen in the doorway, preventing it from closing. Her mind was elsewhere.

The kitchens lay quiet at this time of day. Grabbing a stash of cured and salted meats, vegetables and several rolls of thinbreads, she added them to the pack containing her garments. Down at the stables, a coquettish smile and a flutter of her eyelids had the stable boys speeding to prepare a horse.

'I wish to take some air before the sunset,' she said. 'I'll be back within the hour.'

They thought nothing of it; she regularly rode out and about in the forest around the Citadel.

But today she trotted the horse across the drawbridge with determination etched upon her brow.

She paused at the threshold of the forest and looked back at the citadel. Lights were just being lit in the lower windows as the shadow of the trees began to fall upon its walls.

Then she turned, spurred her steed and urged it to a gallop, heading westwards through the eaves.

'I was summoned to the Tower of the Moon,' Corleth said, relating his tale. 'There to meet, albeit briefly, with one Rorthron, claiming to speak for the Council of the Wise.'

'Of Rorthron I have heard,' Thrall said. 'But not of this council.'

'Rorthron's ruse,' Corleth replied. 'It was he alone.'

'Go on.'

'I was given a mission,' Corleth continued. 'To seek Lord Luxor and his son Morkin and bring them back to Rorthron before the Winter Solstice. This I did.'

'And what interest did this Rorthron have in a Lord of

men?' Thrall queried. 'It is long since the Wise took any interest in Midnight at all.'

Corleth took a breath.

'Rorthron revealed that Lord Luxor was the only surviving heir of the House of the Moon.'

Thrall paused, a mouthful of leaves held halfway to his mouth.

'The House of the Moon was destroyed, long ago. The Witchking's perfidy.'

Corleth shook his head. 'Another ploy of the Wise, it would seem, to preserve the line. Lord Luxor was unaware of it also.'

'And how can we be sure?' Thrall asked.

'Lord Luxor bears the Moon Ring,' Corleth said. 'I have seen him wield it.'

Thrall sat back in his seat and placed his knife upon the table.

'A Moonprince,' he said, considering the news for a long moment. 'And does he rally the Free to his command?'

'He does,' Corleth said. 'Though that road has not been one easily travelled.'

'How so?'

'The Lord of Gard had summoned the forces of the west to the Plains of Blood to deal with an incursion of the Witchking's forces from the gap of Valethor,' Corleth explained. 'Luxor was Gard's vassal and was bound by the traditions of the Free. It was thought that a small band of the Doomguard were causing havoc in the gap. But it was but a feint.'

'We have seen what happened,' Thrall said. 'Smoke rises from the ruins of the Keep of Blood even now.'

'The armies of the Free were defeated and many were lost,' Corleth said with a sad nod. 'The Fey of the west came to their aid, but only prevented further death. Lord Shadows was slain in the fighting. His men are here with me. The Witchking moves further into the south.'

'We have seen their filth all around our borders,' Thrall said. 'An anger has been aroused that would have been best left sleeping.'

Corleth shook his head. 'The Witchking moves of his own accord, my Lord. We encountered his forces in the Forest of Shadows. They somehow penetrated the forests, despite our curation of the trees. The ice-fear freezes hearts once more. Our defences will not hold either. The fell magic of the Witchking stalks our lands ...'

'These are ill tidings.'

Corleth took a deep breath. 'Lord Luxor has bidden me ...
'

'To seek aid from the armies of the Fey,' Thrall finished for him. 'He intends to make a stand against the Witchking at the Citadel of Dawn. This I know.'

'My Lord, then ...?'

'You know the laws that were set upon us after the last war,' Thrall said. 'Lord Dreams set them and they remain. We are not to challenge or provoke the Witchking.'

'The Witchking has broken his promise,' Corleth replied. 'He has assailed the Fey of Shadows. He has the means to penetrate our realms. If we do not come to the aid of the Free they will fall. The Witchking will find it easy enough to destroy us hereafter. The ice-fear is new, stronger, changed. It is more potent than it has ever been ...'

Thrall shrugged. 'I know little of Shadows. I still trust in my forest to take care of itself and those within, we have not been invaded despite many attempts. You know our strength, Corleth. The Fey are not as they once were.'

'We must muster what strength we can. I have promised that the Fey will follow the Moonprince.'

Thrall nodded. 'If Moonprince he truly is, the Fey will follow if Lord Dreams decrees it to be so.'

'We must march now ...'

'Lord Dreams has not given that order,' Thrall replied. 'I cannot defy the standing orders of the Fey not to provoke the Witchking. Dreams and Dregrim are in accord over this. It is not for me to defy the orders of the High Lords of the Fey.'

'Cannot, or will not?' Corleth snapped. 'This is not the time for hesitation. The Free can ill afford …'

'You would seek to order me?' Thrall replied, his voice lower.

'My apologies my Lord … but time grows short. It may mean the difference between victory and defeat for the Free. The Witchking sweeps all before him. As his confidence grows, thus grows the ice-fear, further reducing the ability to resist him. Already he can penetrate our realms. Unchecked he will wipe the Free and the Fey from the face of Midnight. This is the zenith of his power. We cannot wait for distant orders …'

Thrall nodded. 'I hear you, but the decision is not my own. Messengers will be despatched forthwith. If Dreams gives the order, it will be so.'

'Then I must look elsewhere for allies to aid the free,' Corleth replied.

Thrall signalled to attendants and issued hurried orders, writing upon parchments and sealing them with wax seals. The work complete, he turned to Morkin.

'And you, son of the Moonprince,' he began. 'You have not yet told your tale.'

'My father has sent me here in the hope of safe-keeping,' Morkin began.

'Something not much to your liking it would seem,' Thrall said, with a trace of amusement. 'You would stand by his side in such times and undertake some worthy deed.'

Morkin felt his mouth drop open and consciously forced himself to close it again.

'Morkin shares a heritage with us,' Corleth said softly.

Thrall looked across at him, before looking back to Morkin. 'A heritage you say? What heritage?'

'My father is Lord Luxor,' Morkin said. 'My mother was ...'

Thrall's eyes narrowed further.

'Aleisha. No, it cannot be.'

Morkin nodded.

Thrall got to his feet and strode around the table.

'So,' he said, fixing Morkin with a hard stare. 'You are the one she spoke of.'

'She spoke of me?' Morkin looked across at Corleth for re-assurance.

'Giving you up to the world of men broke her heart,' Thrall said. 'She never recovered from that hurt. She was lost to us from that moment forward, lost to the Fey ... lost to me.'

Morkin swallowed at the pain in Thrall's voice and then made a choice.

He knelt before Thrall, his head bowed.

'My Lord, I offer my service to you in her name. If I can serve you, command me.'

For a long moment all was still. Morkin could feel the blood pounding in his ears. Thrall stepped one pace before him.

A hand came down into his field of view, proffered towards him.

'Rise ...' Thrall's voice called down.

Morkin found himself pulled up with a firm grip from Thrall. The Fey looked at him, his gaze firm.

'You have your mother's indomitable spirit,' he said. 'And I see her arrogance and exuberance there too. She was never one for rules or discipline. Oft she found our ways restrictive and sought the companionship of others.'

Morkin didn't answer, so Thrall continued.

'She came to the aid of your father. Nursing him back to health after the last battle against the Witchking. Love, such as it can be between Fey and Free was theirs, you were the product of their union ... at great cost to her.'

'My Lord ...' Morkin began.

Thrall held up a hand. 'She was a great lover of our heritage, well versed in the lore and history of our people. That she would fulfil that lore seems only fitting.'

'Fulfil?' Morkin echoed, confused.

Corleth stepped forward. 'My Lord, Luxor has tasked me with keeping Morkin safe...'

Thrall laughed. 'Safe? You have told me the Witchking can penetrate my borders and that mighty armies lie at my threshold. What is safe now?'

'What lore is this of which you speak?' Morkin asked.

Thrall nodded. 'The old songs. Better you hear them as they were meant to be heard, Morkin of the Free ...' He looked up with narrowed eyes. '... and the Fey.'

He stepped back and clapped his hands. Servants came to him via doors at the rear of the hall and he swiftly barked orders for musicians. Within moments a quartet appeared bearing instruments that looked similar to flutes and lyres.

'The old song, from the lay of Yanathel.'

The musicians took a moment to prepare themselves and then indicated they were ready.

Thrall nodded and the musicians began; a young Fey-girl singing in a high pitched, yet soft and gentle, voice.

Later Morkin did not recall the music, but the words seemed to light something in his mind and stayed with him for the rest of his days.

Her feet trod silently, the frozen ground below,
Whilst wheeled above skies laced with snow.
The ice-fear touches all, freezes them with cold,
Hearts of stone where once were bold.

The Ice Crown, greatest woe of many woes,
Fear pervades it, so the Wise have told.

188

While it remains, the Witchking reigns,
The frightful Midnight bane of banes.

She thought to save the world, seek that talisman's demise,
To the North she rode, on guidance from the Wise.
She came upon that solitary wretched tower,
Her fall appointed at that fateful hour.

For the Witchking steals away all who near his icy heart,
A greater cold than even Frozen Wastes impart.
Yanathel of all who dared, came closest to that deed,
Yet not by Fey alone was Midnight to be freed.

Too late the truth she did perceive; one part Fey, one part Free,
Laughter and lightness from the forests be.
From men take wild-fire, their passions barely tame,
Thus will melt the ice-fear; in rolling drops of summer rain.

It was many minutes before the spell of the song broke for Morkin. The musicians had gone by the time he came back to his senses.

'This is what Rorthron the Wise spoke of,' he said. 'But how can this be? I am not a warrior.'

'Long we puzzled over the lay of Yanathel,' Thrall said. 'One born of Fey and Free? How could such a thing be? The lives of men are but ersh in the wind to the Fey. But the son of Aleisha and the Moonprince, perhaps this is the time.'

'He cannot go,' Corleth said. 'His father has forbidden it. I have given my word to protect him.'

Thrall turned on him. 'Hold faith in the armies of the Free do you? They have been defeated once already, the Witchking holds the north and the west. The hordes of Doomguard are about us. Even if we receive instructions from Dreams and can rally the Fey, it is likely too little too late. The Wise know this to be true. They have curated and protected the line of Moon all this time, waiting for this moment.'

Morkin absorbed Thrall's words and then turned to Corleth.

'Is this true? Is defeat certain?' he demanded. 'My father sent me away because he was sure he was going to die, didn't he!'

'He will fight bravely, there is much strength ...'

'Tell me the truth, Corleth!'

Corleth swallowed, looked away and then sighed. His voice was heavy when he spoke. 'Barring a miracle your father cannot hope to prevail against the Doomguard. The armies of the Fey are not enough, even supposing we rally in time. The Witchking may have already struck a mortal blow ...'

Morkin raised his head.

'Then I will disobey my father's wishes,' he said, his voice ringing in the hall. 'And relieve you of that burden, Corleth of the Fey. As it seems to be true that by my birth the ice-fear cannot harm me, I will seek the Ice Crown as Rorthron instructed and attempt its destruction!'

'The perils of such a journey,' Corleth said. 'You would be beyond all hope of rescue, travelling in the very heart of the Witchking's realm ...'

'If I do not, Midnight will be lost anyway and then what would become of me?'

The youthful logic was irrefutable.

Thrall and Corleth exchanged a look.

'Now,' Morkin said. 'Somebody had better give me a map.'

'Your father will likely slay me on the spot when next we meet,' Corleth said later. Thrall had set them to work in the great libraries of the Fey and they had spent hours poring over maps and ancient writings, seeking everything that was known of the Ice Crown.

'He will have me to answer to if he does,' Morkin said.

'I have had to turn away from him before this time,' Corleth said. 'He will not forgive me for allowing his son to fall into harm's way.'

'I go willingly,' Morkin said. 'Remember that. My father is proud, but he will understand.'

Corleth looked into the distance for a moment. 'Friendship with your father is something I value most highly. It pains my heart to know he will feel betrayed once more. I would not do that to him.'

Morkin grabbed his arm. 'That you care so much for him is plain to see. If I succeed, it will save Midnight and my father. You will have protected and rescued him by helping that end.'

Corleth smiled. 'You are much like your mother.'

Morkin returned the smile. 'She let me go, my father must too.'

Corleth nodded. 'If your wisdom continues to grow such as this, then Rorthron himself will soon have competition. Come, let us divine your path.'

Corleth spread out a map upon the rough table at which they worked, ensuring it lay flat by placing two candlesticks upon its edges. By the light the candles they examined it.

'The Witchking's realm lies beyond the Mountains of Gorgrath and the Plains of Kor,' Corleth said. 'Here in the far north. It is bound by high and frigid mountains, his fortresses lie in the Plains of Despair.'

'And the Ice Crown is kept in the Tower of Doom,' Morkin said. 'He's not very imaginative with his naming, is he?'

Corleth chuckled. 'It was the Tower of Ushgarak before the Witchking came to power. Men have given these places those names, casting upon it their fears and worries. Doom it will be, that is for sure.'

'How do we know the Ice Crown is there?' Morkin asked. 'Perhaps the Witchking has moved it?'

Corleth shook his head. 'The Witchking keeps it in the best tactical position. The mountains, the forests, even the Frozen Wastes themselves serve as barriers, it is well protected where it is. None, save you and one other, can approach it.'

'One other?'

'I dare say the Witchking himself can approach it, no?' Corleth chuckled. Morkin nodded with a smile.

Morkin looked across the map. 'So all I have to do is evade all the armies of the Doomguard, travel into the far north undetected, sneak into his tower unseen, grab the Ice Crown and make away with it ...'

Corleth raised his eyebrows.

'Assuming I do manage all that,' Morkin said.' What then? How do I destroy it? Rorthron said he did not know.'

'Rorthron said he knew one that did,' Corleth answered. 'Lorgrim.'

'And who is Lorgrim?'

Corleth pointed to the far north east of the map. Morkin could see there were hills marked with the name 'Lorgrim'.

'Another of the Wise, older and more skilled than even Rorthron, if my understanding is correct. Rorthron was but a youngster when the Witchking rose to power. Lorgrim though, he was long since grown to power. He tutored Gryfallon, before he fell to evil.'

'The Witchking's master? Why does he not strike him down and have done with it?'

Corleth shook his head. 'I do not know, but it is not uncommon for the apprentice to overtake the master in skill. Still, Rorthron was sure Lorgrim would know how to destroy the Ice Crown and he has gone to find out.'

Morkin frowned.

'Ere you and your father arrived at the Keep of Blood,' Corleth said, 'Rorthron was already far to the east, travelling by means only the Wise know how. Perhaps he draws nigh to Lorgrim even as we speak. Rorthron thought your quest to be the only way to assure the defeat of the Witchking. We must trust he will find the answer and have a way to bring that news to you.'

Morkin nodded and a brightness sparkled in his eyes. 'The magic of the Wise!'

'Now, we must see how you might reach the Witchking's realm.'

Corleth turned back to the map and traced his fingers across it.

'It would be folly to attempt to cross the Plains of Blood now,' he said, pondering the problem. 'They will be infested with hordes of Doomguard. The same can be said of the gap of Valethor.'

'What of the mountains?'

Corleth shook his head. 'You cannot pass through the Mountains of Ithril in the depths of winter. There are no passes. You would perish in those heights. You might strike to the east, towards the Forest of Dreams and the Citadel of Ithrorn, but that is a long route and the Witchking would be watching it.'

'Then perhaps the far west?'

Corleth considered it.

'The Plains of Ashimar are a wilderness,' he said thoughtfully. 'And the Mountains of Dodrak and the lands thereabouts are not well travelled. There are not fortifications or defences. Few venture there.'

'It sounds ideal.'

'Perhaps,' Corleth said. 'But you must be cautious. It is very isolated. Even in the midst of winter, a land is not abandoned; there will be a reason why folk have fled. If it is not the Doomguard, then what could it be? Perhaps Shadows might have known, or Silence. But we cannot ask them now.'

'If I cannot cross the Plains of Blood, I must go south and west first,' Morkin observed. 'The Downs of Mitharg?'

Corleth nodded. 'The armies of the Witchking have already moved on in pursuit of your father. A dash across Iserath and there will be cover enough in the Downs until you come back nigh to the Forest of Shadows. From there, follow its border north and then north west. The Vale of Dodrak will be before you.'

'And what lies beyond Dodrak?'

Corleth indicated the map.

'The lands are seldom visited. I have not been there myself and I do not know the road.' He pointed a finger to a forest marked beyond the mountains. 'Yet, here of old, were Fey. The Forest of Lothoril was a dwelling of our people. It is from there that Yanathel set out on her ill-fated quest to destroy the Ice Crown. Perhaps it is fitting you venture from there too. At the least it will give you a place to gain provisions and rest after your trek.'

Morkin nodded. 'A warm hearth at the end of my journey north would be a welcome thing indeed.'

'Thrall will write a missive directing them to assist you in all possible ways. From there, two days march will see you to the edge of the Witchking's realm, nigh to the Tower of Doom itself.'

'And the Ice Crown?'

Corleth nodded. 'How you will penetrate his realm and venture within the tower I know not. We must trust in Rorthron and the help of the Fey from the north.'

'Then little remains but for me to prepare,' Morkin said. 'Time is short. I must destroy the Ice Crown before the Doom-guard can crush the Free.'

'So the old songs say,' Corleth said softly. 'I trust we will be writing new songs of your victory before many moons have passed.'

'The lay of Morkin, vanquisher of the Witchking,' Morkin replied with a grin. 'Now that, I want to hear!'

A blizzard hurled freezing whiteness across the landscape. The wind howled, sweeping great flurries of snow into the air. Drifts rose yards high, sculpting the snow into treacherous dunes below which lurked hidden chasms and fissures.

Travelling in such conditions was near suicide even for the well prepared. None ventured out in such weather, only the unfortunate would be caught in it, failing to read the scenes and take shelter.

The storms of Midnight were lethal and those whose business required them to travel knew it well.

No eyes saw it, but had there been, they would have blinked in astonishment at the sight of an old man walking swiftly through the streaming whiteout. He strode with surprising energy, walking with the aid of a long staff, clutched in his right hand, making good progress, unaffected by the raging wind all about him.

Closer still and those eyes would have seen the driven snow arc away from the man, as if he were surrounded by some invisible sphere. The storm did not hamper him. He held the staff slightly aloft, its tip glowing with a faint green tinge. His footsteps lay upon the fallen snow, barely dinting it at all, despite the depth of powder. Before a score of his prints had receded from his progress, they faded, dashed to oblivion by the storm.

Thus none marked the passage of Rorthron the Wise, nor could storm delay him. He was learned in the lore of Midnight and knew many of its secrets. The Wise had long ago learned the arts of travel throughout the realm. There were powers with Midnight that those with the arcane knowledge could avail themselves.

Rorthron smiled to himself.

The Liths, the Henges … arts long forgotten by most, but most convenient in times of urgency! If the Moonprince is judged worthy, perhaps they will assist him too …

He had trudged on for weary hours, penetrating the far frozen north, haste in his gait. The mountains, plains and forests fell away before him, until he stood at last upon the borders of his journey.

The storm began to dissipate, cold air falling around him as the clouds dispersed. Sunlight, weak and feeble, but welcome after the long greyness, flickered across the ground. Visibility improved and the vista of the frozen north came into view.

Rorthron paused in his stride, taking a moment to survey the scene.

He was not far off course. Before him lay the jagged spikes of the Frozen Wastes, a barrier none of the Free or the Fey could pass. Certain death awaited in their icy cores. The received wisdom was that the Frozen Wastes were utterly forbidden. This was almost true, but the Wise knew better.

Ahead was a fissure in the frost-cracked ice, a narrow passage somehow free from the fell magic that had formed the Frozen Wastes.

It would have been invisible to the eyes of men and even the sharpest eyes of the Fey would have failed to see its cunning. Rorthron though, he was familiar with the devices of the Wise.

He slipped within the fissure and found himself on a narrow path between the blade-sharp ice about him. He moved cautiously, careful not to touch the jagged shards around him. The Frozen Wastes were not mere ice, but the bitter remnants of a fell mist that had long ago surrounded the lands of Midnight, hemming it in and cutting it off from other lands. Its icicles were laced with evil beyond mere cold. Their touch was death to all who attempted to pass.

It was not long before the fissure widened into a more easily navigable canyon within the icy walls. Rorthron did not pause, but continued onwards, not breaking his stride. Time remained of the essence.

The path beneath his feet climbed upwards, the canyon flattening out into a valley which led on to a plain. Overhead the sun blazed once more, its radiance dazzling on the bright blanket of snow that lay all about.

Rorthron sighed with satisfaction.

Before him, after many leagues of weary travel, lay his destination.

Another edifice of the Wise, thrusting upwards from the glaciated landscape as if in defiance; the Tower of Lorgrim.

A pathway to the tower was swept clear of snow, a paved walkway leading forward through the drifts held aside on either side. Rorthron recognised the craft employed to do this; control of the forces of nature was a skill that had once been widely shared amongst the folk of the Wise.

He sighed. The perversion and concentration of those abilities was what had brought him here. The Ice Crown was the ultimate embodiment of those powers, combining the arts of nature with the arts of the mind, suffused throughout with the will to dominate and subjugate. There was no other that knew the crafts as Lorgrim did.

But will Lorgrim tell?

He could see the gates of the Tower had been opened. The Wise could little help but announce their arrival to each other. Each manifested a certain sensing of being, a flavour discernible only to others of their kind.

My arrival is expected.

As he approached, a figure stood at the gate. He was dressed in a manner similar to Rorthron, his robes a darker shade of indeterminable colour just short of blackness, tied close about him to ward off the chill air. He was a slight figure, as if an age greater than men could know continued to rob him of his vigour. He leant heavily upon a staff, a thin wispy beard reaching almost to his waist.

'I see the passing of the Winter Solstice awakens many from their slumber. Even Rorthron the young makes a pilgrimage. What news from the south?'

Lorgrim's voice was raspy, as thin as his bearing, cold and mocking.

'Tidings I am sure you already know,' Rorthron replied. 'Are we to bandy words in the cold, or will you allow me within?'

Lorgrim grimaced and then relented. Rorthron followed him inside. The gates closed behind them of their own accord.

The tower was gloomy, its interior lined with obsidian and black marble picked out with silver. Save candles for illumination there was little in the way of colour or decoration.

'If you seek counsel, I offer none,' Lorgrim said as he led Rorthron slowly up the ancient staircase. 'Our situation is little altered.'

Rorthron waited until they had entered the central hall of the tower some halfway upwards within its walls. There at least some comfort awaited, a collection of austere and high-backed chairs clustered around a central pedestal. Lorgrim lowered himself slowly into one and gestured to an opposite one with a vague wave of his hand.

'Counsel I need not,' Rorthron replied. 'Our woes are as they ever were. But the Witchking moves upon Midnight once again. I seek knowledge.'

'Knowledge?' Lorgrim queried. 'You do not seek to slake idle curiosity if you have come this far.'

'Indeed no,' Rorthron answered. 'I speak of secrets known only to you. Secrets entrusted to only one other. Your apprentice.'

Lorgrim visibly shivered.

'I will not talk of such things,' he said, pulling his robes tighter about himself. 'That mistake was long ago.'

'With consequences that last until the present …'

'You think I don't know that?' Lorgrim snapped. 'Do you think a day goes past that I don't regret that decision? I was pressured into taking him as an apprentice. Rushed! We Wise grow few they said, we must train more to replace us as the ages weary us! Well we did, didn't we? Look how that turned out? The few that remain in a self-imposed isolation for fear of bringing his wrath down upon them. The Wise are finished. Midnight belongs … belongs to him now. We will wither and none will remember us.'

'We have a duty, we swore to protect …'

Lorgrim's anger rose.

'Why are you here, Rorthron? He will have noted your passing. He will know where you are bound. You endanger us both with your recklessness. He knows all!'

'Gryfallon is the responsibility of the Wise,' Rorthron countered. 'We allowed his evil to be unleashed upon Midnight. It is us who must undo it.'

'Undo it?' Lorgrim cried. 'Perhaps you would melt the Frozen Wastes whilst you are at it! I know, more than any who remain, of the depth of the arts he used to lock the lands in endless winter. You speak of the impossible and you know this well …'

Lorgrim faltered and looked around at Rorthron.

'What has changed?' he demanded. 'What have you uncovered? Why are you here?'

Rorthron shrugged. 'The Witchking's power waxes at the Winter Solstice. He invades the southland, already he has won a victory on the fields of Blood. The Free fail before him and the Fey seek an uncertain safety in their forests. The peoples of Midnight face extinction at his hands.'

'Then perhaps he will finally be satisfied with his dominion,' Lorgrim said, with a dismissive shrug. 'Peace then, perhaps!'

'You do not believe that,' Rorthron said. 'He will unlock the Frozen Wastes, extend his realm to all points of the compass. The world itself will fall to his malevolence. Untold numbers will suffer at his hands as the cold takes other lands. Midnight and the Icemark have already succumbed to evil, would you see the Bloodmarch fall too? What of Merineth and Varangor? It cannot be allowed.'

'And what do you intend to do that has not been tried before?'

Rorthron shrugged. 'For now, nothing, but in time, if the opportunity presents itself ...'

'Yes?'

'The destruction of the Ice Crown.'

Lorgrim's mouth dropped open. After a moment he shook his head, cold laughter cracked out from him. He dismissed Rorthron with a gesture.

'Impossible.'

'There must be a way.'

Lorgrim shook his head. 'It cannot be done. None can approach the Ice Crown and live be they Fey, Free or even the Wise. Its cold and fear render even the stoutest heart and will to fragments, ripped asunder and cast to the wind. One tried, do you not recall? Her stout heart broken by that power and none like her remain. It is insanity to even approach it. All the crowns have such base powers and the other talismans ... the First Power is ...'

A strange expression crossed Lorgrim's face and he coughed theatrically to cover his words.

'Other crowns?' Rorthron queried.

'Oh, all lost now,' Lorgrim said. 'Myths of long ago; other lands. Only the Ice Crown remains of those arts.'

Rorthron frowned for a brief moment before returning to his questioning. 'But if it could be taken, could it be destroyed?'

Lorgrim muttered to himself.

'Such a thing … no, it cannot be done.'

'It was made, surely it can be unmade!'

'To undo such fell forging, why you would need powers that are not at large in the world today. It cannot be done …'

'What powers?'

'A dragon's fire for a start,' Lorgrim said, grinning and pointing a finger at Rorthron. 'Know you of any dragons then, young one?'

'There are wyverns aplenty within Midnight …'

Lorgrim made a disparaging sound. 'I refer not to the stunted creatures that infest the mountains and the downs. No, Rorthron the young. A dragon, a giant of its kind, pure of blood and strong of sinew. Such creatures no longer roam Midnight as once they did. They issued forth from Varangor. It is a land of fiery mountains, *Eldskjal* they are called in the tongue of that land. Fire and ice. It lies far to the north. Such is the homeland of dragons; I doubt many remain even there. They haven't been seen in Midnight for an age, they are gone from these lands. Myth and legend are all that remain. But such fire as they would muster is what would be but the first component you would require. You see, your quest as at an end before it has even begun!'

'A dragon's fire…' Rorthron repeated, in a whisper.

'That will deal with the ice,' Lorgrim answered. 'But the fear and the substance of the Ice Crown itself … you need something else for that …'

'And what would that be?'

Lorgrim sighed and paced around the hall.

'In truth?' he replied. 'I do not know. The Ice Crown was so constructed as to enslave the hearts of all people. To affect all it had to precede all. Somehow Gryfallon found a way to harness a power before the Free, before the Fey, before even the Wise …'

'Before the Wise?' Rorthron echoed. 'There are none ...'

Lorgrim shrugged. 'We pride ourselves that we were always first. A touch of arrogance on our part? Perhaps the Crown is tied to the landscape in some fashion, but its baleful influence strikes at every soul, every creature in this land. Even we of the Wise are not immune. How can he do this but by some means that predates our influence?'

'We seek something older than the Wise ...'

'And the Witchking forged the Ice Crown in the depths of the icy wastes,' Lorgrim added. 'In the depths of winter, at this very Solstice. From what source did he draw the raw materials to compose the Crown? Perhaps timing is important too, perhaps you have already missed the appointed hour upon which the Ice Crown might be despatched.'

'Someone must know.'

'Only one,' Lorgrim replied. 'Only he who made it.'

Rorthron's expression fell.

Lorgrim chuckled. 'Now you see the folly of such thinking. There are no dragons left in the realm of Midnight, you cannot even begin! And he watches Rorthron, he watches. He forged that crown, he has not forgotten!'

'But it must be possible ...'

'No,' Lorgrim almost spat. 'It is not possible. It is a fool's errand. Dragons with the necessary fire are long dead or flown to warmer climes, locked away and inaccessible beyond the Frozen Wastes. He remains, Rorthron. His power grows. There is none left who can hope to be his adversary.'

'We cannot abandon Midnight to its fate.'

'Midnight is already lost. The Fey are witless and subservient. The Free leaderless. The ice-fear issues forth once more. Nothing can stop it. The Wise are tolerated because they do not interfere. Do not meddle, Rorthron, or he will destroy you too.'

'The Free are not leaderless ...'

Lorgrim laughed. 'You speak of your precious Moonprince? Oh yes, I know of your little game, Rorthron. A distant heir of a moribund house. Even with his half-broken Moon Ring this Luxor has no chance. Against the power of the Witchking none can prevail. Luxor has already lost the game, though he knows it not. He is outnumbered and outflanked. Defeat will come swiftly, mark my words.'

'You will not help me, then?'

'I have helped you,' Lorgrim replied. 'You have yet to receive the wisdom of my words. This road you travel has but one destination, Rorthron. Death lies at the end of it. You do not need to take this route. Stay here if you would. The Wise may have ways to escape this eternal winter. Other lands where we would be welcome, where we could guard against the coming of such evil. Start again, learn from the mistakes of the past and see them prevented. But not here, not Midnight.'

Rorthron slowly rose to his feet.

'No, I will not abandon Midnight to despair.'

Lorgrim likewise rose and turned to face him, a frown on his face.

'I have told you this is folly. The Witchking will destroy you all. There is no way to win a battle that is already lost.'

'Yet, try I must.'

Rorthron walked away. The frown grew on Lorgrim's face.

Chapter Nine

*She stands at a Lith in the domain of Kor,
looking south west to the Plains of Kor.*

A long ride had put Tarithel beyond the borders of her home-land and several leagues into the Plains of Kor. She had been pleased with her audacity at outwitting the captains of the guard. She had ridden swifter than the messengers they had instructed and slipped across the border unseen and unmarked.

As the forest fell away behind her she found herself in a strange landscape. The plain stretched away into distance, but to her left rose a series of ancient monuments. Not just an isolated Lith like the one she knew from her travels in the forest, but row upon row of them. She rode a little further and found herself in a gently sloping valley, flanked by the Liths down its length. The valley was unnaturally straight, clearly purposeful in its construction and oriented directly to the south east. She gazed at it for a long while, wondering what the reason could have been to undertake such a mammoth construction.

So much I don't know about the world. So much I would know, but the Fey keep their secrets and their ignorance well hidden.

She had ridden onwards, westward into the sunset and still onwards even as the stars sprung into the sky above her. They were bright and clear, their light casting a faint blue glow on the snowy landscape around her. Bright enough to see by, just, but she had slowed her horse as the darkness closed about her.

She had been able to discern no path in the wilderness. Behind her, the forest of her home was receding towards the horizon, here and there hidden by the rising land. Ahead she could see nothing at all but a faint mist that clung to the horizon. It was cold, but the warm layers of clothing she wore were more than adequate protection. She was well-versed in the lore of travelling about Midnight, having accompanied her father on many jaunts through their forest realm. Oft they had camped in the darkness.

But this was the first time she had been truly alone.

Doubt and guilt gnawed at her. She would have been missed by now, first by the stable boys who would have reported that she had not returned as she promised. Her father would be apoplectic and an unpleasant reception awaited her should she return. She'd been on the receiving end of punishment before, but it had done little to tame her. She considered it a worthwhile trade.

She almost turned around, but her curiosity burned all the brighter.

Just a day, I can ride across the plains and be back by sundown tomorrow. I must know what they try to hide. My father has no son, one day perhaps I will be Lady Dreams herself. Is it not right that I know about the world? Why should he keep secrets from me? I am no child who needs to be protected!

She carved herself out a burrow in the snow, saw to the needs of her horse and then took refuge in the frozen darkness. It took her a little while to fall asleep, thoughts of legends and lore spun about her mind and all the while the fell voice assailed her nightmare. But it was swept away each time it threatened her slumber. A vision of a man upon a stallion came to her mind. Sword in one hand and a bright ring clenched in the other.

Another image too. Younger, a boy barely grown to manhood, blonde hair tied in a braid. He sat astride a red-haired mare of a type favoured by the Fey. It seemed they might be of a similar age. She felt some strange kinship with him. A sense of rebellion and longing for adventure. Distant lands they had never seen, calling them yonder. On the edge of dreams she tried to focus on his visage. He was strong and firm in the manner of men, but his features were fair in the likeness of the Fey. His eyes sparkled with mischievous intent, something about him held her interest and a faint flush of warmth spread throughout her body.

Who are you?

In her mind's eye he turned, as if he had heard her. A frown creased his face as he looked about himself in surprise.

The dreams faded and she fell into a deep sleep.

It had come swiftly, out the whirling maelstrom of snow and thick grey cloud that had issued out of the North. Herath had been on his guard, but he could see what lay ahead of him. Somehow the Witchking's armies had navigated the pass in the foul weather, perhaps protected from it by the enchantments of the Witchking himself.

No such facility was available to his own men however. Herath could see at a glance they had little hope of defending the keep against the army that had appeared out of the gloom. Fear stalked his men. Herath knew his duty.

He summoned his riders and warriors. They numbered just over a thousand. An army of no small note, but not sufficient to stand against the might that was bearing down on them.

Unannounced and unwarned. The Witchking moves upon us with stealth and strategy. I fear for our comrades in the west. We must get word out!

Herath had already despatched his swiftest riders to the south and to the east, hopeful that one or both groups would be able to reach the Citadels of Marakith and Kumar. There a greater force might be mustered in time to hold back the Witchking's forces.

His words to those riders had been bleak.

'We will hold them here until we can hold them no more, it is imperative you get word to Kumar and Marakith. They will need time to prepare.'

They had ridden off into the swirling snowfall.

Herath gestured for his helmet and sword. The helmet was fastened into place and he reached out, grabbing the pommel of his sword. About him his warriors and riders were ready.

He signalled for the portcullis that led outwards from the keep to be raised.

His sword aloft, he rode, galloping at the head of his armies, out to face his doom.

Rorthron had since departed. Lorgrim walked further up the interior of his Tower, pausing for breath at intervals during the climb, yet finally reaching the summit. From there the tower commanded a view that stretched far and wide. To the east the Frozen Wastes stretched as far as the eye could see. Lorgrim well remembered how it was before the cold.

Far to the east lay the sea, something that failed the imagination of the people of Midnight. Lorgrim had been there in his youth and recalled the surf crashing upon the rocks of the coastline. Who knew what lay across that stretch of water? Other lands with other woes perhaps. It was no concern of his.

His gaze drifted to the left. Northwards, the Frozen Wastes stretched for many leagues, but from the tower's height he could discern their edge. The faint impression of a distant mountain range could just be seen. There lay the land of Ice-mark, a land of giants and dwarves, yet still dominated by the same icy evil unleashed upon Midnight.

The daughter-spawn …

Lorgrim shivered involuntarily. He feared the Witchking's daughter more than he feared the Witchking. For whilst the Witchking's malice was deep and abiding, it was at least predictable. Shareth mixed her own evil with her passions; anger and lust.

Should the Witchking ever fall, her vengeance would be swift and deadly …

But she lay far away, countless leagues to the north, beyond the Mountains of Anvulane. She need not feature in his concerns, not for now. He turned his thoughts back to the puzzle that preoccupied him.

Rorthron might be young, but he is no fool. The Ice Crown cannot be unmade, none can approach it. So why consider even fighting a hopeless battle? Even if there were a dragon …

Lorgrim pondered for long minutes, staring out across the wilderness of Midnight.

What does Rorthron know that he's not telling me?

Perhaps answers lay to the west.

He turned his gaze in that direction, his vision tracking far beyond the Frozen Wastes that ringed his small domain. Across plains and downs he gazed until at last he spied the mountains that marked the boundary of the Witchking's abode.

The instant his gaze fell upon the easternmost vanguard, the Citadel of Grarg, he found his movement arrested. A wall of implacable fury rose before him, cutting off his vision and tunnelling it down into a swirling maelstrom of darkness.

DO NOT SEEK TO SPY UPON ME!

Lorgrim braced himself against the cold and the hate. He concentrated, forcing his mind to form words and meaning.

I have tidings from the south. News …

I KNOW OF THE BASTARD MOONPRINCE. HE WILL BE CRUSHED AS OTHERS HAVE BEEN CRUSHED BEFORE.

Lorgrim permitted himself a moment of satisfaction, not even the mighty Witchking saw all.

That is not what should concern you …

The darkness rose up about Lorgrim, strong and suffocating, blocking out light, blocking out heat, blocking out any feeling other than abject fear.

TELL ME WHAT YOU KNOW.

Lorgrim took a deep gasp of air before replying.

First you will honour our arrangement …

I COULD SMITE YOU WHERE YOU STAND, OLD ONE.

Yes, I believe you could, but that would take a portion of your power you can ill afford to expend. You know I speak the truth …

The blackness flickered and faded, the light of the sun flickered faintly in the tower once more.

THE ARRANGEMENT WILL BE HONOURED.

There could be no negotiation on such a point. The Wise made their incantations, not just with mere words, but with emotions and feelings. To fail to honour such a promise would break asunder much that had been made. Promises were not easily abandoned. It was not their way. Even the Witchking was bound to his word.

Then I have news for you.

The darkness wavered, uncertain. Lorgrim enjoyed the moment before speaking once more. He felt little remorse for what he was about to do. Let Rorthron pursue his dreams as he saw fit, there was no escape other than by the will of the Witchking. Lorgrim knew his apprentice well, knew the scope of his powers. He might save himself, but others were doomed.

Rorthron the Wise came seeking counsel. The knowledge of how to destroy the Ice Crown …

Now there was fury, dark and threatening. Lorgrim felt it buffet him, but held his hand out to stop the tempest.

Of course I did not reveal your secrets, save the obvious use of a dragon. Even Rorthron would have been able to comprehend that himself. You have nothing to fear from him, he does not have the wit to divine more …

I DO NOT FEAR THAT UPSTART!

The voice remained wreathed in fury and impatience.

Lorgrim pushed forward, wrestling subtly with the gloom. Images spun about him: crowns, runes, swords and spears. He could sense the Witchking's desire to scour all of Midnight and the lands around.

Fear … but not the ice-fear. Fear of his own mortality! A driving ambition …

The blackness snapped back so abruptly that Lorgrim staggered and almost lost his footing. His vision was wrested away. He blinked, now seeing only the Frozen Wastes from the tower. He sank down, lowering himself to the floor, waiting until his strength returned.

So then. The Witchking seeks more than just the subjugation of Midnight, that is just a means to an end. But what end? Yet still he fears the knowledge of the Ice Crown being widely known. Rorthron has kept the secret of the Moon Ring for a long time, why reveal it now? The bearer cannot approach the tower … so … is there another? It must be. Someone can approach the Ice Crown! But who? And when?

Lorgrim took a deep breath.

So my choice is come at last. Reveal the Witchking's weakness and hope he is felled by Rorthron and the childish Lords of Midnight, or cast my lot alongside my apprentice and try to divine his purpose…

For fair or for ill, Midnight's fate was about to be sealed.

211

Far to the south, a lone rider and his steed traced a path across the lonely Downs of Mitharg, riding west into the darkness. High above the Moonstar glimmered in a darkening sky. None noticed his passing and he was many leagues from any hint of civilisation when he ceased his flight. He too made his camp without fire, hoping not to attract attention from the eyes of the enemy.

Morkin was familiar enough with the ways of the wild not to be overwhelmed by it, but the loneliness was intense now. The comforting confidence he had felt in the warm halls of the Fey had long since deserted him. Midnight seemed cold and unwelcoming now. He dared not go further, dusk had long since fled away. The Foul would be abroad, seeking the demise of isolated travellers.

And his success depended on his stealth. If he was seen, they might decide to run him down and slaughter him. How long would it be before the Witchking somehow sensed him coming?

Too late the seeds of doubt awoke in his heart.

It is too late to turn about now, and what would be thought of me? I will not have songs of Morkin the Coward sung whilst my cheeks sting with shame. I am the son of a Moonprince, and as such will I be remembered!

He scolded himself and tried not to think upon it. A good night's sleep would be essential for him. He would have to keep up a punishing pace to reach the desolation of Ashimar and scant safety of the Mountains of Dodrak. The Plains of Blood and the lands immediately around had to be considered dangerous in the extreme, the sooner he was away from them the better.

He looked north across the Plains of Blood. He could see no lights, no fires. That was encouraging. Lord Thrall had told him that the armies of the Doomguard had crossed his borders both to the North and the South of the forest. They had been moving more slowly than anticipated, perhaps fearing some counterattack. It would give Luxor time to consolidate his defence at the Citadel of Dawn, and perhaps, for the Fey to rally some force to assist him.

Nothing more could be done now. Tomorrow would see him reach the Forest of Shadows once more. From there ... north into the territory of the enemy.

He was beginning to doze when he sensed something. He held his breath, fearing that he had been discovered by a Doomguard patrol. But he could hear nothing. For long moments he lay immobile, listening intently.

Then, as weariness took him, it came again. A voice. This time he heard words.

Who are you?

He blinked. For a moment a girl stood at his feet, looking down on him with curiosity etched on her face. He gasped, for he had seen none as beautiful as her before. He felt his heart lurch painfully within him at her comeliness. She was beyond fair, a Fey-girl, green eyes that matched a dress of forest garb.

And then a sense of familiarity came over him, he had seen her before ... at least, he had dreamed of her before – prior to the battle of Blood. Then she had been in distress, now she seemed more at peace.

Even as he looked again her image was fading, the next moment she was gone and there was nothing but the faint chill breeze.

Morkin blinked.

A portent? And if so, for good or evil?

He made ready to sleep again, settling down within his sleeping robes. Howls came on the wind. Wolves were abroad ...

With the wounded tended, and preparations made as much as they could be, a council of war was called within Dawn's grand hall. Torches and candles lit the room with a warm glow, food had been cleared away, though the wine remained. The servants left the Lords in counsel.

'To business then,' Shimeril said, as the doors to the hall were barred. 'It seems outright war is upon us.'

Luxor nodded. 'A tally of our woes at this point seems appropriate.'

Lord Blood got to his feet.

'Of the seven thousand who assembled at my keep.' Blood paused momentarily. 'Only just over three thousand remain. The Witchking has struck us hard and his army lies but two days march from our gates. Reinforcements from the south and east are on their way …'

'They should reach us before the Witchking,' Gard said. 'Yet he has the numbers to surround us. Do the remainder of the Free have the resources to break a siege whilst still holding the plains to the east? I think not.'

'And we have no strength to the west,' Shimeril said. 'The Foul will tread its roads unimpeded.'

'If the Witchking has come in strength here,' Blood said. 'It is likely he has forces assailing Herath, Marakith and Kumar.'

'Is there no treating with him?' Dawn asked. 'We have had relative peace for years …'

'He seeks our complete demise,' Luxor said. 'Subjugation of all Midnight to his whim and command. We are an anathema to him, he means to end us all. This time, he has the means to do it.'

'Then we must rally,' Dawn said. 'The question is where. I am happy enough if my Citadel is the bulwark of our stand against him, but we are not prepared for a long siege. Why, only a moon ago I considered letting go of some of my soldiers, for we had little enough for them to do!'

'What is the Witchking's goal?' Blood demanded. 'Victory on the field of battle is all very well, but what is it that he wishes to achieve? His strategy we must divine, if we are to counter it.'

'Xajorkith,' Gard said, and many others nodded. 'If our capital falls, then all hope will be lost to our people. If he can take that, we have lost. He has already taken one strategic step with the capture of the Plains of Blood, from there he can dominate the remainder of our lands. He will drive a wedge deep across the Downs of Athoril, split our remaining forces and swiftly extinguish them. Then his might will be concentrated on Dawn and Xajorkith. Both will fall against such numbers.'

'We must concentrate our forces then,' Luxor said. 'And thwart his plans.'

'Xajorkith might reach us in time,' Shimeril said.

'Xajorkith is our last defence,' Blood said. 'We must fortify that citadel too.'

'But we can make a stand here,' Luxor replied. 'If his strategy is to divide and conquer, then we must not let ourselves be divided. We make our stand here, at the Citadel of Dawn.'

'Easier to defend for sure,' Gard said. 'With mountains either side and reinforcements from the south and east.'

'There is something else you must consider.'

Her voice was soft but firm. All turned to look at Silence. She waited for a moment before she continued.

'He now seeks you, Moonprince,' she said. 'If the legends of the powers accorded to you are even half true, you are perhaps the greatest threat to him. You can deflect the ice-fear. You can command the armies of those loyal to you at great distance. If he could eliminate you …'

Shimeril nodded. 'If you fall, we all fall.'

Luxor pondered her words for a long moment. 'The reach of the powers of this ring have yet to be tested, but it will not turn a battle for us. Strength of arms alone can do that. I hear you Silence, but we need more warriors! Is there any news of Marakith, Kumar and Ithrorn?'

'The messengers have yet to return,' Dawn replied.

'And our total strength here?' Luxor asked.

'Some four thousand warriors and two thousand riders all told,' Dawn replied.

Gard shook his head. 'It is not enough. We can hold for a few days, but against the might the Witchking will unleash … we will fall.'

'What of the Fey?' Dawn asked. 'Will they not come to our aid?'

Gard, Shimeril and Blood looked at Luxor.

'Make what fortifications you can,' Luxor said. 'Prepare for war. I will summon what help there is to be found.'

Dawn, Gard, Shimeril and Blood watched as Luxor strode from the hall.

'What does he mean?' Dawn asked, after a moment.

Blood raised his eyebrows. 'The Moon Ring. Magic.'

'Magic?'

'Our faith in sharp-edged steel has not served us well thus far,' Shimeril said. 'We must look to other powers for our salvation.'

Corleth had ridden hard out of the village, turning ever eastwards as the sun tried to shed the faintest of warmth upon the land. Once more it failed, its glory sundered by thin icy clouds. The Forest of Thrall had fallen behind him and the Plains of Dawn rolled by beneath the horse's hooves. Weary days of travel had allowed the Downs of Athoril to roll past. The land was flattening out into the east. Dawn broke across a vast plain, empty and featureless.

216

A keep guarded the boundary. Corleth knew of it, but had never ventured this way before. One of the minor Lords, tasked with keeping the downs safe. Lord Athoril himself.

Before him was a road, well-trodden, running from the north to the keep. It was mainly used for the passage of goods and trade in more peaceful times, but today Corleth could see men innumerable, armed for war and marching swiftly southwards.

Three banners flew high in the breeze. It didn't take Corleth long to identify those who marched beneath their bold colours.

Marakith, Kumar and Athoril. Some relief for Luxor at the very least!

He spurred his horse onwards, heading toward the very front of the combined army. Scouts spotted him ere he drew near and rode out to meet him. Their countenance was gruff and unpleasant. Swords and spears were readied as they surrounded him.

'Hold Fey! What business do you have in these parts?'

'I bring tidings from the west,' Corleth replied, deciding not to draw his own sword. 'Word of the Moonprince and his kin.'

'Moonprince?' the scouts looked at each other. 'Then you come with us, our Lords will decide what to do with you. Your name?'

'I am Corleth.'

Corleth, with the armed riders all about him, was escorted through the army. It was a fair size, perhaps two and a half thousand riders and a smaller contingent of foot soldiers. It was a strength that Luxor would sorely need. They were clustered around the keep, as it was too small to house them all.

A tent had been hastily erected at the vanguard of the army. Corleth was ushered inside.

'My Lords,' the scout announced. 'This Fey was spotted

riding down our right flank. He claims to know of the Moon-prince.'

Corleth watched as the three Lords before him looked up from the maps they had been studying. Marakith was a younger man, with dark brown eyes and a neatly cropped full beard. He had some of a reputation as a lady's man, but his prowess in battle had been demonstrated before. He had taken control of his domain only a few years before when his father had been killed by wyverns when hunting in the Downs of Athoril. Kumar was older, heavyset and stern, his faced lined and careworn by many long years of leadership, admin-istration and battle. An unpleasant scar marked his cheek. Corleth had never met him before, but had heard he was loyal and an accomplished strategist, but not swift to trust newcomers.

The third Lord was thinner and paler, a tall wisp of a man. Corleth knew little of Lord Athoril save his name, but knew him to be one of the lesser Lords of the realm.

'And you are?' Marakith demanded.

'Corleth, sire. Of the Thrall Fey.'

'And what is your business in these parts?' Kumar asked, his voice rough and gravelly.

'I am seeking to raise a host of Fey in the service of my liege, the Moonprince.'

Corleth saw Athoril glance across at the other two Lords. Kumar's grizzled features frowned a little and Marakith drew a breath.

'What know ye of the Moonprince?' Kumar grunted.

'That he sent me on this quest,' Corleth answered. 'I have sworn loyalty to him in the face of peril from the Witchking.'

Marakith smiled. 'Then this is a meeting looked for,' he said, holding out a hand to Corleth. Corleth took it and was rewarded with a firm shake. 'We come in summons from the same source.'

'Summoned?' Corleth questioned.

'Aye,' Kumar said.

'Rorthron the Wise,' Marakith said. 'He came to us short days ago, bid us rally our forces and come to the aid of the Moonprince. We have been sore delayed en route by the hordes of the Witchking. You say you are the Moonprince's liege?'

Corleth nodded.

'Then who is he, this legend from the past?' Marakith demanded.

Corleth blinked in surprise. 'Why, he is Lord Luxor.'

'Luxor!' Kumar spluttered. 'Luxor of Odrark? That ramshackle fort on the edge of Gard's domain? Luxor is barely a Lord, much less a Moonprince.'

'He is heir to the House of the Moon,' Corleth replied, raising his voice. 'Keeper of the last War Ring of Midnight.'

'War Ring?' Athoril asked. 'What is a War Ring?'

'Doggerel from the past, myth, legend and nonsense,' Kumar said. 'I told you this was a fool's errand and now we hear we are called to serve some upstart who happens to have a bauble ...'

'I think we should listen to his tale,' Marakith interrupted, watching Corleth closely. 'Truly a Moonprince? Such a thing ...'

'... has not happened for generations of men,' Corleth said, before raising his voice. 'Luxor would have shared your astonishment and disbelief but a moon ago, Lord Kumar. But hear my tidings and you will understand all the better.'

Kumar straightened, but didn't say anything.

'Rorthron the Wise summoned Luxor and his squire to the Tower of the Moon,' Corleth added. 'I accompanied them. There it was revealed that Luxor was the lost heir of the line of the Moon. Rorthron himself gifted the Moon Ring to Luxor, having kept it safe all these years. It was no accident that

Rorthron sought you out, it was by Luxor's express wish. He rode forth with the battle cry of Midnight upon his lips.'

'Arise Midnight …' Athoril whispered. 'We all heard it in our minds …'

'A dream, nothing more,' Kumar said.

'If dream it was,' Marakith said. 'A dream many of us shared.'

'A call to swear fealty to the Moonprince, my Lords,' Corleth said. 'Will you so swear?'

Marakith nodded. 'I will so swear.'

Athoril followed him, both looked to Kumar.

'I see not the need for such utterances,' he muttered.

'The Moon Ring draws its strength from the one who wields it,' Corleth said. 'Those who swear loyalty to him are protected by it and he gains sight over them …'

'Sounds like so much nonsense to me,' Kumar said, looking at his fellow Lords. 'Oh very well! I swear! Satisfied?'

A faint sense of warmth drew close about the group for a moment, lifting the all-pervading gloom of the ice-fear.

Kumar grimaced. 'I care not for magic spells and talismans. We were sent to the Citadel of Dawn, upon Rorthron's express command. Are there other tidings?'

Corleth nodded. 'The Witchking has already taken the Plains of Blood, a battle was fought and lost there. Luxor and the armies of the west plan to make a stand at Dawn against the Doomguard. Your assistance would be warmly welcomed.'

'Then we are beset upon all sides,' Marakith said. 'Just prior to Rorthron's message we received evil tidings from Lord Herath's domain. He fought a hopeless defence against the Witchking in the passes of Ithril. His sacrifice gave us time to make good our own departure for Dawn.'

'And you? What errand does our Moonprince send you upon?' Kumar demanded of Corleth.

'I seek to rally the Fey to his banner,' Corleth said. 'I journey to Dregrim, from there I will turn northwards and seek out my kin of Whispers and Dreams if they have not already come hither.'

The three Lords exchanged a look with each other.

'You would be advised to stay with us then, until you reach the southern end of the downs,' Marakith said. 'A direct ride to Dregrim from here will take you into the realm of the Targ.'

'And they do not receive strangers in their land,' Athoril said. 'I have lost many scouts to their depredations.'

Corleth had heard of the Targs, but had never ventured into their realm. Situated at the very east of Midnight, just shy of the Frozen Wastes, their lands were bordered in the south by the Forest of Dregrim, to the west by the Downs of Athoril and to the north by the realm of Kumar. By all accounts they had a fractious relationship with their neighbours. To avoid the Targs, Corleth would have to journey south before turning further east.

'It will take too long,' Corleth said. 'Such a diversion will add days to my journey, I cannot tarry.'

'If you venture into the lands of the Targ,' Kumar said, 'you will find your delay permanent. The Utarg does not suffer foreigners to live.'

'He is powerful then?'

'Powerful?' Marakith chuckled. 'Aye, powerful indeed. Barbarian blood I would say, from out of the remote north. He commands a thousand riders from a keep in the centre of his realm. We have treated with him in the past, but he is mercurial, difficult to predict …'

'… and has a habit of flaying the skin off emissaries as the mood takes him,' Kumar added.

'He is a traitor and a backstabber,' Athoril said. 'A usurper. Those lands he calls his own, stolen from my people in the time of my grandsire. The Plains of Targ they call them today, the Plains of Athoril is what they are!'

'But if he could be persuaded to join us,' Corleth said. 'A thousand barbarian riders would give the Witchking pause ...'

'It would give anyone pause,' Athoril said with a shudder. 'His men, any one of them is twice the strength of our greatest warriors. But such an attempt would be foolhardy. Utarg is no respecter of Free or Fey. He will not receive you.'

'Would he receive the Moonprince's liege?' Corleth asked.

Kumar rubbed his chin. 'You risk much. Wiser to head to Dregrim, at least there you have kin you can rally for sure.'

'I would be forced to venture into the Utarg's lands regardless,' Corleth said. 'His lands stand between Dregrim and the northern Fey. I will try my luck with this Utarg.'

'Then I wish you all the luck there is to muster,' Athoril said. 'You will need it. Be sure to call him Utarg of Utarg.'

'Utarg of Utarg?' Corleth asked. 'Why?'

'I am not sure,' Athoril replied. 'Something my father told me in the days after we lost the Plains of Athoril to him. He believes he is the one true 'Targ', whatever that might mean.'

Corleth nodded. 'The Witchking attacks on all fronts, both west and east. He makes his way south at speed. Make all speed to Dawn, my Lords. Time is not our ally.'

'It never has been,' Kumar said, with a grimace.

Luxor paid little heed to the small room he had been assigned in one of the towers of Dawn's citadel. His mind was preoccupied with the flight from the Plains of Blood and the task ahead.

The Witchking's power has waxed to its fullest extent. With each victory his confidence grows and with it the strength of the ice-fear! Soon it may be too great to resist ...

He felt a warmth upon his hand and looked at it. Around his finger was wrapped the Moon Ring Rorthron had given him, pulsing with its strange power.

He closed his eyes.

Rorthron …

The walls of the Citadel of Dawn fell away from him, even Midnight itself grew distant, as if he were looking down on it from a great height. He could see the armies of the Free, the forests of the Fey and, like a shroud creeping across the land, the baleful influence of the Witchking. The ice-fear was like a wraith, creeping across Midnight, sapping strength and hope wherever it was concentrated.

Curious, he looked northwards, rolling over plains and mountains, see the vastness of the Forest of Dreams appear before him. His gaze turned north west to the ramparts of the Witchking's realm …

A painful wrench caused him to cry out, agony flashed across his temple, a burning headache which crackled across his brow.

A face swam into focus, old and wrinkled, but with a certain gentleness about it.

My Lord Luxor. You must be careful where you look. Those that spy upon the Witchking's realm may find their very minds are lost to the ice and fear …

Luxor struggled to focus his thoughts.

Rorthron?

The figure nodded.

Aye, it is me.

Luxor concentrated, framing words in his mind.

How fare you?

Rorthron's face grimaced.

I have learned much and revealed less, so I hope. The fate of Midnight remains in your keeping Moonprince. How has your faith in the strength of the Free served you?

Luxor sighed.

We are sore oppressed. We fled the field of battle at Blood and at Shimeril and now make preparations to stop the Witchking's advance at Dawn …

Rorthron's visage was stern.

I have sent what support I can from those loyal to you. But mere thousands of warriors will not decide this fight. You know what must be done.

Luxor shook his head.

I do not believe in your legends of the past. I will not risk my kin on a flight of fancy.

Rorthron smiled. Luxor felt his heart lurch within him.

I would say that what you believe and what you wish is now immaterial. Your son has taken matters into his own hands. He believes in his destiny …

Anger flared in Luxor's mind.

What have you …?

I? Nothing. Morkin has the bravery of the Free and the enchantment of the Fey. He has embraced his destiny, as must you …

No!

Luxor stumbled back, breaking the connection. The dimly lit room swam into focus, grey stone walls silent around him.

With trembling hands he focused again, searching frantically across the Forest of Thrall. His mind roved north and south and from east to west without finding what it was looking for. In the blink of an eye his sight had moved westward, still searching.

And then a warmth, a familiar presence.

Morkin!

Dawn broke over the eerily quiet Forest of Shadows. Morkin had ridden hard for two days, stopping only when the light failed or to eat a meagre meal from his supplies. He'd made good progress, covering many leagues through ersh, sleet and snow. His horse, a Fey-breed animal, seemed at ease with the pace for now, but he was wary to rest the animal when he could.

Fortunately the eaves of the forest had opened up to him once again, allowing some shelter and, a real blessing, grazing for the horse in a glade somehow protected from the frosts outside.

Thus emboldened, Morkin had continued onwards, skirting the valley where he'd stood with his father only a few days before at the Tower of the Moon.

And what would he think if he knew what I was doing now? Anger certainly! He sought to protect me from this and he has little faith in the legends of the past. But it seems I am one of those legends, I must fulfil this …

The forest eaves were thinning now, a cold wind blowing from the north. The land was flattening out once more, a desolate and dreary expanse opening up before him. The map the Lord of Thrall had given named the area the Plains of Ogrim. In the far distance two mountain ranges, Ashimar to the west and Dodrak to the east, flanked a pass northwards. Several days of weary riding lay before him, following this pass until the mountains were left behind. Then he would strike north-east, skirting the Downs of Mirrow and making for the Forest of Lothoril.

And then hope the Fey of that realm will receive me, distant cousins as they are of the southern Fey …

Little point in worrying about that now though. It might take him a week to reach them, even if the way remained clear.

He could see nothing moving about him at all. Everything lay still, almost unnaturally so. Other than the wind, there was no sound, no hint of habitation. He'd seen no sign of deer, rabbits, or the marks of trolls or wyverns. Nothing since those wolves he'd heard at night in the Downs of Mitharg. The land seemed abandoned by all.

He patted his horse's neck.

'Let's go.'

They rode off into the endless white of Midnight.

The snow played tricks with the eyes of those who weren't wise to it. Sparkling lights might dance in their vision; they called it the blindness, it even drove some crazy. Morkin knew well enough to take his gaze away from it at intervals to break the spell. Even so, the unchanging landscape made the journey tedious in the extreme. The lack of contrast across the plain numbed the mind and froze the brain. Morkin found his concentration failing …

Nearby howls snapped his attention back. His horse whinnied and charged away, Morkin hanging on for dear life. He managed a glance behind him and his heart jumped within his chest in shock.

Wolves!

A pack of them were chasing from behind, they must have picked up his scent when he left the downs days before. He counted five, dark furred and heavily built, running across the snow, spread out in a phalanx. They were perhaps a hundred yards behind him and closing fast; his horse's hooves unable to grip the snow as effectively as the pads upon their paws.

They were going to overtake him.

Morkin hauled his horse around, swinging from the saddle and drawing his sword in one smooth movement. With one hand he held firm to the reins of his frightened mount as the wolves surrounded them, pacing in a circle, their hot breath drifting upwards in the cold air, their yellow eyes fixed on him. Their lips were drawn back showing yellowed teeth as they snarled and licked their chops.

One crouched and made to jump, Morkin swung his sword and it retreated, growling. As he listened Morkin began to hear each one make different sounds; here a yelp, then a growl and a snap.

Almost as if they speak to each other! Do they scheme and plan?

The circling continued. His horse reared and he struggled to hold it.

'Easy ...'

One of the wolves leapt in, taking advantage of his distraction. Morkin saw it coming, all teeth and fury. He twisted his sword arm, bringing the blade around in time and, despite the pull of the horse on his arm, crouched down and jammed the pommel into the snow as he'd been taught by his father.

The wolf, taken unawares, could not slow its momentum and impaled itself upon the blade, yelping in pain before its weight bore it to the ground. It flailed around for a moment before it lay still, its blood staining the snow crimson.

The other wolves were looking from him to the body of their fallen companion.

Morkin raised the sword again and the wolves snarled. Morkin slowly backed away, pulling his horse with him. The wolves advanced, their horrible cries and yelps filling the air. Once he had retreated far enough they pounced upon the body of the slain wolf and began ripping it to shreds.

My cue I think!

Morkin retreated a little further before jumping up upon his horse and galloping away. He looked behind him and was relieved to see the remaining wolves were not following.

Not following for now at any rate. I will have to be cautious. Hunger drives them and there is little prey in these forsaken lands!

He kept the horse at a gallop until the wolves were left far behind and then he reined it back, conscious that there was a long ride ahead. Midnight became lonely and desolate once more, he was alone in the stark whiteness.

Morkin?

Morkin blinked. He could have sworn he'd heard his father's

voice. Before he even had a chance to wonder at it, a warmth enveloped him, as if the sun had suddenly blazed twice as bright.

Morkin!

But the warm glow was replaced with the burning heat of disapproval.

What are you doing? I left strict instructions for both you and Corleth ...

Morkin spoke direct into the air around him, sure his father could hear him by the strange power of the Moon Ring. 'Lord Thrall told me the history,' he said. 'The Fey are not strong enough, nor are the Free ...'

That is not your concern, it is mine. We are prepared for battle. I command you now, return to safety, head back to the Fey and wait for me there ...

Morkin shook his head. 'No. I will not!'

You defy me?

'Yes, father!' Morkin yelled. 'Because you lied! You know you have no chance to defeat Doomdark, that the Free will fall in battle and you will be slain.'

Do not underestimate our valour. We may yet prevail ...

Morkin's voice dropped. 'You sent me away to keep me from that, didn't you.'

He sensed his father's reluctance to answer the question.

'Didn't you?'

The ephemeral voice was softer now.

Morkin, we cannot win, I have a fell and evil duty here, but you will be safe within the forests of the Fey. The Witchking cannot assail them ...

'But he can!' Morkin replied. 'Corleth saw the Forest of Shadows penetrated by the Doomguard, the ancient protections no longer work. The Fey are being killed just as the Free. Doomdark intends to end us all. The forests of the Fey are no more safe than anywhere else.'

Then you must flee south, our home ...

'Father, we are bound on every side by the Frozen Wastes, death will come everywhere in time. You heard Rorthron's tale, I am supposed to do this, he believes in me ... will you?'

There was another long pause.

You are my son, I have no doubt in you, but I fear this task the Wise would lay upon your shoulders. You're ...

'I'm not just a boy,' Morkin answered back.

No, you are not. Yet, we don't even know how this is to be accomplished ... to steal into the Witchking's very realm.

'Rorthron went to find out,' Morkin said. 'Ask him. Then tell me of his counsel.'

I will. My son ...

'I know. But do not worry! You are the one facing the Doomguard, not me.'

The glow returned, surrounding him like a warm embrace.

Farewell then, I will speak to you when I can. Take no unnecessary risks and beware of ...

'I must go father. If you do not let me, Midnight will be lost anyway, and then what would become of me?'

Morkin could well imagine the sigh.

Go then, my son. Seek the Ice Crown and attempt its destruction. I wish you all the luck in Midnight!

'Don't wish me luck! It's Doomdark who will need it.'

A moment of mirth, a pleasure and a pride that surged through the magic that connected them. Morkin smiled at the feeling, even as it faded away and the bleakness of the landscape came back to his senses.

He took a deep breath.

That could have gone worse! I would rather travel with my father's blessing than without ...

Coming to a rise in the land his horse whinnied in alarm. Morkin gasped.

Before him, not a quarter of a league away, was a troupe of warriors.

Doomguard!

He was unlucky. One of them looked up the moment Morkin recognised them. He got a brief flash of red eyes. Yells followed. They ran for their own black-clad horses.

Morkin spurred his horse around.

Flee! But where?

The Mountains of Dodrak were alongside, brightly lit in the noonday sun, their foothills a league away or so. There was no other shelter, nothing but the stark whiteness of the plain. Nowhere to hide …

He rode hard towards the mountains, their grim grey sheer sides rising up around him like primordial teeth. He spared a glance over his shoulder and gasped.

Behind him the detachment of horse-backed Doomguard were in pursuit, spread out in a V formation to cover the width of the pass he was following, to ensure there was no possibility of retreat. They were riding closer, the fierce breath of their horses trailing behind them like wisps of smoke.

If this is a dead end …

He spurred his horse onwards up the slope. Mist fell about him. The pass became treacherous, narrowing under his horse's hooves and causing it to whinny in fear and alarm. Snow and ice slipped under foot as he tried to steer it away from a precipice that materialised out of the gloom. Something snapped through the air nearby and he saw two dark fletched arrows dig into the ice covered mountainside.

Above, something blotted out the sun for a moment. Morkin looked up but saw nothing.

Another arrow struck. Morkin was splattered with blood, having only a moment to realise his horse had been slain beneath him. His grip on the reins was wrenched from his hands and he tumbled into a snow-flecked abyss. He hit a steep slope and knew no more.

Tarithel woke early. She was up and ready in moments, seeing to her horse before preparing a quick breakfast of wrapped breads and vegetables. She looked about her as she ate. The mist was thick and heavy this morning, she couldn't see far.

She pondered the strange dream she'd had, the young blonde haired man. In her dream he had turned to look upon her as he had somehow known she was watching. She could still remember it vividly and it had none of the ephemeral quality that characterised dreams she'd had before.

As if it were real ...

But she had never met anyone like that. She had met precious few outside of her own people if truth be told. The daughter of a Lord did not mix with many, particularly strangers.

Her thoughts turned back to home. A punishment awaited her for certain. Already it would be hard to explain where she had been all night, but she had been absent before, though within the boundaries of their home forest, never out here on the plains.

If I am to find out what this forbidden knowledge is I must ride swiftly!

With the sun still aglow around the misty horizon she set off, riding swiftly westwards across the Plains of Kor.

Her Fey senses were sharp and attuned, but the mist was dense all around her. Fortunately the sky above was clear and she could keep her bearings by putting the sun behind her as it rose. A faint trace of warmth pierced the cold and the mist began to burn off.

And as it did, the Plains of Kor stretched out before her.

She knew the maps well enough. A huge tapestry of Midnight was arrayed on the walls within the Citadel of Dreams and she had studied it for many nights by candlelight. Ahead lay the Forest of Kor, where their cousins, the Fey of Kor, under their leader, Korinel himself, lived.

She rode on as the mist continued to clear, the land falling away before her. Her horse trotted down an icy path between the hills and the forest came into view.

She gasped in horror.

The forests of the Fey were almost as permanent a feature of the realm of Midnight as the mountains. Unchanging and dependable, they were home and hearth, shelter, food and protection. Long association with them had woven an enchantment over them that only the Fey understood, and it took long years for the younger Fey to understand its complexities. Tarithel herself was still learning of those ancient mysteries.

The forests were unassailable. Strong and inviolate.

Burnt!

The Forest of Kor was a smouldering wreck. Even from two leagues away Tarithel could see it was ash, a smoking ruin. Her heart thumping in her chest, she guided her horse onwards, despite it whinnying and signalling its dislike and uncertainty.

'Easy ...'

Smoke trailed away to the south in a gentle northerly breeze. Flakes of snow danced around her as she reached the edge of what had once been the borders of the forest. Now only burnt stumps remained, the ground strewn with blackened branches. Nothing moved, nothing had survived the flames. She could still feel a little heat from the embers.

Who would do such a thing? And where are my Fey cousins?

She dismounted and stepped carefully forward amidst the ash, securing her horse to a blackened trunk. Larger trees, fallen and stark barred her progress. She spied something nestled amidst the roots of one of the burnt stumps and bent down to take a look.

She screamed, flailing backwards to lie in the midst of the ash. Her horse snorted in alarm.

A blackened skull, its head adorned with a mangled tiara, teeth white against burnt skin stared back at her.

Tarithel's gaze took in a burnt and mangled body, festooned with the remains of blackened arrows. She crawled backwards, coating herself in dust and ash, scrambling away in terror until the ash was replaced by snow and ice once more. Bile rose in her throat and she retched, gagging and doubling over on to her hands and knees.

She spat out the foul taste, gasping for breath.

The Fey of Kor … murdered! Did my father know? Why would he conceal this?

She rolled on to her side, trying to catch her breath. Her horse pawed the ground nearby, skittishly moving backwards and forwards.

Tarithel got to her feet and moved to comfort the horse.

'There, it's alright. Shhh …'

A faint noise reached her above the breeze. She turned, looking for the source. Nothing moved, so she took the horse by the reins and led it back the way they had come, away from the remains of the forest.

The path they were walking would take them back across the plain, but the view to the north was blocked by a slight rise in the land. She could still make out a faint noise, but she couldn't place it. A rumble on the edge of hearing.

She led the horse away from the path, pulling it up the rise. It resisted, digging its hooves into the ground and refusing to be led forward. Tarithel yanked on the reins, but it was immovable, shaking its head and snorting.

'Then wait here,' she scolded and ran up the rise, leaving the horse behind.

She reached the top and looked over, blinking in the strengthening sunlight.

She caught her breath. The Plains of Kor stretched away into the far north where a jagged series of dark mountains split the horizon. She knew it well enough from the maps, the realm of the Witchking, none of the Fey ventured that way. Yet it was not the mountains that drew her gaze.

Across the plain she could see banners and flags, groups of them in organised arrays, all dark, all held aloft and fluttering in the breeze. Hoisted by men clad in black armour. To the east the mist still rolled.

Thousands … and the mist has hidden them. My people won't know. Kor is already burnt …

She gasped.

That's why they destroyed Korinel … to keep news of this from us!

The noise she had heard was the distant thump of their footsteps upon the snow. They were leagues away and yet the noise of their passing still reached her on the wind.

The Doomguard march south! I must get back and warn …

She turned and ran back down the hill, grabbing the reins of her horse and leaping up into the saddle. She spurred it around, heedless of the attention it might bring and then raced away eastwards on the path.

Her horse was fleet and in good condition; barring anything unforeseen she'd make it back to the forest before nightfall.

The horse's hooves pounded through the snow, ice flung up behind Tarithel as it galloped on.

A man, directly before her.

She yanked on the reins. Her horse scrabbled for grip, desperately trying to turn aside in time, but lost its balance. Tarithel leapt from the saddle as the horse began to fall, rolling into the thick snow below. The impact drove the breath from her lungs, but she staggered up, her hands pulling twin knives from her belt.

She spun around, one knife head high, the other held low in defence.

An old man …

He was standing beside the trail, watching as her horse staggered upright, snorting and whinnying. Tarithel moved between them, studying the man all the while. He was tall, but a little bent, dressed in some kind of dark mauve robe. His hair was grey and long and he leant upon a metal staff topped with a strange symbol.

'Unusual to see a Fey alone on the plains,' he said, looking at her. 'You will not need the knives. I mean you no harm.'

He seemed completely at ease, not startled in the slightest at almost being run down by her.

'Who are you?' she demanded, keeping her knives ready.

'I am a traveller in these parts,' he responded. Tarithel looked about him and was surprised she could see no footprints. It was as if he'd materialised right out of thin air.

'And who do you serve?' she asked. 'Witchking or Moonprince?'

His expression changed at her words.

'Moonprince?' he asked. 'What know you of the Moonprince?'

'Answer me!'

He nodded. 'Very well, young Fey. I am Rorthron the Wise and yes, I serve the Moonprince.'

Tarithel's eyes widened in surprise. 'The Wise?'

'And you are?'

Tarithel relaxed a little, lowering her guard. 'I am Tarithel the Fey, daughter of the Lord of Dreams and Lady of the Forest, since my mother relinquished the title on the Solstice.'

'Are you indeed,' Rorthron responded. 'Out here at his bidding, I assume.'

He caught the look on her face.

'Or perhaps not,' he added with a faint grin. 'Regardless, it is not safe out here Lady of the Forest. We should take steps to avoid being seen by unfriendly eyes.'

'You mean, hide?' she asked. 'From the Doomguard?'

'In a manner of speaking.'

Tarithel watched as he used the tip of his staff to draw a circle around them in the soft snow. When he completed it, he gestured for her to bring the horse within. Then he turned the staff around and tapped it into the snow. Tarithel fancied she felt a faint flush of warmth around her.

'There,' Rorthron said. 'Enough for now. We are hidden. Away from prying eyes and ears. So, Tarithel, you have sought answers in the wilderness ...'

'The Doomguard have razed the Forest of Kor,' Tarithel said. 'And now they march southwards. My father has kept all this hidden from our people. He says we will turn inwards and look only to ourselves ...'

Rorthron held up a hand. 'The Witchking seeks to divide those who would stand against him. The Moonprince has ridden forth and the Free come to his aid. The Fey might rally too, and yet ...'

'My father will not,' Tarithel said. 'He says he will not provoke the Witchking.'

Rorthron smiled. 'And what say you, young Lady?'

Tarithel blinked. 'I would not dare to defy my father.'

Rorthron laughed. 'Yet here you stand, outside his realm despite his wishes? I think to defy him is precisely what you intend. And I heartily approve!'

'Why?' she asked.

'Why?' he replied. 'I have some ancient kinship with the Fey. I would see them join this battle as they should. I cannot go myself, thus this task falls to you, young lady.'

'What do you mean ...?'

'Only this,' Rorthron said. 'I did not tell you of the Moonprince, you heard that for yourself. For you to hear his cry from here is remarkable in itself. I would say you already know what you must do.'

'I must save my people from the Witchking,' Tarithel said, her eyes wide.

'And?'

'They must rally to the Moonprince's call.'

Rorthron smiled. 'Just that.'

'But my father forbids it!'

Tarithel looked at him. The old man seemed expectant, gazing at her with a keen expression on his lined and aged face.

'Your quest then,' he said.

Her mouth hung open. She meant to say something, then thought better of it.

'Is there something else?' he asked. 'Something you would know?'

An image came to Tarithel's mind.

'I saw this young man, a boy,' she said, stuttering. 'Twice I have seen him. Alone in the wilderness, far from home, astride a red-haired mare. His vision came to me ...'

'Did it indeed,' Rorthron replied, a faint smile playing on his features.

'Do you know of this?'

'I might,' Rorthron said. 'Your loyalty to the Moonprince has been recognised I think. Was he blonde, fair of face ...'

'Yes!' Tarithel said, her enthusiasm getting the better of her.

'You see the son of the Moonprince,' Rorthron said. 'Morkin half-Fey.'

'Half-Fey ...' Tarithel echoed.

'He also undertakes a dangerous quest,' Rorthron said.

'Can I help him?'

Rorthron's smile grew. 'Yes, but in ways you do not know. Watch for him in your mind. If he calls, answer.'

'I don't understand ...'

Rorthron's smile faded and he looked around him, as if suspicious.

'You will,' he said. 'But I cannot tarry. You must arrive in good time to alert your kin.'

Tarithel shook her head. 'But the day is already half spent, I will not reach them before nightfall and I will face some punishment for my impertinence.'

'Perhaps that is one thing I can help you with.'

Tarithel watched as he took something from within his robes. He brought forth a small golden cup and scooped some snow into it before running a finger around its lip. Then he handed it to her.

'It's safe enough,' he said. 'Drink.'

She took the cup, and held it up.

'This was no chance meeting Tarithel of the Fey,' Rorthron said. 'Go with my blessing. Rouse the Fey from their slumber and you will have done more in the service of the Moonprince than most. Watch for Morkin half-Fey!'

Tarithel took a sip from the cup.

Sunlight flashed above her, shadows moving impossibly swiftly across the ground. She looked up in surprise to see the sun arc across the sky, returning to a position just above the horizon. The mist flickered around her, cold and damp.

It was dawn.

She looked about her. Rorthron, the cup and the circle had vanished as if they were a dream. She stood in the wilderness, her horse beside her as the sun rose for the second time.

A voice came to her, the old man's tones.

It is the dawn of the day upon which you rode out. No one will note your passing when you return. Now, ride!

Luxor cast forth the searching beams of the Moon Ring's power. Rorthron was easy enough to find, his own power radiant to Luxor's gaze. Rorthron seemed preoccupied for a moment, but his attention turned as he sensed the Moon Ring's focus.

So, you are willing to listen now, Lord Luxor?

Rorthron's features betrayed amusement as Luxor spoke to him once more via the magic of the Moon Ring.

'Tease me not,' Luxor snapped. 'My son is committed to this quest of yours, regardless of whether I consider it wisdom or folly. He has placed his trust in you, thus so must I. I hope for your sake it is not misplaced.'

You cannot intimidate me, Moonprince.

'I seek your counsel,' Luxor said. 'And if this quest is our salvation, I will take back the harsh words I said at our last meeting.'

As well you might. But a measure of humbleness is a boon to a leader. Your apology is accepted.

'If Morkin is to seize this Ice Crown, he must also destroy it. Know you how to do this?'

I will reveal that at the proper time ...

'And?'

The Ice Crown must be unmade by careful steps in combination. I have learnt much of the arcane matters regarding its construction. Needless to say, it is fraught with difficulties I must overcome. But fear not for Morkin. The Fey have already given him much advice. Lord Thrall is knowledgeable in such matters. Now, to other matters of concern to you ...

'How so?'

You saw the Witchking's strength at Blood. You sent Morkin away because you feared the worst. If I told you your fears were founded in reality ...

'The Witchking's armies march upon us.'

Aye, they do, in greater strength than ever before. The Witchking has even found a way to penetrate the forests of the Fey. All will fall before him. Nowhere is safe. He plans for complete dominion over all Midnight.

'Then?'

I have sent what messages I can to the Fey, but they have their own troubles to overcome before they can come to your aid. Corleth continues on his own quest to rouse his people. You must hold the line, Moonprince, though the darkness beats upon your threshold.

'Buying time for your scheming?'

You cannot defeat the Witchking by strength of arms alone, you never could, even with all of the Free and Fey under your banner. He has laboured long in preparation for this moment, but he does not know all. He does not know of Morkin. That is our strength, the secret we must keep for as long as we can.

'Draw his attention,' Luxor mused.

You must occupy his every thought. If he believes his own victory lies in the subjugation of Midnight's people and the death of the last revealed Moonprince, perhaps he will not notice an audacious plan to unseat the very power that underpins him.

'You peg all our hopes upon my son,' Luxor said. 'If he dies in this quest, the little friendship we share will be at an end, Rorthron the Wise.'

If Morkin fails in his quest, Luxor, Moonprince of Midnight, everything will be at an end. Yet the closer he gets, the easier will be your task. I will work my utmost to his success, will you do your part?

'I will wreak what mayhem I can upon the Witchking's hordes,' Luxor answered.

Let us hope it will be enough. Until next time, Moonprince. Farewell.

Chapter Ten

*He stands in the Mountains of Dodrak,
looking north to the Tower of Coroth.*

Morkin woke, his head sore and throbbing. He winced, but almost welcomed the pain. At least it proved he was still alive. He shifted slightly and was rewarded with a series of aches, but none seemed to be too serious.

He opened his eyes and looked about him.

He'd fallen down a smooth U-shaped ravine in the lee of the mountains and come to a stop at the bottom. Though half buried in snow, he was able to pull himself out and stagger upright. Brushing himself down revealed no broken bones or other injuries.

No sign of anyone else. Had he eluded the Doomguard?

The small gulley that held him showed light a little brighter in one direction, so he cautiously moved forward to investigate. The gulley widened and soon he was blinking in the bright sunlight, overlooking a bowl-like valley nestled in the mountains. He was standing at the southern end and could see a lake before him, sparkling blue in the sunlight, and what looked to be the ice-bound remains of a village not far to the east. Beyond that was a ruined keep and a tower.

One of the Wise? Perhaps I can find some help there!

The sun was lower in the sky. If it was the same day, only a few hours had passed.

The bowl-like valley seemed a curious place, locked on all

sides by mountains. He unshouldered his backpack, relieved to find it undisturbed. Taking out the map, it seemed likely that the tower was that of Coroth. Nothing else was marked. He wasn't too far off track, but he was within a mountain range he had not planned to cross.

Got to get out of here, but these mountains seem set against me. And without my horse …

Dark stains were splattered across his thick tunic. He sighed. A moment's distraction had cost him dear, and his horse its life.

The village looked abandoned. He could see no smoke rising, no obvious evidence of habitation. The ruined keep looked even less inviting. The tower rose, cold and stark, from the landscape. In the manner of all the towers he had seen, it seemed pristine and unaffected by the elements.

He leant against a rocky outcrop to gain some purchase as he descended, being careful not to slip on the treacherous terrain.

Ahead, something moved.

He panicked, staggering backwards and flung himself back behind the rocky outcrop.

The Doomguard? Still looking for me!

His heart pounding, he stayed as still as he could, listening for sounds of movement, expecting to hear coarse cries and the sounds of armour and booted feet.

He tried to calm his breathing, straining his ears.

Nothing …

Somehow that was worse than hearing something. Had they spotted him but lost sight, waiting for him to make a move so they could locate him?

He waited for long minutes, but there was nothing but the faint whistle of the wind over the rock.

Can't stay here forever.

He turned and peered over the rock, taking a quick glance before ducking down. The Doomguard were there, but they didn't seem to have moved at all. He risked another look.

What ...?

He blinked and squinted. It was hard to make out. Figures, but they were stock still, unmoving, black against the snow. A black flag, canted at an angle, flapped aimlessly in the breeze. That was the movement he'd spied. He could just make out spears cast about the ground. Some of the figures lay full length on the floor, others crouched, a few stood upright. It was if they had been frozen in the midst of a battle. Other than the flag, nothing moved.

What magic is this?

He moved forward, dashing from outcrop to outcrop until he got close enough. It was only as he drew near that the true nature of what had happened to his pursuers became clear.

Burnt ...

There were perhaps forty or fifty of them. As far as he could tell it was the same group that had pursued him up the mountain. Bodies, all blackened and burnt, some recognisably men, others so incinerated they were little more than shaped piles of blackened ash. Metal armour was scorched and darkened, along with swords and spears. Anything leather or wooden was gone.

Morkin stepped amongst the dead, turning to look at the face of the cliff that backed the gulley. It too was blackened, a huge arc of soot cast upon it, with the imprints of man-like shapes upon it, showing where some of the Doomguard had stood when whatever it was had assailed them.

Morkin bent down to examine one of the swords. It was buckled, the metal distorted as if it had been in some monstrous furnace. He looked in the other direction, but there was nothing to see other than the snowy landscape.

Above him, there was nothing, just a pale sky laced with thin clouds drifting through the mountain peaks.

He shivered, but not with the cold.

Shimeril and Blood were waiting for Luxor when he returned to the battlements. They exchanged a look at the Moonprince's stern visage.

'Tidings?' Blood inquired.

'I made contact with Rorthron the Wise,' Luxor replied. 'He has despatched Kumar, Marakith and Athoril to us. I can sense their progress via the ring, they are not far away, but they are harried by encounters with the Foul. Whether they arrive in time … how go preparations here?'

'All the garrisons here about have reported in,' Shimeril said. 'We have as many soldiers as we are going to have. Word has been sent to Xajorkith. We expect news from them upon the morrow.'

Blood was eyeing Luxor closely.

'Something else, my Lord Luxor?'

Luxor nodded. 'My son, he has … taken up a quest of sorts.'

'A quest?' Shimeril asked.

'I trust you both,' Luxor replied, 'but this may go no further than between us three. I would not see it discussed for now. False hope and folly go hand in hand.'

'Of course,' both replied.

Luxor related Rorthron's account of the Ice Crown, its forging and the myth regarding the one who might approach it. How he'd sent Morkin to Thrall, but the boy had taken matters into his own hands.

'And this Rorthron thinks it is your squire, your son, Morkin?' Shimeril said. 'The one who can approach the Ice Crown?'

Luxor nodded.

'That young lad was resourceful and keen,' Blood said, 'and of no mean courage if he will seek a way into the Witchking's realm with such a quest. But how does one destroy the Ice Crown even if one can wrest it from its foundations?'

'The lore of the Wise will tell us,' Luxor replied. 'So Rorthron assures me, he seeks those answers even now. It seems our strategy must change.'

'How so?' Shimeril asked.

Luxor smiled. 'My friends, I will speak only the truth to you. You know as well as I do that despite our valour, our skill with weapons and the stoutest defence we can muster, we cannot hope to defeat the Witchking's hoards on his own terms. As his confidence grows, thus grows the ice-fear. It will continue to wreak havoc upon the hearts of the Free. And yet ...'

'If we could strike at the source of his power,' Blood murmured. 'If the Ice Crown were threatened, stolen away, even destroyed ...'

'The ice-fear would reduce, even in part – it might be enough,' Shimeril agreed. 'Why, even the winter would end if that talisman were cast down!'

'Much rests upon that quest,' Luxor said. 'Too much. I would have feared to go myself, let alone send my son, the knowledge of whom spans just a few days! But, in truth, he is born of both Fey and Free. If it is not him, it is not anyone.'

'Then our task is not quite as it seems,' Shimeril said.

Luxor nodded. 'No indeed. We fight on here as if we expect to win. We defend our realm as we should, but we are drawing the eye of the Witchking. We must make such a battle as to keep his attention focussed here, to ensure that he does not spy my son encroaching day by day on the source of his fell power.'

'He will smite us anyway,' Blood said. 'Concentrate the full force of his power upon us. We may have to fall back further, even to Xajorkith.'

'And if Xajorkith falls ...?' Shimeril began.

Luxor held up his hand. 'I know. If that comes to pass we are lost, Midnight belongs to the Witchking.'

The ice-fear crackled about them, as if hearing their words. A pulse of terror and anguish washed across them. Luxor groaned and then raised his own hand. The Moon Ring pulsed once more and the ice-fear was driven back once more.

Luxor staggered, grasping at his head.

'My Lord!' Shimeril called, reaching out to steady him.

'It is alright,' Luxor said, after a moment.

'You combat the ice-fear constantly,' Shimeril observed. 'This Ring may be a mighty talisman, but it demands a heavy price of you.'

'It seems to feed upon my very soul to take the fight against the ice-fear,' Luxor said. 'It drains me. Yet I must fight it. Without the Moon Ring ...'

'Courage,' Shimeril replied. 'You are the Moonprince, chosen by fate for this hour. We have no doubts in you.'

'Quite so,' Blood said. 'Come, Luxor, we have never laid all our hopes upon myths and legends. Valour will see us through, I do not believe that the words of the Wise are the unvarnished truth. What do they know anyway, locked up in their towers and unconcerned with the dealings of the Free? Morkin is a brave soul, if he can destroy the Ice Crown, so be it. Let's defeat the Witchking's hordes on the field of battle regardless!'

'Aye!' Shimeril said. 'We have routed him before, let us rout him again, chase his foul minions back to the gates of Ushgarak and have at the walls of his own citadel. Nay! Raze it to the ground. Xajorkith has never been taken in the history of Midnight. Damn his impertinence for sullying our lands. We will rally and turn him about.'

Luxor clapped them both fondly on the back.

'Ah, my friends,' he said. 'How could I ever doubt the strength of your hearts? With you beside me I have nothing to fear.'

Blood and Shimeril continued recounting stories of long ago, battles fought and won against the Witchking in times past. Luxor joined in, but his thoughts were elsewhere, across long tracts of frozen landscapes, across forests and downs, to a lonely figure struggling northwards into certain peril as he approached the very lands of their uttermost enemy. The Moon Ring glimmered in his mind.

Without a horse the going was long and weary. Morkin was no stranger to long hikes in the snow, but the traipse through the mountains inexorably drained his stamina day after day. He was rationing the food he was carrying and hunger was already gnawing at him. Water was difficult too. Here in the mountains was the occasional spring, still free from the ice via some warmth deep in the heart of the rocks. Out on the plains ahead it would be in short supply. Snow and ice was no substitute. He already felt pinched and weak.

But it seems likely the Doomguard may have alerted others to where I am. It's only safe to assume they are hunting me …

He shivered thinking about it.

Something else had changed in the last day. He could sense the ice-fear growing around him, it seemed unable to penetrate his mind, but it was there, seeking a way to hinder him, flowing around him as if trying to slow him down. It felt as if it were stronger, more confident somehow.

Which does not bode well …

Long hours of trudging onwards finally saw the mountains falling behind him. Plains widened before him to the north, flat and bleak as far as he could see. On the edge of sight rose some low hills. Consulting his map, Morkin recognised the Downs of Mirrow. His destination in the Forest of Lothoril lay many leagues beyond.

No point in delaying …

Stowing the map carefully he set off again, pondering the events of the last day. The plain opened out before him and he strode on. He was making for Lake Mirrow which, according to the map, lay in the south eastern edges of the downs. It seemed likely that there would be no way for him to replenish his water supply in the meantime. The lakes also attracted animals, so there was a chance he might snare some food and perhaps have a chance to tame one of the wild horses that roamed the Plains of Midnight.

And then there is the fate of the Doomguard that assailed me. What happened to them? What power can burn men to ash in the winter of Midnight?

He had seen nothing that could do such a thing. There had been no tracks, no smoke, no other signs of anything. It was as if something had swept out of the sky and incinerated them.

But what could do that?

Certainly there were flying creatures in Midnight. Morkin thought of the wyverns that he'd oft seen circling the forests near his home in Odrark. Some claimed they had seen them breathe fire, but Morkin had never seen it himself. Even if they did it could only be small puffs of flame. The wyverns weren't big, perhaps as long as a man but with lightweight and fragile bodies. Morkin had never heard of them hunting in packs nor attacking Free or Fey, let alone heavily armed Doomguard warriors.

There were stories, of course. According to legend Midnight had once played host to dragons, creatures akin to the wyverns that infested the mountains and hills. Many folk embellished their tales of encounters with the beasts and they were often referred to as 'dragons'.

But real dragons …

They would have been mighty both in strength and cunning. If they had been real, it seemed they were another victim of the eternal winter curse brought upon Midnight by the Witchking. Snow and ice surely did not mix with dragonfire. Morkin could only suppose that with prey in short supply the real dragons, presumably having quite the appetite, had moved to warmer and more hospitable climes. Could one be left? It seemed unlikely, though it might explain Corleth's fears; why this part of Midnight was virtually uninhabited.

But if not a dragon, then what? A fire from within the earth, perhaps?

It would remain a mystery. He was grateful to whoever or whatever it was that had spared him from a fate at the hands of the Doomguard, but unnerved too. If a fire could flare up from beneath the very ground …

Minutes blurred into hours as the sun moved through its arc in the sky. Before long the twilight was upon him. Behind the mountains had receded, but ahead the downs seemed little closer. The plain was hard to judge, defying his ability to determine how far he'd come.

As was the custom for travellers in the wilderness, he spent the last hour of daylight digging out a shelter in the snow, ensuring he was protected from the prevailing wind. He was glad to drop his backpack into the shelter and unbuckle the sword about his waist.

As he was finishing he heard a noise and was instantly alert.

Scurrying feet …

He grabbed his sword and peered around him. The light was fading fast and he could see nothing within the limits of his vision. He trusted his ears though, got to his feet and moved in the direction he thought the sound was coming from.

Still nothing …

He stood still for long moments, straining his ears, alert for any further sound. Try as he might he couldn't hear anything other than the faint whistle of the wind, blowing gently from the north.

He took a few steps further forward and saw something on the ground.

Footprints! Small …

They weren't animal prints, not toed, clawed or padded. It looked for all the world like a small child's prints in the snow. They were fresh. Morkin spun around seeking the source of them.

Wait a minute …

He rushed back to his makeshift shelter with a cry. There, close to his backpack, stood a small creature, upright.

With a yell of fear it leapt backwards, sprawling on the snow. Morkin advanced, his sword extended towards it.

'Don't move!' he yelled.

The creature raised its hands in supplication. It was in size, rather like a child, but stocky, wiry and strong looking rather than thin. It was short, barely reaching to Morkin's waist, covered in long hair from head to foot, wearing a rough tunic and leather covers on its feet. Gnarled hands gestured at him and a rough weather beaten face turned towards him, dark eyes glinting with fear.

'Khlee!' the creature hissed. 'Khlee!'

Morkin stepped forward and the creature huddled down in the show, bowing over and over again. Muffled noises came from it and Morkin could just make out words.

'Surely master, surely, no hurt Fawkrin. Fawkrin means no harm.'

It speaks!

Morkin looked at the creature anew, wondering what it might be capable of.

'Stand up,' Morkin said. 'Fawkrin, is that your name?'

The creature looked up and nodded. 'Surely is, master. Fawkrin, yes Fawkrin is my name.'

Morkin gestured with his sword and the creature retreated, holding up its short arms in defence.

'And what are you doing hereabouts?' Morkin asked. 'Spying for the Witchking no doubt.'

The creature shook its head rapidly, making a blubbering sound as it did so. 'Surely not, master. Not rotten Doomdark, never! Khlee!'

'You've been following me?'

The creature shook and blubbered again. 'No young master, Fawkrin knows this land well, trolls and wolves all about, make a meal out of you they surely will.'

'I am not scared of trolls and wolves,' Morkin retorted.

'Surely not,' Fawkrin replied. 'But the skulkrin know ...'

Skulkrin ...

Morkin had heard of the creatures. It was said they lived in the far north of Midnight, hidden deep in the snow most of the time. Rarely were they seen, and never in the southern lands. Some accused them of being the Witchking's lackeys, others that they were slaves. Others still named them vermin. None of the stories Morkin could recall had ever mentioned they could speak.

'... the ways of Midnight. Lost on the plains, you need a guide.'

'I know where I am going,' Morkin said. 'I have a map.'

'Map you say?' Fawkrin's wrinkled face split into a grin revealing two notably fanged teeth. 'Not mark chasms and falls though, does it? Eh?'

'Chasms?' Morkin asked.

Fawkrin beckoned him closer. 'Look see, look. Secrets I can show.'

Morkin watched as the skulkrin began to draw in the snow with his finger trip. He leaned over to get a better look.

'Chasm, see?' Fawkrin said, 'Not so far north, hard to see, no bottom! Goes down forever. Khlee!'

'But …' Morkin began, frowning to see what Fawkrin was drawing.

In a flash the little creature ducked a hand inside its grubby tunic. Before Morkin could move out of the way a spray of white powder hit him in the face. For a moment it felt like snow, but he got a brief impression of glowing star-like points of light and then the darkness smothered him like a blanket.

Travelling in a way known only to the Wise, Rorthron's progress had been swift. Tarithel had barely reached the eaves of the Forest of Dreams before he had already crossed the Mountains of Gorgrath and made his flight south and west. There was another task that needed Rorthron's attention. He played back the conversation with Lorgrim in his mind. A single sentence had jarred him and was sitting uncomfortably in his thoughts.

All the crowns have such base powers …

What had Lorgrim meant by that? More than one Ice Crown? Impossible, not even the Witchking, with all his fell power could have forged more than one such device. He had poured his essence into its making. A duplicate would be a waste and unnecessary. No, Lorgrim had been thinking of something else and Rorthron knew it had been a slip of the tongue to reveal it.

… and the other talismans … the First Power is …

Rorthron had been considering these words too. Lorgrim kept secrets that he would not tell. Rorthron chuckled at Lorgrim's flimsy denial.

So, there are other crowns. Gryfallon used one as the basis for his capture of Midnight. There are more, and other talismans besides. Where might they be found, and what potency might they have? And this First Power …

Rorthron had never heard the phrase before, which meant it was a close secret of the Wise. Lorgrim wasn't going to reveal any more. Answers, if they were to be found, lay in the libraries of the Tower of the Moon from whence his journey had started.

Dawn was breaking, it was time to go.

Fawkrin watched as the boy fell to his knees and slumped sideways. It seemed that stars had fallen from the sky to settle on the boy's face. One by one, each glinting speck faded and disappeared as the sleep-frost melted into his skin. Fawkrin waited until the last glimmer had died, then edged closer to the boy. He sniffed at the boy's tepid breath, his nose wrinkling and twitching as he tested its warmth and texture. Then he giggled in delight.

The boy stirred. Eyes still closed, his arm rose mechanically and his hand wavered, grasping in the snow for his sword. The skulkrin scurried away with a squeak of terror but the boy's arm fell back, lifeless, to the ground. Fawkrin crouched in the darkness a full minute before he found courage enough to crawl back to his side.

He snuffled at his face and shoulders and chest.

'Mmmm. Fresh! And so warm!' he declared.

Fawkrin tugged another pouch from his tunic and poured some more white powder into his palm. Sparingly, he sprinkled it over the boy's arm. No melting glow could be seen for this time the white dust was more mundane; it was salt. Fawkrin opened his jaws wide and ducked eagerly forward.

Just as the skulkrin's fangs were about to sink into the morsel the boy stirred again, rolling over and nearly crushing Fawkrin. The skulkrin stumbled back in alarm.

'Must be Fey blood, resisting the sleep-frost, surely!' Fawkrin mumbled. 'Not safe, surely not safe! Khlee!'

The skulkrin scampered to one side, seeing the backpack nestled in the shelter Morkin had dug. Quickly Fawkrin went through it, tossing the contents aside until he found the food and drink within. He loaded up his own backpack.

Laughing at his good fortune Fawkrin snatched the provisions and made off into the gathering gloom, swiftly disappearing from sight.

Chapter Eleven

He stands in the Village of the Targ,
looking north east to the Keep of Utarg.

Corleth found little shelter or comfort in the village, it had been abandoned by its folks, fearful of the Doomguard. The desolate hamlet was nestled on the eastern edge of the Downs of Athoril, a few leagues north of the keep. A well-travelled road ran north and south, joining the Citadel of Kumar to the trade route down towards Dawn.

A vast plain that stretched out in all directions, desolate and barren even by the harsh standards of Midnight. Corleth could see the ancient Forest of Dregrim just visible on the southern border, its boundaries blue in the distance. He knew it to be one of the greatest of the Fey's homelands, but it was one of the least travelled, being so far to the east. Corleth had never met the Lord of Dregrim and knew of him only as a remote and distant figure.

To the north the Mountains of Kumar could just be seen, wreathed in high cloud and mist. Kumar himself would be far to the south now, marching with all speed on the Citadel of Dawn, there to thwart the Witchking's forces if he could.

Ahead of Corleth rose a keep.

Even from several leagues away it was clear that it was no ordinary keep. Its battlements and crenulations were stark and ugly. The keep was much larger than most, more of a fortress. It rose upon a small hillock, dominating the surrounding plain, its stonework dark and stained with the marks of fire and war. It seemed the Utarg cared little for aesthetics. As Corleth rode closer he could see that repairs to the fortress were done with little care for retaining the lines or form of the ancient building. Fires were burning on the heights.

Corleth knew he would have already been spotted by the Targ sentries, but he was not challenged on his journey.

As he rode closer he turned his horse on to a road that swept up to the gated entrance to the keep. It was silent, all about him the plains seemed deserted. The road was marked by torches hoisted on metal spikes, fuelled by burning pitch on either side. Thin plumes of foul-smelling smoke drifted upwards, making his eyes water. But still his progress went unremarked.

Ahead a huge portcullis loomed. It was down and shut in place. He rode closer and jumped down from his horse. Through the portcullis he could see the courtyard of the keep, but that too seemed deserted, yet lit by more of the torches.

Too quiet, in a time of war there should be guards …

He stepped back and looked up at the walls above him. He could see no sentries, no guards on duty.

'I am Corleth of the Thrall Fey,' he called. 'Here to seek an audience with the Utarg of Utarg.'

His words echoed off the walls and then faded into the gloom. He listened, but not even his acute hearing could detect anything. It was as if the keep were abandoned.

'Will you not hear me, Utarg of Utarg? I come bearing greetings from the Moonprince of Midnight and tidings of the war in the west.'

Again his words faded into silence. His horse whinnied nervously, its hooves clicking on the cobblestone road.

Whatever Corleth had expected, it was not this. To be completely ignored! He stepped forward and pulled at the portcullis in frustration. It didn't even rattle in his grasp, the metal cold in his hands, but immovable.

No reception from the Utarg then. At least the warnings of Kumar and Marakith were unfounded. Perhaps the Utarg is not the terror they described. So, to Dregrim then!

Corleth retreated from the threshold of the keep and mounted his horse, turning it about. He rode off, leaving the keep behind.

The crunching sound of stonework and metal heaving aside reached his ears. He stopped and turned to see.

With a rumble and thunderous clanking the portcullis was rising into the stonework of the gatehouse above. Corleth watched as it fully retracted, stopping with an echoing thump. A faint hiss sounded, which then faded away.

Corleth regarded the open portal for a long moment, straining his ears to pick up any other sound, but nothing else had changed. He rubbed his chin before making a decision. He turned his horse and rode into the keep.

As he cleared the gatehouse the hiss sounded again and the portcullis slid back down, before crunching into the stonework below.

The courtyard within was wide and expansive with a sand covered floor, but otherwise empty. An internal balcony ran alongside the inner length of the external wall, giving guards and sentries a means to access the battlements. Before him the keep itself rose, almost like a tower, a building festooned with jutting metal barbs, wires and rusted implements of war. It seemed as if unused weapons had been formed into the very structure of the building. It rose far above him, an intimidating confusion of metal and stone, torn and bent, stained with rust.

Corleth looked on in distaste as he saw that, here and there, skeletons hung from the metal barbs.

Impaled there. For sport? For torture? For punishment?

His horse started in fright as movement came from the

base of the fort. Men, so it seemed, emerged. Corleth fought to control the animal, backing it up against the gatehouse.

From either side they came, dozens of men from two darkened access ways. They moved slowly along the outside walls, circling close, hunched down and ready.

Corleth eyed them. They were huge bulky men, dressed in thick and heavy furs, their heads covered in brass helmets that gleamed in the firelight revealing only their eyes, fierce and furious. In their arms they held spears, but spears beyond any that Corleth had ever seen. These were poles, massive beams of wood sharpened to a point and held before them.

They advanced slowly, wordlessly, the only sound their footfalls and their heavy breathing.

'I seek an audience with the Utarg of Utarg,' Corleth called.

The men continued their advance. Corleth looked about him. No escape to either side, the semi-circle of spears was converging on him. He drew his sword and held it before him, preparing to rear his horse and make a fight of it.

A drum sounded. A single beat that echoed off the walls. 'Halt!'

The men paused in their advance.

The imperious cry had come from an alcove in the fort above, perhaps ten feet from the ground. Corleth looked up and could make out a silhouetted figure. Torchlight blazed in the background now, lit at some unspoken signal.

Then, to Corleth's surprise, the man leapt down from the height, landing on the ground with both feet with a heavy thud. He stood up, towering above even the enormous guards before him. Corleth stared at him, the man had to be eight feet tall. He could almost look Corleth in the eye whilst he was still in the saddle.

The men moved aside as he approached.

'Your wish is granted, Corleth of the Thrall Fey. I am Utarg of Utarg.'

'I thank you for your welcome …' Corleth began.

Utarg interrupted him. 'There is no welcome, Fey. You are trespassing in my realm. State your business.'

Corleth waited a moment before sheaving his sword and dismounting his horse. He walked towards Utarg, looking up at the towering figure before him.

'I seek to recruit you and your warriors in a fight against the Witchking,' he stated.

Utarg looked down at him, leaning forward. 'The Witchking is no enemy of mine. Why should I seek to make him one?'

Corleth held his ground. 'The Witchking's armies have moved south, sweeping all before them, Free, Fey and others alike. He means to take all Midnight.'

Utarg grunted. 'He has no reason to attack me.'

'He needs no reason,' Corleth insisted. 'His power is at its greatest extent, he will come for you, sooner or later.'

Utarg laughed and gestured. From the far right of the tower two more giant men emerged dragging a figure between them. Corleth squinted, the figure was slumped in their arms, its feet dangling behind it. Corleth stepped back in horror as the body was dumped at his feet, a disembodied helmeted head dropped alongside it. The body was beaten and bloody.

Doomguard!

'The Witchking has already sent an emissary to us, asking much the same as you,' Utarg replied. 'He failed in his quest.'

'Then …'

'Who sent you, little Fey?' Utarg asked.

'Luxor, Moonprince of Midnight.'

Utarg chuckled again. 'Moonprince?' he repeated, mocking the name. 'This Moonprince, does he stand with you here?'

'No,' Corleth answered.

'Then you represent his interests, little Fey.' Utarg replied. 'You seek my loyalty on his behalf?'

259

'I do.'

Utarg nodded. 'So be it. The challenge is yours.'

Corleth narrowed his eyes. 'Challenge?'

'I will not ally myself with the weak or enfeebled,' Utarg replied. 'Best me in combat and I will pledge my allegiance, fail and ...'

The men about him chuckled. Corleth looked down at the battered remnants of the Doomguard emissary.

Utarg stepped away, signalling to his men. They also re-treated, backing against the walls of the keep, their spears still held ready. Corleth was left standing in the middle of the courtyard. Utarg faced him, drawing two huge knives from his belt. They were so large they would have served as swords for a lesser man.

'Let's see if you and your Moonprince deserve my loyalty, little Fey,' Utarg taunted.

Corleth undid the clasp on his cloak and furled it away, drawing his sword and turning back to face Utarg, dropping into a ready stance.

'Do you swear to honour this agreement should I prevail?' Corleth asked.

'Witnessed before my kin,' Utarg replied.

'And to serve Luxor, Moonprince of Midnight? To take him as your liege lord?'

'I will go to him and swear my allegiance. Enough words!'

Utarg charged towards him with a gruff yell. Corleth stepped aside, swinging his sword in an arc to strike at the big man's midriff. The blow was blocked by one of the knives. A flurry of blows followed. Corleth backpedalled away, skil-fully deflecting the assault.

'So, you know how to handle a sword,' Utarg said. 'Good. Already better than your rival.'

Utarg moved in again, swinging at Corleth's head. Corleth ducked and blocked the secondary blow he knew was coming.

His sword rang with the impact and the shock vibrated up his arm. Such strength and power!

More blows followed, forcing Corleth to give ground. He was being pushed back against the ring of spears that stood proud all around him. He ducked and rolled out of the way, avoiding another swinging lunge from Utarg.

'Very pretty, Fey,' Utarg said, heaving a deep breath. 'But you can't run forever.'

Corleth knew this to be true. Utarg's strength was far greater than his. He could turn the blows from the knives, but he couldn't block them. If he tried he would likely break an arm; that would be the end of him.

And his stamina might be more than I can bear too!

Warily he circled Utarg, stepping sideways as the big man continued to stalk him. Around the pair the other men watched on, their breaths floating upwards in the chill air.

Without warning, Utarg threw one of the knives. Corleth avoided it by less than an inch, lurching to one side. The feint was well timed. Corleth saw the kick coming but couldn't regain his balance in time. The blow caught him in the side, knocking the breath from him and jolting his feet out from underneath him. He crashed on to the sandy floor, dazed and stunned.

The other knife!

It was plunging down towards him. He rolled aside as the point flashed past his vision, impaling itself in the rocky flagstones. He brought his sword up in defence only to have his wrist caught in a grip.

A grip that began to crush his bones. The sword fell from his hands, pain shocked up his forearm and into his shoulder. He kicked out, desperate to free himself. He might as well have kicked one of Midnight's oldest trees. The pain was excruciating.

'The Moonprince will be disappointed,' Utarg said, twisting

Corleth's arm. Through the pain Corleth saw Utarg readying the other knife, ready to strike.

The blade came down. Corleth didn't flinch, but relaxed the arm in Utarg's grip, allowing his full weight to fall forward. Utarg overbalanced and stumbled, releasing Corleth and throwing out his hands to arrest his fall. Corleth leapt aside, grabbing the first knife with his other hand.

It was at Utarg's throat before he could get to his feet.

Corleth took a step forward, the knife point pricking Utarg's skin under the chin.

'I'll have your oath now,' he said.

Utarg went to move, but the knife pressed in further.

'Kill me and you die,' Utarg said. 'My men will see to that.'

'Fail to swear and I will see you branded a coward in all Midnight,' Corleth replied. 'Think not that there is no way for me to send a message to my own kin.'

Utarg stared at him for long moments.

Then he began to laugh. Great peals of laughter shook his mighty frame. Corleth warily backed away, keeping his eyes upon the man as he guffawed upon his back. Corleth picked up his sword, nursing his right hand, it was pulsing with pain.

The laughter subsided.

'I like you, little Fey,' Utarg said, getting to his feet. 'I shall ride to meet your Moonprince as agreed. Luxor, was that his name?'

'It was,' Corleth replied.

'Then I have much to do,' Utarg said. 'An army to assemble.'

'The Moonprince.' Corleth struggled for breath. 'He will be pleased to greet you.'

'I'm sure he will,' Utarg said. 'I heard tell the Fey were cunning and fleet of foot. I will not underestimate them again. You fought well.'

Corleth watched as Utarg performed a bow. Around him the men lowered their spears.

'Would you eat?' Utarg said. 'We have much to talk through.'

Corleth nodded. 'I would.'

Utarg nodded and clapped his hands. The men dispersed.

Utarg waited until they were gone. 'You spoke true of the Witchking,' he said in a lowered voice. 'He has sought me out, he intends to take all the lands as you describe. This emissary … ' Utarg kicked at the body lying on the ground. 'Came yestereve, promising all manner of empty rewards for my loyalty.'

'Luxor will see your lands your own forever should we prevail against the Witchking,' Corleth replied.

Utarg nodded. 'Then let us plan the death and dismemberment of these cursed fiends!'

Corleth staggered under the blow across his back. For a moment he thought Utarg had struck him once again, before he realised it was, perhaps, a hearty thump of comradeship.

An ally hard won!

Morkin woke, confused and bewildered. Light hurt his eyes as he blinked in the brightness. He couldn't remember where he was or what had happened, his mind raced with panic for long moments before he remembered his quest.

Mountains, the chase, the dead Doomguard …

His memory shifted and blurred, there was something else.

The skulkrin!

Morkin sat up and looked about him. Snow fell from his clothing. He was half buried. It was lucky he was wearing his thick leather tunic and furs. If he'd been exposed, he might have died from the cold and never woken up.

No sign of the creature. It had been almost nightfall when he'd met the skulkrin. Now it was dawn. How had he fallen asleep? For how long too? He racked his brain trying to remember.

Fawkrin ... threw something in my face. A powder!

The creature had tricked him, what was it after?

The answer was obvious. Morkin turned to see his backpack lying in the snow behind him. He grabbed it searching through the contents. The map was there, along with his knives and camping equipment.

But food and water ... stolen!

Morkin knew he had to eat a certain amount of food each day. Travelling in the cold of Midnight burnt energy fast. If you didn't eat, you died. It was that simple. Your strength would fail and the cold would take you. Untold numbers of travellers had been lost over hundreds of moons. Everyone knew the danger, you packed provisions for your journey and made sure you never strayed too far from villages and keeps.

But out here.

He pulled out the map, his fingers already chilled.

The nearest village was behind him in the Mountains of Dodrak, but he'd already been there and it had seemed abandoned, plus it was on the wrong side of the mountains. Next was far ahead in the Downs of Mirrow, at least two days hard march away. There was nothing to the south that he could reach, and that would delay his quest intolerably. Lothoril, and the Fey of that realm, were even further north.

If he didn't make the Village of Mirrow, he would die.

Unless ...

The skulkrin had his provisions. Perhaps he could track the creature down and recover them.

How fast can a skulkrin travel?

He didn't know. Without his horse he would have to pursue on foot.

A few minutes of careful investigation showed him the tracks of the skulkrin, the snow had yet to completely cover the small prints. It would not be easy, but it might be his best chance. The footprints led north anyway, in the general direction of Mirrow, so he wouldn't be losing much regardless.

North it is then.

Morkin shivered, but hoisted his lightened backpack and began the trudge through the snow.

Corleth had taken his leave of Utarg after a hearty meal of red meat. There seemed to be little else on offer. The Fey typically ate sparingly of such fare, preferring fruits and vegetables where possible, but the harsh environment of Midnight dictated that sufficient food had to be consumed to survive.

Utarg's forces would ride to Dawn. An army of one thousand riders astride huge shaggy horses. They were not the fleet and elegant chargers favoured by the Fey and the Free, but they were tough draught beasts, sturdy and dependable, able to withstand whatever the weather of Midnight might throw at them. Corleth thought how alike the men and beasts of Targ were.

Utarg would march south upon the following morning, aiming to join the defence of Dawn in time to halt the advance of the Witchking's forces from the west.

With Marakith, Kumar, Athoril and Utarg, perhaps Luxor can stem the tide at Dawn …

Now Corleth's own attention turned south. He had another recruit in mind, this time one of his own people, the Lord of Dregrim.

Dregrim was a forest on the far eastern borders of the realm of Midnight, perhaps the biggest of the forests of the Fey, though of less importance than the Forest of Dreams to the far north. Of Dregrim himself, Corleth knew little, he had never met him. Lord Thrall had said little of him either. In the hierarchy of the Fey, Dregrim was subservient to Dreams.

Utarg's keep had long since disappeared to the North as Corleth rode swiftly in the other direction. He reached the eaves of the Forest of Dregrim by nightfall, but both he and his horse were weary after the long ride. Corleth, rather to his surprise, saw no scouts or signs of habitation. He thought the borders of the Fey's realm would be watched closely, but he could detect nothing.

The darkness came and went without incident. As dawn broke Corleth resumed his journey south, pushing into the shade of the forest.

It was unlike any other forest Corleth had ridden in before, in fact riding soon became impossible. He scouted around for an hour without finding a path. The undergrowth and vegetation were thick and obstructive. Even to his Feyish instincts the way was difficult, for the Free or the Foul it would have been impassable. Even the Forest of Shadows had not been so unwelcoming at the outset. The going was slow and he made only a few leagues by the time the faint light of the sun reached its zenith.

Utarg had advised him that the Citadel of Dregrim was directly south as the wyvern flew, but within the tangled mess of the forest it was easy to lose direction. More than once Corleth found he had to retreat and try a new route, finding the forest itself seemed intent on confounding his movement. His return route north was never impeded, nor his attempts to strike east or west, but when he turned south once more brambles, thorns and barbs erupted in his path as if summoned against him.

Less than three hours of the day remained. He stopped to rest, weariness overcoming him. His sword had been dull by constant hacking through unforgiving undergrowth. Trying to force a path for both himself and his horse was impossible. Leaning against a thick tree he considered his options.

He hadn't come far enough. At his rate of progress thus far it might be days before he could reach the Citadel, days he could ill afford to lose. Dawn might already be under attack. With luck some of the Fey might have responded to Thrall's messages in time. Either he had to turn aside now, or strike on.

With the forest not set against him, he might ride to Dawn in a couple of days, but that would forfeit the Fey of Dregrim. Corleth didn't know their exact strength, but a Citadel and a realm such as this required hundreds if not thousands of men at arms, strength that would be of much assistance in the battle of the Witchking.

We need them! Yet why is this accursed forest set against me?

There could be only one answer. Dregrim did not desire visitors.

He could feel a strange taint to the forest, which preyed upon his mind. It was Feyish for sure, but not in a manner with which he was familiar. It was dark and unsettling. He almost fancied that enchantments were upon the very trees about him, whispering tales of the Fey from long ago, before they had come to the lands of Midnight.

So long ago.

The Fey of Midnight were united for the most part, but it had not always been thus. The Fey had not originated here, but far to the south in the lost warm climes of the Bloodmarch. Oldest were the Dawn Fey, pure of heart, strong of limb and long of life. It was they that had first tamed the forests of the world. But strife had beset them, fracturing the Fey into their own fiefdoms. So were born the Golden Fey, isolated on the isle of Immiel; the High Fey of the west, masters of the fire …

And the Dark Fey …

Corleth shivered. The old songs told tales of the Dark Fey, how their power and lust for domination caused strife and misery for the lands of the Bloodmarch. None of the Fey of

Midnight knew what had transpired in the rolling years that had passed since Midnight had been locked away within the Frozen Wastes.

And it seems that their influence may yet be at work here.

Corleth took a sigh and shook his head. Lord Dregrim was no Dark Fey, but he might take the view that any power was worth using in defence of his home. It was clear that he desired to be left alone, cut off from the rest of Midnight.

But he has no choice, he must hear the summons of the Moonprince.

He made up his mind, he would go on. Reluctantly he dismissed his horse, muttering gentle words of comfort to it while shooing it away. Here it would be a hindrance he could do without. After taking a bite to eat and a gulp of water, he pressed on, pushing through the dark eaves of the forest.

Morkin had struck out northwards across the Plains of Ogrim in pursuit of Fawkrin. The weather stayed fine for the most part, despite a northerly breeze, but it was not strong enough to wipe away the faint footprints of his quarry.

The skulkrin seemed to be travelling just as quickly as he. Morkin had hoped to catch up with the creature within the day, but these hopes were soon dashed when he realised the trail he was following was getting no fresher as he progressed. Weary hours of toil lay behind him and the footprints were the same as ever, with the distant Downs of Mirrow seemingly no closer at all.

To the west he could see another mountain range jutting up out of the mist, the map had it listed as 'Toomog', but it mattered little to him. Ahead one of the mysterious Liths could be seen, and, some way beyond it, the ruin of a fort of some kind. Both looked lifeless and uninviting.

The trail was veering west though. It seemed the skulkrin was making for the Lith, perhaps using it as a waymarker.

Perhaps he will rest there, it might be a chance for me to catch up. He might suspect, but he can't know I'm following.

Thus emboldened, Morkin quickened his pace.

Corleth sensed them before he saw them, but they were accomplished hunters and they had him surrounded before he could even think about escape. He stopped, holding up his hands. Fey, clad in dark green apparel, emerged from the wooded gloom of the trees, bowstrings taut about him, arrows poised to fly.

One stepped quickly up to him, taking his sword, knives and bow before pulling his backpack off and casting it upon the ground.

'Your name, trespasser.'

'I am Corleth, of the Thrall Fey.'

'And what business have you in our realm?'

'My business is with the Lord of Dregrim,' Corleth said. 'Not his guards.'

It was the wrong answer. Corleth heard bowstrings tighten further.

'If you were not Fey, and your people known to us of old,' the guard said. 'You would already be slain. Our Lord requires all to state their business on pain of death.'

'Your welcome in my realm would be much the warmer,' Corleth answered. 'We have not forgotten the customary hospitality of the Fey. My business concerns matters only for the ears of your Lord. I have not been entrusted with missives I can bandy with those unknown to me. Now, slay me, if you will, or take me to Lord Dregrim!'

The guard before him hesitated for a moment, staring hard at Corleth.

'My apologies,' he said. 'It is not my place to question you, but our Lord has given orders that all must be restrained upon entering our domain.'

'Why so?'

The guard shrugged. 'We do not know. You come from the lands beyond our realm. What news of Midnight?'

Corleth sighed. 'News is woeful indeed. The Witchking has exerted his might and both the Free and Fey recoil before him. I come seeking help from my Fey kindred.'

The guard pursed his lips.

'I fear you will receive little from us,' he said. 'We are forbidden from leaving or travelling beyond the borders of the forest. You would be best advised to turn back now.'

'I must speak to your Lord,' Corleth insisted.

'Very well,' the guard said. 'You cannot approach the Citadel unescorted, nor take knowledge of our paths away with you.'

They are terrified!

'Bind him,' the guard called.

Corleth's arms were pulled behind his back and secured. Then a bandage was tied across his eyes.

Tarithel rode within the borders of the Forest of Dreams. Despite her worst fears the forest seemed still at ease. The destruction she had seen to the west a memory here, not a reality. The forest felt warm and wholesome, unusually so, even for these well tended lands.

Earlier, she had crossed the strange line of Liths that marked the south western corner of her father's realm. She had crossed it before, but the snow had been thick and she'd not been able to see much. This time, with clearer weather, the strange architecture of the place was clear to see; twin lines of the ancient stone monuments running from the north west to the south east. It was clear that there was some purpose to it all, but what it might be she couldn't guess.

She felt a strange call, a wish to follow the obvious pathway, but she knew from the maps that it didn't go anywhere particular. Perhaps once there had been a reason for it all, but it was now lost to living memory.

She heard birds upon the air, looking up in surprise to see them perched in the higher branches of the trees.

Yet, it is just past the Solstice, the heart of winter! How can they be here?

A strange brightness grew ahead. Curious she urged her horse in that direction and after a few moments they trotted into a glade. She looked about herself in wonderment. The glade was free from snow, green and lush and edged with wild flowers of all types. Above, the sun peeked out from behind the clouds; she could feel its warmth, wholesome and strong in a way she had never felt before.

What is this?

She stopped at the threshold, dismounting and looking around. She knelt down, feeling strong thick grass under the palms of her hands, coated in just the finest film of dew. The smell of pollen was upon the air. Birds clustered around the boughs of the trees above. She could see a small lake towards the centre of the glade, around which were deer, rabbits and other creatures of the forest seldom seen in winter.

Cautiously she made her way forward, leading her horse by its reins, walking through tall grasses and flowers that reached to her waist. The lake opened out before her and she stood upon the shore, looking out across lily pads and rushes. She could see ducks and the ripples left by fish in the water. She gasped in pure delight at the air of colours and warmth about her.

Some pocket of the forest kept clear of the curse of winter, why has no one spoken of this before ...?

'Because none have ever seen it before, Tarithel, Lady of the Forest.'

She turned at the sound of a man's voice, her hands grasping at the knives secured in her belt, swiftly pulling them out and standing in a defensive posture.

She caught sight of a man standing just along the shoreline. Where had he come from? Had he been there all the time? Impossible! She had been watching carefully.

And how does he know my name …?

'Who … who are you?' she managed.

'A friend,' he replied, with a smile. 'You have nothing to fear from me.'

'How do you know my name?'

'I know a great many things,' he answered.

Tarithel studied him for a moment. He was tall in the manner of men, with the dress and appearance of one of the Lords of Midnight. Yet he was none that she recognised from the catalogues and tapestries in the Citadel of Dreams.

He was sitting on a tree stump, overlooking the lake, peering into the fine mist that hovered above it.

'You are a trespasser in my father's lands,' Tarithel said. 'Tell me who you are?'

'Your father's lands?' the man replied with a chuckle. 'I suppose I am a trespasser. Though your father would have no lands if it weren't for me.'

Tarithel frowned. 'My father has lived here for many lives of men, and his fathers before him. Our line is long, long indeed in the reckoning of men.'

This seemed to amuse the man further, eliciting a laugh. There seemed little harm to him. Tarithel replaced her knives into her belt.

'So strange, to meet those you have …' He stopped as if thinking through what he wanted to say.

'I would still have your name!' Tarithel called.

The man nodded. 'I have many names, but here and now you may call me Midwinter, for I am its Lord.'

'Lord Midwinter?' Tarithel queried. 'I have never heard of such a Lord. Where is your keep or citadel?'

Midwinter looked at her. 'It lies … in another realm than this.'

Tarithel gasped. 'Beyond the Frozen Wastes?'

Midwinter nodded. 'The hard edge of Midnight? Ah yes, far beyond those.'

'And what are you doing here, in my father's lands? And how do you know my name? And how have you done …?' Tarithel gestured around her at the spring-like glade. 'All this?'

'So many questions!' Midwinter replied. 'I had no idea you'd be so inquisitive, young lady!'

Tarithel frowned. There was a strange otherworldly quality to the way he spoke. His accent was peculiar, softer and more melodious than those of the Free she had encountered. She sensed no ill intent, but she stayed a safe distance away.

'Answers will satisfy me,' she replied.

'I am here to seek the safety of Midnight,' he said. 'These lands … they are important to me.' Tarithel watched as he looked around the glade. His expression was peculiar; she picked up a sense of care, pride and love for what he saw, a strange impression of ownership and responsibility. He looked at her with a grin. 'Yes, I love these lands, they are dear to me. I would see the wrongs righted and Midnight restored to its original beauty.'

Before she had a chance to think that over he spoke again.

'And as for you, Lady of the Forest,' he said. 'I have known of you for many years.'

'How?' Tarithel demanded. 'We have never met!'

'I cannot say,' Midwinter replied. 'You have met dear Rorthron – this I know. He speaks wisdom. You will meet others of no less import in the coming days. Much hardship lies ahead of you, but your part in all this will become clear. Have faith in yourself. You have strength within that you do not yet realise.'

Tarithel frowned, not liking the answer. 'Hardships? What do you mean?'

'I have said enough,' Midwinter replied. 'Perhaps too much already. I wished to gaze upon Midnight one last time.'

Tarithel shook her head. 'I don't understand, what do you mean … one last time?'

Midwinter turned his head. 'I cannot tarry here. Other realms call me. Other stories, other lands … so much to do …'

Tarithel followed his gaze out across the lake, wondering what he was looking for. His gaze fell on her and he smiled.

'You must not delay,' he said. 'Your home has need of you.'

'But, this glade … I want to understand …'

'You will, but not now,' he replied. 'There is much for you to learn. This glade is the merest glimpse of how this land was supposed to be. Through your works, and those of others it can be restored. That is my desire.'

'You speak in riddles …'

'I know, but there is much I cannot tell you,' he answered. 'But you are Lady of the Forest, claim that right, seek your inheritance. You are precious to this land and the forest will be your ally in the days and moons ahead.'

'Lady of the Forest … it is just a title of the Fey, given on the eve of the Solstice to …'

Midwinter shook his head. 'No, it is more than that …' the thought seemed to amuse him. 'So much more …'

Tarithel watched as Midwinter got up and walked towards her. She felt no fear, but rather a strange reassurance. She trusted him implicitly, without doubt, without second thought. Much later she sought to explain why, but she never could.

He stroked the horse she had ridden in on.

'A good steed,' he said and then looked at her. 'It is time for you to return to your home.'

Tarithel stared deep into his eyes. She got a sense of something ageless, timeless and unfathomably deep about the gaze he returned. She could not resist, but nodded and mounted her horse, pulling the reins to her in readiness.

'When in doubt,' he said. 'Seek the Liths. Much purpose they still have. They will answer.'

The Liths? The Stones?

She turned in the saddle. A sudden sadness crept across her like a damp veil.

'I won't see you again, will I?'

He shook his head. Tears sprang into her eyes. An awful sense of loss, of conversations started yet unfinished, stories that might have been told but never would be, of humour and mirth that could never be shared again. She shook with a grief she could not explain.

'But I will always be here for those that remember Midnight,' he said.

He patted her horse's rump and it began to trot away.

'Farewell Tarithel, Lady of the Forest.'

The horse reached the edge of the glade, the birdsong faded. She shivered in the sudden cold as the snow and ice closed about her once more. The sunlight faded into gloom and the familiar dreariness of the forest was all around once more.

She turned to look behind her.

Of the glade and of the Lord Midwinter, there was no sign.

Did I dream this? A pleasant one if so …

The Lith towered into the sky above, its sheer stone sides mysteriously bare of snow and ice. Morkin had seen this phenomenon before and always wondered about it, but he'd never found a satisfactory answer. The snow and ice didn't melt on the Liths, it merely seemed to avoid them. They were dry and slightly warm to the touch.

Morkin reached the standing stones by noon, and quickly scouted around them. He could see no sign of Fawkrin. Worse still, the tracks led up to the stones, but, try as he might, he could find none leading away. The wind was blowing fiercely now, snow slowly beginning to drift across the icy landscape as he searched. The footprints were lost to him.

He climbed the stones to get a better view of the landscape in hopes of seeing the elusive skulkrin, but he could not see any sign of habitation in any direction.

At least the downs look a little closer now.

A gale was rising, it would do no use to venture out on the plains if the snow was drifting. As he watched the clouds were building. Before long, snow came plummeting out of the heavens, thick and cold. No one walked when the winds were high. He was already tired and in need of a rest. On cue, his stomach rumbled. He could feel the cold seeping into his bones despite his clothing.

And no food. This breaks every law of traipsing in the wilderness. But that skulkrin is out there somewhere, caught in the blizzard.

He crouched in the lee of the stones and took out the map once more. As best he could determine the downs were about two leagues away, with the village perhaps another three beyond. He would make the downs, but an uncomfortable night awaited him. Without provisions the death-like grip of the cold would be stalking him closely. Walking kept you warm, but it burnt energy ferociously. Sitting still conserved that same energy, but then the cold would take you. He had to survive.

Will I reach the village? Or will cold or hunger, or even both, take me first?

The last few of the Doomguard warriors lay dying on the ground before them. Few of the Free had fallen in the battle and the army had made good account of itself.

'Another victory!' Athoril said, wiping his sword before sheathing it.

Kumar grimaced. 'The Witchking does not seek to defeat us, merely to slow our progress south.'

Marakith nodded. 'We are forced to engage with them every other league. They are harrying us, delaying us. If we do not make a good distance today we will not reach Dawn in time.'

Kumar nodded.

'The Witchking is more than aware of what we are trying to do,' he said. 'We must push on with all possible haste, or we will be too late to make a difference and there is something else afoot too …'

Marakith glanced at him.

'What do you mean?'

Kumar gestured to tracks on the ground.

'Not all of these belong to the Doomguard, nor our men. Another army has made its way through during the cover of darkness.'

'Another?' Athoril asked. 'Who?'

Kumar studied the tracks further. 'Who else? There is only one other power in these parts.'

Athoril's face blanched. 'Utarg?'

Kumar nodded. 'Either he moves of his own accord, or our Fey friend has sent him this way.'

'He has moved at speed then,' Athoril said.

'And unopposed by the Doomguard,' Marakith said, his voice low.

'What does it mean?'

'It means we must reach Dawn all the sooner,' Kumar muttered, 'I do not trust the Utarg. That he reaches Dawn ahead of us does not fill me with joy. Let us move out with haste.'

Marakith nodded and gave instructions to the runners nearby. Flags were hoisted and the message sent forth.

'Let us hope for better luck this dawn.'

Corleth was led for perhaps a league or more by his own count of footfalls. A breeze ruffled his hair, they must have come to some open space within the forest. The bandage was removed and he blinked in the bright light. He had a brief moment to take in the sight of a lofty and elegant building set in the midst of what once must have been elegantly manicured gardens, now frozen in ice and snow awaiting a spring that might never come.

The building rose up above the level of the forest canopy into a series of spires decorated with magenta banners, with a golden lion and a cyan eagle emblazoned upon them. Only one coat of arms was mightier in the reckoning of the Fey, that of the Lord of Dreams himself.

A firm shove in the back propelled him forwards. A pebbled path, well tended and swept clear of snow, led up to the entrance of the Citadel. The guards escorted him to the entrance and the gates ahead swung back at an unseen command. Corleth walked through the gatehouse. The Fey guards stationed on either side watched him suspiciously, not venturing a single word.

There is fear here, that they will not welcome a distant cousin of their own ...

One of his captors walked forward a few paces to talk to another guard stationed within. The conversation was brief, but Corleth could not hear the words spoken. Both turned and gave him a look before they nodded and his captor returned.

'You are fortunate indeed,' his captor said. 'Lord Dregrim has deigned to see you. Speak well and wisely is my advice. I wish you luck.'

Corleth was escorted by two guards up a spiral staircase, lit by torches at intervals. On the next floor he found himself in a hall decorated with greenery cut from the forest. Somehow plants and trees had been encouraged to grow within the structure of the building. He could see that some masterwork of the Fey had been crafted in the construction, the building had been put together around existing trees and cunningly worked into their own living strength. He would have liked to have seen more of it.

Ahead though was a figure that commanded his attention. Corleth's bounds were released and the guards stepped back against the wall behind him.

'Corleth of the Thrall Fey, so I hear,' a voice intoned, deep and sepulchral. 'Come hither.'

Corleth hadn't expected such an old voice. The Fey were long-lived, that was no secret, but here was one that had seen many more moons than he.

Corleth walked forwards and bowed in the customary manner.

'You may rise.'

Corleth looked up into a lined and drawn face. Dregrim was old, even to look at. In the reckoning of the Fey that meant his time within Midnight might be measured in a long counts of moons, perhaps even back to the long summer of legend.

'I regret our welcome is not as it once was,' Dregrim said. 'But these are evil times and our borders are closed. Closed to all.'

'It was not my intention to trespass,' Corleth answered. 'But I ...'

'Bring missives from afar,' Dregrim answered for him. 'Tidings of woe, of war and pestilence. This I know.'

'Then you can anticipate my request,' Corleth said. 'I am sent by the Moonprince himself to gather under one banner all those who would resist the march of the Witchking.'

Dregrim looked at him for a long moment before chuckling. 'You would have us swear allegiance to a childish lord of the Free bearing a trinket of the Wise? I know well the tales of the House of the Moon. They were vanquished before by the might of the Witchking or the folly of the Wise, perhaps both. They will succumb once more.'

'Lord Luxor bears no trinket,' Corleth replied. 'He has with him the Moon Ring, last of the War Rings of Midnight.'

'Such rings did his sires have of old,' Dregrim replied. 'And it availed them not. This Luxor is doomed, doomed to fight a hopeless battle. The Lords of the Free are perishing, their end long foretold.'

Corleth shook his head. 'No, I will not accept that.'

Dregrim shrugged. 'It is already certain. The Free unleashed this woe upon themselves by their fawning subservience to Lord Ushgarak, proclaiming him King of Midnight. Their pride and arrogance led to the rise of Gryfallon. Now they reap the whirlwind they provoked.'

'The Witchking will not stop with the Free,' Corleth said. 'The Doomguard have already despoiled the realms of the Fey to the west, they will do the same here in time. If we do not join forces with the Free we will all be overrun.'

Dregrim shook his head. 'The great forests of the Fey retain a greater power than do the poor thickets and rotten woodlands of the west. Our powers are not in decline. We are quite safe from the Witchking's foul hordes here. None can enter without our permission.'

'The Witchking's power waxes,' Corleth said. 'I have seen it. The ice-fear is rising, I have seen it take on form and penetrate the woodlands, wresting our own defences apart.'

'Then you have perceived incorrectly,' Dregrim replied. 'You are young, Corleth of the Thrall Fey, and have much left to learn. The High Lords of the Fey have seen such battles before, seen the futility of any allegiance with the Free. Despatch one darkness and another will replace it in a short span of moons. The Witchking has no quarrel with the Fey unless we thwart his plans. Dreams and I are in agreement. The Fey will not march upon the Witchking.'

'Then you doom the Free to extermination,' Corleth whispered.

'Their time is at an end,' Dregrim replied. 'There is no future in resisting the Witchking. They should sue for peace.'

'Peace! With the Witchking?' Corleth shook his head. 'If you will not heed the call to arms I will seek others that will. Whispers, Thimrath …'

Dregrim shook his head. 'That is not the will of the High Lords of the Fey. We will not join the fight against the Witchking, in return he will leave us be.'

'He will come for us,' Corleth retorted. 'Once he has finished destroying the Free he will come for us. He seeks dominion over all Midnight, he will not tolerate anything else. The future of the Fey …'

'The future of the Fey is the responsibility of the Lord of Dreams and I will not see his will thwarted in this,' Dregrim replied. 'His instructions are clear. The wisdom of ages will prevail over the idle fancies of youth. We will not see the Fey cast on an altar of sacrifice in a vain attempt to save the men of the Free.'

Corleth took a deep breath and straightened.

'Then I will take my leave of you and seek allies elsewhere.'

He bowed and turned, striding away. As he approached the doorway to the staircase the two guards blocked his exit.

Corleth paused and turned back to Dregrim.

'You should remain here, Corleth of the Thrall Fey,' Dregrim said. 'It is not safe to travel beyond the borders of the forest.'

'I must go,' Corleth insisted. 'Luxor will require my assistance, even if the rest of the Fey will not come to his aid.'

'You should remain here,' Dregrim repeated, giving a brief gesture.

The two guards moved forward.

'A prisoner?' Corleth asked.

'A guest,' Dregrim said, with a nod.

'Tell me,' Corleth said. 'When did the High Lords of the Fey decide that cowardice and fear were the hallmarks of our people?'

A muscle twitched in Dregrim's face.

'You are a fool, Corleth of the Thrall Fey,' he replied. 'You know nothing of the world at large. The darkness is not something you can destroy, it is something you must embrace and contain. There is a balance and it swings hither and thither. The Fey of old knew this, but they insisted in indulging in moral stances, fracturing our people and throwing our old kingdoms into disarray. There is always evil in the world, even amongst the Fey.'

Corleth frowned. 'Evil?'

Dregrim laughed. 'The Fey are no different. We are not blessed with all grace and beauty. Our darker sides are just as prevalent as those in the Free or the Foul, perhaps even more so. Evil is part of our nature too. We cannot suppress it. Here in Midnight we must stand together and not let the ebb and flow tear us apart. Sometimes good prospers, sometimes evil. This is the way of life, it is folly to resist it.'

Corleth shook his head. 'No, evil must be resisted, or it will take us all!'

'You are wrong.' Dregrim dismissed him with a wave of his hand and the guards stepped forward. 'But you will have plenty of time to learn. Take him away!'

Chapter Twelve

They stand at the Citadel of Dawn,
looking north to the Downs of Dawn.

'There!'

Shimeril's eyesight had not failed him. The faint light of torches could be seen sparkling against the far horizon.

'They're venturing around the Downs,' Dawn said, squinting into the gathering gloom as night fell. 'Probably using the caverns to the north as cover.'

'A night attack then,' Blood muttered. 'Oft they prefer the cover of darkness for their foul works.'

'Day or night they are coming,' Luxor said. 'Scouts?'

'Many did not return,' Dawn said. 'Those who did report a mighty host, tens of thousands, machines of war, but they have travelled far more swiftly than expected.'

The Lords shifted uneasily at the news.

'And our strength?' Luxor asked.

'All are ready for battle,' Blood reported. 'And the citadel is prepared for war as best it can be.'

'We are still sore outnumbered,' Dawn said. 'The Witchking's hordes ...'

'Will go no further,' Luxor said. 'He has come this far into our realms and we will halt his advance.'

'Is there news of Marakith and Kumar?' Shimeril asked.

'They make slow progress,' Luxor said with a heavy sigh. 'They still engage with smaller armies of the Doomguard.

The Witchking throws doggerel in their path to delay them. Another day at least.'

'They will find it hard to break a siege from outside,' Blood observed. 'Worse still they may find themselves exposed to attack by the Witchking's forces. Holed up here, we will not be able to come to their aid.'

'Both are seasoned warriors,' Shimeril said. 'They will not be rash.'

'Dare we ask of the Fey?' Dawn said. 'Will they not stand with us in our time of need?'

'Messengers have been sent,' Luxor replied. 'But none have yet sworn any loyalty to me it seems. I do not perceive them via the ring. The Fey will not help us here at Dawn, alas.'

'The might of the Free will have to see us through then,' Blood said. 'As it has always done. Less of this gloomy talk. Our men are worth two of the enemy, we have strong walls and provisions enough to withstand a siege. Let them come and batter themselves weary against our fortifications!'

'Our strategy then,' Luxor said. 'We defend Dawn. If this citadel falls all the roads to the south are open and exposed. The Witchking will march on Xajorkith.'

They watched for an hour, seeing the armies of the Foul grow in number, frustrated that there was nothing they could do to prevent it.

The torches were brighter now, held high aloft by the warriors as they marched. The glow of them was spreading out on the plains before the citadel, widening in an ever increasing arc.

Around the Lords of Midnight the ice-fear gripped once more, almost a tangible grasp, clutching at their hearts. Once more Luxor raised the Moon Ring to send forth the warmth of his mind, grimacing with the effort, his forehead creased.

The sounds of horns echoed faintly from the mountains behind the citadel, deep and intimidating. Warriors were stationed on the walkways atop the walls, with every loophole manned by archers. Further ranks of bowmen were stationed below in ordered formations, ready to unleash their weapons into deadly arcs over and above the walls.

Now the heavy thump of booted feet marching in unison echoed across the plains. The army of the Witchking continued to spread before them, hidden in the darkness, only revealed by the light of the fires burning. Horns blared loudly now and the ugly cries of the Foul reached their ears.

'Will they not treat?' Dawn asked, staring at the gathered hordes in dismay.

The others turned to look at him. Luxor took pity on him.

'This is no war of politics my friend,' he said. 'The Witchking means to smite us all, utterly vanquish the Free and all we stand for. We fight for our survival. They will show no mercy, neither must we.'

Snow began to fall, obscuring the furthest reaches of the Doomguard army, but its size and strength were impossible to ignore.

At some unspoken command the noise of the approaching army stopped. A hush fell upon the attackers and defenders, there was no sound other than the wind whipping past the high towers of the citadel, fluttering the banners.

Then, far below, the fires grew brighter; spreading, becoming pairs and then doubling again and again.

'Arrows,' Blood called. 'Shields!'

The defenders on the walls and those far below in the courtyard raised shields. Luxor looked on in horror as streaks of flame lit the darkness from beyond the citadel. They arced far into the sky, silent and majestic, yet deadly. The lights arced back down, the sound of their passing ripping the air asunder. Flaming arrows embedded themselves in shields with heavy thuds, knocking some of his warriors down. Some shields were even penetrated completely. A few warriors were unlucky, with arrows finding the gaps in their defences. Luxor saw two of the guards upon the walls yell out and tumble from their positions.

'First archers! Return! Loose!' Blood yelled, his voice carrying across the citadel and echoing all about.

The archers of the Citadel, Dawn's own people, returned the attack, hundreds of flaming brands took to the air, just clearing the walls and then slamming down on to the hordes of the Foul before the walls.

The battle had begun.

Crossbow bolts scattered across the stone of the walls, striking down more of the defenders. The Foul were close now, running quickly across the plain before the Citadel. More fires could be seen behind them, larger now. As Luxor watched, huge flaming balls abruptly took to the air and swarmed towards the Citadel in a coordinated strike.

'Trebuchet!' Shimeril yelled as the fire descended.

Flaming pitch splashed into the walls, across the walkways and into the courtyard. Some poor souls were incinerated on contact, others fell, screaming, consumed by the flames. Luxor could see men running to and fro, trying to douse the fire.

The main gates rocked with blasts of fire directed at them, smoke rose, dark and evil smelling, causing men to cough and splutter.

Then rocky debris showered about the defenders. Huge pitons had jammed into the solid walls beneath them, dragging chains from somewhere far below. As the Lords of Midnight watched in horror, metal ladders were hoist into the air, many with the Foul clinging to them.

'Ladders! Defend the walls!'

As one the defenders of Dawn drew their swords. Amidst a hail of arrows the Foul came on, clambering up the ladders and vaulting into the ranks of the Free, hacking and slashing with dark metalled swords already slick with blood. Luxor found himself face to face with a ghastly beast of a man with a sword notched and dented. A swing knocked him back and he was forced to use all his skill to defend himself. The man roared incomprehensibly and came on, wielding his sword like a bludgeoning cudgel, striking down all before him. Luxor timed a swing and then thrust forward as the invader's swing went wide. The beast fell, cursing in some evil tongue, then crunched into the courtyard below.

The Foul attack as if they are possessed! No reason, just mindless savagery!

More arrows pierced the darkness, the screams of the injured and the dying rent the air. Within minutes it was clear the outer walls were being lost and the defenders pushed back. Luxor could see Gard, Blood and Shimeril leading vanguards of their men forward in an attempt to hold station. Of Dawn there was no sign.

Then, with a rumble of collapsing timbers and a spray of sparks, the gate in the main wall burst inwards. A huge roar went up from the Foul.

Blood was pointing downwards into the courtyard. The Foul were coming in like a flood, swords and axes raised, striking about them with abandonment. Ranks of archers fired into them, piling dead upon dead, but still they came on. Silence and her band of warriors were fighting to defend the archers, but the sheer number of the foe were beating them back.

'We'll be outflanked!' Blood yelled. Luxor nodded.

'Fall back! Fall back!'

The defenders abandoned the walls, retreating to either side of the courtyard, reinforcing the lines of archers.

Then, from behind the archers, riders issued forth. Dawn had rallied his men, and their fair white steeds rode upon the massing ranks of the Foul. Swords slashed down, dark blood flew. Blood, Gard and Shimeril sounded their horns and the armies of the Free came about as one.

Archers and swordsmen flanked the riders, and the Free marched forward methodically, pushing back the Foul, littering the ground with their bodies. Archers crouched in the shelter of the Free army, picking off the invaders on the walls.

The Foul advance faltered and began to ebb. Deep horns echoed in the darkness beyond the citadel. The men of the Free looked about themselves and then pressed their advantage.

'Have at them!'

The horns of the Free blared all the louder. The Foul turned and fled, routed from the courtyard as the riders pursued them to the gate. The attackers on the walls grew fewer in number and retreated as swiftly as they were slain.

'Victory goes to the Free!' Dawn yelled, as he rode his blood splattered steed up to the other Lords.

'They've retreated,' Blood said, eyeing the now empty threshold of the walls and the smouldering debris of the main gate with suspicion. 'But why?'

Shimeril was uncomfortable too. 'They had merely to push their advantage and they would have had us.'

Luxor climbed the stone steps to the walls of the citadel. Bodies lay everywhere, Free and Foul alike. The army of the Foul could be seen by the light of their torches in the distance. A retreat for sure, but were they merely biding their time?

'What can you see?' Shimeril demanded.

'They stand half a league away,' Luxor yelled back. 'They wait for something. There's ...'

To the right, more torches could be seen, rising and falling in a swift and regular rhythm, banners just visible in the glow.

Another army!

'An army approaches from the east!' Luxor called. 'I cannot yet see their banners. The ring tells me nothing ...'

Luxor vaulted back down to the courtyard to stand with the others.

'Who can it be?' Silence demanded. 'Friend or foe?'

'Kumar, Marakith and Athoril,' Dawn said. 'Surely it must be them. Why else would the Witchking's forces retreat? They fear an attack on two flanks and have realised they cannot stand against the might of the Free.'

Luxor shook his head. 'It is not our friends. Not yet. They stand more than a day's march east, delayed by other armies of the Witchking.'

'Kumar and our allies would not have marched through the night,' Morning said, speaking for the first time. He was a quiet fellow for the most part, with a nervous stance and abrupt manner.

'Then who can it be?' Luxor asked. 'Let us find out.'

Surrounded by their defenders, the Lords of Midnight walked out through the shattered gates of the citadel. Before them the slain figures of the Foul lay all about, with fires burning here and there, thick plumes of smoke drifting up into the blank dark sky.

The army of the Foul could still be seen, now perhaps a full league away, but their attention was turned to the east where another army swiftly moved towards them. The sound of galloping hooves reached their ears and before a minute had passed the army was swinging around in front of the citadel.

Luxor, Dawn, Blood, Shimeril, Morning and Silence stood with weapons poised as the line of riders formed up. The horses were huge, bigger than even the war chargers of Midnight. Atop them rode massive men clad in furs and leather. One rode forward, a huge beast of a man with an axe strapped across his back.

'Who is this?' Luxor demanded.

Dawn swallowed. 'This is Utarg of Utarg. A barbarian from the plains to the far east and south of Kumar.

Luxor stepped forward. 'I will treat with him.'

Dawn raised a hand. 'Allow me, Moonprince. I have had

some small dealings with him in the past. He is a fearsome opponent, but if he would align himself with us …'

Luxor nodded.

Dawn walked forward until he stood a few feet from the enormous horse upon which Utarg sat.

'Welcome Utarg of Utarg,' Dawn said. 'We have not seen you in these parts for many a moon.'

Utarg regarded Dawn for a moment without saying anything. Then he climbed down from his horse and strode forward. His height and girth were impressive. Dawn had to look up at him, his head coming only to the bigger man's shoulders.

'I had emissaries,' Utarg said, his gruff voice echoing off the citadel walls. 'Tales of woe and rewards for loyalty offered.'

'Emissaries?' Dawn asked.

'One Corleth of the Fey,' Utarg said. 'With a tall tale of a Moonprince and a call to arms. Another from the halls of the Witchking himself.'

Luxor stepped forward.

Corleth has sent an ally?

'I am the Moonprince,' Luxor called out. 'And you speak of my friend, Corleth of the Thrall Fey.'

'A warrior worthy of his mettle,' Utarg said, looking across at him. 'He promised me my lands in perpetuity, Moonprince. And that you would honour that agreement. Is this so? The realm of the Targ, undisputed?'

Kumar, Marakith and Athoril have claims on those lands. Athoril most of all for crimes in the past. But they are not here, and we sorely need the help!

Luxor pondered the matter for a moment.

'Whatever my servant Corleth has promised in exchange for your loyalty,' Luxor said. 'This I will see done.'

Utarg nodded.

'Fair words indeed from the Free,' he called back. 'But

290

promises are easily spoken and easier to break. What guarantee can you give me of your intentions?'

'You have my word,' Luxor returned.

'The Moonprince is beyond reproach,' Dawn said. 'His word is sacrosanct.'

'I have no reason to doubt his word,' Utarg replied. 'Yet he asks much. The Witchking's hordes lie beyond. They are powerful. Standing with you might be folly.'

'Folly or not,' Luxor replied. 'We will fight the evil of the Witchking and stand against his domination of Midnight. Will you stand to see your lands returned to you, Utarg? I will guarantee it.'

'A generous offer,' Utarg said, bring his axe around. He placed it before him handle down in the snow, leaning upon the head.

'Then you will swear loyalty to the Moonprince,' Dawn instructed.

Utarg smiled and nodded.

'No.'

With a swift move that belied his size, the horrified onlookers saw the axe hoisted and swung with terrifying power and speed. Dawn managed to bring his own sword up in defence, but it was a futile move. The axe crashed downwards, shattering the sword into glittering fragments before striking down.

Dawn was cut down, his body hewn in two from shoulder to opposite thigh.

The onlookers staggered back in horror. The ice-fear rose up around them, causing the warriors of the Free to flinch and cry out as the ethereal dread rolled over them. Luxor gasped in pain as the Moon Ring burnt hot on his finger.

Utarg stood over the bloodied body of the Lord of Dawn, raising the bloodstained axe in both hands.

'Your answer, Moonprince,' Utarg said with a grin. 'The

Witchking guarantees my lands too, and more besides. Starting with those you stand upon now. Vacate the citadel, or our forces will scour every last one of you from within its walls. You have an hour.'

Utarg leapt back upon his steed, turned the mighty horse and his army came about and retreated into the darkness.

Tarithel rode into the Citadel of Dreams having ridden all day, trying to hide her astonishment at the indifference to her return. She had been fully two days away, and yet somehow Rorthron's magic had taken her back to the same day. She was left unchallenged. The sun was setting once again, but to all intents and purposes she had not been away at all. She half expected to meet herself fleeing through the forests as she rode back. Other than a growing weariness at the extra hours she had been awake, everything was as it should be.

The magic of the Wise is potent indeed if it can change the course of time itself. But Rorthron and that strange Lord have left me another problem.

Tarithel knew what she had seen, but how could she explain it?

The bustle of the Citadel was as it had been as she returned to the stables. She handed in the weary horse to the stable boys and cast a coquettish smile at them. They looked at her with bemusement. She merely smiled in response.

I said I'd be back within the hour ... and I was!

She was about to make her way up to the palace when horns sounded behind her. Turning around she saw a group of riders, perhaps six all told, ride into the courtyard atop warhorses decorated with bright chivalric symbols. A banner fluttered in the air above them.

Tarithel was well versed in the devices of the Lords of Mid-

292

night and recognised this one immediately. A white lion on a scarlet background. A Lord of the Free.

Men! Here? It's the Lord of Ithrorn!

No retainers were present; it seemed Ithrorn's arrival was unexpected. She hurried across, bowing before him.

'Lord Ithrorn,' she said, curtseying. 'I am Tarithel, daughter of the Lord of Dreams and Lady of the Forest. Such honour as I can offer is yours and I bid you welcome to our realm.'

Ithrorn climbed down from his horse and his men did likewise. He was an elder man; she tried not to stare at his white hair and full beard as it streamed backwards in the breeze. She was surprised by his eyes; they were a bright blue not often seen amongst the Free.

'And I thank you for it,' he replied, with a nod of respect. 'We have ridden long and hard to reach you.'

The stablehands came across to tend to the horses as Ithrorn's escort also dismounted.

'How so, my Lord?' Tarithel asked. 'What news from beyond our borders?'

'Foul news,' Ithrorn said gruffly. 'Foul news indeed.'

'The Witchking's hordes trouble your lands too?' Tarithel asked.

Ithrorn looked at her in surprise. 'I thought the Fey not to be concerned with affairs beyond their borders?'

'Many are not,' Tarithel said, her voice lowered. 'Some fear that we should be.'

Ithrorn looked at her for a long moment. She saw his moustache twitch as he thought her words over.

'I would speak to your lord directly.'

Tarithel curtseyed again. 'Of course. If you would follow me.'

She led them up to the marble palace atop the Citadel and knocked on the great white oak doors to the hall. They opened to her and she saw her father and his chief advisers gathered around a table. Dinner had just been cleared away and servants were bringing dessert, fruits, pastries and other delights.

'Tarithel? What brings you here at this hour?' Dreams demanded. 'Have you not your chores to occupy you?'

'I bring a visitor,' she responded, jutting her chin forward jauntily.

'I have not time for your games,' Dreams said. 'Run along and bother me not.'

'I fancy my presence is not a mere game,' Ithrorn said from behind her. Tarithel gave her father a pointed look and stepped aside to reveal him. Dreams frowned as he took in the sight of the Lord of Ithrorn.

'May I present ...' Tarithel began.

'Yes, yes,' Dreams said. 'My welcome to you Lord Ithrorn. To what do I owe this visit?'

Ithrorn looked at Tarithel. She rolled her eyes and stepped back. Ithrorn stepped into the room.

Tarithel waited. Her father glared at her.

'You may go, Tarithel.'

She sighed and pulled the door closed slowly behind her, listening for as long as she could.

'I bring ill tidings,' Ithrorn was saying. 'The Foul ...'

But the rest of the conversation was muted as the great doors closed and locked behind her.

Dawn broke over the beleaguered land of Midnight, rolling from the east, casting a pale glow over the Downs of Athoril. Men stirred, breaking camp and organising the packing tents and equipment. The men were weary from constant embattlement, another day of pitched but inconsequential battles lay behind them. Another long march lay ahead.

Lords Kumar, Marakith and Athoril looked out as the sunlight grew. The mist was thin today and the ground covered in a faint outline of ersh. But it was not that that drew their attention.

'I fear the worst,' Athoril said.

To the south west a black plume of smoke was rising, drifting high up into the sky before arching away, carried by the wind.

'We must reach Dawn as soon as we can,' Kumar said. 'Sound the march, let us set a goodly pace.'

Marakith turned and gave direction to the heralds, who ran about the camp giving directions to each section. The army formed up and organised itself. Warriors girded their weapons and packs, riders mounted their steeds. Within minutes they were on the march.

'The bloody sword of battle has brought death in the domain of Dawn,' Kumar muttered. 'Let us hope we can still make a difference. I fear the Witchking has not been idle.'

Athoril nodded. There was a taint upon the air. A pressure, a feeling of desperation and peril, a premonition of evil yet to come. The Lords shivered as it swept about them, and not with the cold.

'The ice-fear grows stronger,' Marakith noted.

Kumar nodded grimly, but made no further comment.

The army moved out, marching hard through the ice and snow underfoot.

Tarithel had run to the staircases of the citadel, quickly striding up them two at a time and then secreting herself in the bell mechanism room above the hall. She wriggled into place as quietly as she could. She had never had to do this with people already below. Satisfied she hadn't been heard she gazed down through the slatted hatchway above.

It seemed she hadn't missed much. Lord Ithrorn was still standing, her father had not bid him to sit at the table. The conversation was already stilted and sharp.

'We have been assaulted thrice at my very walls,' Ithrorn said, his voice gruff. 'One of my keeps has been razed and the land about defiled. My people are demanding action. The ice-fear stirs once more, you must have felt it!'

'We are safe from the depredations of the Witchking's power here,' Dreams replied.

'I have received emissaries from the southlands,' Ithrorn continued. 'The enemy has moved on the Plains of Blood and scored a victory. The Lords of the Free rally to Dawn to defend it. Kumar, Marakith, Shimeril! All are summoned. War is upon us! The Fey ...'

'The Fey did not start this war,' Dreams replied, his voice even and calm. 'It was the Free and their lust for kingship and power.'

Ithrorn looked aghast. 'Then you will not help us?'

'The Witchking seeks the demise of the Free, not the Fey,' Dreams replied. 'He gains nothing from attacking us, and we gain nothing from provoking his anger. You ...' Dreams pointed at Ithrorn. 'You have defied him, taken up arms against him.'

'We?' Tarithel saw Ithrorn recoil and felt his outrage.

'Yes,' Dreams replied. 'Do not suppose I do not have my own knowledge of events in Midnight. Your Lord Gard attacked the Citadel of Gorgrath with no provocation. Then this Moonprince declares himself the ruler of men having found some heirloom from the past, doubtless a plaything of the so called Wise! He has determined to rid Midnight of this foolishness. Let the evil lie I advised – my advice has not been followed. No ... I will not help you. To do so would put my own people and my kin at risk.'

Tarithel stifled a gasp.

My father knows of the Moonprince ...

She saw her father pause, looking around for a sound. Tarithel held still whilst he looked about him, but it did not occur to him to look up.

'This was no provocation,' Ithrorn replied. 'The attack at Gorgrath showed he was ready, prepared for invasion. This was no whim! He came in force, he intends to take all Midnight!'

'He intends to eradicate the Free, perhaps,' Dreams replied. 'But not the Fey.'

'Do you not see?' Ithrorn replied. 'Once he has finished with us, he will turn upon you. Divide and conquer! A trivial ploy, an obvious stratagem.'

'The Witchking knows our power remains potent,' Dreams replied. 'He would not dare attack us.'

Ithrorn frowned. 'You have not been attacked? Not at all? Lothoril? Korinel? Whispers?'

'All at peace and undisturbed,' Dreams replied.

Tarithel couldn't help herself. The words we out of her mouth before she could silence them.

'Korinel is dead!'

Both Ithrorn and Dreams jolted back in surprise. Ithrorn drew his sword, looking around himself in bewilderment, but Tarithel found herself staring into her father's eyes.

'Tarithel!'

She jumped back, dislodging the rafter she was perched on. With a creak it shifted. She rolled to the side, crashing into the slatted hatchway. It gave way beneath her. She felt her body fall through and screamed, reaching out her hands to grasp at anything as she tumbled downwards. Dust and shards of wood cascaded about her, covering her clothes and causing her eyes to water.

She caught hold of something, and swung, suspended above the dining table as debris showered down about her. Before she had a moment to react or even look she fell the rest of the way.

She thumped into something soft and sticky. For a moment she fought for the breath that had been knocked from her. Momentary relief as she realised she was unhurt gave way to bewilderment. Her dress was drenched. She was covered head to foot in thick milky goo. Only then did she realise she'd fallen full length upon the desserts that had been prepared upon the table. All around her had splattered the remainder of the repast. She scrambled to rise, but a slick of cream took her feet from under her and she fell on the floor. Ithrorn was looking at her in astonishment; he had stepped back quickly enough to avoid getting covered himself. With dread, Tarithel looked behind her.

Her father was glaring at her with absolute fury, his visage stern and severe despite being covered with the debris from the table.

Tarithel gulped.

'What did you say?' Ithrorn demanded.

'She said nothing,' Dreams snapped, dragging Tarithel unsteadily on to her feet. 'To your room! Get yourself out of my sight!'

Tarithel resisted, pulling back. 'No! You lied. Korinel was attacked!'

'Enough with your silly girlish stories!' Dreams said. 'To your room! I will deal with you later!'

'... And the Forest of Kor is ablaze!' Tarithel continued, raising her voice. 'He and his people are slain ...'

'Stop it!' Dreams shouted, yanking at her again.

'And you knew!' Tarithel screeched. 'And you did nothing. We skulk here whilst all around us fall before ...'

'Enough!'

Her father swung his arm out, as if meaning to strike her. She staggered back, bracing herself. She could see he was trembling with fury.

'How dare you defy me!' he snarled, his eyes ablaze.

Tarithel cowered in fear. Her father had never threatened to strike her before. She had never seen him so apoplectic. She flinched as he pulled his hand up.

The blow did not fall.

Ithrorn looked set to intervene, his sword hung in his hand, but she knew there was nothing he could do.

'Guards!' Dreams shouted. 'Take her away! Lock her in her chambers!'

The doors opened. Tarithel saw the guards coming for her.

'It's true,' she shouted at Ithrorn. 'The Fey are attacked too! I have seen it …'

The guards grabbed her under each arm and yanked her away, dragging her backwards.

'The Fey must fight! We must! The Fey must follow the Moonprince!'

She struggled as they dragged her away, twisting and writhing in the grip of the guards, trying to break their hold.

As she was dragged to the threshold she heard Ithrorn's voice.

'I see the Fey no longer hold the truth and old allegiances of any value,' Ithrorn said, his voice raised.

'She is a child,' Dreams snapped. 'A wayward child who will be dealt with. Heed her not.'

'I am the Lady of the Forest!' Tarithel squealed. 'Heed my words!'

Ithrorn shook his head.

'I came to inform you that my host will be marching south in defence of Dawn. I intend to swear loyalty to this Moon-prince. I hoped to extend the hand of comradeship to you and your kin.'

'Listen to him, father!' she pleaded. 'We must help! Before it's too late!'

Tarithel felt the guards pause. She saw her father turn to Ithrorn as he sheaved his sword.

'But that offer will not be made,' Ithrorn continued. 'The Fey are not those I would stand shoulder to shoulder with against our ancient foe.'

Ithrorn strode towards the doors. Tarithel looked up at him in despair.

'Save one,' Ithrorn said and bowed towards her. 'I would stand with you, Lady of the Forest.'

Then he was gone and she was unceremoniously wrestled away.

The army topped the rise and marched down the other side. Marakith and Athoril gazed in dismay. Kumar raised a gauntleted hand and the army came to a halt.

Silence reigned for long moments, interrupted only by the idle flapping of the banners in the breeze.

Ahead, the snow covered ground was dotted with bodies; hundreds … thousands of twisted figures all still. Here and there fires burnt, black smoke billowing upwards into a misty sky. Cast upon the ground were spears, swords and the blackened remnants of fighting machines.

Beyond them lay the Citadel of Dawn.

What remained of it.

Its walls were burnt, streaked with grime and the marks of fire. Sections had completely collapsed into rubble revealing the buildings beyond. Fire could still be seen raging within. The tall minarets that had marked its corners were shattered and broken, cast down to destruction.

'We're too late,' Marakith said, aghast.

Riders appeared, scouts that had been sent out to reconnoitre the area. Their reports were subdued and breathless.

'None remain alive, sire,' the scout reported. 'The citadel is burnt, nothing remains. We saw the Witchking's armies assembling south west of the citadel, some three leagues away. They will march into the gap of Corelay ere the day is out.'

'What news of the Free that stood in defence?' Marakith demanded.

The scout shook his head. 'We could not ride around the enemy's army sire. None survive on this side. If they retreated in good order they might be ahead ...'

'Yet the way to the south now lies open,' Kumar said. 'It seems our last stand is already upon us and the war has barely started. We have been caught unawares and will rue our complacency. The Witchking has moved swiftly and swept all before him.'

'What do we do now?' Athoril asked.

'Xajorkith,' Marakith said, his voice barely above a whisper. 'But we cannot follow the Doomguard, we must circumvent them somehow.'

'We must indeed,' Kumar said. 'Within a quarter moon the Witchking's hordes will be at the gates of our capital. If Xajorkith falls all is lost. The Free will never rally again.'

'And our route?'

'We have no choice but to ride south westwards,' Kumar said. 'We must ride hard across the Plains of Trorn. We can recruit Lord Trorn to our campaign upon the route. From there we must ride to Corelay and then approach Xajorkith from the west.'

'It is a long and weary road,' Marakith said.

'Made no shorter by talking about it,' Kumar replied.

Kumar blew a blast on his horn and the army began to move once more.

'This was a battle of defence and tactics, but no more.'

He looked grimly at the other two Lords as he turned his horse. 'Now we fight for our very survival.'

Chapter Thirteen

He stands at Lake Mirrow,
looking north east to the Plains of Glorim.

Morkin struggled on. A tempest battered at him, snow swirled around, a blizzard that had swept through the downs within minutes. Greyness had blanketed him.

The cold stung his face, penetrating his clothing and chilling his bones, threatening to freeze his flesh. He had never felt anything like it before.

The tracks he had been following were a distant memory. They had quickly been obliterated by the rising gale, dashing any hopes he had of tracing the path of Fawkrin. He could only hope he'd been travelling in a straight line but in the reduced visibility he might be walking in circles.

If so, he was doomed.

His strength was already ebbing, worn down by exertion, cold and lack of food. Through the blizzard he could see little around him, just a snowy wasteland. The snow was deepening, further slowing his progress. Before long it was up to his knees causing him to stagger impotently against the worsening weather.

It was to no avail, he tripped and fell headlong into the icy grip of the storm and lay unmoving.

I have failed ... my father was right. I should not have taken this quest. I will not even reach the Ice Crown ... so much for the songs I hoped might be sung! Morkin's folly and death in the snow!

The village could not be that far away, but he had no idea in which direction it might lie. He was shivering violently now and he knew he did not have long to find shelter.

But there was none to be had, there was nothing out here. He was lost deep in the Downs of Mirrow. Despair clawed at his mind, the guilt of failure and the desperate need to survive. His body would not respond to his commands, too weary now to move.

He tried to raise himself but his arms gave way and he collapsed back into the snow.

Morkin, son of the Moonprince!

Morkin heard the words but could make no sense of them. They had been uttered by a light and melodic voice ... a girl's voice. He was tired, sleep was beckoning, a long sleep from which he wouldn't wake, no longer to be troubled by the perils of the world.

But the voice was insistent and would not let him go.

Morkin!

'Leave me,' he mumbled. 'Tired ...'

Morkin! You must rise, it is not far. See the lake!

Annoyed now, he managed to peer ahead, looking over the drifting snow about him. The wind whipped at his face, forcing him to squint into the whiteness. He could see nothing.

Look harder!

He screwed his eyes up further and for a brief moment caught a glimpse of a shoreline perhaps half a league away, nestled between the hills. He was close.

You can reach it, you must!

He blinked, fancying that he could see a girl standing before him. He had seen her before. Eyes green and hair a fiery red, her face soft and impossibly beautiful. A Fey-girl. He saw her smile and beckon to him.

It is not far. Come!

She was dressed in forest garb, not the heavy travelling

304

gear essential to survive in the wilderness. Morkin frowned. She could not possibly be …

Morkin!

He could not resist her call. He stumbled to his feet and staggered towards her, rewarded by a growing smile upon her features. She reached out a hand towards him and he stretched out his own towards her.

Their fingers almost touched, but his foot struck against something hidden in the snow and he tumbled forward.

The snow gave way around him, slipping away and dragging him forwards. He was rolled around as the snow pummelled down the side of the hill, its momentum irresistible, helpless in its grasp, expecting every moment to be dashed to oblivion against some rocky outcrop.

But the motion slowed and he came to rest, struggling to pull himself upright.

He heard a strange sound. A sound that brought back memories of his childhood in the warmest days of the south-lands when the sun was at its height and some of the ice that bound their land actually melted in the sunlight.

Running water …

He looked up.

Before him lay a vast expanse of water. It surface was smooth and undisturbed. Barely a ripple marked its mirror like surface despite the faint breeze that reached him. It seemed unnaturally still and quiet.

Water!

Thirst took him and he staggered on the final few feet to the shoreline. The snow stopped to reveal a stony beach of pebbles free from the ice. He fell to his knees, cupping his hands to scoop the water into his mouth.

It was lukewarm, heated by whatever mysterious powers lay beneath the land of Midnight, yet fresh and clean. Sunlight glittered off the surface, the cold retreated.

He looked up, a wave of wellbeing and vigour surging through him. Energy rushed back through his body, revitalising every extremity. He rose to his feet and gave a cry of exaltation, the sheer joy of survival thrumming through him.

Truly they are the waters of life!

He turned, looking for the girl, but she was nowhere to be seen.

A dream? If so, a pleasant one! Whomsoever she is, she seems to watch over me. But who can she be? And why does she …?

He would find no answers here, but at least he had found the lake. At least he now knew where he was. He was at the east end of the Downs of Mirrow. The storm had blown him off course from finding the village, but had inadvertently steered him directly to the lake. The Forest of Lothoril was not far away now. Whilst refreshed, the pangs coming from his stomach told him that he would need food, and soon. If he could trap some animals or perhaps even fish at the lake side he might be able to continue on.

Not out of danger yet.

Above him the storm continued to clear, the greyness rolling back to reveal a steep sided valley in which the lake was contained. He was at the south western end, with the Downs of Mirrow behind him. Beyond the lake the land opened out once more into the wide expanse of the Plains of Glorim. As the visibility improved he could see further. His heart leapt with joy when he could make out the distant shape of a forest.

Lothoril! There perhaps I can find help in this wilderness.

The downs ran right up to the water's edge in places, overhanging the surface of the lake in curious twisted shapes worn by the age-old motion of the water. Further on down the shoreline he could see caves. They might provide some shelter. A rest and a good night's sleep safe from harm would help restore his strength sooner. He might even stumble upon some old camp. The lake would be an obvious stopping point for any travellers in these parts.

He walked on down the water's edge for a while, making his way towards the caves. They rose above him, dark and mysterious, but when he reached them he found them empty, with no signs that anyone had ever used them. He sighed, it had been too much to hope for.

He walked back outside and down to the shoreline, pondering his next move.

A shadow moved across him, swift and silent. He looked up in surprise, but could see nothing against the glare of the sun. A faint sound in the air, like the brief rumble of distant thunder. But the skies were clearing and he could see nothing.

You're tired, imagining things.

He turned, hearing something.

A group of horses had trotted down to the lake some hundred yards from him.

Wild horses!

Morkin approached them cautiously. It was a long shot, but if he could tame one his journey to Lothoril would be far easier than on foot. He called to mind the lessons of his father and the habits of the Fey, approaching slowly and crouching low.

He'd made his way halfway along the shoreline when a sixth sense somewhere in his mind alerted him. The hairs on the back of his neck rose and a shiver traced its way down his spine. He neither saw, nor heard or even felt anything, but he looked up regardless.

Flames burst out before him, exploding out of the rocks on the shoreline ahead. There was a brief whinny of fright before the horses were consumed in the sudden inferno. Morkin stumbled back and fell on to the stones beneath him, gasping in surprise and fright.

Smoke billowed. Something dark and huge moved within the cloud and then was gone.

Morkin got to his feet cautiously and moved forward. The fire quickly burnt itself out and the smoke cleared. The ground thereabouts was scorched and blackened, but of the horses there was no sign.

It couldn't be …?

Rocks tumbled down behind him. He turned, dreading what he might see.

Above the caves, something lurked.

Baleful eyes stared back at him, cat-like, yet enormous.

Tarithel found herself thrown in her room. Before she could get up she heard the sound of a key turning in the lock. She leapt to her feet and battered at the door in rage, but it was to no avail. The door was solid and held fast. She knew there was no escape that way.

Like many of the high ranked members of the Fey her room was within one of the tower minarets of the Citadel, narrow windows looked down from high above. She sat on her bed, pawing at her filthy dress.

My father lies! Why does he lie? He has never raised a hand to me thus before. I have never seen him so angry … is he ill? Burdened by some other woe?

She could hear a vague commotion from outside. She got up and threw open the window, gazing down. From her vantage point she could just see the courtyard and the gates. The men of Ithrorn were assembled, awaiting their Lord.

As she watched he appeared, striding quickly to his waiting horse. He mounted and turned it about, giving a brief signal to his men, who lined up alongside and followed him. The guards of the Fey stood aside to let them through, but there was no send off, no acknowledgement of his leaving as tradition demanded.

My father insults the Lord of Ithrorn. The Witchking has some hold over him … a pact? A promise? What deal has my father made with the evil of this realm?

She watched as the men of the Free rode through the gates. She couldn't see them for a few minutes, but then they appeared in the clearing beyond, circling the citadel before turning east and heading for their home three days travel away.

Tarithel watched them go in misery.

Have I failed in the task Rorthron set me? Rouse the Fey from their slumber he said! The Fey will not rise to help whilst my father remains of this mind. Now I am locked away. What can I do? So much for being Lady of the Forest. I haven't roused the Fey, and if the Witchking's hordes do decide to come our way my beloved forest will burn before them. What should I do?

She closed the window and slipped out of her dirty dress, washing her face in a bowl before changing into fresh clothes. Then she returned to sit on her bed, wringing her hands with frustration. Unable to stay still she returned to the window and gazed out.

It was snowing once more, dark clouds coming down from the north. The winter was gripping the land tighter in its freezing grasp. Snow flurries danced before her, hypnotic.

Her vision blurred. In her mind's eye she saw something, a figure …

The young man I saw before …

He was trudging through heavy snow, staggering with weariness, on the verge of collapsing with exhaustion. She felt her heart lurch in sympathy, involuntarily reaching out towards him.

His name was sweet on her lips.

Morkin …

Somehow she knew.

Morkin! Son of the Moonprince! As Rorthron said ...

He looked up as if he had heard her. She felt a thrill of excitement as he reached out. She smiled, warmth and a strange glow lighting her body from head to toe.

Her gaze wandered. It was as if some strange power directed it, not wholly against her will, but she was not entirely in control of it either. Somehow she rose far above the land of Midnight, seeing the world fall below her. She could see a distance she could not comprehend, whole mountain ranges, vast plains ...

Before she could make sense of it she was descending, a vast forest spread to the limits of her vision, stretching out from horizon to horizon. A citadel appeared, tall and proud, not dissimilar to the one she knew. Her vision was drawn to a minaret much like the one she was in.

Her gaze travelled within. She could see a Fey, pacing back and forth. He was dressed in travelling apparel, his face drawn with worry and concern.

He is imprisoned too! Why would he be locked up so?

As if he heard her, the Fey looked up, catching her gaze. She heard words in her mind ...

I am Corleth, I swore allegiance to the Moonprince. I am held at the Citadel of Dregrim in the far south. The Fey must rise before it is too late ...

Before she could reply, harsh sounds echoed in her head.

She turned, her vision blurring again as her gaze was wrenched away, travelling at a dizzying speed over downs and mountains, frozen rivers and desolate plains before sweeping over the vast expanse of another forest. It was so disorienting that it almost caused her to fall.

Then it slowed and she could see a keep, nestled in the midst of a clearing cut in the deep forest. It was like her homeland, but less well tended. She recognised it. One of the kin of the people of Dreams. Friends and relations.

The Forest of Whispers!

But the keep was beset. Dark figures swirled around it, machines of war launched missiles and flaming balls of fire. She gasped as the defenders on the walls struggled to repel the invaders. She saw fire leap against the gates of the keep, threatening to overwhelm them.

Fey warriors fell from the walls, arrows flew, the shrieks and cries of the dying reached her ears.

Tears coursed down her face.

Words came to her. She heard Rorthron's voice carried above the mayhem.

The bloody sword of battle brings death in the domain of Whispers …

'No!'

Her cry jolted her out of her reverie. Her room swam back into focus around her, calm and peaceful.

She gasped for breath for long moments, feeling her heart pounding in her chest.

We must go to their aid!

She stood up and ran to the locked door. She pummelled on it with clenched fists.

'Guards! Unlock this door!'

She banged again, raising her voice and shouting as loud as she could.

'The Lord of Whispers is sore oppressed! We must go to his aid! Is anyone there? Listen to me!'

She flailed against the door, thumping her fists against it over and over again, fury and frustration mounting to an incendiary rage.

'Heed me!' she yelled. 'Whispers! We must help!'

But there was no answer from without.

She screeched in pure frustration, screaming at the indefatigable door that barred her way and then kicking at it. She achieved nothing but hurting her foot, the pain brought her back down to earth.

Broken by sobs she uttered a final cry. 'The … Fey … we must rise!'

She collapsed on the floor, sobbing in grief, rage and sorrow. The jewel about her neck pulsed, glowing brightly in the darkness of her prison.

Outside, beyond the citadel, the forest began to stir.

The storm clouds were thick and heavy over the Tower of Lorgrim, buffeting the exterior with squalls and blizzards. Wind howled around the alcoves and buttresses, but no sound or movement penetrated the interior. The Towers of Midnight were inviolate, no mere natural phenomena could render any harm to them.

A man, or what seemed to be a man, sat at a gnarled and battered desk, parchments and scrolls scattered about him. The room itself was lit by the few candles perched upon the desk, casting a warm yellow glow.

One such parchment was a map, clearly ancient, with the baroque decoration of the ancient scribes marking its antiquity. Names both strange and familiar were marked upon it and the old man was feverously first looking at the map and then making notes with a feathered quill on another piece of parchment.

'Midnight to Ustor, to Varangor and hence Erandor … No, no! Merineth. It must be Merineth!'

Lorgrim the Wise continued to mutter to himself.

'Or not. Varangor of old was home to the dragons though … perhaps Valahar or Berin? No, too far. Arillon and Isheril are too far west to be considered.'

Scribblings on the parchment were struck through to be replaced with more.

'Aost … those lands I know not. Sarandar, Qadim Haraj?

The southern lands are closed until … events run their course. The Bloodmarch I will give my attention to in time. That leaves the Icemark, home of that she-devil!'

Lorgrim paused and reviewed his notes.

'Crowns, runes … a bow, a spear and an axe. Spells of swiftness. A sword and a hammer. Then the War Rings. Gryfallon sets his daughter to watch upon the Icemark …'

Lorgrim pieced together the fragments of memory within in his mind. A shocking conclusion broke forth, making him tremble.

'No … he couldn't … not that!'

Could it be done? The reconciliation of the First Power?

The more Lorgrim thought about it, the more it seemed it might be the Witchking's intent.

Midnight itself is just a move in his game. He has a crown, and his daughter doubtless seeks for the talismans of the Icemark. He knows of the Eye of the Moon and the Ring itself …

A creeping doubt came across him.

Long ago, when he was my apprentice, we talked at length …

Lorgrim recalled those conversations. Idle chats, or so they had seemed then, before a roaring fire, in the high halls of this very tower. Two powers, master and apprentice, refining their craft. They had talked long about the history of the Wise. How the Wise considered themselves responsible for the safety of the lands. How, long ago, they thought they had too much power and that they should leave the world to the new peoples; the skulkrin, the Fey and the Free. How they pooled their power and then set it within dozens of talismans, to be distributed to the leaders of those people. Power shared, power evenly spread.

And how our power was diluted to the point of impotence!

Despite the honourable intentions, it had been a monumental error. Some talismans were used for good of course, most lay unused as family heirlooms and were lost to the ravages of time. Others were corrupted and used for ill.

It was thought that the Wise retreated from the affairs of the world, but that was not true.

Our greatest folly!

Lorgrim sighed. Gryfallon had wanted to return the Wise to their pre-eminence. When the rest of the Wise refused, he struck out on his own.

Yet I told him of it ... there is a way to bring back the First Power, if the talismans could be united once more ... the Last Book of the Wise and the Solstice ... the Solstice is when it could be done!

Lorgrim shivered.

He seeks them all. Not just the Ice Crown, but the powers of Icemark, the rings and all powers that remain in all the lands!

Lorgrim ground his teeth, and looked out of the windows of the room, gazing at the whirling snowstorm outside.

If he gains more power, none will ever stand against him. Imbued with the First Power he would be utterly irresistible, all the lands would fall under his dominion. Midnight is just the start ... and he will have no need of me!

Morkin thought of drawing his sword, but knew it would be a foolish gesture. The creature was huge. It was clearly a wyvern, but huge beyond any tales he could recall. Wyverns were perhaps the length of a tall man, with a similar wingspan, creatures of cool scaled skin and long sinuous tails, their most notable features being rows of sharpened teeth within a pointed snout.

They were accomplished aerial hunters, taking prey on the wing, rodents and the like, perhaps even a small deer.

But this!

It was vast. Morkin couldn't see all of it as it was crouched above him, staring steadily down at him with eyes that must have been a similar size to his head. That head was the familiar shape of a wyvern, but grown to proportions that were terrifying in their enormity. Ridged eye sockets rose out of a skull taut with red-tinged skin framed by a mane of bony protrusions that rose just forward of the creatures neck. The body was hidden from sight beyond the ridge above the caves.

Morkin took a step back, raising his hands as if to ward it off. The creature's body remained motionless, only its gaze followed him. He stepped into the water of the lake, he could retreat no further.

Morkin flinched as the creature opened its mouth, revealing teeth akin to those of the wyverns, only dozens of times larger. A roar shook the ground as the creature sucked in breath. Morkin saw its tongue vibrate, curl and then straighten again before the jaws came down. The creature swallowed and then resumed its stare.

Morkin didn't move.

The creature turned its head, cocking it to one side.

IF YOU WERE GOING TO RUN, YOU HAVE LEFT IT RATHER TOO LATE.

Morkin blinked. The creature blinked back.

The voice was deep in a manner Morkin could not fathom, it was like enormous boulders rubbing against each other as they were shifted reluctantly from a resting place deep within the ground. It echoed around his mind, but his ears had heard nothing.

'You can … talk?' he managed.

The creature lowered its snout and looked down at him.

EVIDENTLY.

'But you're a wyv–'

Smoke billowed about him, blasting him off his feet to lie sprawled in the water. He coughed, acrid fumes burning his throat. He rolled out of the way, trying to find some clear air. The smoke about him was thick and impenetrable.

A thump and a rush of air blasted across him; he turned over as the smoke cleared. The creature was before him, its true scale now revealed. The monstrous head was supported by a vast muscular body. It was four-legged, with each limb as wide as a tree, ending at feet from which claws, each bigger than a man's foot, twitched, retracting in and out as the creature sought its balance.

Morkin looked up, his whole body trembling as the creature towered over him.

From its back, wings unfurled, stretching out perhaps fifty feet from tip to tip. Morkin was thrown back along the shoreline as it flexed them, performing a single down stroke.

DO NOT INSULT ME WITH THAT NAME. THEY ARE LESSER CREATURES THAN I.

Morkin propped himself on his elbows. 'Who are you?'

The creature brought its snout closer. Morkin could smell ashes and cinders.

I AM FARFLAME.

Its voice thudded through Morkin's astonished mind.

LORD OF THE DRAGONS OF MIDNIGHT.

Truly a dragon …

AND YOU ARE?

'I am squire Morkin,' Morkin stammered, trying to assemble his courage. 'Son of Lord Luxor, Moonprince of Midnight!'

The great dragon moved, sitting back on its haunches, folding its wings and then peering back down at the young man before it.

A MOONPRINCE OF THE FREE? BUT I SMELL THE SCENT OF FEY UPON YOU, BOY.

'I am half-Fey, my mother …'

ONE BORN OF FEY AND FREE?

Farflame snorted.

I HAVE HEARD THIS BALLAD. YOU SEEK THE DEMISE OF THE WITCHKING.

'I …'

THE TRUTH BOY. DO NOT WASTE TIME WITH LIES. I AM NOT HUNGRY, BUT YOU WOULD BE LITTLE MORE THAN A SMALL MORSEL IF I SO DESIRED. IT IS LITTLE TROUBLE TO ME.

'Whose side are you on?' Morkin demanded.

SIDE?

Farflame shook his head.

MINE, OF COURSE. OH, I AM NO FRIEND OF THE WITCHKING'S FOULNESS, BUT NOR DO THE WORKS OF THE FREE HAVE MUCH TO RECOMMEND THEM TO ME. THE FEY I WILL TOLERATE, THOUGH THEY ARE DEATHLY DULL.

The dragon moved forward, looking at him closely.

YOU DON'T SING, DO YOU?

Morkin frowned and shook his head. 'Er … no.'

THANK THE FIRE FOR THAT. I HATE SINGING. SOME OF THEIR WRETCHED BALLADS GO FOR ON FOR INTERMINABLE HOURS.

The dragon moved again, the ground trembling as it turned around. It began to stride off.

Morkin watched it for a moment before chasing after it.

'Wait!' he called. 'Where are you going?'

WHAT BUSINESS IS THAT OF YOURS, BOY?

'I need your help,' Morkin said. 'I was after those horses but you …'

HORSES?

Morkin could have sworn something akin to a guilty look crossed the dragon's face.

'Yes, you ate those horses,' Morkin said. 'I needed them!'

Farflame stopped and craned his neck around.

I NEEDED THEM TOO. THEY WERE HORSES. I AM

**A DRAGON. THEY WERE TASTY IF THAT IS ANY CON-
SOLATION, THAT IS THE END OF THE MATTER.**

'No it's not!' Morkin ran to get ahead and stood defiantly
before the dragon. He drew his sword. Farflame stopped
before him.

The dragon's eyes narrowed, peering at the sword in
Morkin's hand. The beast emitted a deep rumbling sound.

**YOU ARE BRAVE, BUT RATHER FOOLISH. IS YOUR
SWORD IS EMBUED WITH MAGIC OR SOME OTHER
POTENCY? PERHAPS YOU FANCY YOUR BLADE IS
CALLED 'DRAGONSLAYER' OR SOME SUCH? IT WILL
BE OF LITTLE USE AGAINST ME.**

'You will help me.'

AND WHY WOULD I DO THAT?

'Because you already have,' Morkin said with a grin. 'You
slew those Doomguard back in Dodrak didn't you? You've
been following me!'

I HAVE NOT.

Morkin fancied that the dragon's innocent expression was
not very convincing.

'You won't eat me, because you didn't eat them.'

EAT DOOMGUARD?

Farflame snorted, his dragon features registering disgust.

I WOULD NEVER SULLY MYSELF!

'You slew them to protect me … and you were waiting,
standing guard. Why?'

Farflame affected a look of unconcern.

I WAS CURIOUS.

'And you owe me a horse.'

Farflame stepped back a few paces, lowering his head to
the ground. Morkin heard a ghastly choking sound as the
dragon undulated its neck. A moment later a crushed pile of
bones, dripping with saliva and tattered shreds of entrails lay
steaming on the lake side.

ONE HORSE.

'Very funny.'

Farflame closed his eyes and emitted the odd bass vibrato rumble from his throat again. It took Morkin a moment to realise it was the dragon equivalent of laughter.

VERY WELL, SQUIRE MORKIN, SON OF LORD LUXOR, MOONPRINCE OF MIDNIGHT, HALF-FEY AND HALF-FREE … BUT I CAN DO BETTER THAN A HORSE.

One of the great wings was lowered to the ground before Morkin. Farflame bowed his great head.

To ride a dragon …

Morkin hesitated for a moment, feeling his heart pounding in his chest.

Flying!

He ignored the trembling in his legs and strode forward, climbing aboard the heavily muscled creature, grasping one of the exposed vertebra that jutted up from the dragon's back.

With a mighty down-sweep of his wings Farflame launched into the sky in a blast of snow and ice.

WHERE ARE WE BOUND, YOUNG SQUIRE?

Morkin could barely frame a thought, let alone speak. The sudden uprush whipped his breath away; his hands were clenched on the dragon's back, his knuckles white. The ground fell away at a dizzying rate; rocks, boulders, trees, even the lake shrinking fast below.

The fear passed and exhilaration overpowered him. He yelled out in sheer delight as the air whistled in his ears. Beneath him, Farflame roared in counterpoint.

The tracks of the skulkrin were long lost, whereabouts the creature had gone he knew not, nor was he ever likely to know. He needed provisions and support before he could tackle the journey to the Tower. There was only one place left to him.

'To the forest!' Morkin shouted above the air blasting past him. 'To the Fey. To Lothoril!'

Chapter Fourteen

He stands at the Citadel of Xajorkith,
looking north to the Plains of Corelay.

It rose from the ice a thousand feet in the air, dominating the landscape around it. Sheer white towers and mighty walls overlooked plains, hills and forests. Flags and banners flew from lofty minarets, proud and defiant. This was no minor keep, nor understaffed city. This was, in the minds of most, the capital of the Free. The Great Tower. The Citadel of Xajorkith.

Its situation, south of the great valley of Corelay, gave it a masterful strategic position. Any attacker would have to fight their way through that valley, cordoned in by mountains on either side leaving no alternative but a frontal assault. The architects of the citadel had anticipated this, and its construction favoured defences in this direction. Any adversary trying another approach would have to divert far to the east or west and those routes had their own perils; long distances and the unseen hindrance of the deep forests.

With such a commanding position, Xajorkith was famed for being the only Citadel that had never fallen to an enemy. Few had even reached its walls. It was held that if Xajorkith ever did fall then the world of the Free would be at an end. Xajorkith was the last bulwark, the mightiest citadel, the very core of the Free's territory.

To the south of the citadel, now separated by a barren icy plain, lay the deserted shipyards. They had been icelocked for moons beyond count, but there were etchings and tapestries which depicted them in the days of the long summer when the blue waters of the river Imilvir ran down from the Vale of Corelay, past Xajorkith and onwards under the Bridge of Whispers and through the Dawngate, until being lost to the south in lands that were now only vague memories; Saranar and the Bloodmarch.

The Lord of Xajorkith was a young man, having taken over the Lordship when his father passed away just a dozen moons before. He had been but a child at the time of the last war against the Witchking, but he recalled his father's chilled words and melancholy tones as he explained the desperation of the fight against the cold and fear.

Xajorkith himself stood on the walls of the citadel, looking north. The day was clear and the valley of Corelay stretched out to the distant horizon. He squinted into the distance, hoping to see something. Guards and lookouts were posted and would have alerted him immediately of course, but there was no substitute for personal attention.

Beyond that distant horizon lay the lands of Dawn.

And the tidings had not been good.

Rumours spoke of great conflicts taking place in the lands to the north. Traders had been fleeing from the wide plains and the villages in the realms of Shimeril, Dawn and Athoril for days, with ever increasing tales of woe and fear. Some spoke of the armies of the Witchking on the prowl, razing villages and settlements, with the armies of the Free falling back before them, powerless to resist.

And they had felt it, even here. A touch upon the heart, a pause in the breath and a tremor in the voice.

Xajorkith didn't need his father's words to know what was seeping through the very air around them, slowly tightening its grip on the hearts of men, women and children in his care. Terror was stalking them, invading like a subtle but irresistible plague, sapping their will and their resolve.

The ice-fear.

It had been growing stronger, yet in fits and spurts. Now it seemed to be growing more assertively, chilling the hearts of the folk of Xajorkith and sapping their strength. Such potency had never been felt in these southern lands before.

A short trumpet blast sounded across the frigid air. A sentry had seen something. Xajorkith squinted into the distance, seeing sparkles in his eyes as he strained his vision into the whiteness.

'Riders, sire!'

'How many?'

'Just a handful sir, they bear a banner ... the device is ... The Lord of Morning, sire!'

'Open the gates,' Xajorkith instructed. 'I will meet him directly!'

By the time Xajorkith had descended the many layers of his realm, the riders had reached the Citadel. Xajorkith could see at a glance that they were battle weary.

There were five, four men at arms riding to protect their own liege. Their horses were drenched with sweat, almost staggering with exhaustion. The men looked little better, eyes bloodshot and countenances downcast.

Morning dismounted and pulled himself up to stand straight. Xajorkith could see it was an effort even to do that.

'My Lord,' Xajorkith said, 'Your men ... we must see to you ...'

'No time,' Morning said, his voice strained and hoarse. 'We must prepare ...'

'What news then?' Xajorkith asked. 'What has happened?'

Morning coughed and staggered. Xajorkith reached out a hand to steady him.

'Doom is upon us,' Morning said. 'In every sense of the word. The Witchking's army marches at pace.'

'But the defence at Dawn,' Xajorkith said. 'It ...'

'Overrun,' Morning said. 'Whether it be their numbers, the foulness of the ice-fear, or the treachery of the barbarian …'

'Utarg?' Xajorkith said. 'Treachery? What treachery?'

'He slew Dawn before our very eyes,' Morning said heavily.

'Dawn … is dead?' Xajorkith staggered himself, unable to take it in. 'My father and he fought side by side for endless moons.'

'Utarg hew him as he went to treat, the vile scum,' Morning continued. 'The Citadel of Dawn has been razed. We hoped for aide from Kumar and Marakith, but it did not come. If they survive then the Doomguard lie between us and them.'

'Then the Doomguard …'

'What remains of our armies is but a day's march to the north with the Witchking's foulness less than that behind them. We have ridden all night and day to reach you. The enemy are driven ahead of storms of snow and ice, the very weather fights against us!'

'They are coming here?' Xajorkith said, the blood draining from his face.

Morning looked at him and then nodded curtly.

'The progress of the Doomguard has proved unstoppable thus far. Hordes of the Foul are but short days away. The armies of the Free retreat before them, their numbers sorely reduced.' Morning looked around at the bright citadel above him. 'Our last stand is already upon us.'

'But, I heard news, good tidings,' Xajorkith said. 'A Moonprince, a power with which to combat the rise of the Witchking …'

Morning pursed his lips.

'I fear the legend of the Moonprince has grown too large in the telling.'

As he stepped away from Xajorkith, his shoulders slumped.

Night fell over the walls of Xajorkith, but the gloom had settled hours before. Dark clouds full of the strength of winter had blanketed the citadel, cutting off the light of the sun long before it reached the frozen horizon. The temperature, already low, fell precipitately, penetrating within the buildings and rooms inside the walls.

Throughout the day the exhausted armies of the Free had made their way through the gates under the watchful eyes of the Xajorkith sentries. Luxor and the other Lords had arrived in their midst, weary and downcast. Food and warming beverages had been provided by the city folk, wounds tended by the healers, but there was little anyone could do for the mood.

Scant thousands of warriors and riders remained, less than half of those who had stood and defended Dawn from the approaching vanguard of the Witchking's forces.

The great Lords of the Free held a council within the palace atop the citadel mount.

'As near as we can tell,' Gard reported, his face even more dour than usual, 'the Doomguard is split into two main forces. One proceeds apace from its victory at Dawn down through the Plains of Corelay. It will be in position to attack within two dawns.'

'And the other?' Luxor asked.

The other Lords paused, seeing the weariness on his face. Luxor looked waxen, his skin paler than the candlelight that lit the hall.

'Mustering further to the west,' Morning said. 'Those that issued from the gap of Valethor. Reports indicate that the Citadel of Shimeril was seized ...'

Lord Shimeril grimaced, but didn't say anything. Blood looked across at him.

'We will see it taken back, my friend.'

Shimeril nodded. 'Both of us will rebuild what has been smashed down. We've done it before ...'

'And their strength? Luxor asked.

'Fifteen, perhaps twenty thousand when all counted,' Morning said. 'We expect them to join forces and proceed south directly towards Xajorkith, or perhaps a pincer movement from the west.'

'And our strength?' Luxor asked.

'Less than eight thousand, and provisions for only days if under siege,' Xajorkith replied. 'We did not plan on hosting so many.'

Luxor rubbed his chin, thinking through possibilities. Each one led to a dead end in his mind, each more futile and hopeless than the last.

'What of the Fey?' Gard demanded. 'You sent missives.'

Luxor shook his head. 'If they intended to stand with us, we would know by now. I sense nothing via the ring, none have sworn their loyalty to me. They are not coming.'

'But they must know if we are lost that the Witchking will eradicate them too, they cannot hope to stand alone.'

Luxor nodded. He had tried to contact Corleth via the Moon Ring, but he had been unable to locate the Fey at all. Was he already dead, perhaps slain by the traitorous Utarg? Or was some other power preventing their contact? Perhaps that explained the lack of response from the Fey? Neither the Fey of the north nor the south had been seen. Did they think their forests would protect them? Not even that power could stand against the invigorated might of the Witchking. Shadows had seen that, Corleth knew it too …

So where is he? A Fey army might turn this battle, but without them … Corleth, you have failed me in my time of need …

'Whatever we must do,' Luxor stated. 'We must do without the fickle Fey.'

'What of Kumar and Marakith?' asked Silence. 'And Ithrorn to the North?'

'They have been forced through the domain of Trorn,' Luxor

said. 'Neither would shrink from a fight, but they cannot fight their way through the Plains of Corelay. As for Ithrorn, who knows what has transpired in the lonely north now ...'

'Then what is to be our plan?' Morning demanded, looking around at Luxor. One by one all the Lords turned and did the same. Conversation dropped and only the faint spitting of the tallow candles sounded through the hall.

Luxor sighed. 'At this point? I have none ...'

To their dismay, he stood and walked out, slamming the doors behind him. Shimeril made to get up, but Blood caught him by the arm.

'Let him go,' he said softly. 'A heavy weight to bear and the Moon Ring has drained his vigour, we must trust that it does not break him.'

The libraries of the Tower of the Moon held tomes more ancient than the lives of the men of the Free. There were documents here that predated even the Fey and the skulkrin. The Wise had long chronicled the history of Midnight and the lands about. Many were histories, or long ledgers of the forgotten realms of the world long before the Lords of Midnight and their houses came to be.

Rorthron knew of records of the long summer and the days before the sundering of Midnight, maps of other lands, names both familiar and strange.

He had studied much in his time, but he had only been a boy at the end of the long summer and, even for him, such days were far in the past.

Yet this clue Lorgrim inadvertently spoke of. The First Power ...

Rorthron knew the tales that the Free and the Fey told of the Wise, that they had failed in their duty to prevent the rise of the Witchking and thus holed themselves up in their towers, there to disappear from history, abrogating themselves of care and responsibility. Rorthron recalled the severe faces and frowning countenances of those he had looked up to in his youth.

I didn't understand enough, I was too young. But the Wise should have been able to counter the Witchking. He was one, we were many! But we retreated and gave him free rein ...

Rorthron knew the answer. It had not been revealed beyond the confines of their own people.

We lost our powers. We could not have challenged the Witchking even if we had wished to. Yet, Gryfallon was one of the Wise. He retained a power ... why were ours so weak?

The Witchking's rise had always been attributed to the fell arts he had learnt elsewhere, knowledge he brought back and used to support his rise to power.

Yet Lorgrim was his master and he was the apprentice. Lorgrim knows more of course ... but what?

Rorthron spent weary hours reviewing the books within the library, but there was no mention of Lorgrim's phrase anywhere.

The First Power ...

His back aching from the toil he collapsed into one of the softer chairs within the tower and pondered the problem.

Our powers were too weak as the Witchking rose, but they had been stronger in the past. Lorgrim spoke of Talismans and the First Power, what did he mean?

Rorthron pulled back more memories of that conversation into his mind, pondering them over and over again. There was another phrase, another utterance that felt out of place, disjointed and accidental. Lorgrim was old and let things slip inadvertently.

Rorthron frowned. Lorgrim had said something else.

Even with his half-broken Moon Ring ...

Half-broken? The Moon Ring was pure and unsullied! Rorthron had kept it safe for many moons of men, ever since Gryfallon had come in force and destroyed the Citadel of the Moon. He could remember the discussions he had with Lorgrim in those times. How they planned to keep the ring safe, hidden away from the Witchking. How they had kept a child safe to continue the line of the Moon. How the Citadel had been razed, the forest burnt and only the Tower of the Moon left untouched ...

Rorthron got up once again, dragging down more books from the shelves above him.

There must be something, something that links all this together. What did the Wise do? Of what does Lorgrim speak? Half-broken ...

He continued studying the books and tomes, delving ever deeper in the old lore of Midnight. The further he retreated into the past, the more difficult the task became. History became fragmented, mixed with myth and the strange poetic styles of scribes from long ago. Magic and all that went with it fell in and out of vogue under the hundreds of leaders that had gone before. Scribes often had to couch their words in riddles to avoid detection. It made for wearisome reading when trying to establish ...

Rorthron blinked at a passage. He turned the book over, to remind himself what he'd been studying.

The Annals of the Bloodmarch.

The passage was peculiar. He read it again, speaking out loud, blinking through strained eyes.

In Varangor, the Daughter of the Seventh Sky;
Arch Priestess of the Goddess.
Visions from above she saw,
Yet from a talisman not so blessed.

Sent forth she did, for vengeance sake,
Five kings danced to her cry.
Yet a greater power did deceive,
Woven by the Moon's eye.'

Rorthron re-read the passage several times. The Bloodmarch was far to the south, sundered from Midnight by the impassable harshness of the Frozen Wastes. But it had not always been so, travellers had traipsed the length of the world unhindered at the time this author had lived.

Talismans ... and the Moon's Eye?

He continued reading, hoping to learn more, but there was no further mention of anything he could see was relevant.

A half-broken ring, which is yet whole. An eye, a talisman and this First Power ... how does it all fit together? What did the Wise do?

He had to know the answer. He braced himself and cast his mind back into the past, seeking any lost memory he might find.

Luxor walked out from the Citadel, looking southwards across the sunlit snow. He could still make out the outlines of the river Imilvir, locked in ice for moons beyond count, stretching away until it was lost in the hazy outline of the Frozen Wastes.

Despair gnawed at his mind.

They look to me for answers, but I have none. The might of the Witchking, the treachery of the Utarg ...

The Witchking's forces marched upon them. The Free endured defeat after defeat. Blood, Dawn ... would Xajorkith be next?

Xajorkith falling on my watch, such a thing has never occurred in the whole history of Midnight. Perhaps I should relinquish command to Gard, or even Xajorkith himself. We might fare better ... I have led them all to ruin.

He gazed upon the ring on his finger, extending his hand. On an impulse he wrestled it free, looking over the walls of the citadel to the frozen landscape far below.

I might just be done with it, it has brought me nothing but grief! All look to me for salvation and I have none to offer ...

He clenched his hand around the ring and made to throw it ...

'You should not be alone, Lord Luxor.'

Luxor turned to see the young Lord Xajorkith standing alongside him.

'I have my thoughts for company,' Luxor replied. He slid the ring back upon his finger, it glowed softly.

'Ill company I would think,' Xajorkith answered. 'This responsibility lies heavy upon you, and this talisman of good you bear seems to have a deadly call upon your strength from all accounts.'

'It is mine to bear,' Luxor replied.

Xajorkith nodded and stared out at the whiteness for a long moment.

'You have not led us astray you know.'

Luxor turned to look at him and scoffed. 'We have lost Blood, Shimeril and Dawn,' Luxor said. 'Under my so-called leadership. The way to Xajorkith lies open. You said it yourself, we cannot last more than a few days, and we are outnumbered whilst a confident foe bears down upon us. The Moon Ring demands a price from me I am not sure I can pay. Did I miss some element out? The Witchking's victory is sure.'

'If you believe that we have already lost,' Xajorkith replied.

Luxor shook his head. 'This is no time for some brave speech rallying the troops, for us to summon up some old tale to inspire courage in the face of certain death hoping for some uncertain and miraculous victory. Such things belong in the books where the harsh light of reality cannot penetrate!'

Xajorkith didn't answer for a moment, but stood alongside Luxor and gazed out over the snow covered plains to the south of the Citadel.

'The weight of history is a burden that drives many men to madness,' Xajorkith said. 'Do not shoulder it.'

Luxor frowned. 'What do you mean?'

Xajorkith smiled. 'My father told me that he felt the responsibility of being custodian of the only Citadel in Midnight never to have fallen to the enemy. He hated it. He told me it was only by luck, being positioned so far south, that Xajorkith had been spared. Foul Doomdark never made it this far – he would say. That's all. We could hardly call ourselves the only Citadel that had never had a proper fight could we? Not very grand for the murals and tapestries. No, so much the better to say we'd never been conquered. Far better.'

Luxor chuckled. 'I remember your father, he was a good man.'

'What we achieve can be judged by the scribes only after the event,' Xajorkith said. 'But they do not face the hard choices without knowledge of what the outcome might be. What we do now is what we do, for good or ill. Do not fear their judgement. They aren't the ones who face the foe. What you must do is what you feel is right, here and now.'

Luxor nodded, rubbing his chin with his hand.

'Come,' Xajorkith said. 'I have something I want to show you.'

Intrigued, Luxor followed Xajorkith down through the Citadel walls and out into the landscape beyond. They rode half a league or so, before Xajorkith turned about. Luxor could see they were heading for the frozen river he'd been watching from the heights.

Ahead a series of low buildings with sharply pointed roofs jutted upwards from the landscape. Snow had been cleared from them and it was plain to see that they received much care and attention.

'My father instructed me to take care of this, alongside all my other duties,' Xajorkith explained.

Luxor looked about him. 'What are these buildings for?'

Xajorkith gestured to a nearby set of double wooden doors. A quick rap of his knuckle upon them and they opened, manned by guards stationed within.

Luxor followed into what he first took for a dimly lit hall.

Within, torches blazed on metal fasteners attached to the walls at intervals. The hall was massive, stretching perhaps two hundred yards in length and fifty wide. As his eyes adjusted to the gloom Luxor could see it was no hall, but a vast empty space, centred around a wide berth, in which lay ...

A ship.

It was a proud looking vessel, with an upturned bow and scalloped stern. Two masts jutted upwards from the hull, necessitating the strange roof design of the building. Its hull was painted black up to what would have been the water line, but gold above, stretching fore and aft. Luxor could see the bow was carved into the shape of an intricately realised bird.

'The Cormorant,' Xajorkith. 'Swiftest of all the ships of my domain.'

'Such vessels I have read of,' Luxor said, staring wonderingly at the ship. 'But never imagined I would see the like. I thought them all perished and destroyed after the long summer.'

'Most were,' Xajorkith said. 'Useless in the winter of course, and a great source of wood and provisions in time of need. My father had this one preserved though, the finest of the fleet that once graced our port. It remains here, awaiting a chance to sail again.'

Luxor walked down past the vessel, running his hand against its sleek sides. He could see the craftsmanship that had gone into its construction; the smoothly planed wood, the decoration of the paint, the brasswork that edged the gunnels and portholes.

So old!

Luxor heard a thump from above and looked up. Xajorkith was peering down at him with a grin.

'Come aboard!'

Luxor climbed up a rope ladder thrown over the side and stood upon the decks. For a moment he got the faint impression of wide open seas, swirling water and the wind blowing through outstretched sails, but it was a hard image to keep in the mind. The ship was drydocked, with no hint of water about it, imprisoned and unable to move as once it had.

Xajorkith beckoned him towards the rear where a door led inwards under another deck.

'This would have been the captain's cabin,' Xajorkith said. 'From where he would have issued his commands, directing the vessel this way and that.'

Luxor followed him in, squinting in the gloom.

Inside was a desk, secured to the floor, upon which were festooned a series of brass instruments the like of which Luxor had never seen. He cast his gaze over them, wondering what they might be for.

'The art of navigation at sea, no small thing,' Xajorkith said. 'We have the records, perhaps one day we will be able to try our hand at this again. Our ancestors accomplished it, why not us?'

Luxor continued to look at the instruments, the heritage of a time long vanished. One in particular caught his eye. It was circular, bolted upright against the wall so as to be easily seen. Its front was covered in glass and within he could see numbers rising from a low count to a higher one around a dial. The numbers were bold and stark, unlike the gothic writing he was used to.

'A timepiece,' Xajorkith explained. 'It counts off the hours and minutes whilst the ship is out at sea.'

'They could do that?' Luxor said, in wonderment.

'That and more besides,' Xajorkith answered. 'Quite the

masters of their craft were our forebears. But here, this is what I wanted to show you.'

Xajorkith took out a scroll from a shelf at the back of the cabin. Reverently he unrolled it.

'This is perhaps as ancient as can be,' he said, securing each end with a heavy brass weight from the table.

Luxor gazed at the scroll. He could instantly tell it was a map, but a map of some fair and pleasant land far away. Green hills and lakes stood out immediately, with fertile plains and cities dotted around …

He recognised a name and frowned, leaning in closer.

A city was marked at the edge of a bay, from which a river ran southwards.

'Xajorkith …'

'Aye,' Xajorkith said with a smile. 'A map of the world as it once was, before the Witchking, before the winter came. A map of the world as it should be.'

Luxor looked at the map for long moments, seeing the familiar landmarks of Midnight all anew. He straightened slowly, with a long sigh.

'Why did your father save this vessel, this place?' he asked, his voice a whisper. 'And why do you keep it still?'

Xajorkith smiled. 'Hope, my dear Luxor. Hope.'

The ice-fear twinged about them, and the Moon Ring glowed that little stronger.

Rorthron had spent two days further within the library of the Tower of the Moon, working feverously through its contents. Piles of books lay about him, scribbled notes and parchments scattered everywhere.

He had been working through the lineage of the House of the Moon when he stopped at a drawing of one of the Lords of yesteryear. He frowned, examining it closely. He had traced back the line for generations. Across all the renderings of those Lords, some flattering and others perhaps more accurate, each had always had their right arm clenched across their chest, proudly displaying a ring upon their finger. Some iconography displayed the ring accurately, a plain golden band, others seemed to take a more symbolic approach, thus the ring occasionally appeared to be wreathed in flames of red. The further back he went, the more common this representation appeared to be.

As if the ring has lost potency over all this time …

One image had a Lord holding the ring up for inspection, the artist had been keen to stress the ring was not upon the Lord's finger, but held up for all to see, pinched between thumb and first finger. Yet the Lord's expression was not one of joy or pride, but fury, or perhaps despair.

Rorthron turned the page.

The last image was of another ancient Lord, but this time there was no ring. Rorthron looked closer. Instead of a ring the Lord wore what seemed to be a medallion, swinging on a golden chain about his neck. The image was stylised again, difficult to read, but Rorthron's gaze was drawn to the medallion. It seemed to be …

A blue eye, set in a circle of red. An eye … a ring. A half-broken ring …

Rorthron sat back.

'A ring, but not just a ring!' he said out loud. 'It was a talisman, an ancient one. The eye and the ring were separated. The ring we still have … but the eye …'

He scrutinised the image again.

A gem perhaps? Set in the ring? But if the ring is broken and has lost potency over the years … So Corleth was not quite wrong when he told the tale of Rarnor. How Rarnor tried to impress a maiden, something was stolen that day. The Eye of the Moon!

336

Memories flooded back into his mind, a sudden rush of realisation. The Ring, festooned with a gem; sparkling, tantalising, somehow possessed of its own will and agency.

He blinked.

I knew this ... my memory ... how could I have been so careless, how did I forget about the Eye?

Rorthron knew enough about the ancient magic of the realm to fear his next thought.

These talismans were imbued with power by the Wise long ago ... and they have been put to good use and foul ... and they have their own wills. The Eye wants to be forgotten ...

Such power had a way of twisting the device and any who wielded it to a purpose hard to see. The Ice Crown itself was the most obvious example, but there had been others throughout history.

And if such a device were broken in two ... each part not whole. Its purpose would be further muddied, impossible to foresee ...

Broken magic, its original purpose cracked and scattered. There might be no telling what it might do. Magic had its own whims and desires, far beyond the reach of mortals.

Then, without the Eye, the Moon Ring's power may not be what we think it is, incomplete, fractured, broken, as Lorgrim said! It may be as much a danger to Luxor as the Witchking himself!

As he was reeling from his unexpected revelation he sensed a presence around him. He turned to see a figure glowing in the shadows of the library.

'Lorgrim!'

The Wise had their own means of communication between their kind. Lorgrim was a master of it.

'I am in haste, Rorthron. And we must be cautious. I know of what you seek.'

Rorthron tried to empty his mind of what he had been

researching, but Lorgrim's chuckle made a mockery of that attempt.

'If you sought to be stealthy, it is much too late,' Lorgrim said. 'I set you on this course, your work is at my bidding, though you knew it not.'

Rorthron said nothing.

'Come, come,' Lorgrim said. 'The broken Moon Ring? The First Power? Questions enough to pique your interest. The Wise love their lore, you are no different.'

'Why come to me now?' Rorthron said.

'Because you were right,' Lorgrim said. 'Though it pains me to admit it. The Witchking's power waxes and will sweep all before it. Not just Midnight, but all lands about.'

'You care little for those lands by your own admission,' Rorthron replied. 'Perhaps you fear for your own salvation?'

'I have my own motivations,' Lorgrim replied. 'Do you want my counsel or nay?'

'I would hear it,' Rorthron said. 'I am in haste, and those that seek to defend Midnight have little time remaining.'

'Very well then.' Lorgrim paused for a long moment, licking his lips and clasping his hands together, slowly clenching his fingers one by one.

'I told you that Gryfallon must have found a way to harness a power older than even the Wise in the creation of the Ice Crown,' Lorgrim said.

'Yet there are none,' Rorthron replied.

'Oh but there are,' Lorgrim said, with a grin. 'They are not what they once were, but they retain their craft and knowledge in some measure. And it is from them you need help to undo the potency of the Crown, willingly given in sacrifice. Only bravery, courage and a selfless nature can overcome fear. You need their magic!'

'Magic? Who are these people of which you speak?'

'You know them as skulkrin.'

'Skulkrin? You jest!'

Lorgrim laughed at the look on Rorthron's face.

'Oh, I'll admit they are considered little more than parasites or infestations by most. Rodents scurrying underfoot, ignored by the haughty Fey and hunted for sport by the men of the Free. But it is from them that the oldest native blood of Midnight comes … but that is not all …'

'There is a third?' Rorthron prompted.

'The very substance of the Ice Crown is not mere water,' Lorgrim said. Rorthron watched as his expression grew dreamy. 'No. The arts of Gryfallon were more subtle than that. To tame the cold and enslave the heart, that was complexity enough, but then, to take the land of Midnight itself and bind it to your will … that was mastery indeed.'

'The third,' Rorthron said again.

'Take the waters that infuse Midnight with its own lifeblood, the wells that rise up through the ground and, even now, provide us with warmth and food …'

'The lakes …' Rorthron murmured.

'Yes … the lakes of Midnight,' Lorgrim said. 'One particular lake I believe. Long study leads me to conclude that only in the waters of Lake Mirrow could you cause the Ice Crown to dissolve away. Only there, for from that water it must have been made long ago.'

Rorthron blew out a deep breath.

'And this First Power of which you spoke?'

Lorgrim looked aside. 'Long ago, the Wise feared the abuse of their power. They determined that it would be best spread amongst the peoples of the wide lands.' He laughed. 'Perhaps it made sense …'

'And what happened?'

'Talismans were crafted,' Lorgrim replied. 'The Ice Crown is the youngest and foulest of them. Given to Kings and Lords they were, both in Midnight and beyond these borders. It was hoped that they would use them well ...'

'And yet?'

'It was foolishness in the extreme,' Lorgrim replied. 'The Wise were diminished, leaving the likes of the Witchking to rise. The Free fell to petty squabbling. Over time the talismans were lost to history.'

'I don't understand ...'

'The power of the Wise,' Lorgrim snapped. 'The First Power! Broken asunder it was and now ... now he seeks to reunite it all.'

Rorthron stared. 'The Talismans still exist?'

'Enough of them,' Lorgrim replied. 'Midnight is but the beginning, he seeks more power than he can command with just his beloved Ice Crown ...'

'Then ...'

'I have done my part,' Lorgrim said, mirthless laughter upon his lips. 'And I will do no more. Use this knowledge wisely, young Rorthron. Use it wisely.'

Lorgrim's image crackled and faded into the darkness.

At last, the secret to his doom. Now the quest has a chance to succeed. And succeed it must, for it seems far greater peril lies before us if the Witchking achieves his goals!

The books were left untidied. Rorthron was already gone. Snow flurries swept up around a path that led swiftly to the east. The Forest of Shadows stirred briefly before all trace of his passage was lost on the deserted Plains of Blood.

Lord Morning pulled his cloak tighter about him, shivering in the chill wind blowing from the north. The Plains of Corelay remained clear of any intruders, but all camped within the walls of Xajorkith knew it could only be a short reprieve. An

340

army bigger than any of them had ever faced was massing on the borders of the realm, ready to march south and extinguish the Free from the history of Midnight.

'Feeling the cold?' Gard said, standing alongside him.

'The ice-fear grows,' Morning said. 'Doubtless the Witchking feels his victory is close at hand.'

'He has been overconfident before,' Gard said. 'Such pride oft goes before a fall.'

Morning shrugged. 'If I were he I would feel as confident. We are outnumbered perhaps two to one. We can't hold a siege, we have no allies to come to our aid and we are pressed back against our last defence scant days since first assailed. His strategy has been masterful.'

Gard nodded.

'And our leader sore lacks the traits of leadership,' Morning said, half under his breath.

'Lord Luxor of Odrark,' Gard said. 'You do not think him worthy of the heights to which he has risen?'

Morning turned to face Gard. 'I put more stock in experience and wisdom. You have fought this enemy all your life. I would rather serve you than an upstart Lord with a magic ring. It seems to have done little to aid us ...'

Gard raised his head slightly.

'I faced the Witchking at Valethor in the shadow of Gorgrath,' he said softly. 'I have felt the ice-fear time and again, stealing the cold from my heart and turning my limbs against my wishes. I have seen the bravest men reduced to abject cowards before my eyes, the stoutest hearts turned to blithering fools.'

Morning frowned, Gard looked directly into his eyes.

'I tell you truthfully,' Gard said. 'Had Lord Luxor not been there that day, I would not be standing here now. The Witchking has curated the ice-fear, focussed it somehow, projected it into the perfect weapon. None can withstand it. Until Lord

Luxor raised the ring we were all helpless, from the newest recruit to the most seasoned warrior. He combats it day by day, hour by hour. He defends us all by his will. Have you not seen the struggle he has with this magic? The Moon Ring is a potent ally for sure, but it has a price, and Luxor pays it on our behalf.'

'Then ...'

'I'll grant you he is young,' Gard said. 'But he has fought his share and his courage is not in doubt. If salvation is to come to the Free, it will come through Lord Luxor. History tells us that the House of the Moon retains the power granted to it by the Wise. There is none other who can wield it. For good or for ill, the choice of the Moonprince is made by fate. We have a choice too.'

'A choice?' Morning demanded.

Gard clapped him hard upon the shoulder.

'We can choose to be loyal to him,' Gard said and then fixed him with a stare. 'Or not. My choice is already made, I suggest you make up your mind ... and quickly.'

Far to the north, wind blew chill about the Liths to the west of the Forest of Lothoril. A group of four scouts were patrolling the land, preparing to ride back toward their home having conducted a search of the lands to the west of their realm. Riders from the Fey of Lothoril.

This particular route was much favoured by the scouts for many reasons. It took them further away from the Witchking's realm and it was typically peaceful throughout. The western-most reaches of Midnight were hardly populated at all, apart from some very small wandering communities that lived a miserable existence in the Snowhalls that had been built to offer some small shelter against the elements in these parts during the winter. They traded fish for cloths and utensils, contributing to a small economy the Fey availed themselves of. For their part, the Fey patrolled the lands and kept a measure of order.

The route took them across the Plains of Moon, a curiously named land, harking back to the old legends of the Free. The Tower of the Moon lay far to the south, many leagues distant. What connection there was between the two the Fey did not know, but it was written upon the ancient maps and so it was called.

The halfway mark of their journey was Moonhenge, an ancient assemblage of stones, at the far end of a line of Liths that extended many leagues from the Forest of Lothoril. Their alignment could be no accident, they ran straight and true, a clear path directly east to west, with the Henge at their most westerly point. What the purpose of such an arrangement might mean, none knew.

The weather was clear, but blustery, a teasing, dancing breeze which ruffled cloaks and jostled the riders as they drew close to the Henge.

'The Henge looks peaceful enough,' one said as they drew close.

'Aye,' said the leader. 'Let's make our search and head back. The weather will be taking a turn for the worse if I'm any judge of it.'

The others grumbled their agreement. Being caught outside in one of Midnight's wintry blizzards was not something they relished, not when the warmth and comfort of the Keep of Lothoril lay less than a day's ride away.

Moonhenge itself was a huge structure, built with some care and craftsmanship. It seemed to be of a similar age to the Liths, but whilst those were relatively common throughout Midnight, the Henges were less so, but the two seemed to be interlinked in some fashion. The Fey held that the Henges were ancient temples of a sort, meeting grounds for followers of some religion that had long since vanished from the world. The Fey were always careful to respect the stones however, there was a strong sense of power lurking around many of them, and those powers didn't always feel benign. If there was evil here, it was older even than the Witchking and best left undisturbed.

The Fey never ventured within the circle of Moonhenge, but only patrolled its outermost perimeter. Moonhenge had the touch of fear upon it, as if it had been cursed in the distant past. The Fey left it well alone.

The leader led his group in a slow trot around the silent stones. Snow had drifted up against them in places, but it was fresh and untouched. They completed half a circle around the northern most side and then turned to the south, following the line of stones.

They had completed the southern quarter when the leader reined in his horse and held up a hand, swiftly dismounting. The other scouts could immediately see what had caught his eye.

On the south east corner of the Henge, the snow had been pushed aside. Something had forced its way through the drift, a trail of footprints leading away towards the Downs of Mirrow.

The other scouts joined their leader, careful not to trample on the prints.

'What do you make of this?' he asked. 'No animal could make prints like this, and no reason to venture within the Henge either.'

The footprints were small and close together. He put his finger to his lips to indicate the need for stealth.

'A child perhaps?' one volunteered, his voice low

'Out here? Half a dozen leagues from the nearest outpost?' the leader replied. 'No, there's only one creature this can belong to. A skulkrin.'

'Up to mischief no doubt,' his companion replied.

'We had better investigate,' the leader said reluctantly. 'Two of you stay here and keep watch. You ...' he gestured to the nearest scout. 'With me. Let's see what we may happen upon.'

They left their horses behind and warily stepped within the circle of stones.

As they did so, the breeze dropped. The change was dramatic, causing both of them to look uneasily around. No sound, it was as if a door had been silently closed behind them. Not even the merest hint of wind, yet they could see it ruffling the hair of their companions still standing alert outside.

'I don't like this,' the scout whispered.

'Silence,' the leader hissed, with a confidence he did not feel.

Within the circle of stones the ground was flat and, for the most part, completely empty. Snow covered the ground, but without the wind, it lay flat and even, the trail of footprints leading from where they stood towards the very centre.

At that centre was another stone, lain sideways, with its long edge oriented north and south, clearly the centrepoint of the Henge, perhaps an altar or gathering stone. The tracks led straight towards it.

Their eyes met and they drew their swords before stepping forward.

As the leader's steps took him onwards, faint colours floated in the air about him. But they were elusive; when he turned to look they were gone, only to return on the edge of vision, tantalisingly out of reach. Sounds also reached his ears, but it was impossible to tell if they were real or imagined. He glanced at his companion, seeing the same bewilderment on his face. Words were cast upon the air about him, unintelligible, murmurings of voices just out of reach, eerie, yet somehow laced with menace.

The leader gestured, indicating that they should move apart as they approached the stone. It was close now, only a few yards ahead. The colours and the sounds swirled more closely about them.

Shadows ... Shadows ... Shadows ...

The leader swallowed, trying to stop his body from trembling, telling himself it was the cold and nothing else, but knowing that his kind was not welcome here.

Then he heard another sound, different from the mesmerizing murmurs all about him. The sound of crying, of despair. The light about them seemed dimmer somehow, as if twilight had come early despite the morning hour.

As both Fey rounded the edge of the central stone they spied a small figure huddled against it, curled up, with its small arms wrapped around its knees, its head buried in its clothing. The sobs came from it, both could see its body shivering, racked by whatever woe had befallen it.

The skulkrin heard them, looking up as they approached.

'No! Khlee! Stay away! The Shadows ... the shadows!'

'What do you speak of skulkrin?' the leader demanded. 'What brings you to this awful place?'

The skulkrin did not respond for a moment, but then broke out into a keening wail. It took a moment for the Fey to realise it was ... singing. Singing a song that they had never heard before.

Yet somehow they knew it and felt compelled to join, adding their own counterpoint to the refrain. The glows and sounds swirled about them stronger still.

A faint wind swept around the tableaux.

Gradually the skulkrin's voice shrivelled to silence and they were left with only its sobs once more.

The Fey wondered at the song, for it had not evil intent; they sensed a feeling of remorse more than anything else.

'Come skulkrin, tell me on what mischief you are bound?' the leader asked.

'None, my Lord,' came the swift answer, but the guilty expression on the creature's face belied its words. 'None of my own ...'

'I need not ask whose ...'

'I have done bad,' the skulkrin cried. 'Khlee! Robbed and stolen I have. Sleep-frost ... but I was hungry and he had food! Even skulkrin have to eat. Nasty boy, prodded me with a knife he did!'

The Fey tightened their grip on their swords.

'I didn't eat him ...' the skulkrin complained. 'Nice boy, kind boy ... surely he was ...'

'Why are you here?'

'Thought to hide, thought to find shelter ... but the shadows ... the shadows of death. I cannot flee ... too tired ... Khlee!'

At the words the lights and sounds curled about them once more, their eerie voices. The leader felt suddenly weary, as if his very energy was being drawn away ... he saw his companion stagger.

'Sire ...'

'Bring him!' the leader said. 'Doubtless Lord Lothoril will want to question him.'

His companion hoisted the unresisting skulkrin up and carried him back the way they had come. The leader paused for a moment, facing into the swirling colours.

'We mean no trespasses,' he said, stepping backwards, 'No offence ...'

The colours swirled, but did not impede their progress. As they reached the perimeter the other two scouts dragged them through to safety.

As they did, the leader fancied he heard words in his ears as the lights faded away.

Shadows of death ... shadows of death ...

Then the wind was back, the colours gone, everything was as it had been before.

The leader blinked the weariness out of his eyes. 'Saddle up, we ride to the Keep of Lothoril!'

Luxor returned to the citadel and made his way upwards to the towers. There, in one of the highest rooms he locked the door behind him and knelt upon the floor. He clenched his fist, trying to slow his churning thoughts long enough to concentrate. The Moon Ring glimmered on his hand, its glow uncertain and unsure.

Think! Be still, my thoughts!

With great effort the walls of Xajorkith fell away before him and the strange vision of Midnight arose about him. Everywhere he cast he felt despair and despondency. The inhabitants of villages hiding out of sight wherever they could, the guards left on duty at the keeps and citadels peering out into the whiteness, wondering when their doom would come.

Midnight's strength falls and it is all down to me. My fault! My responsibility! Did we have a chance to stop the Witchking? Have I failed where I might have succeeded? Or was this hopeless from the outset and it is our time to be written out of the annals of history?

With fear clutching at his mind, Luxor swept his thoughts ever northwards, seeking what might be his last remaining hope. Mountains and hills flashed by, and the ever present darkness in the far north throbbed closer. He dared not approach it, revealing himself to the Witchking directly …

I have barely the strength to use the Ring, and certainly not the strength for that! And if he knew our despair, our end would be all the swifter!

A presence came to him.

'Rorthron!'

Aye, Luxor. I have tidings. At last I have unlocked the secret of the Ice Crown.

Luxor's heart leapt in response.

'You have divined how to destroy it?'

I have ... Morkin's quest is laid out before us.

'Then tell me!'

Chapter Fifteen

He stands at the Citadel of Xajorkith,
looking north to the Plains of Corelay

Luxor stood for long moments, considering what he had heard.

Insanity! And I thought we might have stood even the barest chance, but now …

Rorthron's description of what Morkin needed to achieve still echoed in his mind. Luxor had broken the connection, seething with anger.

Madness. I should have trusted my instincts and not some crazy wish fulfilment of the so called Wise! Time to end this folly now.

The Moon Ring still in place, he sought for long minutes, sweeping his gaze across the icy contours of Midnight, searching …

There!

A sense of warmth and boyish good humour, but something else too, a power he could not identify.

'Morkin!'

Father? Father!

'Yes, my son. Are you well, are you safe?'

Between the ice, the wolves, the mountains and the Witchking's hordes, my days have been full of adventure … and just wait until I tell you …

'My son, it is time to return to me.'

Return? What of the Ice Crown?

'Rorthron has divined the ultimate purpose of your quest, but ...'

How to destroy the Ice Crown?

Luxor sighed. 'Yes indeed. But it is impossible; he has led me astray with false hope. Such is the fell magic that created it. What is required can no longer be found. Perhaps a hundred moons ago we might have had a chance, but not now ...'

Tell me! I must know how to destroy it!

'Rorthron is a fool,' Luxor said. 'The Ice Crown can only be unmade by the arts that made it. It is bound to Midnight itself, connected in some fashion to the land and its people, not a natural object. The means to do so is lost. Morkin, your quest is over, return to me before the Witchking's hordes make it impossible.'

Father, tell me what Rorthron said!

Luxor sighed, but he knew his son's determination. He only wished his own spirit had remained as strong.

'Very well,' Luxor said heavily. 'I will tell you, much good it will do. But you will return to me immediately, the road south should be clear, but stay to the west ...'

Tell me the secret of the Ice Crown.

Luxor sighed, but relented.

'First the ice,' Luxor said. 'It must be unsealed by dragon fire. You see? An impossibility, a dragon such as Rorthron describes has not been seen in Midnight for generations of the Free.'

Luxor could sense his son's earnest excitement through the link between them. What young man wouldn't be enthralled by tales of dragons?

'Then the fear,' Luxor continued. 'A skulkrin's favour. The Crown must be sprinkled with their sleep-frost. But none can summon the skulkrin at will and they will not treat with the Free or the Fey.'

Luxor knew the skulkrin were common enough in the northlands, but none had ever tried to reason with them, let alone seek their cooperation.

'And then the substance of the Crown itself. Ice is from water … there is a lake. Lake Mirrow, within which the Crown can be dissolved, but only once the prior incantations have been performed. Now, enough of this enchantment. I would have you at my side ere it is too late. Make haste to me, son. Time is short.'

Father … no! Listen to me!

Luxor jolted, almost losing the mental link.

'No? Morkin, you must listen. The quest is over, Midnight is almost overrun. Rorthron has failed us, there is …'

Something shifted in the mental image of his son. Luxor watched as Morkin stepped back, his view widening to take in a boulder and icy strewn shoreline.

Father, I have found the lake …

'That is not sufficient,' Luxor said, shaking his head.

Morkin smiled, and then gestured with his left hand. Luxor's gaze travelled with the gesture. He staggered back as a monstrous visage came into view. A vast scaled head, with an enormous sinuous body trailing back from it, atop which sprang two wings that dwarfed the rest of the creature. A whip-like tail completed the ensemble.

Luxor stared aghast. Morkin's face was split by a wide grin.

You see, I found the dragon too!

'You … found …' Luxor managed. 'But how? Where? Morkin, it's deadly dangerous! Run from it, a dragon …'

I WOULD PREFER YOU TO TALK TO ME RATHER THAN ABOUT ME, IF IT IS ALL THE SAME TO YOU.

This time Luxor did stagger back, the mental voice resonating around inside his head as if projected into a vast empty cavern.

'It talks?' he managed.

353

I TALK. YES, I MASTERED YOUR SIMPLE FORM OF COMMUNICATION UNCOUNTED MOONS BEFORE YOU WERE BORN, MOONPRINCE OF MIDNIGHT. YOU ARE LUXOR I BELIEVE, YOU SEEK THE DEMISE OF THE WITCHKING.

'I … yes,' Luxor stuttered. 'Yes, yes I do.'

I HAVE AGREED TO AID YOUR SON IN HIS QUEST. YOU SAY A DRAGON'S FIRE IS REQUIRED TO DESTROY THE ICE CROWN? THIS DRAGON WILL SEE IT DONE.

Luxor stared, unable to form words.

NOT VERY ARTICULATE FOR A MOONPRINCE, ARE YOU?

Luxor swallowed. 'This … this is the first time I have spoken to a dragon. I did not know such a thing was possible.'

Luxor wasn't sure, but he could have sworn the dragon winked at him.

AH, WELL. MUCH THAT IS CONSIDERED IMPOSSIBLE CAN BE DONE WITH A LITTLE APPLICATION AND FORTITUDE. YOU SHOULD NOT BE SO QUICK TO DISMISS THE WISE, THEY CAME BY THEIR NAME FOR A REASON.

'Who are you?'

I AM FARFLAME, LORD OF THE DRAGONS OF MIDNIGHT. THOUGH TRUTH BE TOLD I AM ALSO THE LAST OF THE DRAGONS OF MIDNIGHT, SO MY LORDSHIP IS SOMETHING OF A TITLE WITHOUT MUCH AUTHORITY. HOWEVER, DECISIONS IN MY REALM ARE USUALLY UNANIMOUS.

'Then …'

YOUR SON HAS BEEN TRUTHFUL IN HIS CONDUCT. HE IS A CREDIT TO YOU MOONPRINCE. I AM AWARE OF HIS ORIGINS AND THE MYTHS THE FEY HAVE WOVEN ABOUT HIS PURPOSE. I WILL DO MY

UTMOST TO SEE THIS DONE. THUS YOU HAVE MY SERVICE, SUCH AS IT IS.

Luxor recovered enough to utter, 'My Lord Farflame. Such service is unlooked for in a time of great despair, but you have kindled hope once again. Perhaps the Ice Crown can truly be despatched as the Wise believe.'

And there is more news!

Morkin's voice was excited.

We stand on the shores of Lake Mirrow. It is here we must return. I have also encountered a skulkrin father! He stole my provisions, now I know I will find him again. This quest can succeed, I know it can ...

Luxor shook his head in bewilderment.

'Forgive me, Morkin,' he said. 'I should have had greater faith in my son. But know this. Time is truly short. Fortune has not been so kind to me. Dawn has fallen and Xajorkith will soon be opposed. I cannot contact Corleth at all and the Fey have not come to our aid. We fear defeat in days. If we are to triumph in this, it must be soon. I fear to put this upon your shoulders, but your quest may be all that is left to us now.'

I will not let you down!

Tears sprang into Luxor's eyes and the vision wavered. He fancied he heard Rorthron's laughter in his mind.

'You knew this, you have watched me anguish and burn with fury over your plans, old man?' Luxor cried out.

The laughter faded and Rorthron's voice somehow interspersed itself between them all.

I knew enough. I bear you no malice, Lord Luxor. But a little humility in a leader is no bad thing. The Wise still teach lessons. You have done well enough.

'We will speak in person again at some point,' Luxor said. 'I may have some choice words for you.'

The laughter returned.

Those I may deserve.

Luxor turned the focus of his mind back to his son.

'Midnight hopes with you Morkin. All the Lords of Midnight will shout your name. Go with our blessing and bring about the demise of the Witchking. Morkin of Free and of Fey! Counselled by the Wise and flown by a dragon!'

Luxor heard Farflame roar in approval and then the vision flickered and died.

Luxor staggered, thinking it all through in his mind.

A dragon!

Luxor could scarce believe it. He shook his head in bewilderment.

'Now the quest begins in earnest.'

Farflame flew low over the forest eaves, his pinions and fantails fluttering in the blast of air. Morkin was crouched low, huddled as deep in his clothing as he could manage. Speed was certainly an advantage of riding a dragon, yet the cold! He had never felt such a wind.

Through watering eyes he could make out the forest falling away beneath them. It reminded him of the Forest of Shadows far to the south. Lothoril seemed similar in many ways, a vast circle of trees around what once must have been a verdant valley. Within, Morkin could see a Keep and a Tower, centred around a lake caught between low hills.

Beyond the forest, Morkin could just make out a jagged row of mountains on the horizon. They were dim with distance and had a foreboding aspect in the faint northern light. They almost looked like a row of bleached teeth set upon the ground. **THOSE ARE THE MOUNTAINS OF UGRAK, THE WESTERNMOST EDGE OF THE WITCHKING'S REALM. WITHIN THOSE MOUNTAINS LIES ONE OF**

THE CITADELS OF THE WITCHKING'S KINGDOM, THE CITADEL OF VORGATH.

So close! I am surprised the Witchking tolerates the Fey such a short distance away.

THEY DO NOT BOTHER HIM, HE DOES NOT BOTHER THEM. NOT YET.

I fear that will not remain the same for long if the Witchking gets his way!

A thought occurred to Morkin as he watched the distant line of mountains.

With a dragon, my journey to the Tower will be so much easier …

He felt a rumble between his legs as the dragon drew breath.

I DARE NOT APPROACH THE TOWER, YOUNG SQUIRE. THE MOUNTAINS ARE A BARRIER I CANNOT PASS. THE WITCHKING KNOWS OF DRAGONS, THERE WERE MANY OF US LONG AGO. DO YOU NOT THINK HE HAS THOUGHT LONG AND HARD HOW TO SAFEGUARD HIS OWN DOMAIN? EVEN DRAGONS ARE NOT IMMUNE FROM THE ICE-FEAR. YOU MUST FIND ANOTHER WAY HE HAS NOT CONSIDERED.

Morkin cursed under his breath. It would have been too good to be true.

So how will I get across those mountains? There seems to be no way!

NOR WILL I FERRY YOU EVERYWHERE. I AM NOT AS YOUNG AS ONCE I WAS.

Farflame banked through the air, Morkin could see he was making for the keep.

'Don't go too close,' Morkin yelled. 'I don't know how they will react to seeing a dragon swoop down from the sky!'

TERROR AND PANIC IS THE USUAL RESPONSE. IT'S VERY TEDIOUS.

Morkin smiled to himself. Farflame back swept his wings and thudded to the ground some three hundred yards from the keep. Morkin could see a troupe of guards between their position and the keep, they were armed with pikes and halberds, nervously advancing.

Morkin dropped down.

'I suggest you stay here.'

AGREED.

Morkin walked across towards the keep, stopping short of the advancing guards. Morkin could see they were dressed in the sturdy leather armour common to many of the Fey, but there was something rougher about their appearance than would be acceptable to the Fey of the southlands.

'Who are you?' one demanded, stepping forward with a pike outstretched. 'What is your business in the domain of Lothoril?'

'I am Morkin, son of Luxor the Moonprince,' Morkin said. 'I seek shelter.'

'Moonprince?' the guard replied. 'We have heard rumours … but … and is this your dragon?'

Before Morkin could open his mouth again the rumbling dragonspeak thrummed through their minds.

NO, I AM NOT.

'It talks?' The guard stuttered in amazement.

Farflame let out a blast of air, the dragon equivalent of a sigh.

'Will you help me?' Morkin asked. 'Time is short and the fate of Midnight hangs in the balance.'

The guard recovered himself. 'You will follow me. Lord Lothoril will likely be interested in your tale. What of your dragon …?'

I AM NOT HIS DRAGON!

'He will likely hunt,' Morkin began and then reconsidered his words as the faces of the guards blanched in horror. 'Horses! Wild Horses … we don't taste good apparently.'

THE VERY THOUGHT.

Behind Morkin, Farflame shook his mighty head and then launched into the air, circling above the keep.

CALL FOR ME WHEN REQUIRED. I MAY RETURN.

Morkin looked back to the guard who had been questioning him.

'Shall we?'

'This way,' the guard said, turning on his heel and walking towards the keep. The rest of the troupe surrounded Morkin. He noticed they kept their weapons ready.

Lord Morning continued to walk the walls of the citadel, trying to ease the cold out of his limbs. The conversation with Gard had left him undecided. The defeat at Dawn had sown doubts in his mind. They were trapped here at Xajorkith. His own keep lay undefended, he'd evacuated it, down to the last man, woman and child, sending them all south to the capital. He held little hope that the Doomguard would leave it undefiled.

Luxor's fault, Luxor's responsibility! And now he cowers from the fight. What if he fails to regain his resolve, do we trust in Gard who failed at Blood? Shimeril and Blood, old men with many tales to tell, but of no greater worth now ... is everything already lost?

'You seem upset my Lord.'

The voice caught him by surprise. He turned to see Silence standing alongside him on the battlements.

'I have a right to be,' Morning replied. 'We all do.'

'That the Witchking hunts us down and tries to slay us?' she answered. 'Such are the fortunes of war, yes?'

'More that we have no leader worth following,' Morning grumbled.

Silence turned and walked towards him.

'You do not trust in Luxor then?'

Morning sighed and then shook his head. 'I see blind faith, a little luck, a trinket from the past, but I do not see a leader.'

'And what would a leader be to you?' she asked.

'Bold and strong, defiant in the face of adversity,' Morning replied. 'With some measure of success to point to!'

'You were not in Gorgrath then,' Silence replied. 'You did not ...'

'Gard has already spoken of that, perhaps he hopes to hide his own ineptitude in that battle ...'

'You speak of what you do not know,' Silence said, raising her voice. You did not stand there and watch as the ice-fear ripped through the hearts of men and women unhindered. I heard those screams, they haunt me still.'

Morning looked at her, her gaze was locked on his, unwavering.

'I rode with the Lord of Shadows, he of the Fey, that day. Even they succumbed to the Witchking's bane, a despair so awful none could resist it. Hardened warriors and mighty Lords fell before its power. Lord Gard knows the truth, and a humbling lesson it was for him. Had he listened to Luxor earlier, more might have been saved, perhaps we would have even scored a victory.'

'Victory!'

Silence moved closer. 'It was only by the power of the Moon Ring that any of us still live today. Luxor may have only been a minor Lord and I know well the humiliation of that position in the ranks of the Free! But he is the descendant of royalty of old. The House of the Moon remains, protected by the Wise until this hour and he is the one who can wield that ring. Only him. Without it, the full force of the ice-fear would descend upon us and reduce us to mindless creatures crawling in the snow, cowering at the Witchking's feet and begging for death ...'

'What are you saying ...?'

'You already owe Luxor your life. As all of us do. As holder of the Moon Ring Luxor protects us all, he is bound to that fate, unasked for. Do you not see the toll it takes upon him? Why, every hour of every day of every moon he is drained, fighting the unholy weapon of the Witchking! Do not assume the ring works alone, it uses Luxor for its power.'

Her gaze remained unflinching.

'What do you ask?'

'Only this,' she said. 'Listen to your heart on this matter. Do not despair. Have faith in this power, without it we are bereft …'

Morkin looked about the keep as he was led inside. The Keep of Lothoril was very different from the distant Keep of Odrark where he had spent his childhood as a squire. There cold stone walls lit with candles and decorated with tapestries were his overriding memory, here the keep seemed fused with vegetation, enormous trees were somehow woven into the fabric of the building, serving as buttresses and supports, even bridges and walkways. Damage to the stone work from nameless battles in the past had been repaired, not by stonemasons, but by gardeners – cunningly weaving different plants throughout the rocks.

Instead of flagstones, the ground underfoot was grass, somehow kept green against the endless winter. Morkin smelled the scent of flowers upon the air, reminding him of a spring he had only dared hope for.

Yet all about him the Fey were ready for battle. All were armed with short bows, standing in ordered rows as he was escorted forward into a central courtyard within the keep. There, sitting on a throne within the carved out ruin of an ancient tree sat a Fey, bearing a silver coronet.

He was already scrutinising Morkin has he approached.

'Our visitor from the distant south,' he said, his voice reaching out across the courtyard.

Morkin bowed low.

'Rise dear fellow. I am Lord Lothoril and you are welcome here.'

Morkin rose to his feet as Lothoril got up himself and came down to meet him. Lothoril raised a hand. For a moment Morkin thought Lothoril was going to strike him, but found his chin grasped and his head turned from side to side.

'Half-Fey and half-Free, eh? Not a bad mix it would seem. Handsome enough, tall enough, bright eyes and a face that has already seen more than it would care to recall. Arrives on a dragon, unannounced. You must be Morkin, son of Luxor, I presume?'

Morkin was momentarily lost for words. Lothoril grinned.

'No doubt you expected to have to plead your case and explain all to us lost northern brethren of the southern Fey,' he said. 'We are not so cut off as they would have you believe. We keep our own council, and none traverse our lands without us knowing all about them.'

'Then …'

'Yes, we know your mission, son of the Moonprince,' Lothoril said. 'We know of the legends, we know of the history and the lore. You seek to enter the lands of the Witchking and destroy the Ice Crown.'

Morkin nodded. 'You speak the truth. And I am in haste …'

Lothoril nodded. 'The Witchking focuses his fury on the south, his armies sweeping all before it. We have seen it here too.'

'I was told you would help me,' Morkin said. 'Did the Fey of Thrall speak truly?'

Morkin pulled out a crumpled parchment and handed it to Lothoril. Lothoril took it and read it aloud.

'To our northern brethren, I Lord Thrall of the southern Fey, do beseech, request and require that you render all service such as our kindred is known for, unto he that presenteth this petition, being truly Morkin, son of Luxor, the revealed Moonprince of Midnight.' Lothoril stopped. 'Well, my people, we have been duly tasked!'

A chuckle rumbled around the courtyard.

'Rather pompous old Thrall, isn't he?' Lothoril said, with a grin.

Morkin smiled and nodded.

'Fear not then,' Lothoril said, standing straight and putting on a mock stern face. 'We shall thus render all service to you young Morkin. Beseech and request what you will. We will see it done.'

'Food, clothing and a rest is all I need,' Morkin replied. 'And then, everything you can tell me about the Ice Crown.'

Lothoril grew serious.

'Aye,' he raised his voice and gestured to waiting staff. 'See to it! Make up a room! But first – food!'

Luxor summoned the Lords back into the hall of Xajorkith. The fire had been made up, its ruddy light flickering around the lofty beams. Along the walls hung tapestries and shields, variations of the magenta coat of arms of previous Lords of Xajorkith dating far back into the past. Many were battered from battles long forgotten, but all proudly bore the golden lion and cyan star of the city.

'I have been remiss in my duties,' Luxor began, looking around the assembled throng. He took a moment to note them all. Friends in Blood and Shimeril, support from Xajorkith and Gard. There was doubt from Morning and from Silence ... she merely observed, clearly waiting to hear what he had to say.

'But that ends now,' he continued. 'We have been forced out of our homes by overwhelming force. The Witchking has put forth his full strength upon the Solstice and caught us unawares. We stood at Blood and fell back, we stood at Dawn and fell back, now those of us that remain stand here at Xajorkith awaiting our doom.

'We have fought hard and fought well, but none knew of the might the Witchking had assembled, nor that the Fey would abandon us in our time of need.'

'Abandoned us?' Morning interjected. 'They will not come?'

'I have no news,' Luxor said. 'I sent a friend to recruit them. It seems he has failed. I sense neither him nor the Fey via the ring. The Fey are not coming.'

A mutter of dismay went around the hall. Clearly most had still hoped for some salvation from that quarter.

'Marakith, Kumar and Athoril attempt to reach us, and they bring Trorn too from the east,' Luxor said, 'But an army of Doomguard lie between them and us. They have turned to the south west, journeying as fast as they may though the domain of Trorn. They will reach us, but not for some days. I will not lie to you. We are outnumbered two to one, perhaps three to one. We are ill-prepared for a long siege.'

'Then, other than a bloody sword or a short but ignoble lingering death,' Morning said, his voice disparaging. 'What sage counsel do you offer, Moonprince?'

Luxor smiled grimly.

'I am not one of the Wise,' Luxor said. 'I am no lore master, I know not the history of the House of the Moon or what it once was. All I know is that this ring came to me from one Rorthron the Wise, the only one of their ilk that has deigned to help us in our struggle against the Witchking. It allows me to combat the ice-fear, to turn it aside for a time for those close by. It means a fight equal in skill, without our courage deserting us when we need it most.'

'Such a blessing is not in doubt,' Gard said. 'Many of us have experienced this, but that still leaves us facing odds no gambler would take.'

Luxor nodded.

'Here my tale grows strange,' Luxor said. 'For us, warriors used to putting our stock in weapons and tactics of war, it took me a long time to accept that despite our skills and fortitude, we might never prevail against a power such as the Witchking. In prior battles he has looked to fortify his own holdings in the north. This time he exerts his full strength, his plan to consume all of Midnight and turn it to his will. You have all felt the ice-fear grow and seen me struggle to defy it with this Ring of mine. It burns upon my very soul …'

'The answer lies not in swords and shields and bows,' Silence said, speaking for the first time, 'but elsewhere?'

'But you've already said the Fey aren't coming,' Morning replied. 'They are the only other power capable of resisting the Witchking. They have magic, but they selfishly defend their own interests within the safety of their forest realms …'

Luxor held up a hand.

'I speak not of the Fey,' he said. 'The Witchking's power emanates from a talisman, safely locked away within his domain.'

'We know of legends,' Morning replied. 'You speak of the Ice Crown, what of it? It is untouchable, indestructible.'

Luxor straightened.

'It cannot be destroyed,' Luxor said. 'But it can be unmade. Rorthron the Wise has discovered how that can be done.'

'Unmade?' Gard said.

'But none can approach the Ice Crown,' Silence said. 'It would freeze the heart of any that tried, not even the Wise can approach, so the stories tell.'

Luxor nodded. 'This has long been held true, but there is one who can.'

The Lords looked amongst themselves, talking in urgent tones before turning back to Luxor with the obvious question.

'Who indeed?' Luxor said. 'I was not at all happy to find that the one Rorthron revealed to me was my own squire, Morkin, whom I then discovered was my son!'

'Your son? The squire? The boy that accompanied you?' Gard said. 'Why did you not say sooner?'

'I did not believe it,' Luxor said. 'I sought to protect Morkin from what I saw as the folly of the Wise. It is they that let the Witchking rise, after all, but matters were taken out of my hands. Morkin is my son, and a son of a Feyish woman of Thrall from long ago. The Fey have legends which tell of one born of Fey and Free and by virtue of the gifts of both our races the ice-fear rolls from him like drops of rain in a summer shower. Morkin can approach the Ice Crown … and live.'

'And do what? Unmake it? How?' Gard demanded.

'The process is arcane,' Luxor said,' And unlikely. A combination of a skulkrin's sleep-frost, drowning in a lake and a dragon's fire.'

'Dragon's fire?' Shimeril said. 'There are no dragons in Midnight, not since the moons of our forefathers.'

Luxor closed his eyes, raising the hand which bore the Moon Ring. All within the hall suddenly beheld a vision in their minds. A monstrous head, a vast array of teeth and scaled skin …

Some yelled, others jolted back out of their chairs in shock and surprise.

'You … you have a dragon as an ally?' Silence managed, recovering first.

Luxor nodded. 'Unlikely as it sounds, Morkin has ventured into the far North. Even now he approaches the realm of the Witchking.'

Conversation dropped as all considered the plan.

'If the Ice Crown were to be unmade,' Shimeril said. 'Then the Witchking's power …?'

'Ended at a stroke,' Luxor said. 'Rorthron's firm intention from the beginning. Winter itself would be ended, the Frozen Wastes unlocked, the ice-fear banished to memory …'

'Our battles …' Blood said.

'All in vain,' Luxor said. 'In terms of outright victory at least. I did not want to see it, but now I reveal the truth. We cannot prevail against the Witchking in terms of military prowess. Perhaps even with the help of the Fey that would have been impossible. But we do not seek to beat him in battle.'

'A decoy,' Gard said. 'Our entire host, a decoy. A feint, to distract him …'

'We keep the Witchking's focus on ourselves,' Luxor said. 'We make such a battle that he has no choice but to divert all his attention here, to the heart of our domain. The Free look to Xajorkith as the capital of our people. But you are right – it is a feint, a feint to allow Morkin to slip within his realm and destroy his power from within.'

'So you ask us to sacrifice our lives for the poor chance of a boy venturing into the heart of the Witchking's realm hoping to steal away the source of his power?' Morning spluttered, looking around him for support.

Heads turned towards Luxor and a stillness fell upon the hall.

Luxor straightened and pursed his lips. For a moment he stood there silent before he looked up and gazed at Lord Morning.

'Yes.'

'So, young squire,' Lothoril said. 'A weary way you have come! A strange route indeed even when borne on the wings of a dragon!'

Morkin almost forgot to reply, so fixated was he on the food about him.

Unusually for the Fey there were meats aplenty. Morkin helped himself with abandon once given permission by his host, though he did comment upon it.

'The southern Fey have warmer climes,' Lothoril said with a chuckle. 'Softer beds and easier lives no doubt. The forest hereabouts provides for us. We tend it and the animals within, that trade goes both ways. Eat your fill, you will doubtless need your strength for the travails ahead.'

Morkin did as he was bade with no reluctance, his hunger was extreme. Only after several minutes was he able to slow and listen to Lothoril once more.

'I will leave this part out of the songs my people will doubtless compose in moons to come,' Lothoril said with a chuckle. 'The gallant choice of the ages, with fat dripping from his chin won't make for the best chorus I fear!'

Morkin laughed and wiped at his face.

'I thank you for your hospitality,' he said. 'It is a welcome relief after my travels. From Thrall to here was a weary road and cold for the most part.'

'And yet it seems you are the half-Free and half-Fey of legend,' Lothoril said. 'The son of a revealed Moonprince, if I am to trust my southern brethren.'

'Scant days ago I would have laughed at such a thing myself,' Morkin replied. 'But it was revealed to me by Rorthron of Wise ...'

Lothoril nodded, 'Ah ... the Wise. Yes. We have one here-abouts, locked deep in his tower. A taciturn fellow. We haven't seen him in generations of our folks, save when he chooses to vouchsafe some small doggerel of fact. Tricky folk by all accounts. You are fortunate indeed to have conversed with one at length, few have that privilege!'

'And it is he who started me on this quest.'

'To destroy the Ice Crown. No small feat.' Lothoril grew serious. 'It has been tried before you know, it is not a happy tale.'

'Yanathel,' Morkin whispered.

'Aye,' Lothoril said. 'A distant cousin of mine, many times removed of course, but still a relative. The stories said she was especially light and fleet of foot, able to travel half the length of Midnight in a day. Fanciful stuff perhaps, but she was marked out as different from an early age. Utterly confident, utterly bold she was. The spirt of the Fey was strongest upon her in an age; there have been none like her since.'

'What happened to her?'

Lothoril sighed. 'She travelled far and wide through Midnight, some said she ventured beyond the Frozen Wastes somewhere in the north, rumours of a passage to another realm. I doubt that, but she knew the whole of Midnight well. She spoke to all she met, even the animals of the realm. She longed for the end of the winter and a return to the summer of ancient song. Perhaps she fell in love with that desire, for it consumed her, until her every thought was focussed on bringing it to fruition.'

Morkin listened without interruption.

'Of course, the Witchking stood between her and that outcome. She determined that she would bring about his end if she could. She consulted with the Wise, journeying to their towers and harrying them for their lore and understanding. She thought herself immune to the ice-fear, and it seemed she was. She fought in many battles against the Foul, still valiant whilst others crumpled around her in despair. What she learnt in her travels I could not say, but one day she was gone.

'We followed her trail as far as the Mountains of Ugrak, before the gates of that cursed citadel, Vorgath. We could follow no further. We knew what she had tried to do.

'The Ice Crown,' Morkin whispered.

'We were in hiding,' Lothoril said, his own voice dropping to sepulchral tones. 'Waiting, hoping for her to return – when a blast of fear so extreme, so cold and terrible, swept across us. Strong Fey warriors fell where they stood, their hearts stopped dead by the terror. None of us who survived were left unscarred. Even today I tremble at the memory.

'But we were far from the heart of that detonation of wrath. It spun out, a great circle of horror and dread from the lands of the Witchking. From then on we all knew where the Ice Crown lay, the maps are clear enough. The shock came from the Tower of Doom itself. What it must have been like to be at the centre of that horror I cannot begin to fathom, but it was there Yanathel met her fate. The event went unmarked by the Witchking, there was no body, no word, nothing. Some hold she might still be alive, locked inside some dungeon without hope of rescue, driven to insanity by the constant fear, a plaything of the Witchking. But she was lost to us that day, none have ever tried again. Lost, long ago.'

'Until now.'

Lothoril looked at him. 'I cannot in good conscience recommend the path you take. But, if you have come this far, I doubt any words of mine will dissuade you from your quest. Yet, even if you could retrieve that fell talisman, what then? It must be protected by spells more powerful than any weapon the Fey or Free can bring to bear.'

'I know how to destroy it,' Morkin said. 'Did you not see the dragon I rode in on?'

'I did,' Lothoril replied. 'And most impressive it was. A dragon's fire is a potent weapon indeed, but set against the Witchking's might? Is it enough?'

Morkin shook his head. 'Two other things I must secure. The Ice Crown must be taken to Lake Mirrow ...'

'I know it,' Lothoril said. 'It is not far from here ...'

'There to be cast into its waters,' Morkin said. 'But not until it is cast insensible.'

'What do you mean? Insensible?'

Morkin sighed. 'Something I have yet to find. The sleep-frost of the skulkrin ... I encountered one on the way here, he tricked me and took my provisions, I nearly died as a result. I was tracking him when the dragon found me ...'

Lothoril sat back and rubbed his chin. 'Perhaps fate does favour you then, son of the Moonprince. My scouts captured a skulkrin yestereve! We caught him prowling the edge of our domain to the west, the Liths of Moon. They brought him back, cursing and spitting; we were to drive him to our borders and cast him out ...'

'Say you have not!' Morkin gasped.

'Nay,' Lothoril replied, 'He is locked safely away, but I would not count on him for help. A unpleasant enough creature ...'

'If he is the same one I met,' Morkin said. 'Perhaps I might persuade him to help me.'

'The skulkrin are not trustworthy,' Lothoril replied. 'They are vermin, you should not expect anything.'

'Yet a skulkrin I need, 'Morkin said. 'Or I cannot destroy the Ice Crown.'

Lothoril sighed. 'Very well, I will take you to him. But there remains the small obstacle of reaching the Witchking's realm.'

Morkin frowned. 'I have seen it on the maps, it is not far now – two days hard march? I cannot delay, Luxor and the Free are in peril. Xajorkith may fall at any time ...'

'I do not seek to delay you, but to aid you,' Lothoril said. 'The Plains of Lost lie between here and the mountains of his homeland. They are treacherous and infested with his armies. Do not think he leaves those lands unguarded! Without a guide, you will not find a path … and I daresay a dragon may be rather too conspicuous.'

'Do you know such a guide?' Morkin asked.

Lothoril smiled. 'As a matter of fact, I do …'

Pandemonium in the hall! All about Luxor the Lords were arguing, gesturing and shaking their fists at each other. Luxor let the debate run.

'I see no chance here,' Morning said. 'The boy will be found and killed, our chance destroyed. Luxor has sent his son to his end. None can penetrate the circle of the enemy.'

'If we cannot prevail in battle,' Silence said, 'such a ploy has merit. I would do it myself if my ancestry allowed me to approach the Witchking's realm. The Witchking has a vulnerable spot, we have a chance to exploit it and end his power forever. A scant chance, but worth the risk …'

'At the price of all our lives on the stake?' Morning answered, shaking his head. 'There must be a better plan than this! Even if Morkin does succeed, what then? What would be left but a ruined Midnight, razed to the ground by the foe!'

'Midnight burns whatever we do,' Blood rumbled. 'The blame for that cannot be laid at Luxor's feet, or the feet of any others save the Witchking himself.'

Gard raised a hand. 'Our lives were forfeit the moment the Witchking decided that all Midnight must bow the knee to him. He has planned this invasion for a generation of the Free. We could not have withstood him even if we had prepared for moons. He seeks our complete eradication, we must seek his.'

'It will be the death of us all!' Morning shouted.

'Enough!'

Luxor stepped back into the fray. All eyes turned to him once more.

'I would prefer an honest fight,' he said. 'We know we can best the Doomguard on equal terms. But he refuses to fight on equal terms so that option is denied us. The Witchking is a fell power, we must fight like with like. We must hold Xajorkith against his might for as long as we possibly can. Engage his armies and keep them occupied. Lord Xajorkith?'

All eyes turned to Xajorkith, who had stood closer to the fire, observing the other Lords. He rubbed his chin and looked from one Lord to another, nodding at Silence as she returned his gaze.

'It is true that this city has never fallen to the Doomguard,' Xajorkith said. 'I would hope that such a horror would not occur whilst I was its Lord. I have faith in our strength, and hope that events may still turn in our favour. Marakith and Kumar are mighty men at arms. Yes, the strength of the Free will be sore tested. If we are to stake all upon this throw, let us put all our weight behind that throw. The Witchking will not have Xajorkith without a fight, and we will make him pay dearly for every yard he tries to take!'

Luxor nodded.

He held forth the Moon Ring once more and it blazed with its strange unearthly light. Luxor grimaced as the ancient Talisman scoured him for its energy, but he braved the pain and pushed on. The Lords stood transfixed by a power and a magic older than history, older than lore, older even than myth or legend. All heard words echo in their minds.

Arise Midnight! Arise the Free! Peril and doom lie at our gates! Waken your valour, arm yourselves with courage! Our chance to conquer Doomdark forever! Arise Midnight, arise!

A fast and heavy knock came at the doors to the hall. Guards opened them and a messenger came running in, flustered, cheeks puffed ready with exertion.

'My lords!' he gasped. 'Doomguard armies have been sighted in the valley of Corelay to the north and to the west. The Keeps of Corelay on the borders have already been over-run. Our warriors retreat … they … the enemy … they march towards us!'

Luxor lowered his arm and the light of the Moon Ring faded. He drew his sword.

'Follow me, my Lords,' he said. 'Arise!'

For a moment none moved. Luxor turned to regard them all.

'This I perceive to be our duty, Lords of Midnight,' Luxor said. 'Will you arise and follow me? Or will you find another? Make your choice this hour.'

Blood and Shimeril drew their swords, quickly followed by Gard and Xajorkith. Silence's knife glittered in her hand as she held it aloft.

'Arise!' they yelled. Silence looked across to Morning. He grimaced and made as if to turn away.

Yet he turned and drew his own sword.

'Let us make of this what we can then,' Morning said. 'Arise!'

Luxor nodded to him.

'So it begins.'

The few that remained were weary, utterly exhausted from their flight. Many were wounded, many had dropped from exhaustion, their comrades forced to abandon them in their despair. Only one figure could they afford to protect and he lay upon a bower, wounded beyond their immediate ability to heal.

The last few warriors of the Keep of Whispers trudged on-wards.

The Doomguard, servants of the Witchking had descended

on their keep, assailing its walls and overcoming their defences. More armies were seen to the south and north, cutting off escape in either direction.

They had received no warning as the Forest of Whispers had been put to the flame, no missives, no tidings, nothing. The Fey had not challenged the Witchking for hundreds of moons. None could explain why his fury should have descended upon them now.

Riders heading south had been slaughtered, there was no way to warn their kindred that way. The Witchking's forces already controlled the route. To the North was possible shelter courtesy of the Free. Lord Ithrorn's citadel remained a power in these parts, but the Fey could see he was already oppressed.

The only open route was to the north west, to the capital of their realm, the Citadel of Dreams.

Yet why hadn't Dreams advised them? A watch must have been kept upon the eaves of the forest and its borders. Dreams should have known …

The weary band of Fey, less than a score that had escaped the devastation of their home, took it in turns to carry the bower of their fallen leader. The Lord of Whispers lay, wounded by the dark metal weapons of the Doomguard, his skin pale and his breathing shallow as the survivors tried to reach safety.

Their long flight had brought them to the Citadel, yet its gates were locked and closed as they approached.

'Hail Dreams,' a young warrior called. 'Open unto us.'

'Speak your name,' came the answering call.

'Terinel, of Whispers. We need urgent help. Our Lord Whispers lies here, injured! Open the gates!'

There was no immediate answer, but a few seconds later the gates were unlocked and open outwards. The Fey of Whispers moved inside.

Within the walls there was no one save the guards of the

Citadel. The streets, stables and stores were empty and bereft of civilians.

Terinel looked around him in surprise.

'Where is everyone …?'

From the Citadel emerged another troupe of guards, this time with weapons drawn and surrounding a Fey dressed in robes and royal attire.

'Lord Dreams!' Terinel gasped, bowing the knee.

'Rise,' Dreams said. 'What business do you have with us at this late hour?'

'My Lord,' Terinel said. 'We come hither from our home in the Forest of Whispers. The Doomguard have razed our home, there was no warning …'

'You lie,' Dreams snapped. 'The Witchking would not dare to assail …'

Terinel and his companions stepped aside revealing the bower of Lord Whispers, his body wrapped in bloodstained bandages. They saw him gesture with a raise of his hand.

'They came …'

'No …' Dreams shook his head. 'No, he would not dare. The peace has held, the peace will hold! I have his promise …'

Terinel stepped forward. 'The Doomguard pursued us sire, to the borders of your domain. They are everywhere, north, south, east and west. Ithrorn is under attack as we speak. They will march upon the Forest of Dreams as sure as …'

Dreams threw aside his cloak in a rage.

'No!' he yelled into the air. 'No … you promised!'

A darkness swept across them, billowing clouds of thick grey, cutting off the light.

PROMISED? PROMISED!

Cruel laughter echoed around them from a source unseen.

A RUSE, NOTHING MORE! TO SEAL THE FATE OF THE FREE IN THEIR TIME OF NEED. EVEN NOW THEY

HOPE FOR SALVATION FROM THE FEY AND IT IS TOO LONG DELAYED!

'It cannot be!'

I HAVE PICKED OFF THE FEY ONE BY ONE UNTIL THEY ARE WEAK AND HELPLESS! LOOKING FOR THE UTMOST FOLLY? YOU MUST SEEK THE LORD OF DREAMS AND HIS LACKY THE LORD OF DREGRIM!

'No …'

YOUR INDECISION WILL BE THE END OF ALL YOU HOLD DEAR.

Shrieks and howls came from behind them. All turned to look. In horror they saw Doomguard warriors pouring through the still open gates. Horns sounded in alarm from the city walls behind them. The guards drew their swords, but were already beaten back by the oncoming warriors.

Terinel stood before them, his own sword drawn ready to lay down his life to protect his own Lord. Whispers lay behind him, defenceless. The Doomguard came on, en masse, ready to kill …

The ground shook beneath his feet, causing him to stumble. A deep rumbling issued forth from it.

Truly! This is the end of all things! Despair overtakes us, the very earth cries out beneath our feet.

Yet it seemed the Doomguard were caught off guard too, they stumbled back, their charge halted and their footsteps uncertain.

Not of their doing?

It might have been his imagination, but Terinel thought he saw a flash of green light as the trembling continued.

The ground shook again, great shivers underfoot signalling sudden cracks which widened, casting Doomguard and Fey to lie helpless on the ground. In horror, Terinel saw vast roots grow out of the ground, snapping upwards, growing at a terrifying speed.

The very forest is possessed!

The roots whipped upwards, still growing, fastening their tendrils on to the nearest Doomguard warriors lifting them aloft, screaming, into the air before dashing them against the walls or back down upon the ground, with fatal force.

The Fey backpedalled as the roots turned upon the invaders. The Doomguard tried to flee, but outside the walls of the Citadel the vegetation was more intense. The screams and yells died within seconds.

The roots retreated into the ground as if they'd never been.

The Fey sat upon the threshold of the Citadel, staring into the open gates that led into the forest, trembling with fear.

Something moved. A shadow against the trees.

Hands grasped swords, bows were gathered and arrows slotted by trembling hands.

'Stand ready,' Terinel managed to gasp, getting to his feet. 'Stand …'

Morkin followed Lothoril down into the deeps of the keep past guards and metal linked gates that sealed off the lower levels. Lothoril took a torch from the wall and led him down a steep set of stairs hewn into the rock.

'I do not keep prisoners as a matter of course,' Lothoril said from ahead, 'but this skulkrin was found in a peculiar place, clearly up to mischief.'

'What do you mean?'

'He was found within the circle of Moonhenge,' Lothoril replied. When Morkin didn't answer he continued. 'It lies a day and a half's ride from here.'

'Moonhenge?' Morkin asked, frowning.

Moon? Why would something be named Moon up here so far away from the ancient lands of the House of the Moon?

'An ancient ring of stones suffused with some strange power of the ages,' Lothoril continued. 'Unwholesome and unclean so my people have long held. We never go within, but this skulkrin had done so.'

'Why?'

Lothoril shrugged. 'A good question. The stones seem to have had some unhealthy influence on him. He was exhausted beyond measure when he was captured, unable to lift an arm in defence. Those who trespass in our lands are subject to my judgement.'

'And the penalty for trespass?' Morkin asked.

'Most are turned away at the borders,' Lothoril replied. 'There is no precedent for such as he stirring up magic in our realm.'

'Then what will you do with him?'

'I have no wish to harm him,' Lothoril said. 'And the Fey do not kill prisoners. But I sense the touch of the enemy close by. He could be a spy, or a sorcerer. I must look to the safety of my own people first. He will stay in this dungeon. The Henge and the Liths that lie close by are a power I would rather leave undisturbed.'

'Would you turn him over to my keeping?' Morkin asked.

Lothoril stopped and turned.

'Yours?'

'If what I have been told of the lore of the Ice Crown is true, I need the cooperation of a skulkrin to destroy it. If he languishes here in a dungeon he is of little use to me and a nuisance to you ...'

'He'll escape the moment you take your eyes off him.'

Morkin grinned. 'You forget. I have a dragon at my disposal; a little threat alongside the hand of friendship.'

Lothoril smiled. 'Perhaps ... I have no idea what the word of a skulkrin is worth ...'

'Let's find out.'

Lothoril led Morkin down the final few steps into the dungeons deep below the fortress. There were a series of cells there, all but one unused. A single torch blazed, fastened on the wall and casting a flickering light across the stony floor and walls.

'Skulkrin,' Lothoril said. 'I bring someone to see you. I believe you have met before.'

Morkin could see a small body asleep on a pile of blankets … no not asleep, he could just make out a glint of light reflecting from eyes that were almost closed. The skulkrin was awake, observing warily.

'Fawkrin,' Morkin said, stepping out from behind Lothoril. 'Remember me?'

Morkin saw the skulkrin's eyes widen in recognition.

'I see you do,' Morkin replied. 'Sleep frost wasn't it? A trick of your kind. You stole my food and water, leaving me for dead in the snow …'

Fawkrin was on his feet in a moment.

'No, no, my young lord, no!' Fawkrin stammered. 'Surely not. To lead you I meant, to stop you falling in chasms and holes …'

'Spare me,' Morkin said. 'I know what you were about. I guess I was lucky you didn't decide to feast upon me too.'

A guilty look crossed Fawkrin's face. Morkin shook his head.

'You planned that too?' Morkin asked. 'And now you are a prisoner, caught trespassing in the realm of a Fey Lord. Woe betide you, Fawkrin!'

Lothoril took his turn. 'To trespass in the realm of the Fey is no small thing, skulkrin,' he said. 'My laws are strict.'

Fawkrin was looking between the two of them, rapidly turning his head from side to side.

'Mercy great and powerful Lords, mercy! Khlee! I meant no harm!'

'How can I believe that?' Lothoril demanded. 'Magic you stirred, at Moonhenge. My men saw it, do not deny it!'

'I sought only rest and shelter from the storm,' Fawkrin mewled. 'Didn't know of the wraiths and spirits. Scared I was, they kept chanting ... always chanting ... stole away my strength, left me so tired I could not move ... the shadows of death ... the shadows of death!'

'You are in the service of the Witchking,' Lothoril said. 'A spy. Do you know what we do with spies, skulkrin?'

Fawkrin trembled, unable to answer.

Lothoril pulled out his sword, swung it about in a flamboyant manner before pointing it directly at Fawkrin. It glinted in the dim firelight.

Fawkrin swallowed, backing away from the bars of his cell. His gaze moved to Morkin.

'Kind boy, nice boy, lovely boy!' he entreated. 'You would not see this happen. Fawkrin doesn't want to die!'

Morkin affected a look of unconcern. 'Why should I concern myself with you?'

Fawkrin rushed forward. 'You are half-Free and half-Fey. I know this, I smelt it! You seek to destroy the Ice Crown!'

Morkin frowned. 'What do you know of the Ice Crown?'

Fawkrin sighed. 'Long ago, my people, used they were. We had magic then, yes, strong magic. But the Witchking, he took it, cast us out ... the winter, it was never supposed to be ... The Fey tried to destroy it long ago ... but ...'

'Yanathel,' Morkin whispered.

'Yes, but not her,' Fawkrin said. 'Not her ... you!'

The skulkrin's eyes looked distant all of a sudden and he seemed to be seeing things that neither Morkin nor Lothoril could see.

'Frozen she was, frozen in horror everlasting ... in the vaults of the tower ... high above it lies, its power shining with a cold black despair ...'

'Wait a minute,' Morkin said. 'You've been there? You've seen the Ice Crown?'

Fawkrin backed away from the bars again. 'I was young and foolish, thought I knew best. Thought I would see the Witchking himself … he laughed at me and let me live … my friends … frozen long ago … my people threw me out … an outcast … Khlee! Alone, poor Fawkrin, alone forever!'

Fawkrin collapsed on the floor of the cell, sobs coming from the blankets he had fallen upon.

'Leave him,' Lothoril said. 'It's all lies anyway. You can't trust a skulkrin.'

The skulkrin howled and threw himself at the bars, they echoed with a thud.

'Not lies, not lies!' the creature snarled.

'I don't believe you,' Lothoril returned, readying his sword and preparing to plunge it between the bars of the cell.

'But I might,' Morkin said gently. 'Will you turn him over to me, Lord Lothoril?'

Lothoril grimaced. 'He has committed crimes against the Fey …'

'I will answer for his conduct,' Morkin said, before turning back to Fawkrin. 'Will you swear allegiance to me, if I make the Fey spare your life?'

Fawkrin looked from one to the other again.

'You are right,' Morkin added. 'I go to destroy the Ice Crown. You can help me, or …'

Lothoril raised his sword.

'Swear I do!' Fawkrin said. 'Swear all service and duty to you young master. Nice boy, lovely boy! Khlee!'

'Do not think to cross me,' Morkin said. 'I stand with Farflame, Lord of Dragons. He will find you and roast you alive should you even think it!'

Morkin watched as Fawkrin swallowed again.

'Swear young master. I swear!'

Morkin stepped back.

'Open the cell.'

'Are you sure?' Lothoril asked, looking warily at Fawkrin.

'Let him out,' Morkin replied. Lothoril took a set of keys from his belt and unlocked the cell door. It swung open. Fawkrin remained within.

Morkin held out his hand.

Fawkrin shuffled across and stretched out, his small knurled fingers grasping at Morkin's.

'I will trust you,' Morkin said, looking directly into Fawkrin's eyes. 'The past is behind us. Let us seek the Ice Crown together.'

Fawkrin nodded.

'Swear it once again, skulkrin,' Lothoril rumbled. 'Swear to your new Lord. Morkin of the Free, for it is he who has saved your life. You now owe that life to him.'

Fawkrin looked at the tall Fey with a grimace, but turned back to Morkin.

'I swear, my Lord Morkin. I will serve you.'

'Heard and witnessed,' Lothoril said. 'Do not be quick to break your word, skulkrin! For if you do, if any perfidy comes to my ears, I will see your end is swift. Heed my words!'

'Come,' Morkin said. 'Let us prepare.'

He pushed Fawkrin ahead of him, and the small skulkrin began climbing the stairs out of the dungeon.

'You enjoyed that,' Morkin whispered to Lothoril.

'Was it too much?' Lothoril replied with a grin. 'I so rarely get to proclaim anything any more ...'

Morkin chuckled.

'I wish you well with this,' Lothoril said. 'But great peril still lies ahead ... I hope it does not come from him.'

Morkin nodded, watching Fawkrin ahead of him. 'I hope so too.'

Chapter Sixteen

She stands in the Forest of Dreams,
looking east to the Citadel of Dreams.

Deep within the Forest of Dreams the Fey stood, weapons ready, watching the forest all about them for signs of movement. Then came footsteps, soft, yet firm. A figure appeared, a green glow emanating from a jewel around its neck.

Twin roots broke out of the ground. One grew over the figure's head in an arch, sprouting yellow flowers as it did so. The second formed itself into a stool beneath, awaiting they who had summoned it.

The figure stepped into the light and sat down. Swords were lowered, mouths gaped in surprise.

'I am Tarithel the Fey. I am Lady of the Forest,' she said, her voice sweet and soft.

Before anyone could stop him, Dreams was on his feet, his face a mask of crazed rage and apoplexy.

'I had you locked away …' he yelled, stumbling forwards. 'How dare you defy me!'

He did not get far. Roots swarmed about his feet, binding him in place. He struggled for a moment. Green fire flashed about him.

'The forest has its own will, Father,' Tarithel said. 'It would have us counter the evil in the world even if you would not.'

Dreams recoiled from the blaze that flickered in her eyes.

All who gazed upon her stumbled back as her form was lit by an unearthly green glow.

'It is our duty, long derelict!' Tarithel called out, her voice echoing around the empty courtyard. 'Midnight is as much our responsibility as it is to any other of the races that call it home. We are not separate, not apart from it. Evil has kept us sleeping long enough. If we do not help, everything will be lost. We must arise from our slumber and face the foe!'

Terinel looked from Dreams to Tarithel and back again, uncertain.

'The pact you made with the Witchking is over!' Tarithel cried out. The green glow expanded, flickering over the people, the grounds and the citadel.

About him people muttered in horror, the words whispered back and forth between them.

A pact? With the Witchking?

Dreams fell to his knees, sobs racking his body. The root released him and Tarithel ran to his aid.

She wrapped her arms about him, pulling him close.

Dreams looked up, his face tear streaked, fear and terror etched upon his features.

'I sought only to protect my people … yet I have led us all to ruin …'

'No father,' Tarithel replied. 'We have survived long due to your wisdom, but we cannot make a peace with evil. When we do nothing – evil prospers! We can no longer hide. We must resist it …'

'It is too late, we cannot prevail …'

'We can and we must!'

Tarithel stood, her hand on her father's shoulder, he still trembled at her feet.

'Rouse the captains. Assemble the army. Messengers to their steeds. The Fey will ride!'

The assembled Fey about her stood and stared.

'Now!' she yelled.

They scattered, heeding her commands.

She turned back to her father, kneeling before him.

'Such blessing as the forest can bestow, be yours father.' She closed her eyes, willing his mind to be free from the fear and horror he'd immersed himself in. 'Come back to us! Come back to me …'

She felt his thoughts, despair turning to barely credible hope. He looked up.

'Yes, look to me for hope anew,' Tarithel said. 'All is not lost.'

Her father shuddered in her grasp. She could see the emotions writhe across his features, fighting a battle for his soul.

Father, listen to me. Resist the evil, fight it! We need you. We need the Lord of Dreams! Cast off the nightmare and dream once more …

Her father blinked and his eyes focussed. For a long moment he stared at her as if seeing her for the first time.

'Tarithel?'

'Father?'

'I have been blind. Blinded by fear and the chains of my own making. My precious daughter, how can you ever forgive me?'

Tarithel hugged him close, tears in her eyes. 'You were lost, but now you are found once more!'

'I …'

'There is little time, come!'

Tarithel pulled him to his feet and drew his sword from his scabbard. She handed it to him. The green light from the gem around her neck flashed out bright and sharp. Dreams looked at the blade in bewilderment, before looking back at her.

'Lead them!' she cried. 'Lead the Fey. Fight for Midnight, save the Free, slay the Witchking!'

Dreams raised the sword, looked at it once more.

She saw determination frame his features.

'So shall it be!' he shouted. 'To arms! To arms all of you!'

About them the voices of the Fey cried out and they set about their tasks.

Tarithel watched in surprise as her father bowed reverently before her.

'You truly are the Lady of the Forest.'

They had ridden hard across the Plains of Lothoril, past the great Tower of that realm, through villages, and skirted the great lake that supplied the people of the valley with much of their food. Great fish lived there, enjoying the strange warmth of the lake, fed as it was by heat from far below the ground, untouched by the harsh winter above.

North east they had ridden, entering the dense eaves and protection of the Forest of Lothoril until at last the trees thinned out once more and a plain opened before them. Far ahead, Morkin could see mountains. They looked cold and stark against the east, wreathed in mist and shadow in the faint morning sunlight.

'Aye,' Lothoril said, in response to his question. 'Those are the Mountains of Ugrak, the edge of the Witchking's realm.'

'A land of torments and woes,' Fawkrin said. Morkin had ridden with the skulkrin perched in front of him on the saddle. He felt the small body of the creature shudder.

Around them all, a legion of Fey riders had accompanied them to the forest edge.

'Ahead lie the Plains of the Lost,' Lothoril said. 'An empty land through which none venture if they have a choice. We keep watch of course …'

To the north Morkin could see another forest on the limits of vision.

'What lies there?' he asked.

'Part of my realm long ago,' Lothoril said. 'It was sundered from us in the last war, the forest here burnt by the Witchking when he assailed our realm. Now it lies forlorn and untended by the Fey.'

A swirl of snow whipped about them. Fawkrin squealed in fear, but Morkin leant in close and shouted in his ear.

'Fear not, it is a friend!'

With a heavy thump a dragon descended from the sky, wings unfurled in a mighty downstroke to cushion its landing. The snow settled slowly, the Fey wrestling with their horses to keep them under control. Some of the Fey yelled in surprise and fear.

TELL THEM I WON'T EAT THEIR HORSES, MORE IS THE PITY.

Morkin laughed.

'Farflame! It is good to see you once more.'

The dragon arched its neck and gave a trumpeting sound, which further spooked the horses. He took a step back and shook his great head.

I BRING ILL NEWS. ARMIES OF THE WITCHKING SEEM AWARE OF YOUR PRESENCE. THEY PATROL THE PLAINS OF THE LOST TO THE EAST, EVEN TO THE EAVES OF THE REALM OF THE FEY. I SMOTE A FEW, BUT THEY ARE TOO NUMEROUS. THERE IS NO WAY FOR US TO APPROACH THE MOUNTAINS WITH-OUT BEING SEEN. SHOULD I ATTEMPT TO LAND I FEAR A STORM OF ARROWS WOULD AWAIT ME …

Lothoril rode swiftly over to Morkin. It seemed he too had heard Farflame's words.

'I see no reason to distrust your dragon …'

I AM NOT HIS DRAGON!

A faint roar issued from the dragon's throat. Lothoril's steed whinnied and bucked before he brought it under control.

'… this is the Witchking's realm. I do not have the strength to force a path direct to the Citadel of Vorgath, let alone through it. Even if I did, secrecy is your best ally here. If you are found, your end will be swift indeed. The Plains of the Lost are being watched. You cannot go that way and I fear a dragon might be a little too noticeable.'

'But is there another way?' Morkin asked, his voice high with desperation. 'I cannot tarry. Xajorkith …'

'I do not know another way in,' Lothoril replied. 'But if the fate of Midnight rests upon the success of your quest then we must take all precautions. There is one who might know a way, unwatched and less likely to be spied upon.'

'Who?' Morkin demanded.

'Follow the forest wall north, not east,' Lothoril replied. 'Some leagues hence you will see a range of mountains, turn west around their base and you will see a Citadel.'

'A Citadel?' Morkin answered. 'Whose?'

'An outpost of the Free,' Lothoril said, his voice low.

'The Free?' Morkin replied. 'Here in the north? What lord resides here?'

'I know not his real name,' Lothoril replied. 'We have had few dealings with him. He does not bother us and we do not bother him. His Citadel lies against the Frozen Wastes themselves …'

'But his name!'

'We call him the Lord …' Lothoril said slowly, 'the Lord of Gloom.'

'Gloom!' Morkin replied. 'Why he sounds a cheerful fellow indeed.'

'I know not enough about the history of the Free to tell you much more,' Lothoril said. 'But he was loyal to the Free. His people lived in these lands long before King Ushgarak came to power, he may know a better way for you to assail the Witchking's realm.'

'How do you know he's not in league with the Witchking?' Morkin demanded.

'He does not tolerate them to cross into his realm,' Lothoril said. 'This much I do know. His lands may have been invaded, though the Witchking concentrates his fury in the south.'

'Will he tolerate me?' Morkin demanded.

'You are the son of the Moonprince,' Lothoril replied.

'That isn't a yes,' Morkin said, with a frown.

Lothoril smiled. 'I am sorry I cannot tell you more, but his realm will afford you more safety than a passage across the Plains of the Lost. I will strike out east for a while and be as much of a decoy as I can.'

'You have risked enough already …'

'We would see you succeed, Morkin, son of the Moonprince,' Lothoril replied. 'My realm will be the next to fall if you do not succeed and the Witchking's power waxes to its fullest extent. I do not have the strength to resist him in a pitched battle. But a skirmish … that I can win, on the edges of my forests. Wish me luck.'

'Then we will depart,' Morkin said. 'All the luck in Midnight to you!'

Lothoril grabbed him by the shoulder and pulled him into an embrace.

'You are your father's true son,' Lothoril said. 'I look forward to meeting him. He would be proud of you, your conduct speaks well of him.'

'And your hospitality, despite your troubles, has been most welcome. I sought shelter, but found a friend.'

Lothoril released him. 'Farewell, Morkin. Seek the Ice Crown, destroy it and end this winter!'

A rumbling snort came from behind them both, which unsettled the horses once again.

ARE WE READY TO GO NOW?

Morkin dismounted and gave the reins to one of the Fey

before climbing aboard the dragon, lifting a squealing Fawkrin into place beside him. Farflame launched himself into the air. Fawkrin shrieked. The forest fell behind them as they began the journey across the Plains of the Lost.

Doom and Gloom awaits! Not a cheerful prospect!

BETTER THAN BEING IMPALED UPON THE SWORDS AND ARROWS OF THE DOOMGUARD.

'Have you ever heard of this Lord Gloom?' Morkin asked Fawkrin, who clinging on, huddled in front of him.

'No,' Fawkrin whimpered. 'I do not visit the Lords. They try to skewer me!'

I DOUBT HE WILL BE VERY PLEASED TO FIND A DRAGON HEREABOUTS EITHER …

Morkin chuckled. 'Then it will be up to me to seek his hospitality. Let us see what he is about!'

Behind them the Fey moved east and were soon lost to sight against the whiteness of the snow.

Before long there was no doubt of the messenger's words. The valley of Corelay was straight for nearly ten leagues, bordered by austere mountains on either side; a path that led directly north and south. Long ago it had been a fertile land, cut by a sinuous river, and even now it was the main thoroughfare from the central plains to the south lands guarded by the Citadel. It afforded a commanding view of any who dared to approach.

And dare they did.

The ice-fear was cold and sharp.

Lord Xajorkith could see the approaching army to the north, a dark stain against the bright white ice and snow. The heavy black banners of the Doomguard. Before long would come the chants, the noise of weapons of war, then fear, clamour, pain and blood.

From the west another army was spread out around the blazing wreckage of the nearby keep, some three leagues away. The Doomguard were razing everything as they came. Villages and settlements, keeps, even the old ruins were trampled anew. Only the Liths and the towers were left alone by the rampaging hordes.

All the nearby villagers had been evacuated in the previous days, now all were contained within the protective walls of the city, huddled in close against the threat from outside.

War was upon Xajorkith for the first time in living memory. Preparations had been ongoing for days, ever since news of the defeat at Dawn had reached them. Provisions had been stockpiled, weapons prepared, armaments and projectiles readied. Scouts had provided updates on the progress of the enemy. They were marching quickly. They would be at the gates by nightfall.

'The Doomguard oft prefer to fight at night,' Luxor said. 'Here in the south, despite the Solstice, the sun is at its height and they hate it.'

'We will need more than sunlight to defeat this foe,' Xajorkith said. 'We would need a miracle.'

'Then we must hope for one,' Luxor answered.

'And another army lies beyond,' Xajorkith said with a grim chuckle. 'Perhaps a pair of miracles should be sought.'

Luxor didn't respond, but turned his gaze to the North, watching the slowly advancing army of the Witchking, the Moon Ring glowing upon his finger. The great Vale of Corelay was filling, filling with the dark stain of the Witchking's foul hordes. It was a vast army, terrible to look upon with the knowledge that all that malice was bearing down upon the last Citadel of the Free.

The Plains of the Lost provided little obstacle to the flight of a dragon, and Farflame's keen eyes ensured that they were not seen. Neither Morkin nor Fawkrin were able to see much in the biting gale that was the result of the dragon's swift flight northwards, but Farflame's gaze roved far and wide.

DOOMGUARD PATROL TO THE EAST, ALONG THE BORDERS OF THE MOUNTAINS. BUT THERE IS NOTHING TO THE NORTH. SEE? THE FROZEN WASTES!

Morkin squinted and could just make out the band of jagged inhospitable ice that framed the horizon before him. They rose up abruptly from the Plains of the Lost, an implacable and impassable barrier, the northern most tip of Midnight itself.

Even from their altitude Morkin could not see an end to them. They seemed to stretch to the horizon no matter how hard he tried to see past them. He found himself wondering again what they were. They were clearly unnatural, not subject to the decay and erosion of everything else in Midnight. They never changed no matter what the season and any attempt to penetrate their reaches led to a swift death amidst a field of sharp icy daggers.

Farflame seemed aware of his thoughts.

THE WITCHKING'S DOING, LONG AGO. OTHER LANDS DO LIE BEYOND.

'Have you been there?' Morkin asked as the dragon began to descend.

NOT FOR MANY MOONS. TO THE NORTH EAST LIES THE ICEMARK, TO THE NORTH WEST VARANGOR ...

The dragon's voice echoed for a moment. Morkin fancied that a sense of homesickness had come upon the great beast.

THE ICY WASTES ARE NOT JUST A PHYSICAL BARRIER. THEY TAKE YOUR WILL, EBB AND FREEZE IT. NOT EVEN ALOFT CAN I CROSS THEM.

Morkin got the distinct sense that the dragon had tried this at some point and been thwarted. The last dragon in Midnight? Sealed off by the Witchking's magic? Had the dragon left family and friends behind somewhere?

His ears popped and Fawkrin squeaked as the dragon banked sharply and the frozen landscape of the Lost plains became clear below them.

NOW TO THE WEST.

The dragon was banking around, one wing tilted low. Morkin could see a citadel before them, hewn out of the mountains ahead and nestled in amongst them. It was a superb tactical position, protected on three sides by a combination of the Icy Wastes and the sheer mountains. To Morkin's eyes it looked impenetrable, even to a mighty host of warriors.

'The Citadel of Gloom?' Morkin wondered.

'It does not look friendly,' Fawkrin said, his voice quivering, although the terror had gone out of it.

'Nothing in the north does,' Morkin replied.

The last few leagues fell away beneath them. Farflame circled and landed fifty yards beyond the gates of the Citadel.

The gates were closed. There seemed no life anywhere, even the wind was sombre and slight. No guards atop the battlements. Everything seemed still.

PERHAPS YOU SHOULD KNOCK.

Farflame shook his body and folded his wings. Morkin looked at Fawkrin, who shrugged.

'Maybe I should,' Morkin said with a sigh.

The sun was westering as the army drew up before the gates of the citadel. Thick and heavy clouds had accompanied the arrival of the Witchking's forces, but those clouds seemed unable to assail the Citadel. Those within watched as the clouds rolled across the city, but were mysteriously diverted around it, leaving the great tower basking in the fading light of the sun. Even the elements struggled and fought against each other.

No treating, no parley. The Witchking's armies formed ranks below whilst the defenders of Xajorkith lined up above on the towers and battlements. Weapons were held ready, waiting for some unspoken signal for the battle to commence.

The lowering sun touched the jagged pinnacles of the Frozen Wastes to the west. Twilight sprang into the sky. Horns bellowed from the massed ranks of Doomguard below and were quickly taken up by the whole army. Trumpets returned a higher note from the pinnacles of the citadel.

Atop the battlements the Lords of Midnight drew their swords.

The battle of Xajorkith had begun.

A mass of arrows erupted from the ranks of the Doom-guard, scattering against the thick walls. Xajorkith signalled for a return volley. Dozens of the Doomguard were cut down, but within seconds they had reached the walls en masse. Crossbows dealt with many of them, but the defenders began to fall too, they were easy targets for skilled archers further back in the ranks of the enemy.

'Ladders!' Xajorkith yelled.

Already the Doomguard were hoisting them, crewed by dozens of mail clad figures, by some unseen machinery at the base.

'Wait ...' Xajorkith called, watching the rising ladders. 'Wait ... now!'

At his signal, a group of men worked some contraption on the wall. With a harsh grinding of gears a mechanism spun rapidly. Luxor saw great levers rise out of the walls of the citadel, heavy ropes strung between them. The ropes caught the ladders before they were fully upright, arresting their movement with a shocking jar, spilling those who vainly tried to cling to them to the ground below. The ladders, unbalanced, crashed back down, crushing many beneath their weight.

Luxor grinned. 'The legends of Xajorkith's prowess in battle were no exaggeration I see!'

'We have a few tricks of note!' Xajorkith returned. 'Weapons from the far south, before the Frozen Wastes closed about us. Ballistas!'

Atop the towers, men uncovered more weapons. To Luxor's eyes they looked like huge crossbows mounted on sturdy emplacements. As he watched a huge bolt issued from one of them, hurtling down into the ranks of Doomguard and dispatching dozens into oblivion.

'We will make good account of ourselves before the night is out, mark my words!' Xajorkith shouted.

'These youngsters with their new-fangled contraptions,' Blood grumbled. 'Warfare isn't what it used to be.'

'Envy, old friend?' Shimeril said, with a smile.

'I never liked ranged weapons,' Blood said, hoisting his sword. 'Have at them, up close and personal.'

'We need every advantage in our struggle against the Witchking,' Luxor said. 'I fear the battle you seek will be on us soon enough.'

Stars were shining through the ever darkening sky, the blue of twilight fading into the darkness of night. Lurid flame now lit the citadel as bolts of fire were exchanged between the defenders and attackers. Time and again the Doomguard tried to assail the walls but were thrown back, unable to breach the defences of the citadel.

Through the smoke and fire Xajorkith strode through the battlements.

'They're pulling back!' he said, a fierce and joyful grin upon his face. 'They've lost hundreds to mere dozens on our side and have made no progress. We have given them a bloody nose.'

Luxor clapped him on the shoulder. 'A defiant stand. Let's see what else they have to bring against us.'

The Lords peered out into the smoke that wreathed the battle, seeing the Doomguard army now more than a hundred yards from the walls.

'Trebuchets,' Shimeril said, squinting.

'They can pound these walls with rocks all night long,' Xajorkith sneered. 'They will not breach them, my father reinforced them moons ago, they are dozens of feet thick. It will not avail them.'

'And the gatehouse?' Luxor asked.

'Metal bound wood of great sturdiness,' Xajorkith replied. 'Not stone of course, but strong enough to resist this.'

Luxor nodded and looked at Shimeril and Blood.

'The Witchking must know how strong Xajorkith is,' Luxor muttered. 'He would not have been ill prepared for such an assault ... or is there hope that we might prevail after all?'

Rocks flew through the air, smashing against the high walls of the citadel. Tremble ran through the battlements, but the great defences were unmarked and unaffected. More rocks crashed down upon them, some spiralling over the walls to crash down in the courtyards. A few were caught by the debris, but the Citadel stood firm.

The pounding continued for some long minutes before it too ceased. An eerie silence crept across the battlefield, punctuated only by the moans and cries of the injured.

Then they felt it, crackling across their minds and hearts, as if splinters of ice were forming inside their bodies. Men yelled, women and children screamed as the terrifying weapon of the enemy was brought to bear.

Ice-fear!

Men stumbled on the battlements, their weapons cast aside as they clutched at their chests in panic and alarm, some over-balanced and fell to their deaths from the height. The sweep of power emanating out of the cursed northlands was palpable, almost visible as a deadly beam of unwholesome light casting every man woman and child into an evil shadow of despair and hopelessness.

'Luxor ...' Shimeril gasped.

Luxor raised his arm, the Moon Ring upon his finger, his hand outstretched.

The Ring gave forth its power, glowing a fierce blue in the lurid red about them. Luxor cried out, collapsing to his knees as the Ring shrieked forth its own baleful influence.

In the sky above, great flashes of light crackled and spat about them. Those who still had presence of mind looked up in fear and wonder as the strange magics of Midnight fought their ethereal battle.

All felt a strange warmth, the glow of humanity, the comfort of comradeship, wholesome and renewing. Eyes turned upwards once again, seeing Luxor standing on the battlements, the Moon Ring aloft.

Arise Midnight!

The ice-fear retreated, unable to assail him.

A cry of defiance went up from all those on the battlements as the ice-fear relented. Hope was kindled again. Clouds swirled away once more revealing a star-spangled sky.

But the Witchking was not so easily thwarted.

Far to the north, mist swirled about the Citadel of Ushgarak. Doomguard warriors patrolled its cold and ice-shocked boundaries. Far within, the architect of that ice stood poised, a hand outstretched toward the hated south.

SO, LITTLE MOONPRINCE OF MIDNIGHT. YOU BE-LIEVE YOU HAVE THE POWER TO RESIST ME? THAT YOU CAN TURN THE ICE-FEAR GIVES YOU HOPE? YOUR

ALLIES ARE LOST TO YOU. YOU THINK YOURSELF SAFE WITHIN YOUR PRECIOUS WALLS OF STONE?

A brief gesture sent the command.

Silent laughter shook the foundations of Ushgarak to the core.

YOUR WALLS WILL CRUMBLE! AS WILL YOUR RESOLVE. YOU HAVE ALREADY LOST, NOW YOU WILL BEGIN TO REALISE IT ... AND THE MOON RING WILL BE MINE.

Morkin approached the gates of the Citadel of Gloom. There was still no movement, nor did any sound reach his ears. Behind him Fawkrin had remained under the protective wing of Farflame.

He reached forward, ready to rap his knuckles on the great gates.

Just before he touched them they gave a creaked and swung outwards. Morkin backed away, peering into the darkened interior.

With a thundering of hooves, armoured horses surged through the gates, covered in metal plates. Atop them were knights, themselves armoured in a similar fashion. Each carried a lance in their hands and a mighty broadsword at their sides. They organised themselves in a semi-circle, lance tips pointing towards Morkin, but in such a way that they could keep a wary eye on the dragon in the distance.

One rider, high above him, called down in aggressive tones.

'What business do you have in this realm, traveller? Speak well or face the consequences.'

'I have travelled far,' Morkin managed, watching the tip of the nearest lance. It was mere inches from his face. 'From the south. I seek counsel.'

'From the south?' the rider replied. 'With a dragon and a skulkrin in tow? Your business, stranger. Speak!'

'I seek the Lord of Gloom.'

The lances pressed in closer. Morkin recoiled, stumbling back. The horses shuffled forwards, snorting in the cold air.

'I do not care for that name,' the rider rumbled.

Morkin took a step back and bowed low.

'If you will give me your name, I will honour it in my speech,' Morkin said. 'But I know it not, only what I have heard from others.'

The rider gestured and after a moment's pause the lances were lowered.

'You have manners,' the rider replied. 'Uncommon in a southerner. Give me your name and you will have mine.'

'Morkin, sire. Son and squire of Luxor, revealed Moonprince of Midnight.'

'Moonprince?' the man seemed surprised. 'Moonprince indeed! And by what right does your father call himself the Moonprince?'

Morkin stood tall. 'Thus revealed by one Rorthron the Wise at the Tower of the Moon, less than a moon ago. He commands the power of the Moon Ring.'

'You speak of events out of the past long since thought dead and buried,' the rider replied, his voice low. 'I know much of the House of the Moon.'

'Know much ... what do you know?'

The rider interrupted him. 'First, your business here in the north?'

'You promised me a name,' Morkin replied.

The rider chuckled. 'So I did.' He reached up and pulled away his helmet, revealing a strong but weather worn face, a crop of tousled brown hair and a grim expression.

'I am Balor. Lord of this realm. Your Feyish friends of Lothoril call me Gloom so I hear. It is an apt enough name.

There is little to be cheerful about in these times. We keep ourselves out of harm's way.'

'My Lord,' Morkin bowed low.

'And what seek you in the frozen north lands, Morkin, son of the so-called Moonprince?'

Morkin looked him in the eye.

'Over a cup of something warm, you have a tale to hear.'

From out of the darkness below, more missiles were hurled. Men shouted in warning as they crashed down upon the Citadel walls anew.

They were not rocks, nor were they fire.

They were ice.

Men laughed and pointed as the projectiles crashed down spectacularly, spraying ice in all directions with a strange tinkling sound. They did no harm to the stout walls.

'The Witchking must be a fool if he thinks ice will prevail in this battle ...' Xajorkith began.

Luxor held up a hand. 'Hold fast, this is some fell magic.'

As they watched, the ice abruptly melted, turning to water despite the cold. Men watched in growing apprehension as it flowed across the flagstones, slowly sinking into the cracks and mortar.

Then, in a split second, it froze again.

Great cracks rent the paving and the exposed walls wherever the ice had struck and turned to water.

'Clear the ice away!' Luxor yelled. 'Clear it before it melts ...'

Men struggled, but the ice turned to water the moment they touched it, making it impossible to deal with. The water seemed aware of its mission. Men watched, slack-jawed, as it flowed uphill in some places, finding small cracks and imperfections in the stone work, filling them before freezing and bursting them asunder.

With a loud roar, one of the towers toppled, casting men and equipment down to lie in ruins upon the courtyard below. Men scattered in all directions to avoid being crushed.

'He can rend the very rocks and elements ...' Xajorkith muttered.

'The defences will not hold much longer,' Luxor said. 'Summon our best to the gates. It will soon be time to meet the foe with cold steel.'

Lord Ithrorn's plan to march south in aid of the Moonprince had come to naught. Word had swiftly reached him that Doomguard armies had been spotted on the Plains of Herath in greater numbers.

Herath knows the strategic value of his realm. He would not have abandoned it. For the Doomguard to reach that means that Herath has been overrun and the realms of Kumar and Marakith sore oppressed.

Then they had seen the smoke. Riders reported that the Forest of Whispers was ablaze, its keep sacked and its people put to the sword.

The foolishness of Dreams! He refused to see the danger when it prowled around in the dark, now it will be the end of us.

Ithrorn had few alternatives left. With the way to the south now fraught with peril and the buffer of the forest removed, any movement in that direction would be suicide. The disposition of the west was uncertain. The Citadel of Dreams remained, but it was no ally now. If the Witchking truly was sweeping all before him, Ithrorn had none to come to his aid. The southlands were too far away and the Fey had abandoned him.

Other scouts reported that Doomguard armies were moving to cut them off from the north as well. The Citadel was prepared for a siege, but with no hope of rescue, their situation was grim.

'Night is falling,' one of his captains said.

'And the Foul are abroad,' Ithrorn replied. 'I can smell their reek upon the air.'

'As well we didn't venture south,' the captain nodded. 'They have come in force.'

'Had we ventured so with the Fey at our side, we might have turned the battle in our favour. As it is we are bereft, and powerless. We cannot flee, nor can we assist those in the south. We are impotent. The Fey's inaction may have sealed our doom.'

Stars were shining in a sky streaked with wispy clouds. To the west the sun had dropped into a thickening bank of gloom, a wall of impenetrable murk that was edging in their direction. Under that, the storms would gather, snow and ice would follow.

Ithrorn had felt it before, the clutch of horror, the shiver in the spine that would not relent.

'The ice-fear grows stronger,' he muttered. 'The Witchking's confidence grows. He has rent asunder the old alliances. His victory grows ever more certain.'

Fires sparkled in the distance. Both men knew that dawn would bring the bloody sword of battle.

Tarithel climbed to the highest tower in the Citadel of Dreams. From there she could see over the forest and down upon the Citadel itself. Before it, clad in the armour and weapons of the Fey, the mighty army of the Lord of Dreams stood ready; thousands of riders and thousands of foot soldiers. As she watched a cry went up. Together they turned and began to ride and march, following the forest roads to the east.

She could just make out her father leading the army, with his captains and generals about him, the proud banners of the Citadel fluttering in the breeze. With pride she saw her father's own standard unfurl and rise above the others; blood red, with a golden lion atop a cyan eagle. Royalty of the Fey the men of the Free would call it.

He had begged her forgiveness and she had granted it.

'In my weakness I departed from wisdom,' he said. 'Yet your heart was unsullied by the lies and deceits of evil. I would take back what I have said, but I cannot. I allowed my anger and my fear to overcome my love and care. I am truly sorry, Lady of the Forest.'

Her father had never spoken to her in such terms, always treated her as his child, never his equal. She had pulled him close again.

'It is not too late,' she instructed. 'Go to war, make amends. We can still turn the tide against the Witchking. I will stay here to safeguard the Citadel and all who remain.'

'We cannot spare many ...'

'The forest will not see our lands unmade,' Tarithel said. Somehow she knew this without doubt. She had felt it, the same power that had wrenched her from her imprisonment, the very trees responding to her cries for help. She had watched in terror as the windows had been wrenched aside and her prison broken. The forest had come to her aid and she was its servant, yet it would respond to her own wishes too, and the safety of the Citadel was uppermost in her mind.

'Go with all the blessing our land can give,' she said. 'Do not look back, but hurry to the service of the Moonprince. Ithrorn needs you! Our hopes and dreams rest upon the Moonprince's salvation and those who serve him. If we fail this time, the Witchking will dominate us all.'

'It will be done, Lady of the Forest.' Dreams' face had crumpled and he dragged her into a close embrace. 'My daughter.

You have warmed my heart, my pride in you is more than I have words to tell.'

He had turned then, striding forth to assemble his armies. Only Tarithel had seen the tears upon his face.

A breeze brushed past her, the scent of pollen upon it. She heard a faint cry, echoing from below as the armies moved out. She recognised her father's voice. Yet it was not just his voice, something deeper had been stirred. She felt the forest thrill to it. Leaves rustled as branches and limbs responded.

The trees rejoice! The Fey are alive once more.

Carried upon the wind, the forests spread the news. In an ever widening arc, cascading out from the Citadel the enchantments of the Fey communicated the imperative.

Through the remnants of Whispers, across the wreckage of Kor, even to the far west in Lothoril it sang, a breath of joy upon the evening air. Further south it touched the Forest of Thrall. Children and mothers looked up expectantly, feeling a change upon the air. It touched the sombre trees of Shadows and swept onwards. Dregrim rang to its news, its vast and ancient trees stirring for the first time in many moons.

Onwards still, until it echoed off the Frozen Wastes themselves, until gently caressing the distant Forest of Thimrath far away. There, where the sun was strongest and the Witchking's influence the least, flowers bloomed spontaneously, seeking the last rays of the sun before it was lost in the westering gloom.

The Fey ride …

Tarithel felt her pulse quicken.

All is not lost!

Lord Trorn had not been in the least bit enthusiastic about finding an army camped about his keep. Kumar looked upon him with disgust. The man was thin and unfit, with a receding hairline and a weak jaw.

'But, my lords!' he stammered. 'Would it not be best if I held this route secure against the Doomguard? Surely you do not want them to attack from behind. If I leave for Xajorkith with you, why all these lands would be undefended.'

'They're defended now?' Marakith said mischievously.

Kumar fixed him with a glare.

'We need all to come to the defence of Xajorkith,' he rumbled. 'There will be no defence of these lands. If Xajorkith fails the Doomguard will come swiftly to despoil them, you will face an even greater darkness.'

Trorn trembled. Kumar watched as his face few even paler.

Marakith nodded alongside.

'There is safety in numbers though,' he said jauntily. 'We all stand a much better chance by combining our might. Why, the Doomguard might decide to come this way in strength ...'

'Safety?' Trorn said, 'In numbers? Yes, I see ...'

Kumar rolled his eyes.

'In that case let us make all haste,' Trorn said, getting uncertainly to his feet. 'March upon the foe and whatnot. What are we waiting for? Let us depart immediately.'

Kumar and Marakith got to their feet too and watched as Trorn gingerly retreated from his hall.

Marakith smiled.

'Shall I remind him to take a sword, or will you?'

Kumar grimaced.

'Let's hope his men are in a better state than he is.'

Dawn broke, grim and cold, about the Citadel of Ithrorn.

Standing on the battlements, Ithrorn could see the fires burning from the ruined villages to the south west. They had been evacuated before the Doomguard armies had reached them. He glared out at the blaze, his hand upon his sword hilt as he watched the destruction.

Already the keeps to the west had been overrun. They too had been abandoned in advance, with all their men, equipment and provisions hastily moved within the Citadel. There was no way to defend them, so, at Ithrorn's order, they too had been put to the torch. Better that than for them to be used by the enemy.

But now that enemy lay around them. Through the night they had come, until dawn brought a host about the walls of his home.

At a glance Ithrorn could see there was little hope. With thousands contained within, the Citadel could not hold out long against a siege even if the Doomguard merely camped outside. There was little enough food for such a wait. Ithrorn could not venture forth and hope to prevail, they were outnumbered perhaps three to one. Safety, tenuous as it was, lay firmly within the walls.

'Archers on the walls!' he called, seeing the trebuchets of the Doomguard being readied through the morning mist. 'Loose!'

Arrows smote their targets, the Doomguard fell, but more always took their place. The machines of war advanced upon the walls and soon began hurling rocks and iron missiles. Parapets were struck, rubble cascaded into the streets. Men were hurled from their positions.

The answer came from within as firebrands were launched by the Citadel's own defences. Dozens of the Doomguard were consumed by the flames, but on they drove. Rocks crashed at the mighty gates of the Citadel. The oaken doors trembled with the onslaught and began to splinter.

Below warriors stood ready to meet the inevitable flood that would pour through the stricken gates. Above Ithrorn shouted more orders as the Doomguard pressed forth.

CHAPTER SIXTEEN

'Ladders!'

From the ranks of the Witchking's hordes, mighty ladders rose in ordered procession. A few were struck by firebrands but most were secured against the outer walls, locking into place with huge wrought iron claws fashioned into the shapes of fell beasts and the twisted evil imaginings of a cold and unfeeling mind.

Ithrorn was a seasoned warrior. He knew well the ebb and flow of a battle. The Citadel's fall was approaching. The defenders were making good account of themselves, but the overwhelming might of the invading force would determine the outcome. It was only a matter of time.

Ithrorn drew his sword and fought alongside his men, striding forth upon the battlements and slaying the foe. Blood-stained and yelling obscenities he forced them back across one section of the battlements, his men rallying to his side. Hewn and stricken Doomguard fell about them.

Screams from beyond made them raise their heads. Across the battlements men were falling back, hacked as they tried to retreat by the oncoming Doomguard, their blackened swords now stained with crimson.

'We must retreat, sire!'

Ithrorn growled something.

Better to make an end now, or be holed up waiting for the end? Or more prudent to retreat?

In that moment he heard something. The wind turned, changing from the north to the west, a faint warmth upon it. It felt strangely wholesome, the reek of battle momentarily pushed aside, replaced by the fragrance of summer.

Ithrorn frowned, looking out across the battlements. The timbre of the battle changed. A moment of uncertainty dealt upon the Citadel.

Then there were horns, horns upon the air, calling proudly above the tumult.

'Sire, look!'

Ithrorn's eyes were not what they once had been, he squinted, but could not make the details clear.

'What do you see?'

'A flash of silver sire, horses, riders, warriors. An army approaches from the west!'

'An army? The devices man, whom can it be?'

'Gold and Cyan upon Crimson ... my Lord, it is the Fey! The Fey of Dreams!'

The army was moving fast, with the riders at the fore, the warriors spreading out to each side to protect the flanks. As they watched from high above they saw the riders move into an arrowhead formation. Silver flashed in the air as they drew their swords and charged upon the ranks of Doomguard assailing the Citadel.

Deeper horns sounded as the Doomguard belatedly came about to deal with the unexpected threat.

Yet the wrath of the Fey, now ignited was a fury they did not foresee. The Fey burst upon the hated Doomguard like an immolating fire, sweeping them away. The riders cut through their ranks, sending them into disarray. Doomguard warriors spread to the north and south only to be caught by the ranks of Fey Warriors now spreading out to encircle them. Ithrorn watched in awe at the slaughter taking place below.

'To arms!' he called. 'Open the gates and have at the Foul!'

He vaulted down from the battlements and wrestled his way to the forecourt as the gates unlocked and burst outward. With a cry of hope and anger the men of Ithrorn issued forth, joining the furious fight beneath the walls.

The Doomguard, now assailed on all sides fought back, in desperation, but there was no answer for the wrath of the emboldened Fey and the hope kindled in the hearts of the Free.

The horns blared and weapons clashed, but the Witchking's

forces were annihilated by the strength of two allies too long rent asunder and now rejoined.

Through the wreckage of the battle and the twisted corpse of the Doomguard, Ithrorn stared at the devastation before his gates, hardly daring to believe that his realm had been saved from certain destruction.

Before him a proud figure galloped up on horseback, dismounted with a jump and stood before him.

Ithrorn stared into the eyes of the Lord of Dreams. He looked taller, prouder and more possessed of purpose than before.

Something happened to him …

'The Fey have been bereft in their duty,' Dreams said. 'We stood together once, I would see us stand together again in service to this Moonprince of which you spoke. Your servant, Lord Ithrorn.'

The Fey held out his hand. Ithrorn took it.

'You are most welcome, Lord of Dreams.'

'It is you that have held the line against all odds, and despite my own foolishness,' Dreams replied. 'Your courage is a wonder to behold.'

'We did not expect to see you here.'

Dreams nodded. 'Had it not been for one more courageous than I, you would still be waiting in vain.'

'My Lord?' Ithrorn asked, puzzled.

'You know her as the Lady of the Forest,' Dreams said, a smile playing on his lips. 'My daughter, Tarithel. You may thank her when you get a chance.'

Before Ithrorn had a chance to reply Dreams had hoisted his hand aloft. Then he cried out in a loud voice. The Free and Fey about them looking around.

'The bloody sword of battle has brought death in the domain of Ithrorn, yet victory goes to the Free!'

Cheers and shouts arose about the two leaders and the

chant was taken up, echoing about the frozen landscape around them.

'Victory went to the Free! Victory went to the Free!'

Morkin sat across from Balor, the Lord of Gloom, at a long trestle table. The food was good, if not plentiful, a mixture of dried meats and fish. Both ate in silence for a while before Balor began to talk, his voice deep and slow.

'Strange company you keep,' he said. 'A dragon and a skulkrin. Enough to make even the most jaded watcher of the wastes take notice.'

'I have come a long way,' Morkin said. 'And many strange things have happened to me upon that road.'

'No doubt,' Balor replied. 'But one does not travel idly near the realm of the Witchking. I would know your purpose here, Morkin.'

Balor stopped eating and fixed Morkin with a fierce stare. Morkin swallowed.

'Then I must ask where your allegiance lies,' Morkin replied, trying to stop a waver in his voice.

'My allegiance?' Balor replied and then chuckled. 'Perhaps I have none.'

Morkin frowned. 'Are you not a Lord of the Free, sworn to protect these lands?'

Balor's mirth faded.

'If you knew your history you would not ask with such impertinence,' Balor replied. 'But you are young and such knowledge has doubtless not been given to you.'

'What do you mean?'

Balor sighed. 'What know you of the House of the Moon?'

Morkin shrugged. 'Not much. There wasn't time. Rorthron the Wise told us they had been destroyed long ago and that only a handful survived. He had kept watch in all the intervening years waiting for one to be able to wield the Moon Ring ...'

Balor nodded. 'The truth ... at least in part. Rorthron is right to say that only a handful survived, but your father's kin were not all that remained of the House of the Moon.'

'There were others?' Morkin said. 'You mean ... you?'

Balor chuckled. 'My remote ancestors, yes. You see, the folk of the Moon once lived in these lands, there are monuments to them on the maps and in the naming of places hereabouts. This was before the Witchking rose to power.'

'Here in the north?' Morkin asked. 'Lothoril talked of Moonhenge.'

Balor nodded. 'Before the winter fell of course, these lands were fair enough so it was told. Know you of the rise of the Witchking?'

Morkin shrugged. 'A little. I heard he murdered King Ushgarak.'

'Indeed he did,' Balor said. 'But Ushgarak was a fool by most accounts, relying heavily on his trusted advisor, Gryfallon the Stargazer. Ushgarak's loss was not keenly felt, and when Gryfallon took over, the Lords and laypeople of Midnight were not displeased. They considered that Gryfallon had advised wisely and, knowing nothing of his crime, believed he would see them through.'

'The Lords trusted the Witchking at first?' Morkin echoed.

'He ruled well at the outset, or so it seemed,' Balor said. 'But, in reality, he was fomenting conflict behind the scenes. The Lords did not perceive it and fell to petty squabbling amongst themselves. Arguments over territories became skirmishes and skirmishes became wars. Gryfallon set them against each other whilst all the while building his own strength.'

'But why?' Morkin asked.

Balor shrugged. 'I do not know the Witchking's mind. He seeks dominion over Midnight, that is for sure. That has always been his wish ... as to why ...'

'And the House of the Moon?' Morkin prompted.

'There were many Houses in those times,' Balor replied. 'Yet the House of the Moon was prominent amongst them. They perceived the stratagem of Gryfallon and worked against him, attempting to unite the Lords and promote peace between them. Long and hard they toiled against Gryfallon.'

'And?'

Balor looked grim. 'Then came the sorcery.'

Morkin swallowed.

'Gryfallon harnessed the power of winter to assail them,' Balor said. 'The Frozen Wastes erupted on the borders, the frozen essence of a fell mist of Gryfallon's creation. The ice-fear touched the hearts of all, bringing despair. With the winter came the famine and more war as the Lords fought over what remained. So many perished in short years as the hoped for spring never came.

'The House of the Moon were pushed back. They were chased from their ancestral lands, establishing a new realm to the south. What you know as the Tower of the Moon was once the Tower of Shadows. They renamed it, building a mighty Citadel there. Your fellow ... Rorthron? He aided them in their work, the only one of the Wise to do so. There they continued their task, seeking to unite what remained of the southlands against Gryfallon, now the hated Witchking of the north.'

'The rest you know,' Balor added. 'The Witchking perceived the House of the Moon as a threat and destroyed them, long ago. Few now remember.'

Morkin frowned.

'And you?'

Balor shrugged. 'The remnants of the House of the Moon

that did not flee to the south. My descendants choose not to oppose the Witchking. Thus, he spared us. We remained … we are few in number, but we are all that remain.'

Balor stopped and took a drink from a goblet of wine.

'So, your tale, Morkin of the House of the Moon,' Balor said. 'I'm sure it will be more interesting than mine.'

Morkin took a deep breath. 'If you know of the House of the Moon, you must know of the lay of Yanathel.'

Balor regarded him for a moment, a puzzled look crossing his face, which slowly turned into astonishment.

'You seek the Ice Crown?' he whispered.

Morkin nodded.

'And your mother …'

'Was Fey,' Morkin answered. 'Yes.'

'You think you are the one spoken of in the old songs?'

'I believe it.'

'And you are here …' Balor mused. 'You sought a way across the Plains of the Lost and found them guarded by the Witchking's hordes. Lord Lothoril sent you to me, did he not?'

Morkin nodded. 'He said you might be able to aid me.'

'An unseen way into the Witchking's realm,' Balor said. 'That is what you require.'

'Is there such a thing?' Morkin whispered.

Balor rubbed his chin before answering.

'Yes, there is.'

Morkin took a breath, feeling his pulse racing.

'Then I must know. I have to destroy the Ice Crown, time is running out … will you show me the way?'

Balor regarded him for a long moment.

Morkin waited, a frown growing on his face.

Balor shook his head.

'No, I will not.'

'My Lord …!'

Balor raised a hand. 'To aid you would break the central

tenet of my people's survival. We were spared, because we never took up arms against the Witchking. He does not attack us in return. Long has that ruling been upheld by me and my forefathers. By aiding you I would break that trust and have the Witchking's wrath descend upon my people. I alone am responsible for them now. The Free have long since abandoned us and the Fey care not.'

'But I need your help ...'

'You shall not have it. I will not preside over their demise ...'

'But you seem happy to preside over them as they rot here,' Morkin said. 'You have no purpose, no will. The Witchking honours his promise only because it is convenient for him. He will turn upon you the moment he feels it is to his advantage! He presses his attack on the southlands ...'

'The southlands are no concern of mine, they never have been. Houses rise and fall, my people remain, we always remain ...'

'They will be lost when they the south is defeated,' Morkin replied. 'Do you think the Witchking does not know of your ancestry? That he will suffer even a sundered line of the House of the Moon to live when he has eradicated all others? He will put you all to the sword the moment he has dealt with them, whatever promise you might think you have.'

'The Witchking has kept his word for ten thousand moons,' Balor rumbled. 'Can the Free or the Fey claim better?'

'You cannot trust him!'

'Enough!' Balor replied. 'My decision is made. You may have food and lodging for as long as you wish. Then you depart and your route is your own.'

Morkin pushed the dinner plate aside.

'Then I leave now, for time is short,' he said, striding out of the hall. He turned upon the threshold, seeing Balor looking back at him.

'You are my distant cousin,' Morkin said. 'But I do not see

416

the House of the Moon in you. I go to defeat the Witchking as I believe our forefathers would have us do. Farewell, Lord of Gloom. We shall not meet again.'

The ancient walls of Xajorkith were methodically being reduced to rubble. The Doomguard tactics of fracturing the walls with ice had been swiftly followed up by a more traditional pummelling with rock and stone. Its structure weakened, the defences were failing. Lord Xajorkith had ordered the walls abandoned as the Doomguard artillery turned its attack upon the gatehouse. It too was succumbing to the ferocious onslaught. It was clear the gates would fail before long.

Ice splattered around the mighty oak and steel workings of the gatehouse, turning to water which dripped down into hinges, locks, gears and cogs. The mighty crossbeams that barred the gates remained in place.

Men watched as the sound of water dripping faded away.

A faint crackle, almost imperceptible. All watched as a curtain of ice began to spread across the gates, crystal fingers growing swiftly, expanding across the wood and metal, seeking purchase and a way within. The ice moved, as if it were a living thing, grasping and clutching at everything it could reach, penetrating, working its way into every crevice.

The gates creaked, metal squealed as intolerable pressures came to bear. Hampered by the chilling temperatures, it became brittle, inflexible, tensioned far beyond a strain its designers had ever envisaged.

With an almighty roar the gates fractured in an explosion of fragments, ice and spiralling pieces of metal debris. Snow flew in all directions.

'Hold fast!' Luxor cried. 'Hold fast!'

Then came the Doomguard, charging through the ruined gatehouse, mindless of the debris, dark metal swords aloft, spears slicing through the air and arrows flying. The cavalry of the Lords of Midnight rode at them, hacking them down whilst archers poured arrow after arrow into the morass of men.

The cries of the stricken filled the air. Horns blew, calling all to fight. Time and again the ice-fear struck at them and each time Luxor would raise his arm and strive against it, the light of the Moon Ring casting fear into the Doomguard whom it fell upon.

Back and forth the armies struggled in the courtyards of Xajorkith, first one and then the other holding the advantage. The Lords of Midnight gave good account of themselves, but as the hours progressed it was clear they could not prevail forever.

'If we had but another thousand men,' Shimeril yelled, his armour blood splattered and broken in many places. 'We might turn this Foul horde!'

'I'd ask only for a sharper axe,' Blood yelled back. 'This one is notched and more of a mallet!'

The men were tiring, but their leaders urged them on against the foe, rallying time and again. Xajorkith himself slew a band of Doomguard that had the temerity to attempt to defile his standard, proudly standing aloft on a flagpole in the midst of the courtyard. The corpses of Free and Foul alike lay deep upon the ground.

A glow now lit the eastern sky. The promise of a new day. Clouds cast their mantle across much of it, but in the sky a point of light blazed forth.

'The moonstar,' Luxor said. 'A good omen …'

The Moon Ring warmed upon his finger. In a rush of images Luxor saw new banners in his mind. Some familiar, others less so. His vision widened, taking in the land of Midnight once more. Proud banners, with eagles held aloft.

The Fey? Can it be true? I see the Lord of Dreams! If he turns, might they all turn to our banner?

As he thought it, horns could be heard upon the wind. Horns out of the east. The Doomguard heard them too. Responding to whistled commands and orders barked in the harsh tongue of the north they retreated, flowing out through the gates and leaving the death strewn courtyards behind.

'An army approaches!' A herald cried. 'My Lords! It is … it is Kumar and Marakith! Athoril and Trorn! Approaching from the east! The Doomguard retreat!'

But Luxor, already knew the good news. The Lords cried out in joy, the herald left dumbfounded.

And the Fey begin to march as well, we will see this battle turned!

Tarithel had watched her father's armies until they were out of sight to the east. Two days later word had come that they had reached the Citadel of Ithrorn and freed it from the ravages of the Foul. The Witchking's grip on the far east had been weakened.

She could feel it upon the air, the sun shone a little brighter, a little stronger. It was still the heart of winter, but the days could only grow longer now. A faint hope tinged the landscape.

She had busied herself with her duties, both the defence of the Citadel itself, and her charge, the Lord of Whispers. Long he had lain injured, but tended to by the skilled herbalists of the citadel. His wounds had been dressed and changed. To her delight his deathly pallor had been touched by colour. He would live, perhaps one day strong enough to return to his own forests and start the work of restoring them after the devastation the Witchking had wrought.

With her chores complete she walked the walls of the citadel for a time, sensing the warming in the east and the cold fury to the west and north. The Witchking was not defeated overall, far from it. What little other tidings that had found their way this far north spoke of the Free falling back time and again, beaten in the very battle they had engaged in, retreating further and further until they were forced up against the impenetrable barrier of the Frozen Wastes themselves. Their capital city Xajorkith, a hundred leagues south, already under siege.

Time is running out ... will the Fey reach them in time? And if they do, will it be enough?

She walked out into the forest just beyond the boundaries of the tended lands around the citadel, riding the paths she had learnt from childhood. Without knowing why, she found herself riding to the Lith her father had promised to take her to.

It stood, always miraculously clear of snow and ice. It's ancient stone thrusting up from the landscape, the forest about it strangely clear and tended.

Almost as if it bows in respect for the old stone ...

LADY OF THE FOREST.

She turned, looking for the voice, but there was no one present. She stretched out her senses, still unfamiliar with what she had done before, when the forest had come to her aid, rescuing her from her imprisonment and turning on the Foul that had invaded their lands.

She had seen the Fey at the citadel making way for her wherever she walked, scared of what they had seen her do. True enough, the Fey had always known the forests had their own sentience, how otherwise could their borders be defended? The trees had always barred the way to those unwanted, a craft the Fey had worked long ago. But to see such power manifest itself, wild, dynamic and unleashed in the way it had been ... that was something new and strange.

And truth be told, I wanted to be free, but I didn't command the trees, they took the initiative themselves …

Lady of the Forest she might be, but from whom did the forest really take its instructions?

And this voice …

'Who, who are you?' she whispered.

A faint sense of amusement, nothing more. She could barely perceive it.

COME HITHER.

She walked forward, feeling the ground beneath her somehow warm through the soles of her shoes. She reached out and touched the ancient stones …

Visions flashed through her mind. Armies, battles, proud citadels and haughty towers. Mountains and lakes, great swathes of forests.

MIDNIGHT IS ONLY THE BEGINNING OF THE STRUGGLE. EVIL ROAMS FAR AND WIDE BEYOND THESE BORDERS.

She gasped, thinking to retreat, but found her body would not respond to her commands. She was locked, immobile.

LOOK. BEYOND THE WASTES …

She managed to shake her head.

'But there is nothing, nothing beyond the Frozen Wastes!'

But it was clear she was wrong. Somehow she could see from above, the Forest of Dreams falling away below her sight. With horror she spied the realm of the Witchking, locked behind his gloomy fortifications. Then the Frozen Wastes stretched out before her, endless leagues of razor sharp ice and rock stretching …

… they came to an end.

Beyond lay another land. She gasped, her eyes seeing detail beyond measure. A gateway, broken and worn, clearly the relic of some civilisation that had long ago succumbed to the weight of history.

THE GATE OF VARENORN.

She was swept north and east. A great forest …

FANGRIM.

A mighty city passed below her. She could see people, people alike unto her.

But they are Fey! Fey live to the north of Midnight?

The landscape moved at an impossible speed, soon a range of austere mountains rose up to greet her.

ANVULANE.

She had no time to consider it before they were whisked away behind. A dark and forbidding fortress rose before her, cloaked in grey and unwholesome light. She peered closer, sensing something, a feeling of intense scrutiny as if something were …

KAHANGRORN!

Eyes, dark and malevolent stared back at her. She tried to recoil, but found she couldn't. The eyes were framed by a beautiful yet sinister face, pale stunning beauty mixed with implacable malice.

She got the vague impression of a woman, rounded of body, wrapped about with luxurious hair. The eyes narrowed, as if aware they were being watched.

Who …

Dread fell upon her. She shivered with cold and fear.

THE HEARTSTEALER!

With shock of cold she found herself thrown back into the snow. She was in the glade, just as before, looking at the Lith, trembling from head to foot.

'Who are you?' she cried. 'And why do you show me these things?

MIDNIGHT IS BUT THE BEGINNING, LADY OF THE FOREST. PREPARE YOURSELF.

'For what?' she answered. 'What must I do?'

Her vision clouded again, the swift passage of the lands flickering in her eyes. She saw her father, standing at the

422

boundaries of a forest, thwarted in his progress south. She frowned in confusion.

Why does he stop?

Her vision was wrested away further south where the spires of the Citadel of Dregrim rose above the twisted trees of the forest. He gaze was drawn to one tower, where a Fey stood, pacing a room.

Locked and barred. But why?

No answer, no further revelation. She could sense frustration, fury and impotence. A desperate longing to be free and to serve …

… The Moonprince!

The chuckle came again. This time it seemed closer somehow. She looked about herself, but still saw no one.

YOU HAVE DONE YOUR PART FOR NOW, MY LADY. LOOKING FOR YOUR NEXT DUTY? YOU MUST SEEK THE DEFENCE OF YOUR HOME.

A face swam before her vision, indistinct for a moment, but clear enough to recognise.

Rorthron!

AYE, MY LADY. YOU HAVE WOKEN THE FEY. I MUST NOW SEE THEY JOIN THE STRUGGLE IN TIME …

The connection broke. Tarithel found herself crouched in the snow before the great stones of the Lith, the silent forest all about her.

Chapter Seventeen

They stand on the Plains of Corelay,
looking west to the Citadel of Xajorkith.

'We found the way south blocked,' Marakith reported after the army had reached the beleaguered citadel. 'We could not hope to prevail against their might, so we rode to the east through the Plains of Trorn and approached from that way. It seems the Doomguard discounted us …'

'We would have been here sooner,' Kumar grunted. 'But it is a long and weary road.'

'We are sore glad to have you here,' Luxor replied. 'And I have news from afar. The Lord of Dreams and the Lord of Ithrorn are on their way. If we can but hold out long enough …'

Kumar nodded. 'That is welcome news, we feared the worst when the Forest of Dregrim allowed none to pass its borders. Those lands are closed to us. They might have sped our way even if they refused to join the fight, but we had no assistance, nor even contact from them.'

'I will leave Dregrim to Dreams,' Luxor said. 'We have enough to be doing here.'

'We will welcome what Fey do aid us,' Blood said. 'We must not be saddened when the unworthy turn away. Why perhaps, when we have despatched the Witchking, we can bring those fickle Fey to account as well!'

'Surely they can see that the Witchking will turn on them if we are exterminated?' Shimeril said. 'Fey they might be, but those I fought with long ago were no cowards, I don't understand ...'

'The loyalties and reasoning of the Fey are not always easy for us to comprehend,' Luxor said. 'They are a strange folk ...'

'Bah,' Kumar retorted. 'Let those who will come, come. That's an end to the matter. Let those who are cowards rot like the old wood they are in their forests. The Free will decide the fate of Midnight, as it should be. The hapless Fey can wither away.'

With the arrival of the additional Free army the Doomguard had retreated to the North. They could be seen re-organising themselves, content with the damage they had inflicted on the citadel.

'You are here now,' Luxor said. 'We have much need of reinforcements as you can see.'

Work had begun to make such repairs to the walls as could be achieved. It seemed certain that the Doomguard would attack again at nightfall. Xajorkith had ordered the remains of the gatehouse to be broken down, to form as much of a barrier as possible. Atop the rubble he gazed north, looking out over the plains towards the Doomguard army a league or so away. The internal towers of the citadel still stood proud despite the ruin of the lower battlements.

'We have given them good account,' Xajorkith said. 'But even with our friends' arrival we cannot prevail for long.'

'We said that yesterday,' Luxor replied. 'And yet here we stand.'

Xajorkith laughed. 'Now it is you who encourages me! Yes, your words are true, we fought them well.'

'And Xajorkith has a battle it can be proud of, whatever the final outcome,' Luxor said.

Xajorkith nodded. 'I hope there is some bard or minstrel who will survive to some pleasant future time and tell our tale.'

'Stories will always be told,' Luxor said. 'Many victories and defeats scatter our history. There are always those who survive to tell the tale.'

Xajorkith nodded. 'The Witchking sends reinforcements, doubtless his army waits for still more numbers.'

Luxor nodded. 'He sends all his might against us now. Come, council is meeting once more. We must review our strategy. There is much to do before nightfall.'

With the demise of the Foul the Fey had ridden swiftly south from the Citadel of Ithrorn. Through the Forest of Whispers they charged, their steeds untiring, their men unwearied. Even those of the Free who accompanied them found that the forests somehow sped their way. Lord Ithrorn himself counted the leagues unrolling behind him, astonished at their progress. Nightfall found them far into the Plains of Kumar, with mountains to the west and his homeland far beyond the horizon.

'I cannot account for it!' he said aloud, not realising he was vocalising his inner thoughts.

'The Fey have known the ways of Midnight for many moons,' Dreams replied. 'Such familiarity brings knowledge of things less than obvious.'

'Fey magic?' Ithrorn asked. 'I have heard tales of such things, but I never believed them.'

Dreams shook his head. 'An affinity, nothing more, but powerful nonetheless.'

The following day brought them into the lands of the Utarg, but though his keep was guarded, locked and fortified, they received no challenge as they thundered across his territory. Another day brought them to the eaves of the great Forest of Dregrim, the second greatest in all Midnight.

Riders had approached them from the west. Ithrorn heard them recount the mustering of the Fey. An army was en route from Thrall and would be with them by the next morn. Far to the west Thimrath the Fey had joyously received the word and was already en route towards the defenders of Xajorkith and would surely arrive there before the rest of the Fey. Only Dregrim had not responded to the summons it would seem.

Yet there they found their way barred. The forest would not avail them, its twisted roots and branches blocking their progress. Dreams dismounted and walked to the threshold of the forest. From it seeped a thin mist.

He raised his arm towards the forest and muttered words under his breath. The trees nearest him quivered and shook, but the way remained closed.

Dreams frowned.

'Lord Dregrim, as High Lord of the Fey I demand your presence. We are in haste and your succour is bade!'

No answer came, save for a breeze that blustered around the army, now motionless before the eaves of the forest.

'Lord Dregrim! Your answer!'

Morkin strode across the snow, stamping his feet down, his expression hard and as ice-locked as the land about him. Fawkrin saw him coming and sprung to his feet, nudging Farflame, who had begun to doze. The dragon opened one eye.

SO SOON, YOUNG SQUIRE?

'You must take me to the edge of the Witchking's realm,' Morkin said. 'As close as you dare.'

MUST I?

'Yes,' Morkin said. 'Gloom will not help us.'

THEN WHY IS HE FOLLOWING YOU?

Morkin stopped and looked up.

'What?'

The dragon inclined his head, indicating something behind Morkin. Fawkrin pointed.

'See, young boy, see? Khlee! The Lord of this great citadel!'

Morkin turned and saw Balor standing half a dozen feet away.

'I depart,' Morkin said. 'If you have something to say, say it quick. I cannot tarry any longer.'

Balor stepped forward.

'You are brave, squire of the House of the Moon,' Balor said. 'Your plan?'

'I will find a path through the mountains,' Morkin began.

Balor shook his head. 'There are no passes, those mountains are sheer. Mighty gusts sweep their faces, there is no way through.'

'Past the Citadel of Vorgath then,' Morkin said.

'You would sneak past one of the Witchking's mightiest citadels, with his armies on patrol across the Plains of the Lost and his attention already focussed here – with a wondrous but most conspicuous dragon alongside?'

Morkin spun around, glaring at Balor.

'Then what would you have me do?' Morkin demanded. 'You will not help me yet I will make the attempt ...'

Balor sighed and took something out from within his fur-lined robes.

'You are brave, Morkin,' he said. 'Braver than I. Perhaps you have a chance to succeed where Yanathel failed. You spoke truth that the Witchking will come for my people if the southland falls. I see that. But with this, I sign their death warrant if you fail ...'

He handed Morkin a package, leatherbound, clearly worn with age.

'What is this?'

429

'It was handed to my grandsire, long moons ago,' Balor said. 'Within are the translations in the common tongue of notes penned by Yanathel herself. How the Fey came upon them I do not know. They speak of a cavern east of here, from which Yanathel somehow found a way into the Witchking's realm …'

'A passage!' Morkin's eyes grew wide.

'I know not whether it is even true,' Balor said. 'But I fear it is your only hope … and having given it to you, now it is my only hope as well.'

'How do I find it?'

'Read it.' Balor replied.

Morkin opened the old document and began to read.

'Travel east from Gloom,' he said. 'Along the sharp edge of the Frozen Wastes and hither to the horizon. Many leagues hence you will set upon a Snowhall. Then turn south. Verily you will find the cavern before the mountains. Be wary traveller, such places are oft infested with ice trolls and it lies but a few leagues from the Citadel of Vorgath …'

Morkin looked up.

'A cavern and a passage … does this place have a name?'

Balor nodded and his dour expression was one that Morkin would always remember.

'I know of no name myself,' Balor replied. 'But Yanathel herself referred to it as the Cavern of …'

'Don't tell me,' Morkin said. 'Terror, doom, fear, horror or some such …'

'Death,' Balor said, with a wry grin. 'I will ride out with my warriors and meet with Lord Lothoril. We will harry the Doomguard and thus, I hope, give you safe passage.'

Morkin bowed low. 'I am in your debt then, Balor.'

'Farewell Morkin. All of the hopes of the Free, the Fey and the sundered houses of the Moon go with you. Should you fail, we all fail.'

He turned and strode away towards his citadel, leaving Morkin standing the snow.

Morkin swallowed.

'Thousands of men at arms,' he muttered. 'A dragon, the host of the Fey, the Wise and all their scheming – yet it ends with me. If such is fate, so be it!'

'My Lords,' Luxor said, looking at the assembled leaders of Midnight before him. 'The final throw of the dice may be upon us.'

Afternoon was already fading into evening, the sun westering on the second day of the battle. The Doomguard still held back, preparing whatever strategy they had in mind. Clouds were boiling up from the north, dim and grey against the sky. Soon the vales of Corelay were masked in murk. The elements seemed to have lost their battle against the powers of the Witchking.

The sun faded behind the thickening clouds and a cold winter ruffled the cloaks of the Lords of Midnight.

'I have not the words for long speeches,' Luxor said, looking from one to the other. All looked back at him, waiting, expectant. 'All I know is this. I have seen great valour and courage in these last few days. We have already fought a battle our forefathers would be proud to call their own. Whatever the morrow brings, we can be satisfied with what we have already withstood.

'The Witchking seeks the destruction of all, Free or Fey. Long he has plotted our demise and lain in preparation for this day. We were all caught unawares. We have fought and been defeated. We have fallen back. We stand here, already at our last line of defence.'

Luxor paused and took a breath.

'Perhaps I am not the leader some of you hoped for, scant few days have passed since I was but a minor Lord of an insignificant keep far to the west, with a handful of men at my command. Fate has turned this around. It seems I am Luxor, of the lost House of the Moon. Rorthron the Wise entrusted me with the last War Ring of Midnight. With it I can resist the ice-fear and protect the hearts of all of us from its fell enchantment. That gives us a more even chance ...

'We have worked long in the preparation of this, our capital. Xajorkith has already proved its worth, repulsing the enemy when they thought they could take it. We must do so again. Dreams and Ithrorn stand at the Forest of Dregrim, they make all haste to us. Thrall musters and will join their army. Thimrath of the Fey rides from the west to our defence.'

Rumblings of approval echoed from all around the hall.

Luxor raised his gaze.

'But there is something else that the Witchking does not know. Far to the North my own son, revealed by the Wise to be the half-Fey and half-Free of ancient myth, seeks the very source of the Witchking's power. He is close now, but the most dangerous part of the journey still lies before him.'

Luxor paused again.

'We may not be able to win, yet our best hope is to give my son his chance. By keeping the Witchking's attention focussed here, by making the very best fight we can, we give Morkin his opening. Fate will decide the outcome, but all is not yet lost.'

All remained silent, still waiting, still expectant.

Luxor drew his sword. 'Let us make them pay for every inch of land they wish to take. For Xajorkith! For Midnight!'

Swords were unsheathed, glinting in the fading light.

'For Xajorkith! For Midnight!'

Corleth remained locked in the tower. His captors had treated him well enough, food, water and fresh clothes had been provided at intervals, but he could get nothing out of the guards who attended him, they seemed terrified of the wrath of Dregrim.

Luxor will be sure I have abandoned him once again. Locked here with no news, plans ruined! What will befall us all if the Fey do not join the defence? The Witchking will despatch the Free and turn upon us. We are fools if we believe we can resist him alone. It has always been thus, Fey and Free, keeping evil at bay …

And yet there had been something. He had sensed a presence on at least two occasions, as if someone was watching him from afar. He had tried to grasp it, but it was ephemeral and fleeting. The more he concentrated on it the less tangible it became.

A young woman I do not know …

SHE IS TARITHEL, LADY OF THE FOREST OF DREAMS. YOUR SALVATION LIES WITH HER.

Corleth lurched backwards, looking about him for the source of the voice, but he was alone in the room. The voice had a timbre and a tone that he recognised immediately.

'Rorthron?'

AYE, MY FRIEND. IT HAS TAKEN ME SOME TIME TO FIND YOU.

'I am imprisoned here,' Corleth answered. 'Lord Dregrim will not join our cause. I have failed in my duty to rouse the Fey …'

A chuckle. Corleth got the sense of wry amusement.

YOU WILL HAVE YOUR CHANCE TO STAND AND FIGHT WITH THE FEY. FEAR NOT, LORD DREAMS STANDS AT THE VERY EAVES OF THE FOREST OF DREGRIM AS WE SPEAK.

'But how?' Corleth said. 'I was not able to send any message north.'

I SPOKE TO ANOTHER.

'Who?'

YOU ALREADY KNOW HER. TARITHEL, LADY OF THE FOREST, HAS ROUSED THE FEY FROM THEIR SLUMBER. HOLD FAST. IT WILL NOT BE LONG. I WILL JOIN YOU AS SOON AS I CAN …

The presence of mind faded away again, leaving Corleth to stagger back and rest against the wall.

The Fey are roused! They are coming!

As he did so he heard a tapping at the window. He frowned as he saw twigs and branches scrape against the lead lined glasswork before somehow gripping at the window. With a creaking groan the window was wrenched open and then torn free from its mountings. The branches forced their way within, clutching at the stonework. Corleth saw it crumble and break under some enormous strength, cracking and turning to dust as the vegetation pulled at it.

Dust flew about him, but within moments a hole had been torn in the wall.

Corleth climbed out seeing a huge vine had somehow grown up the side of the citadel, it waved back and forth, enticing him to step into its grasp. A voice came from far away, but clear and direct.

Trust the forest!

He grasped the vine and stepped into it. Branches curled around his arms and legs and he found himself transported rapidly towards the ground. Shouts rose below as the guards who had clustered about the vine pointed up at him.

He was released as he reached the ground, stepping free with the vine rearing up behind him.

Corleth spied Lord Dregrim pushing his way through from the rear.

'What fell magic is this? You are a sorcerer!'

'You wrongly imprisoned me,' Corleth replied. 'This is not the will of the Fey …'

'I will decide the will of the Fey in my own lands!' Dregrim roared. 'Guards, arrest him once more, take him to the dungeons where no root or vine may reach!'

Two guards with halberds moved forward, tentatively approaching Corleth. As they came close the vines whipped out faster than the eye could see, coiled tendrils lashed around the halberds, wresting them from the guards' grasp and then throwing them over the walls of the citadel.

Corleth stepped forward

'The Lords of Dreams stands at your borders, Lord Dregrim,' Corleth called in a loud voice. 'He calls for you. It is time for the Fey to do their part in the war against the Witchking. What is your answer?'

He heard the mutterings of the guards around him. Clearly they had no idea that Dreams was close by.

'I am master here!' Dregrim replied.

'Dreams is your liege!' Corleth replied. 'You are his vassal, do you deny this?'

'I will not parley words with you, Corleth of the Thrall Fey ...'

Corleth turned his attention to the guards about him.

'If your leader will not help, will you? Our brothers stand ready to fight for the realm of Midnight. To stand up against the Witchking and perhaps vanquish him forever! My own liege is Luxor, revealed Moonprince of Midnight, holder of the last War Ring of Midnight. He demands our help. Will Dregrim be the only outpost of the Fey that refuses that call? Or will Midnight from here on curse the name of Dregrim?'

'To fight against the Witchking is utmost folly!' Dregrim almost screamed. 'That way does death and extinction lie!'

'Not while hope is kindled in the heart of Free and Fey alike!' Corleth returned. He gestured behind him. 'The forest comes alive to a new will, our fellow Fey are roused ... will you march upon the foe?'

Neither Dregrim nor his men answered.

Corleth took a step forward and raised his voice.

'Will you march upon the foe?'

The guards around Dregrim looked nervously at each other.

Corleth persisted. 'Will you march upon the foe?' He stared at each of them, one by one, daring them to answer.

One stepped forward, a sword raised.

'I will march upon the foe!'

Dregrim snarled at him. 'You will be killed for your impertinence!'

Corleth shouted him down. 'Will you march upon the foe?'

More swords were drawn. Dregrim looked around him in dismay as all those within earshot raised their weapons with a shout.

'Will you march upon the foe?'

The cry went up from all but one.

'We will march upon the foe!'

And across the land of Midnight the ice-fear faltered for a moment. Far to the south and west, renewed hope was kindled in the heart of the Moonprince.

The Mountains of Death were unguarded, and for good reason. They were impassable. Morkin looked at their sheer and jagged slopes and wondered what magic must have crafted them in the dim and distant past. They erupted out of the ground as if they had burst upon the world, impaling it from below, thrust up through the ground by some mighty force.

Lord Gloom's advice had led him to this most desolate of lands, but the path had been true. The passage across the Plains of the Lost, skirting the strange ring of stones known as Weird Henge had led him to a cavern, the Cavern of Death.

'Cavern of Death, Mountains of Death ...' Morkin muttered to himself. 'The Witchking doesn't have much imagination ...'

The ice-fear was ferocious, as if aware that peril lay nearby. Fawkrin could barely take another step forward, and the cavern was too small for the dragon to enter.

ARMIES PATROL THE PLAINS WITHIN THE WITCHKING'S REALM. STEALTH, NOT FORCE, IS YOUR ALLY. RETURN HERE AND I WILL FLY YOU BOTH TO LAKE MIRROW …

Morkin peered inside the dank entrance, seeing nothing at all. There was bad smell though, his nose wrinkled in disgust.

Behind him Farflame snorted.

GET BACK!

With a roar, a bulky body burst out of the darkness. Morkin only got a brief glimpse of it before he took a blow to the chest which flung him through the air. He heard Fawkrin's squeal of fear as he hit the snow and struggled to get back to his feet.

He could see a massive burly creature striding towards him dressed in animal hide, ghastly purple skin, with a low sunken forehead and a huge pair of dark eyes, clawed hands outstretched.

He struggled to rise, fumbling with his sword, trying to bring it around to defend himself.

Jaws opened, showing a lizard like tongue framed with stained and fearsome teeth. The creature roared again and sprinted towards him.

A blast of fire incinerated it. A flurry of snow blasted around him and the body of the creature was clasped by talons and wrenched away into the sky.

ICE TROLLS MAKE FOR GOOD EATING IF LIGHTLY COOKED.

Morkin looked up in gratitude.

'Thanks!'

YOU MUST BE CAUTIOUS, YOUNG SQUIRE. THERE

ARE MANY SUCH CREATURES BENEATH THE ICE OF MIDNIGHT.

In the shelter of the cavern entrance Morkin reviewed his map and the writings of Yanathel. There were indeed a pair of caverns, one outside the mountains and one within, separated by a distance of perhaps a league or more. Above, the mountains were as perilous as they had been described, but underneath, he would be unseen, unheard, and out of the way of any harm the weather might try to inflict.

Yanathel's notes talked only about finding the cavern, and nothing about what lay beyond. It seemed she must have left it hereabouts before making her way into the passage and into the Witchking's realm, never to return.

Morkin looked deeper within, seeing little but the rocky walls.

'How will I see?' he asked. 'I have a torch, but it will not last me all the way through …'

'What does the Feyish writing say?' Fawkrin asked.

'Nothing,' Morkin said. 'It will be pitch-black, and not even the purest Fey can see in the absolute darkness.'

Behind him, the dragon rumbled. Morkin recognised the chuckle.

THERE ARE OLDER MAGICS THAN THE WITCHKING WITHIN THE REALM OF MIDNIGHT.

'Being cryptic again?' Morkin replied.

A LACK OF LIGHT WILL NOT BE A SOURCE OF FEAR.

Morkin sighed. Farflame screeched up, unfolding his wings and covering the entrance with them. Morkin and Fawkrin were plunged into darkness.

'Great,' Morkin said. 'Now I can't even start, very helpful, Farflame …'

LOOK ABOUT YOU, IMPATIENT ONE.

Morkin blinked. He could see the outline of the rocks and

boulders strewn about him. At first he took the dim illumination to be from the little light that seeped around the dragon's wings, but then he realised it was brighter within. He stepped across towards the back wall of the cavern, peering closer.

'The rocks themselves ...'

It was hard to make out, but the rocks were emitting some kind of milky luminescence. The deeper Morkin went the more obvious it was. The cavern was lit with a strange cold, but steady light. Morkin touched the rocks and was rewarded with a stronger glow for a few short moments, outlining the contours of his outstretched hand.

'Magic ...'

PERHAPS. A WONDER OF THE WORLD, NONETHE-LESS.

Morkin returned to the entrance and shouldered his pack. 'Then I must go,' he said. 'Farewell my friends.'

LUCK GO WITH YOU.

'Travel safe, young lord. Success to you! Khlee!'

Morkin took a deep breath and then walked to the rear of the cavern, a small crack in the far wall beckoned. He slipped through.

It was no smooth and winding track through a lofty cathedral of stone, no well-worn track he could follow. The crevice had widened for a while, but it was a tight squeeze. Around him the strange white light seemed to be stronger, but perhaps it was just his eyes growing used to it.

No sound came to his ears other than his own breathing and he could see little around him in the close confines of the rocky passage. Before long he had scraped knuckles and elbows and narrowly missed hitting his forehead on jutting outcrops of unforgiving rock.

He could not measure his progress, but it was not swift. At times he was able to walk, but more often he found himself squeezing through narrow gaps, or climbing cracked and broken cliffs of rock, or crawling through narrow clefts under great tableaus of rubble. These last were the ones he liked the least, keeping himself as flat as possible as he inched forward, always conscious of a mountain's weight of rock above him, poised to crush him in an instant if it wished.

It was not a pleasant thought.

Two things kept him moving. He knew, of course, that the Free and the Fey were depending on him to unseat the Witchking, but that was a responsibility so great that he found it hard to dwell upon it without trembling and coming to an utter stop. It was easier to set himself a challenge he could rise to.

Yanathel came this way before me, she made it, and so will I!

It was impossible to tell how much time had passed. The rocky walls came and went with monotonous regularity. He was fortunate that there only seemed to be one route for him to take, no choices to the left or right, or even up or down were presented. It seemed like a crack had been rent underground through the Mountains of Death. Morkin wondered how it had come to be, somehow it did not feel natural. Some mage, perhaps the Wise themselves, must have wrought it long ago. A secret route into the Witchking's realm.

Tiredness came upon him and he found a hollow in the rocks to curl up and rest for a while, breaking out some of his provisions and a little water. This he used sparingly, unsure how long it would take him to traverse the passage.

It was then he noticed he was warm.

He couldn't remember where it had happened, but at some point along the route the rocks around him had grown warm to the touch. He reached out to check again. Yes, a warmth, certainly not hot, but enough to have removed the chill from the air. The ghostly white light flickered around his hands as he moved them.

Patterns swirled in the rock, spiralling around a certain point. Be blinked and peered closer.

There, marked on the rock was a symbol.

It is a letter … a 'Y' … Yanathel!

For a moment he could have sworn he saw a woman's face take form in the glow about him, but it must have been his imagination, for when he blinked there were just the eddies of white flickering across the rocks.

'She came this way,' he said to himself.

Thus emboldened, Morkin continued onwards.

The Lord of Dreams stood before the Forest of Dregrim, at the head of an army of thousands, yet was unable to move. The forest barred his way; roots, branches and trunks locked in an impenetrable wall of foliage before him. He had called into the forest in a commanding voice, trying to summon any that might hear his voice, but none had replied.

Ithrorn joined him as he examined the wall of vegetation. Wherever they approached thorns and brambles twisted out of the trees to re-enforce the message.

'It seems your countrymen will allow none to pass,' Ithrorn said. 'We cannot afford to tarry. I fear a siege upon Xajorkith …'

Dreams nodded. 'I hear you, but Dregrim commands a mighty force and he is my vassal. It is not his right to refuse me. We need his army too.'

'If we cannot get his attention …'

'He knows I am here, perhaps the ice-fear has twisted his mind?'

The creeping malaise had been growing all the while during their headlong rush south, giving all a sense of unease and foreboding of worse to come.

'I will march for Xajorkith before the morning is out,' Ithrorn said. 'My own countrymen are in sore need ...'

A rumbling sound halted their conversation. Both leaders turned and saw the brambles and thorns retreating, snaking their way back with the forest. Leaves rustled as branches and trunks unwove themselves, the eaves of the forest taking on a more welcome aspect. Ersh and snow fell about them as the trees moved.

Torchlight could be seen glimmering in the dankness within and before long a troupe of Fey could be seen marching towards them.

'Dregrim responds!' Ithrorn said in surprise.

Dreams signalled to some of his warriors and they formed ranks behind him.

Ithrorn and Dreams watched as the troupe of Fey rode out into the sunlight. They were all dressed in the colours of Dregrim save one.

'Who is this?' Dreams said. 'I do not know him. He wears the colours of the Thrall ...'

'Perhaps Lord Dregrim is indisposed,' Ithrorn chuckled.

The riders came to a halt before Dreams and Ithrorn.

'I apologise for our tardiness,' the lead Fey said. 'I am Corleth of the Thrall Fey. May I present the Fey of Dregrim.'

'Where is Lord Dregrim?' Dreams demanded.

Corleth sighed. 'Awaiting you, my Lord. He would not accompany us to meet you.'

'We cannot tarry,' Ithrorn said. 'We must march upon Xajorkith.'

'Indeed we must,' Corleth said. 'But none other than a Lord may rebuke a Lord.'

Dreams looked at Ithrorn. 'I will not be long.' He turned back to Corleth. 'Are the folks of Dregrim ready to depart?'

Corleth nodded. 'They are prepared, but they will not ride without Dregrim's word, or yours.'

'Then consider it given,' Dreams said. 'Have them ready to depart upon the hour. And take me to Dregrim!'

Morkin emerged from the now comforting familiarity of the cavern into a blasted and crushed landscape. It looked almost as if a fire had swept through the place, but the land about him was not grey with ash, but grey due to something else. He could put it down only to a lack of any kind of colour. There were plants here, but they were grey and lifeless, as if only pale imitations of what they should have been.

The Forest of Doom was how it was labelled on his map, presumably taking its name from the Tower that had long ago been cursed by the fell powers of the Witchking. He paused at its eaves. Long ago these poor trees must have been tended by the Fey who once lived in these parts, long before the Witchking came. There was little enough of their work left. The trees were rent and shrivelled, composed of nothing more than twisted branches encrusted with sharp and brittle thorns that ripped at clothing and pierced the skin. Ice had grown up from the ground amidst their darkened trunks, sparkling crystal shards that were equally as sharp as the thorns, as if small chunks of the icy wastes had uprooted themselves and begun planting themselves anew.

As Morkin moved within them he could perceive a strange noise. At first he thought it was music, but it was too regular; a thrumming sensation that was echoing through his mind and through the soles of his feet. About him the ice tinkled and vibrated every so often. Ahead something pulsed, as if alive and malignant, growing stronger with every step he took.

But there was no life here, not a living thing moved or grew. The trees were dead, somehow preserved from decay by the ice and evil that had subsumed them.

As he continued Morkin could see that the trees were bent, angled away from some point ahead of him. All about him the pattern was the same. The trees were leaning away, as if trying to flee, yet held in place by their roots.

The forest came to an abrupt end, with the trees there bent and blasted away all about him, crushed down by some overwhelming eruption, all lain outwards from the same focal point.

That point was more than obvious. The pulse was emanating from here.

Underneath broiling clouds that swirled about it, wreathed by the occasional flicker of lightning was a vast edifice of rock and stone. Once it had been akin to the other towers of Midnight, and Morkin could see that it must have had the same architect back in the ancient past of the land.

Now though, it was veiled in darkness, its stonework scorched and blackened, the very air about it filled with a dank dark mist.

Morkin gasped, staggering for footing on the ruined edge of the forest.

Backed up against the Mountains of Death, his destination finally lay before him. The Witchking's source of power, the Tower of Doom, wherein lay the Ice Crown.

Morkin could feel the cold about him. The ground vibrated with it, shuddering around him as the ice-fear sought to unhinge his mind and crush his soul. There were no guards, no warriors here. He doubted even the Doomguard themselves could venture within two leagues, such was the potency of the ice-fear. None save the Witchking himself could approach the Tower and survive.

Save one.

'Save me ...' Morkin muttered to himself.

For all the wonders of his shared heritage and the immunity that gave him, Morkin could still feel the ice-fear battering at his mind. He could feel the potency and knew, without a shadow of a doubt, that without his strange birthright that his mind would have been instantly rent asunder by the icy blast that pulsed from the tower.

As it was, the constant throbbing of the ice-fear made it hard to concentrate. Conscious thoughts were swamped as the waves of power pulsed across him and he found it hard to continue onwards, satisfying himself by placing one foot in front of the other.

He trudged forwards, the pulsing of the ice-fear growing stronger and more frequent at every step. Before him the tower reached into the heavens, its heights now lost in the gloomy storm clouds far above. The ground underfoot was a maze of fractured ice, wrought into spikes, buttresses and other treacherous obstacles.

It was perhaps a league or so from the forest boundary to the cracked and ruined rocks upon which the Tower stood, but it was weary hours of travel for Morkin.

He rounded a series of boulders, finding a little respite from the icy blast in their shadow. There he rested for a few moments. His vision was blurring as the ice-fear pounded about him, its evil beat resonating in his heart. He could feel his fortitude slipping away, despair clawing at his mind.

So easy to give in and run screaming, insanity wraps itself about me ...

He gasped down deep breaths, trying to calm his beating heart, which seemed to be attuning itself to the rhythm of the ice-fear.

He stood up, tottering in the thumping emanation of the tower. The pulse was building to a crescendo. About him the very air seemed to be thickening, as if he was walking through water. His eyes could even see the pulse, a distortion of the air itself, that began at the tower and expanded outwards every few seconds; a sphere of power swelling outwards into the lands of Midnight, casting its fell influence to every corner of the realm.

And he stood in the focus, the very core of the Witchking's might.

He stepped onwards, dragging his feet forward. He was almost at the threshold. He could see gates before the Tower and there was something else …

One last step, he pushed through air that seemed to have congealed before him. Then a shocking calm descended. It was as if he had stepped within some unmarked perimeter, an unexpected sanctuary. The pulsing throb had gone.

But the ice-fear rose. Morkin could almost taste the foulness upon the air.

Somehow the sudden silence was worse, the sense of evil palpable. Morkin looked about him.

The Tower gates were just ahead, dark metal standing stark against the frozen ice and snow. But they weren't what drew his gaze.

Before the gates a large stake had been driven into the ground, perhaps half a foot in diameter and eight tall. Morkin stared, a freezing chill seeping into his bones.

From it hung a figure.

Morkin staggered back, his heart thumping wildly. The figure was hanging from its wrists, somehow tied in place by a band of ice. The body was long since frozen solid, but it was plain to see that it had once been a woman.

About her head blonde hair was fanned out, as if a ferocious wind had blown it forward and then it had been locked in place by a sudden freeze. Her clothes were those of the Fey, the greens and blues still visible, though the clothing was rent and torn in places. Her legs were visible, icy white and exposed, her feet limp a foot or so above the ground.

'Yanathel …'

446

Here she had been held captive when the Witchking detonated his blast of ice so long ago. Morkin remembered the haunted look on Lothoril's face when he had told the story. How Fey warriors far from this epicentre had dropped dead, their hearts burst by the ice-fear.

And here, trapped in the centre, caught by the Witchking himself, Yanathel had endured the absolute purest incarnation of that horror. Morkin looked up into her haunted visage. A frozen look of utter horror and despair was locked upon her face. Morkin could almost hear her scream, still echoing off the rocks about him. She had sought to defeat the Witchking. She had failed, and paid a horrendous price for her attempt.

How long her body had been hung there, defiled, Morkin could not guess. What awful scenes she must have witnessed, confronting the Witchking before her death, he could not bear to consider. The ice-fear clutched at him.

She was mighty, fierce of spirit and will ... she came so close, yet she failed.

Lothoril had recalled those times, but they were many moons ago. Tears sprang into Morkin's eyes at the thought of all those who had known and cared for her, unaware of her ultimate fate. What would they say when he brought them news of how she'd hung here, forever inaccessible to those who would see her honoured, with no way for them to lay her body to rest and mark her passing with the rituals and thanksgiving of the Fey?

If I can bring them news ... should I?

Unashamed tears rolled down his cheeks as he looked on at her. He made up his mind to bring news of her plight to those who would remember.

'You will be remembered, Yanathel. I promise!'

Chapter Eighteen

They stand in the Forest of Dregrim,
looking south to the Citadel of Dregrim.

With Corleth alongside, Dreams rode hard through forest tracks only barely opened around them. The forest had been twisted into a great barrier and in places only a narrow pathway allowed them passage. They slowed in sight of the Citadel itself.

'Dregrim refused your entreaty?' Dreams asked.

Corleth nodded. 'He did, and then locked me in the tower!'

Dreams looked at him. 'Then how did you escape?'

Corleth frowned. 'A most peculiar thing. The very vines of the forest sprouted, rising up the side of the Citadel and wrenched my prison open. I received a message from Rorthron the Wise proclaiming that a Fey woman known as the Lady of the Forest would be my salvation … know you of this?'

'The Wise,' Dreams muttered. 'That explains much. The Lady of the Forest … yes I know of her. She is the reason I am here, free from the decay and despair of the Witchking's enchantments. Thus I know what ails Dregrim. Worse than the ice-fear this is, a cloying dampness, weakening the spirit until all hope and free will is stolen away.'

'She must be a powerful enchantress, this Lady,' Corleth replied. 'If she can summon the forest to her will.'

A muscle twitched in Dreams' face. 'She is my daughter, just a few moons ago she was but a child. Now she is grown tall in the lore of the Fey, despite her youth. A power that has not been seen within the Fey for an age.'

'You must be proud of her.'

'Proud, aye,' Dreams said. 'And fearful too …'

They rode out into the clearings before the Citadel. As directed the army of Dregrim was mustering, warriors and riders were preparing to depart. Shouts of joy greeted Corleth and Dreams as they approached the gates.

'My Lords! You are most welcome. The Army stands ready and the Citadel is secured …'

'Lord Dregrim is my concern,' Dreams said. 'Take me to him.'

'He is within,' the guard replied, his expression clouding.

Dreams and Corleth were led into the Citadel and into one of the anterooms on the ground floor. There, Dregrim stood, pacing back and forth, prevented from escaping by two guards.

He turned as they entered, striding forward.

'Lord of Dreams, have you come to end this perfidy?' Dregrim yelled. 'Ah, I see you have recaptured this interloper, this foreign brat! He comes here and incites rebellion amongst my own people. Ah, now we can decide his punishment. Death I think, a fitting example. Dismiss these guards and let's be at it!'

'There will be no execution,' Dreams began.

'Imprisonment then?' Dregrim spluttered. 'Kinder I'll warrant, mercy too. Yes, perhaps that is wise, we cannot create a martyr can we!' Dregrim laughed, but his laughter was cold and mirthless.

'Nor imprisonment,' Dreams replied. 'Corleth has prepared your army for battle. The Fey march south, to aid in the defence of Xajorkith.'

Dregrim's mouth fell open. 'No … no!' He pointed a trembling arm at Corleth. 'This is no Fey, he's a sorcerer … in the service of the Witchking no doubt! I have seen his magic …

he has bewitched you, turned your wisdom to folly. Xajorkith? Aid the Free? This is not the arrangement we had …'

'Arrangement?' Corleth asked, a frown crossing his face.

'A pact,' Dreams said, his voice heavy.

Corleth blinked. 'You had a pact with the Witchking?'

Dreams looked at him. 'To protect our people from endless war and heartbreak? I thought the Witchking had himself tired of the endless fight. We would not interfere with him, nor he with us. It seemed to work, and yet …'

'The Witchking used that time, free to build his strength and then unleash it upon the Free at the height of the Solstice!' Corleth gasped.

'He was right so to do!' Dregrim said. 'The High Lords of the Fey agreed!'

'They did,' Dreams said. 'And we may have thus struck a mortal blow for all who oppose the Witchking. Whilst we slumbered, his strength grew. He has torn us all apart. His strategy was masterful. We must come together now, or perish.'

Dregrim shook his head. 'No my Lord! Your strategy was sound. Sound! Defend and lock our borders, open them to no one, hide within until the storm passes! Storms always pass!'

Dreams shook his head. 'Not this time, Lord Dregrim. The Foul invaded Kor and destroyed it. They came within the Forest of Dreams, to my very gates. The Witchking can overcome us now. Nowhere is safe, nowhere. He will come to every corner of Midnight, Free or Fey notwithstanding.'

Dregrim staggered back. 'He would not turn on us … we agreed.'

'He has betrayed us, as he betrayed all others before. He can do nothing else, it is his very nature. Cold and frozen to the core. He used our weariness to his advantage, lulled us into quiescence. Now he strikes.'

Dregrim fell into a chair.

451

'I ride for Xajorkith,' Dreams said, raising his voice. 'Your army will come with me regardless of your wish, for I am the highest of the Lords of the Fey. I would have you at my side Dregrim. The Fey have much to atone for – and atone we must, before it is too late.'

Dregrim's face was bereft, his skin pale, his eyes hollow.

'The Witchking's power waxes …' Dregrim said. 'We cannot prevail.'

Dreams shook his head. 'Ithrorn and I threw them back at his Citadel, we will throw them back again. 'We must! Ride with me Dregrim, ride to battle as we did of old!'

Dreams strode forward and thrust out his hand towards Dregrim.

'Shake off the trepidation, find your boldness. Be invigorated once more! We remain a mighty force to be reckoned with. Let us prove it to the Foul and to the Free. Let the Fey be strong once more!'

Dregrim, his arm trembling, slowly reached out. Dreams grasped his hand and pulled him to his feet.

'Kindle hope once more my old friend. Our folly lies behind us. I will not see the Fey wither away on my watch. Let us make a battle that will be long remembered.'

A faint glimmer grew in Dregrim's eyes.

'An ending worthy,' Dregrim whispered. 'A place in the annuals of our folk?'

'A place of honour,' Dreams replied with a smile.

Dreams felt Dregrim's grasp grow tighter. Dregrim looked across at Corleth.

'I owe you an apology young Corleth, Fey of Thrall,' he said. 'It seems age has wearied me, the years condemned.'

'None are too old to look with eyes anew,' Corleth replied. 'And no apology is needed. You sought to keep your people safe.'

Dregrim nodded. 'Then, young Fey, ask me one more time!'

Dreams looked at Corleth in confusion, but the younger Fey grinned and pulled out his sword.

'Will you march upon the foe?'

Dregrim pulled his own sword out and held it aloft. It was a glorious blade, emblazoned with fine filigree of Feyish craftsmanship, glinting in the torchlight. Dregrim's voice was bold and strong.

'I will march upon the foe!'

The armies of the Free stood around the ramshackle walls of the Citadel of Xajorkith. Such repairs as were possible had been undertaken, with cracks and breaks mended haphazardly. The major breaches were filled with rubble, but the outer walls no longer had the strength they had enjoyed in the opening battles, many of the weapon emplacements upon the walls were ruined beyond repair and the defenders were fewer in number than before.

Yet the people of Xajorkith remained unbowed. Bleak might their future be, but the warmth of the Moon Ring leant courage to hearts that would have been bereft without it. Luxor went here and there about the people, accompanied by the other Lords of Midnight, overseeing repairs, speaking to the soldiers and encouraging them in their works.

Yet it was not long before the trumpets sounded once again. Luxor and the other Lords leapt up to the battlements.

There, in the distance, drawing ever closer down the long valley of Corelay came an army. Black and crimson banners waved in the distance. Doomguard reinforcements had arrived. Before long the new army would join forces with the one already but a few leagues distant. A force that would surely overwhelm the defences of the Free.

Xajorkith had prevailed once, yet it could not prevail again.

'They will be here by nightfall,' Shimeril said. 'Even after a long march they are likely to attack tonight.'

'Let them come!' Blood replied. 'Let them do their worst! We know our duty, it will cost them sore to take this place from beneath our feet.'

'Aye,' Luxor replied. 'It will cost them sore and we must fight them every inch of the way. I sense the Witchking's hatred bent upon this place. I can feel the Moon Ring, it vies with the Ice Crown in some fashion I care not to dwell upon.'

'What do you mean?' Blood asked.

'I cannot, in truth, explain it,' Luxor replied. 'But this is not merely a power for good versus a power of evil. I sense purpose and intent in the way the Moon Ring acts. I have felt driven today to wander around the city and prepare the battle, not just from my own instincts, but by this ring too ...'

'Your imagination ...' Shimeril said.

'There is more to this than just the power to defy the ice-fear,' Luxor said. 'I will be glad to see the end of these tokens of magic from long ago. A fair fight and a sharp sword alone would leave me far more at ease ...'

'If our enemy employs fell arts, we must counter them with the same,' Blood said. 'I am glad you wield this magic. If it gives us a fairer fight ...'

Blood watched as Luxor's face became strained once more. Both he and Shimeril could see the distant look as the Moon Ring weaved its strange potency about him. Luxor staggered back from the wall.

'My Lord!' Blood said, grasping him to stop him from stumbling.

'It is good tidings, my friends,' Luxor said, catching his breath. 'It seems my friend Corleth has not failed. With Dreams and Ithrorn the Lord of Dregrim has been recruited to our cause. An army of the Fey marches towards us, with sufficient numbers to turn the tide ... if only they can reach us before we succumb!'

They continued to watch as the armies of the Doomguard made their way down the valley of Corelay. There was no way to prevent the rendezvous. Perhaps with more warriors they might have attempted it, but they had none to spare. The defence of the city was their only consideration.

'We count more than fifteen thousand,' Morning said, half an hour later. 'And their numbers continue to swell. They are indeed readying themselves for battle.'

'Then let us meet our fate,' Luxor replied. 'We must hold out – salvation is at hand from the Fey, but we must hold! Set the flags, to the walls!'

The Doomguard army was widening out to flank the beleaguered Citadel on all sides. Their army was mighty enough to fully round two thirds of the walls thousands of men deep. Soon the Citadel was a white pinnacle surrounded by a sea of black; cut off, alone and besieged.

All felt the ice-fear as it crashed upon them once more. Luxor almost felt his skin burn as the Moon Ring leant its own power to the battle, burning hot upon his finger. In the sky above, clouds swirled, crackling with lightning, with the walls of the Citadel echoing to the claps of thunder.

First came the arrows, attempting to smite those defenders upon the walls. The Free of Xajorkith responded to the onslaught, cutting down the Doomguard as they approached the foot of the walls.

But where one fell, two more replaced the fallen. Within minutes the Doomguard had reached the walls, and their practiced strategies were immediately put into play.

Ladders rose in ordered sequences from amidst the attacking army. Some fell, caught by deft moves of the defenders from within the remaining towers of the Citadel, but there were too many ladders and not enough of the defences remained to see them all off. The Doomguard began to swarm the outer walls within minutes of them reaching the base.

The Lords had been ready for that. Archers positioned below slew hundreds of the Foul as they came into view. Thousands of arrows were poured into the foe, but still they came, a dark and rising mass, seemingly unending. The ground was littered with the dead and dying.

'Retreat from the walls!' Luxor cried. 'Retreat!'

The Doomguard continued to pour over. Xajorkith, Shimeril, Gard and Morning led their warriors from one side, Marakith, Kumar, Trorn and Silence from the other. All formed behind Luxor as they met the foe head on amidst the streets and corridors within the walls.

'To the second level!' Luxor called.

The Free retreated again, covered by archers within the inner walls. In ordered ranks their warriors stepped back, fighting to keep the enemy away at all times. Minutes passed as they withdrew further into the citadel, but finally the gates to the second wall were bolted behind them, the Doomguard thwarted for the time being.

Luxor was panting hard by this point, his sword stained with the dark blood of the enemy.

'They fight as if possessed,' he muttered.

'That they do,' Xajorkith replied. 'But we have given good account. I'd say more than two of theirs for every one of ours ...'

'Not enough,' Shimeril replied.

'They will find it hard enough to dig us out of here,' Blood said, looking up. 'The weather worsens, we have shelter, they do not.'

'I fear they do not feel the cold the way we do,' Luxor said. 'Their master has made sure of that.'

The Doomguard had retreated out of range of the archers, clearly revising their strategy. The Lords took the opportunity to rest, climbing to the ramparts of the city, looking down upon its ruin.

'Xajorkith may not have fallen,' Xajorkith said, looking around the ruins of the external walls. 'But it will take some great work to set it right once more.'

'Don't fret!' Blood said. 'My old keep has been sacked more than once, we always put it back together. Stone is stone wherever it may be found!'

'I've seen your stonemasons,' Shimeril replied. 'It's amazing your keep stays upright. Why there are cracks in the walls so big you can place your hand through them.'

'It keeps the halls aired,' Blood said. 'Good for the constitution.'

Luxor chuckled, but turned at a clatter from nearby. A guard had rushed up, face flushed with exertion.

'Sires, Lady!' he said with a bow.

'What is it?' Luxor asked.

'The Doomguard approach once more.'

They stood as one, looking down across the city. A group of men were approaching the lower gates. The archers were trying to deal with them, but the men were protected with giant shields the arrows could not penetrate.

'Barbarians!' Shimeril muttered.

'Aye,' Luxor replied. 'Our friend Utarg of Utarg returns.'

The men were methodically moving forwards towards the gate, the archers unable to prevent them. As they reached it a heavy thump rang out from below.

'Battering ram,' Blood said. 'They'll have that gate down in minutes ...'

'Then to the gate we go!' Luxor cried.

They had barely reached it when the gate began to splinter and crack, assaulted from without by immense force. The Lords drew their swords, formed ranks and waited for the inevitable.

With a final shudder the gate disintegrated in a shower of

wooden fragments. Dust and smoke billowed forth, obscuring everything.

Then they came through, the enormous men of Targ, swing cudgels and hammers about them with abandon.

'For Midnight! Slay the foe!' Luxor yelled, rearing his charger at them and ploughing forward, his sword swinging.

The battle was joined once more.

Men flew through the air, struck and dismembered by the weapons of the Targ warriors. They were deadly, easily twice as strong as the mightiest warrior of the Free. Men cowered before them and were slain, bludgeoned to death.

Blood and Shimeril took one down between them, but the warriors of the Free were thrown back.

Then their leader stepped through the ruined gateway.

'Utarg!' Morning shouted over the fray. 'Utarg is here!'

Luxor and the other Lords turned about to see the enormous man, but they were too far away. Two warriors died within moments as they tried to face him, struck down by a mighty axe, the same one that had dispatched the Lord of Dawn. Blood glistened on its sharpened blade.

The Free pulled back, leaving a space before the invader and a wary hush fell about the battle.

And Silence stepped out.

'No!' Morning called.

She had only her knives, one in each hand.

Luxor and the other Lords pushed to the front of their warriors, ready to stand with her. Her own warriors stood alongside them, ashen faced, worry etched on their features.

'Stay back!' she cried. 'He is mine.'

'I'd heard the men of the Free were cowards!' Utarg roared in laughter. 'But they send their womenfolk into battle in their stead?'

'You are not welcome here,' Silence replied. 'Go back from whence you came, or face your end.'

Utarg regarded her for a moment, belatedly realising she was serious.

'Woman,' he rumbled. 'I will rip your frail body apart. Expect no mercy from me.'

He towered over her, perhaps by five feet or more.

'I expect no quarter,' Silence replied. 'And I will give none.'

Utarg grunted and then hefted his axe. He charged forward with a yell, swinging at her. Silence deftly moved aside, her knives trailing behind her, slashing across Utarg's arm. He stared at the blood running down his mighty forearm.

Then he summoned a madness from with, striking and swinging with abandon. Each time Silence would evade him, each time she would leave a slashing trace across him. Blood flowed in rivulets down his arms and legs as she rolled aside, unharmed.

He sought to pin her down, drive her into a corner, but she seemed to have some sixth sense as to the direction he would move. Time and again she evaded the strike of his axe, causing it to clash upon the stones with a shower of sparks.

He staggered to one side, and she moved in to strike.

It was a feint. From that position he couldn't raise the axe, but he was able to swing a hammer blow with his fist.

It caught her in the side of the head, dashing her to the stony ground. Utarg raised his axe, ready to impale her body. The axe came down to gasps of horror.

But Silence had rolled aside.

In that instant her knife came up, straight between Utarg's thighs.

His scream of anguish was excruciating.

Silence was not finished. She pulled on the knife, using it to haul herself upwards, heedless of the Utarg's screams. Another knife was jammed into his chest and still she rose higher, the first knife pulled free and rammed into the giant's neck.

Blood sprayed across the snow, the scream drowning into a ghastly gurgle.

Silence stepped back a pace and then both knives were cut across each other at the Utarg's throat. He fell his length upon the ground, his body convulsing. The axe crashed down with a ringing impact upon the stones.

Silence screeched a high pitched wail of rage which sent the remaining Targ warriors scurrying back out of range, pushing and shoving to escape.

Silence turned to face the other Lords. All stepped back a pace at the look of fury on her blood splattered visage, the knives in her hands slick with hot blood.

None moved, until Silence staggered and fell to her knees. Lord Morning ran to her and pulled her away.

The faint sound of trumpets cast itself across the air.

'An army!' Someone shouted. 'An army to the west!'

Luxor turned.

'It must be … sight the banners!'

A guard, perched upon one of the ruined barricades, was looking out in the setting sun.

'It's hard to make out,' he called. 'I see green banners, with a white eagle.'

'The Fey?' Blood said, from beside Luxor. 'Can it be?'

'I recognise that banner,' Luxor said, with a grin. 'That is Thimrath! First of the Fey to reach us. How many does he bring?'

'Perhaps a thousand sire, warriors and riders together.'

'Not enough to break this siege,' Blood said. 'I fear there is little he can do to help us at this stage …'

'We cannot let his valour go in vain,' Luxor replied. 'Send archers to the western walls, let's see if we can weaken the Doomguard in that direction.'

A faint breeze ruffled the snow about his feet. Morkin walked on, summoning the courage to pass the wretched corpse of the Fey woman. He reached the gates of the Tower.

They swung back at his touch, much to his surprise, unlocked and free.

The way to the Tower lay open before him. A darkened archway serving as a portal.

There seemed little enough within. Morkin lit a torch and peered inside. The entrance was an arch where a door might have once been. He recalled that the tower had been similar to the others of Midnight long ago. Before Gryfallon became the Witchking he was one of the Wise and would have had similar needs.

Rooms led off from a central staircase of stone that wound its way upwards from the ground, circling around and around as he climbed higher. Each room was entirely bare, there was no furniture, no decoration, each level contained a small mound of snow piled below empty window frames long since bereft of their glass.

The tower might have been an abandoned ruin, slowly succumbing to the ravages of time.

Not what I expected ... but what did I expect? Guards perhaps, magic spells and fell traps ... but this ... nothing?

Perhaps the Witchking considered the ice-fear defence enough, surely none had ever come this way before.

His footsteps echoed throughout the structure, a heavy clanking thud against the stonework. Yet nothing impeded his progress, no creature, no guard, no strange enchantment. All about him the air was stale and dry. The walls of the staircase were scratched with runes that Morkin could not read or understand.

Surely, somehow, the Witchking must be alerted to my presence?

But there was nothing. Morkin fancied that some silent

461

alarm must be ringing somewhere, but for all he knew, the Witchking himself was ensconced in his plans to the south east, deep within the mighty fortress of Ushgarak, directing his minions against the forces of the Free and the Fey.

He reached the top-most stair.

The flickering light from his torch illuminated a room that was similar in size and shape to that in which Rorthron had spoken to him, now far to the south in the Tower of the Moon. But where Rorthron's tower held endless bookcases and a welcome, here there was nothing but a stone cold floor and empty alcoves where windows once had been. Wind blew gently in, making his torch gutter in the gust.

At the centre stood a carved stone pedestal engraved with sinister runes and inscriptions. Morkin squinted. Before him there was a glow, a chilling cyan hue, shining from an object set upon a black velvet cushion which, in turn, had been carefully placed on the pedestal.

As Morkin watched, the faint glow strengthened, revealing a sparkling object surrounded by faint wisps of mist that swirled gently around it. It looked fragile and delicate, Morkin knew it to be have been wrought of the purest crystals of ice in the darkest depths of winter.

He knew it for what it was.

'The Ice Crown!'

The archers on the westerns heights of Xajorkith rained destruction down upon the foe. Dozens were slain, their bodies piled high upon the ruined stonework, but still the Foul were too numerous to count.

A cheer arose as the Fey from the west rode into the dark phalanx of the Foul upon the western side of the citadel. Bright steel flashed in the fading light. The Fey charged in with fierce cries, cries that were answered by cheers and yells from the ranks of the Free far above in the besieged city.

The Fey broke upon the Foul like a wave, forcing them back against the walls where they were caught between both their opponents. The ranks of the Foul crumbled and fell back.

'They reach the walls!' Blood called.

Some of the Free made their way down the ruined stonework of the city to greet the Fey who had arrived at the base.

'Wait …!' Luxor called.

Arrows flew out of the gathering gloom, cutting the men of the Free down. Luxor and Blood retreated for cover as more arrows sought their targets. Likewise the Fey came under heavy bombardments, rocks, arrows and sheets of ice crashed about them. Trying to shield themselves they were forced to retreat.

Luxor watch in frustration as the Fey were beaten back, hordes of the Doomguard rushed in from either side, strengthening their position and forcing the Fey back further. The Free upon the walls were likewise forced back by the rising tide of the foe.

'They cannot break the siege,' Blood said, his cheek bleeding from an arrow he had barely avoided. 'They cannot reach us.'

Luxor watched in despair as Thimrath's army came about and retreated. Dozens of the Fey lay dead at the base of the wall, the Foul cheering and yelling abuse as they moved away.

Luxor knew Thimrath to be no coward, but to ride in again was to ride to certain death. He could not blame him for turning about.

'He will be remembered with honour,' Luxor said, turning away. 'If any of us survive to mark the history of this battle.'

'Aye,' Blood agreed. 'But if Thimrath tries again he and his folk will be slaughtered. Too few of us and too many of them!'

The trumpets of the Fey sounded once more. Luxor turned in surprise and dismay.

'No ... don't Thimrath! It is folly! Save your people ...'

Luxor and Blood could see the army of the Fey had come about, their riders turning their horses back towards the Foul. In a magnificent show of horsemanship they formed into an arrow-like formation, their foot soldiers stepping into line alongside, guarding their flanks.

They didn't charge, but stepped forward slowly, weapons readied.

'What are they doing?' Blood demanded from alongside. 'Charge or retreat ... but not a slow advance!'

The Moon Ring pulsed upon Luxor's finger, almost burning hot. His gaze was wrested to the east.

The Fey!

Men were scurrying back and forth, shouting directions and instructions at each other. Clearly something was afoot.

More Fey trumpets sounded.

Luxor grinned at Blood. The sound had not come from ahead of them, but from behind, from the other side of the citadel.

Luxor saw a messenger jump from the inner walls, making a ridiculous and foolhardy leap towards him. He almost misjudged it, and was caught and hauled to safety by the guards nearby. Undeterred he ran up to Luxor and Blood, breathless and gasping.

'My Lords ... the Fey ... they ...'

'The Fey?' Blood demanded. 'Thimrath?'

'No My Lord ... the Fey ...' The messenger gestured back towards the east, beyond the heights of the Citadel's towers.

Cheers were rising in the air all around them. They pushed through the ranks of men atop the citadel until they could look out to the east.

Before them fires burned in the shattered walls of the city.

Beyond that, the dark armies of the Doomguard, yet, in the distance, across the whiteness of the snowy plains advanced an army, thousands strong.

Banners flew in the wind, all the colours of green, cyan and magenta. Even from here the devices were clear; eagles bold and bright.

Luxor stood, tears upon his face. Blood and Shimeril stood, jaws slack and mouths open.

'The Fey …' he muttered. 'The Fey have come at last!'

Some measure of peace had returned to the forest in the days following her father's departure. Tarithel had seen to the immediate needs of the people with the help of her mother and then retired to her own room seeking solace and sanctuary. She was exhausted after long days of work; sleep had not come easily.

Around her she could sense the life and power of the forest. Something had stirred there which she had not felt before. It both excited and scared her. It had been her salvation and turned the Fey to their tasks once more, but it had used her too, as an instrument of its will.

It is more powerful than I am. It has a will all of its own …

In the quietest moments she could almost hear it; voices out of the present and the past, the nameless thoughts of … what? Fey long gone? Spirits of the woods? The deep forests of the Fey held many secrets.

Yet now, as she sought the solace of her own bedchambers her mind refused to be quiet. Tenseness grew and despite her weariness she found she could not sleep. There was a strange scent in the air, almost as if …

Burning … flames …

She could see no smoke, but she was sure of the smell. She

465

leapt up, expecting to see the lurid glow of fires, but nothing seemed awry in the Citadel.

She walked outside, climbing the steps to the battlements. Her sense of unease seemed to emanate from the west, so she peered in that direction, squinting into the darkness of the forest. The Moonstar twinkled in the clear sky, for once the clouds had been banished and the canopy above was glorious in the darkness.

But on the far westernmost horizon she could see a glow, faint with the distance, but distinct like the sunset.

Yet it was the middle of the night.

Someone has set the forest ablaze!

Below her she saw guards riding through to the gates. She hurried down to meet them in the courtyards below. Their messages were rushed and of ill tidings.

'It is the Doomguard once more,' one said. 'They march on the forest, they carry some strange weapon that spits liquid fire. They are torching the trees and killing them, they march upon us again.'

Tarithel swallowed.

The one thing the forest cannot stand against. Fire! The Witchking seeks to burn us to ash. Is this what he did to Kor?

'They march quickly, my lady.'

Heat flashed about her for a moment, burning, intolerable. She gasped in pain and the guard reached out to steady her.

'My lady?'

She looked up, fire dancing in her eyes.

'I can feel it,' she managed. 'They are burning everything … we must stop them!'

'Banners sire! An army approaches.'

Lothoril looked around as one of his heralds pointed to the north.

'Can you make out the devices?'

'Not the Foul for sure,' the herald replied. 'It's a Red Lion on black ...'

Lothoril chucked. 'It seems Lord Gloom marches forth. Our young acquaintance has stirred him to action.'

It was not long before Balor himself rode up to the waiting Fey.

'Lord Gloom,' Lothoril said jauntily. 'It is many moons since I had the pleasure of your company.'

'Balor will do,' Balor replied. 'And I am sure my presence gives you little pleasure whatsoever.'

'Then what brings you hither?'

Balor glared. 'You know of Morkin and his quest. Do not waste my time. I am here to give him the best chance of success. We are the only powers in this forsaken corner of Midnight. If we are to have a positive influence on the outcome of this near hopeless folly then we must band together, harry the Foul and keep them occupied. Do you not agree?'

Lothoril grinned. 'As it happens, yes, I do. An Alliance of Free and Fey? Such things are written about in songs of yore; shall I send for my minstrels?'

'Not if you know what's good for you,' Balor grunted.

'Then let us seek our doom together,' Lothoril replied. 'The Foul are ahead, in greater numbers than we can hope to prevail against. A hopeless battle and certain death. Let us make of it what we can!'

Lothoril signalled to his folk. The Fey army under his command came about.

'A hopeless battle and certain death,' Balor said, under his breath. 'And they call me Lord Gloom ...'

Morkin stepped towards it, feeling frost creep across his skin, the cold the talisman emanated was palpable, almost as if it were trying to freeze the air around it and prevent his advance. Undeterred he moved closer, now seeing the cushion upon which the Ice Crown rested crackling with ice summoned out of the little moisture in the air.

The cushion shattered into sparkling fragments and the Ice Crown fell down on to the pedestal, giving out a pure ringing note as it did so. Morkin watched, transfixed, as it rotated around for a few moments before lying still. Frost flickered around the pedestal itself, but the stonework was strong and resisted the onslaught of the ice. The ringing tone continued unabated.

Morkin reached out a trembling hand towards it, forcing his fingers against the cold. An inch, another inch. He strained his muscles, finding them reluctant to obey his will, sensing the will of the Ice Crown trying to thwart his progress.

But he was Morkin. Half-Fey and half-Free. He that had forged the Ice Crown out of the heart of winter long ago had not foreseen that the elemental powers of Midnight might combine in ways he could not predict. He sought to master fear and cold, not appreciating that hope and warmth might one day counter them.

Morkin's fingers touched the Ice Crown.

The high sweet tone of the Ice Crown stopped. The breeze halted. All was still. Across all of Midnight winter took a breath. Snow halted in its gentle fall, blizzards paused in their onslaught. For a moment the clutch of winter faltered.

And the Witchking knew.

Far to the south east, deep in the horror that was the Citadel of Ushgarak, in that moment he perceived the final plans of the Moonprince, the plans of the Wise, even the larceny of his old master.

He himself knew fear and uncertainty. His own fate now

in jeopardy. His wrath rose about him like a fire, but his own terror smothered it like a cloak. His gaze turned from the battles of the south and all his hatred was cast back into his own domain.

Within the tower, Morkin saw something. He could not perceive what it was, only that he had been alone, but now a tangible presence had joined him. It was gathering strength and form before him.

He could make out a cloak, wreathed in a mist of icy vapour. As he watched, dumbstruck, the mist wrapped around and spun, weaving out the shape of a skeletal arm that was pointed towards him. Words crackled harshly, unheard, but deafening.

MORTAL BOY! YOU DARE DEFILE MY ABODE? DEATH AWAITS YOU.

Morkin staggered back at the force of the words, watching in horror as the figure continued to take form before him. He tried to flee, but his body would not obey his commands. His legs were leaden, unresponsive. The cold was seeping into him, freezing him …

Just like Yanathel …

Her haunted face came back to his mind in that brief moment. The horror, the sadness, the fear and … the hatred …

He blinked. Before him swam her face, but not frozen in terror, now it was alive once more, her features clear and bright, sparkling with a light that threw the room into sharp relief, shadows etched across the walls and floor.

Morkin could make out her form, glowing in the darkness. Her figure was likewise insubstantial, transparent and ethereal as the darkness that framed the Witchking's nascent form. She moved across the room, the brightness of her shade increasing. Morkin saw the Witchking shudder and retreat, dark smoke reeking up from around him as he sought to evade the light.

Light fought the dark, wrestling back and forth before Morkin's eyes. He gaped in stunned wonder as the Witchking flailed, unable to take his full form.

In that split second, Yanathel's shade turned back to look at him.

'Long I have waited for this moment, so that my sacrifice might not be in vain!'

Her voice was sweet and child-like, her eyes full of tears, yet her face set in a determined expression.

'Go now Morkin, half-Fey! Tell my tale!'

The smoke was billowing once more, gaining strength, swirling about with alarming potency.

'Be swift! I cannot hold him long!'

Morkin grasped the Ice Crown and pulled it from the pedestal. A shuddering cold crackled through him, but he was moving now, his legs given respite by the glowing figure before him. He turned and staggered through the archway, almost falling down the staircase below, stumbling from one stair to another in his hurry to vacate the tower.

He lurched out of the final archway. Flickering bursts of light caused long shadows to be cast first this way and then the other upon the snowy ruin all about.

A final shriek, a long drawn out howl of hatred, a woman's voice tortured down through the ages. Morkin skidded to a halt as the light was extinguished. A horrendous cracking noise startled him and he whirled around to see Yanathel's frozen corpse shattered into untold pieces. The stake held for a moment before it too disintegrated, splinters flying through the air. Morkin ducked out of the way just in time.

All was still for a moment.

Morkin looked up to see smoke begin to billow from the windows of the tower.

Her voice came to his ears for the last time.

'Flee!'

He heeded her last wish, scrambling away from the tower, running as fast as his weary body would let him, the concentrated frozen evil of the Ice Crown clenched in his hand.

Around the shattered walls of the Citadel, the battle raged onwards. The newly arrived Fey pressed hard against the vanguard of the Foul, wrenching them aside and forcing a way to those of the Free surrounded in their ailing fortress.

None who survived the battle of Xajorkith would ever forget that day. Those of the Free, the Fey and the Foul fell in their multitudes, the count of the fallen reached heights never seen in the annals of Midnight.

As the battle raged to the sounds of clashing steel and the yells of cries of the combatants, even the elements surged into conflict above. Thunder and lightning shook the citadel as the Moon Ring fought for dominance against the ice-fear in the hearts of those below.

Several times it seemed that the sheer numbers of the Doomguard would overwhelm even the combined strength of the Free and the Fey. The citadel itself was breached, its walls shaken and torn down, its buildings ruined by fire and the flying destruction wrought by the weapons of the Foul.

Yet through it all the Free and the Fey continued to fight. At the last gasp another presence made itself felt.

The sky lightened to the east. Sunlight burst out strong and warm, a sense of joy pervaded the embattled armies of the Free and the Fey. The defenders looked about them in surprise at the sudden hope and joy that kindled in their hearts.

Luxor knew it for what it was. The burning weight of the Moon Ring was light upon his heart, it no longer was drawing upon his soul to push out the warmth of his heart and mind.

The ice-fear! It has faded! Something ails the Witchking! Can it be Morkin has succeeded?

Yet the ice-fear was still there, much diminished, but lurking, as if biding its time. Luxor concentrated his mind to the north, but it was wreathed in mist and cold, and he could not sense his son.

Luxor cried out and rallied the Free. As the Doomguard sought to battle back the Fey and stop them reaching the relative sanctuary of the Citadel, a bright light burst forth across the plains. The Doomguard staggered before it, cringing and flinging themselves out of its way. Many were struck down, never to move again.

Dawn broke to the muffled cries of the injured and the dying.

Luxor struggled to see through the smoke and the haze. He staggered forward, reaching the edge of the Citadel, where the mighty external walls were now just piles of rubble. He stood there with his sword drawn, the dark blood of the Foul dripping from it as the light of the sun strengthened about him.

Before him lay a plain strewn with the bodies of the dead; Free, Foul and Fey alike.

The smoke slowly cleared in the breeze. The Foul were routed, what few remained fleeing northwards.

Luxor could see figures silhouetted in the distance. Beside him stood the Lords he had fought alongside. Luxor looked about him.

Marakith, Kumar, Xajorkith, Shimeril, Blood, Silence, Morning ...

'Where is Trorn?' he managed.

'Slain,' Shimeril said heavily. 'Defending the southern ramparts, he slew thirty of the foe ...'

Kumar looked at Marakith, who looked back guiltily.

'I had little care for Trorn,' Kumar said. 'But I will see his name honoured now. He died a warrior's death and that should be remembered.'

The smoke continued to clear.

Luxor could see a man standing between the assembled Lords and the figures in the distance. An old man, leaning on a staff.

'Rorthron?'

The figure straightened and walked towards him.

'A victory unseen, Moonprince?'

Luxor shook his head. 'Hardly a victory ...'

'The Foul have fled from your combined wrath,' Rorthron replied and gestured behind him. Luxor looked up and began to recognise those who stood there.

'Ithrorn!'

'Aye, Lord Luxor,' Ithrorn replied.

'A miracle unforeseen!' Luxor said and then looked to the others. 'My Lords Fey ...'

Luxor recognised the Lord of Dreams, resplendent in fine armour. Beside him the older visage of Lord Dregrim and the thin figure of the Lord of Thrall. Alongside them was his old friend, Thimrath the Fey. All four looked weary, but unbowed.

'We had given you up for lost,' Luxor said.

'And my folly might have been the end of your hopes,' Dreams replied.

'How so?' Luxor asked.

'A story for the fireplace, not the battlefield,' Dreams replied. 'But you can thank the efforts of my daughter, and a friend of yours more worthy of honour than me ...'

Luxor frowned.

Another Fey pushed through the ranks, dressed in green and blue, his clothing tattered and torn.

'Corleth!' Luxor exclaimed. 'I thought you surely lost!'

'I came close to it,' Corleth replied. 'But it seems many powers have intervened on my behalf – all unexpected!'

Luxor regarded him for a moment. 'I tasked you with looking after my son …'

Corleth nodded. 'A duty I failed in my Lord …'

'Nay,' Luxor replied. 'It is as well you did, for it seems Morkin holds our salvation in his hands. It was my lack of faith in the legends of the Wise that might have led us to ruin.'

Luxor looked around him.

'The Doomguard have been routed when all hope seemed lost. It was not by the Free, or by the Fey alone that this was achieved. Midnight needs us all, Free, Fey … and Wise, dare I say it skulkrin and dragon too! Only together can we be victorious.'

Luxor reached out and pulled Corleth into an embrace.

'There has been much mistrust between our peoples. I would vow today that we will never let that sully our thoughts again. To the Fey, our salvation in our time of need!'

Behind him the Lords of the Free raised the chant.

'To the Fey!'

'Our tardiness might have caused the end of all things,' Dreams replied. 'Your fair words do us more justice than we deserve. It was you and yours that held the line against the darkness. You alone. To the Free!'

Now the Fey took up the chant, raising their voices in chorus.

'To the Free!'

Rorthron nodded as the chants continued around them. He stepped past Luxor, patting him on the shoulder and whispering in his ear.

'There is hope for you yet, Moonprince.'

Tarithel could hardly breathe, the smoke of the burning forest, though still far off, seemed to be choking her. She could feel bark crackling in the heat, the burning splash of the Witchking's horrible weapon as it smote fire upon the forest.

She was taken inside, coughing and choking, her eyes wild. She was laid down beside Lord Whispers, himself lying upon a bed, badly injured from the assault upon his homeland.

'My lady ...' he managed.

'Fire ...' she gasped. 'They are burning everything!'

Another bout of coughing took her and she feebly waved her hands in front of her face, trying to waft away non-existent smoke.

Her mother tended them both, trying to get them to lie still.

'Who sees to the citadel?' Whispers demanded.

'The guards are on duty,' Tarithel's mother said. 'They will ...'

Whispers shook his head. 'If the Doomguard are burning the forest then they intend to make their way here, we must prepare a defence ...'

'You are too sick to rise, my Lord.'

'If I do not, who is left?' Whispers said, staggering to his feet. 'Bring me a staff, I will make do.'

The inner walls of the Citadel of Xajorkith were stained and damaged, but they had held together under the assault. Beyond them, the outer walls were mere piles of crushed masonry and rock. The courtyards that had once served as a market place and the community forums of the city were a smouldering ruin. Outside the city, huge pyres of the burning corpses of the Witchking's hordes had been set alight, whilst others worked to honour and bury the dead. Thousands had died and the task was immense. Within the walls the sick and injured were treated as best they could be.

Scouts had been sent far and wide, but it seemed the Doom-guard, what little remained, had retreated in ignominy to the north, but their march into the southern realm had torched and razed much of Midnight. There remained few places untouched by their rampage. All the keeps and citadels of the central plains had been put to the fire, villages ransacked and Snowhalls smashed and broken. Only in the far east and west had any been spared.

Reports came back that the Citadel of Gard had repelled invaders. Likewise Thimrath's realm in the south was untouched. Even Luxor's old Keep of Odrark remained intact. Kumar and Marakith still stood, but sorely damaged. Blood, Shimeril and Dawn had taken the brunt of the attack. Many of the forests of the Fey had been set ablaze or twisted by the Witchking's fell powers.

But now it seemed that the Witchking had retreated. Keeps were still occupied, but the main attacking force of the Foul was routed, or slain.

Luxor called a council of the survivors in the great hall of Xajorkith. Some of the windows were cracked and damaged, but it had survived the assault in good order.

'My Lords,' he began. 'With the valour of the Free and the courage of the Fey we have repelled the attack upon our lands. Though we have lost many to the darkness, we have prevailed against our ancient foe.'

Murmurs and nods sounded from around the room.

'Yet, we have returned only to the point where this battle began scant days ago,' Luxor continued. 'The Witchking remains, doubtless preparing some new anguish for us. Time remains on his side, he will rebuild his strength faster than we can and assault us once more.

But there is reason to rejoice! The ice-fear is mild now and for good reason! Kindle joy and hope in your hearts my friends – my son has seized the Ice Crown!'

Gasps of surprise and delight greeted this revelation.

'Yes,' Luxor continued. 'Even as the Witchking threw his might against these walls, Morkin crept within his domain and has stolen away the very source of his power. The Witchking doubts, he fears! His fate now rests in our hands, not the other way around. He has retreated to Ushgarak to lick his wounds, our next decision is upon us.'

'We have little choice,' Morning replied, nursing a badly injured arm held in a sling. 'We must see to our people first, winter is still winter, food stocks are low, sickness and injury will be the end of many in the next few moons if we don't work to protect them.'

'And what use will a few tonnes of fish be if the Witchking returns in force at the end of the next moon?' Blood demanded. 'We must push our advantage. The Witchking is on the back foot, I say we press the attack.'

'Aye!' Shimeril agreed. 'Take the fight back to him. Let him taste the wrath of the Free and the Fey!'

'It is a long trek to his fortress,' Gard replied. 'Our warriors are already exhausted, to mount an assault after such a weary road would not be my choice.'

'Wisdom at last!' Morning said, nodding.

'My son remains in great peril,' Luxor said. 'If the Witchking casts all attention on him, why – imagine the entire host of the Doomguard chasing him across Midnight! We must distract him, the quest to destroy the Ice Crown must succeed.'

Luxor looked over to the Lord of Dreams.

'What say the Fey?'

Dreams pursed his lips before speaking.

'In the past I have always counselled containment of the evil,' he said, his voice slow and even. 'We did this a generation of men ago. Even in the last moon this was my thought, that if we do not bother him he will not bother us.'

'We have roundly beaten him against all the odds,' Morning said, agreeing. 'He would not dare to bother us again after such a defeat, surely!'

But Dreams was shaking his head. 'Such was wisdom, so I thought, but it has brought us to this. The lands of the Free sacked, the domains of my people torched and ruined. Thus it will always be unless we decide to put an end to it once and for all. My people do not seek conflict, but I see no alternative but to agree with the Moonprince. We must destroy the Witchking. We must give Morkin all possible aid. If we do not end the Witchking now, then when?'

'We must make an end of this,' Corleth added. 'All roads have led us to this point. We cannot turn aside, future generations of the Free and the Fey will look to this decision and judge us accordingly.'

Conversation rose to a crescendo as the Lords debated amongst themselves, arguing back and forth the possible outcomes of such a bold move.

Luxor raised his hand, and the conversation ebbed.

'A direct military assault on his realm will give Morkin the chance he needs, the Witchking will have to deal with us, once more keeping his gaze away from his own domain.'

'Do we even know his strength?' Morning protested. 'What armies does he have within the walls of Kor, of Vorgath and Grarg, nay, even Ushgarak? Four mighty citadels guard his homeland, great armies patrol the Plains of Despair so I've been told, strength surely more potent than ours remains to him. A weary march and a certain death awaits those who attempt to assail his domain!'

The point was well made and the Lords fell to angry words and gestures of frustration until a sharp tap echoed through the hall. All eyes turned to the old man who strode into the centre of the room.

'It is true enough that the Witchking's might is at its lowest ebb,' Rorthron said. 'It is also true that he has strength enough to resist us still. The ice-fear is mild now, but it will return to its full potency if Morkin is caught. The Witchking has been touched by doubt, seen his plans go awry. Given time he will rebuild his armies. Boldness now on our part will serve us well, and give Morkin a greater chance of success in his quest to unmake the Ice Crown.'

'You suggest we march upon the Witchking?' Gard asked. 'More than fifty leagues away? How many will be able to fight after such a long march, and against a foe that may still out-number us with a tactically superior position? I am all for valour, but valour without wisdom leads to disastrous ends.'

Rorthron nodded.

'Wisdom indeed,' he replied. 'And I welcome it. Consider this though, if we could arrive at the Witchking's realm un-wearied by the journey, might we then press the attack?'

Luxor looked around the assembled Lords. They all nodded. Even Morning had to agree.

'Then I will seek such a route,' Rorthron replied. 'There are older powers in the realm of Midnight than the Witchking, perhaps it is time they too came to our aid.'

'What do you mean?' Luxor asked.

'It would be hard for me to explain, and the explanation would do little but waste time,' Rorthron replied. 'Assemble your armies, be prepared to march, formulate your plans for an assault.' He tapped his staff upon the flagstones once more. 'Leave the rest to me.'

And with that, the only member of the Wise the assembled crowd had ever seen strolled out of the hall, leaving them nonplussed and puzzled.

'He has not changed at all, has he?' Corleth chuckled.

'I know not of what he speaks,' Luxor said. 'And his ways are often unfathomable, but he has not led me astray yet. If we are to defeat the Witchking we must abide by his counsel.

Make preparations, equip your warriors. Somehow, we will take our fight to the Witchking's very doorstep!'

Chapter Nineteen

They stand on the Plains of Corelay,
looking west to the Tower of Corelay.

The armies of the Free and the Fey had assembled themselves on the Plains of Corelay. Their numbers were sorely depleted, but they were still a host to be feared. The total of a mere three thousand five hundred warriors and four thousand two hundred riders remained after a guard was set upon the citadel. Those too injured to join the force were also left behind in the hope they would heal and perhaps be of some use in its defence should it become necessary again.

Provisions were packed, meagre as they were, in preparation for a long march. Weapons were readied. Scouts had reported that some of the forts along the route had been spared the torch and would serve as resupply points. Without those, the army would not have completed the march, but starved to death in the wilderness of Midnight long before they reached their destination.

After Rorthron's instruction and Luxor's command they had set out west through Corelay, marching with renewed determination in the hope of undoing the damage and ruin they saw all about them.

Nightfall brought them to the western reaches of the valley, on the borders of the lands of Thimrath, there they set their camp.

'My domain still survives the fury of the enemy,' Thimrath

said, after a discussion with the Lord of Dreams. 'We can offer some measure of rest and refreshment on the way.'

'That will see us to Rorath well enough,' Luxor agreed. 'But then? Rorthron, it is time for you to tell us your part of the plan. I would turn north, not west. Where are we bound?'

The old man looked across at Luxor.

'I shall decide when it is time for me to reveal my intentions, Moonprince,' Rorthron said. 'For now the road is enough of a challenge for you I think.'

'I will scout ahead,' Corleth said, nodding to Thimrath. 'And make what preparations we can make.'

Another day saw the army leave the domain of Corelay and enter that of Thimrath.

Lord Thimrath was as good as his word. The army was welcomed within the eaves of the forest and given such refreshment and help as the Fey of that realm could provide. Even Lord Dreams seemed impressed.

'I have spoken harshly of the Fey of the south in the past,' Dreams said to Luxor. 'It seems I have said many words I would have been wiser not to utter.'

Luxor smiled. 'I have been guilty of some clumsy words myself.'

Plans were reviewed, changed and updated. Scouts still reported little of the Doomguard, armies had been seen in retreat, moving north away from the domains of the Free.

'Doubtless holing up in the north,' Blood said. 'Cowards! Brave enough when they outnumber us, but witless and craven at the thought of a fair fight.'

Shimeril was subdued. Luxor knew that far away to the north east lay the ruins of his own home. The Citadel of Shimeril had borne the brunt of many conflicts, standing as it did on the borders of the Plains of Blood.

'Come my friend,' Blood had assured him. 'We will set things right again. We have done it before, we can do it again.'

'Aye,' Shimeril replied. 'That we can.'

They exchanged a look, silently acknowledging what both of them knew in their hearts; that there were more years behind them than years ahead.

From Thimrath the army struck out north west, crossing the Plains of Rorath. Here once again they stopped at Luxor's home, the small yet homely Keep of Odrark.

'I think that if we survive all this,' Gard said. 'We might honour you with a more fitting abode, Moonprince.'

Luxor chuckled. 'A small keep and enough food to put hunger at bay will satisfy me. Legends tell my people had a citadel within the Forest of the Moon long ago, but it is gone now. I am content enough with my lot.'

'It is a wholesome place,' Corleth said, with a grin. 'I remember it well.'

Luxor smiled. It seemed a lifetime ago that the enigmatic Fey had ridden with his wild stories of the Wise. His thoughts turned to Silence, riding alongside. Luxor could see her, riding at the head of her troupe of warrior women, now sadly reduced in number to less than fifty, but still as fierce and indomitable as the day they had first appeared. Of all that had pledged their allegiance, she had been one of the most loyal, unwavering in her support and keeping the other Lords on side.

The slayer of the Utarg! I must see that she is rewarded once this is over. Her lands laid out in manuscript and signed by the Lords, agreed and sealed as law. She deserves nothing less.

From Luxor's home they took the mountain pass, but where Luxor had expected to turn to the North, still Rorthron directed them west. The wise old man rode at the head of the army, staff held aloft.

'What does he seek?' Blood demanded. 'The enemy lies not here, we waste precious time dallying about when we should be wiping the blood of the Foul from our swords.'

483

The combined army of the Free and the Fey found a garrison of the Foul guarding a small keep in the remote west. The battle was short and one-sided and by nightfall the Keep of Ishmalay was returned to the ownership of the Fey.

'Does he toy with us?' Blood said, his voice almost sounding pained to the point of insult. 'A scant few hundred of his Foul horde.'

'Perhaps he has exhausted himself with his southward march,' Shimeril replied. 'Overextended his reach ...'

The ice-fear was mild, barely a taint of its foul feeling could be sensed.

'We draw close to my lands,' Gard said. 'There is shelter there if we should need it.'

'And our Wise friend has yet to reveal our path,' Corleth added.

'A long road remains,' Luxor said, turning his horse and trotting forwards. 'And little enough time to do it. If the Witchking falters, we must press what advantage we have. Rorthron! Enough is enough – we must turn north. I don't know what strange scheme you are ...'

The old man turned with a fierce glare. Luxor stepped back a pace, even Gard swallowed in surprise.

'Do not question me,' Rorthron replied. 'We are close now and my efforts on your part will soon be revealed. We shall not have need of your refreshment, Lord Gard. There are other forces at work here.'

'You speak in riddles once again,' Luxor said. 'This does not usually bode well. Our foe lies to the north, we travel west. Time to explain yourself, Rorthron the Wise!'

'You would seek to fight your way northwards?' Rorthron asked.

'Aye,' Luxor replied.

'Take back Shimeril and Blood, lay waste to Gorgrath?' Rorthron continued.

Luxor nodded.

'Sack Korkith, fight your way on to the Plains of Kor?'

'This we would do,' Luxor replied.

'And then lie hungry, worn and exhausted before the gates of the Witchking,' Rorthron said. 'Easy prey for his own hordes who have been well rested, safe within the grand halls of Ushgarak, waiting for you to arrive? You lead your allies to a slaughter, Moonprince!'

'We must take the fight to the Witchking,' Luxor replied. 'And soon.'

'Fight you must,' Rorthron replied. 'But it must be a fight on equal terms, otherwise you stand but little chance of success.'

'I find nothing I disagree with,' Luxor rumbled. 'But we are south of the realm of Gard, not knocking on the gates of Kor! Half a moon's march lies between us and the Witchking's realm now. You lead us further away from his gates, not closer!'

'Open your eyes, Moonprince.'

Rorthron turned and gestured to the north west.

From the uppermost reaches of the Keep of Ishmalay, Luxor could see a pass through the mountains. Beyond lay the Plains of Gard and the first of a row of Liths that stretched northwards past the gates of Gard's citadel.

'I see nothing but what I would expect to see,' Luxor said. 'What miracle do I look for?'

Rorthron sighed.

'Lord Gard,' he called. 'You know these lands well. Of what do I speak?'

Gard stepped forward and looked where Rorthron had gestured.

'This is the southern end of my realm,' he said. 'There are keeps and some fortifications, villages of course …'

Rorthron shook his head.

'He means the Liths.'

The heads of the three men turned to regard Silence. As was her way, she had stood alongside them, unnoticed and unremarked until she interjected her words.

'The Liths?' Corleth asked.

'Yes!' Rorthron replied. 'The Liths.'

'The Liths?' Gard repeated. 'Of what use are they to us? Those stone markers have been there since time immemorial, they serve no purpose …'

'That is where you are wrong,' Rorthron said. 'You all have much to learn. Come.'

Another hours march brought them to the nearest of the Liths. Luxor could see a line of the ancient monuments stretching northwards to the horizon. He knew that the Liths were occasionally found in these ordered formations here and there about the landscape of Midnight. None, to his knowledge, knew why they were so organised.

'The ancient powers of this realm are, for the most part, quiescent,' Rorthron said to the assembled Lords. 'But there are deeper potencies, older than the Free, older than the Fey, older even than the Wise. Midnight itself keeps its warmth under the unnatural cold of the Witchking. The lakes remain free of ice and the trees still grow, nourished from beneath the ice. That potency is something we can harness in our struggle against the Foul.'

Rorthron stepped forward, holding his staff aloft. After a few paces he began drawing marks in the snow with the tip of his staff. He busied himself for a few minutes and then stepped back from it.

Luxor and the Lords waited expectantly. Moments passed, their cloaks ruffling in the stiff breeze.

Rorthron raised his staff and gestured forward with it.

Still they waited.

Low on the horizon the moon itself was barely a sliver, just a deeper darkness blotting out the glistening haze of the Roads of Light, a glistening trail in the sky which seemed to have oriented itself above them.

'What is this …?' Luxor began.

With a heavy thump of ignition, light flared out before them. All save Rorthron gasped and jolted back, the horses whinnying and snorting in alarm. A wave of heat washed over them.

Ahead the first of the Liths was on fire, or at least that's how it seemed to those who watched. Green tinged flames had burst from upon its rocky sides, surging upwards in a ferocious blaze of light. As they continued to gaze upon it, the next Lith in line flared too, and then the next, until all five could be seen glowing in the gloom.

The fires increased, cascading upwards. At some unknown potency, a beam of energy crackled between the Liths, akin to lightning, but with the same green hue, flickering and sparkling between them, wresting some great energy from within their ancient stores.

Rorthron turned and smiled.

'Midnight itself has judged your conduct and found it worthy, Moonprince,' Rorthron said. 'Behold the power of the Liths of Midnight. March onwards and you will see.'

Luxor exchanged a look with the others about him. They gazed back, waiting. Corleth nodded, gesturing forwards.

Luxor gripped the reins of his horse and guided it forwards. Ahead of him the other Liths seemed somehow closer. Clouds whirled overhead as if swept onwards by a wind swift beyond imagining. The weariness faded from his arms and legs, the fatigue of the long march fading away. Hope was kindled once more in his heart as he basked in the warm radiance of a sun that blazed away on the horizon …

But it is not dawn …

It seemed to him that a voice called out around him, warm and amused at his confusion.

DO YOU WANT DAWN?

Luxor smiled.

Yes! I welcome it!

AND WHAT WILL YOU DO WITH THE GIFT OF DAWN?

I will march upon the Witchking …

THUS IT WILL BE.

He kept on walking, marvelling at how he did not tire. The realm of Midnight seemed ephemeral now, as if time and distance didn't matter, that mountains and forests were mere trifles, small objects of note and nothing more. The sky was a pure azure … a cyan backdrop to the stark beauty of the realm, the sun blazed on the horizon.

He knew not how long he marched, only that he reached another Lith. The mountains and the forests were not as he had expected.

He blinked. Before him stretched a plain. To the east a forest.

'These are not the Plains of Gard!' he exclaimed.

'No indeed.'

Luxor turned to see Rorthron beside him, with the Lords and the host of the Free and the Fey not far behind. He could see everyone looking about themselves in wonderment.

'We stand at the very threshold of the Witchking's realm,' Rorthron said. 'It is dawn once more, no time has been lost.'

What do you mean?' Luxor asked.

'It is the morrow of the day we set out from Xajorkith and you stand upon his doorstep,' Rorthron answered. 'You asked why the ice-fear should be so mild. Morkin has the Ice Crown and you have brought fear and confusion into the heart of Ushgarak. He grows alarmed at your sudden appearance, fearing you have magic arts he does not comprehend.'

'Then he is entirely right,' Luxor said. 'I do not comprehend either!'

'Nor need you,' Rorthron replied. 'The Liths have many purposes, only one of which is the roadways you have seen. Midnight itself has aided you, Moonprince. The rest is up to you.'

Luxor frowned and shook his head, 'But if this is the morrow of the day we left, then we are both here and …'

Corleth stepped up beside him.

'I fear madness lies that way,' he said. 'Trying to divine the ways of the Wise might lead us all to question our sanity. Perhaps we should just accept this good fortune.'

'The Fey can be wise after all,' Rorthron said, with a chuckle.

A company of the Doomguard assailed the Citadel of Dreams. Whispers, despite his wounds, had seen to the defence as best he could with the few soldiers that remained. The Fey shot arrows down into the hordes and gave good account of themselves. Yet the Doomguard pressed in. Equipped with crossbows and some heavier weapons they picked off the defenders one by one, each loss making the task of defending the walls of the great city harder and harder.

Whispers could see the battle was hopeless and that they would be overrun.

Doomguard were already beginning to mass at the gates, shields held above them to protect them from the arrows of the defenders. The gates themselves began to shudder.

Whispers winced against the pain in his body, propping himself up with the help of a nearby guard.

'See to the messengers on the walls, we must prepare for the gate to be breached! All warriors must stand within the courtyards and fight to the last to protect the people within …'

The guard wasn't paying attention, he was looking to his right.

Whispers turned and saw Lady Tarithel standing on the threshold of the wall.

She looked deathly pale, her body twitching spasmodically as she staggered forward. Her mouth opening and closing, her face twisted with pain.

'My lady!' Whisper's gasped and then pushed the guard towards her. 'Help her!'

Tarithel screeched.

'No! I cannot bear the touch. Fire is upon me!'

'My Lady, you must withdraw ...'

'No! There is no solace to be found whilst the Foul burn my forest! I must stop them ... make way!'

Whispers and the guard stepped aside as Tarithel crept forward, her limbs jerking and mechanical, every step an agony. Whispers could almost see flames about her, licking at her skin, as if she was being burnt and yet somehow not consumed.

She screamed in torment, but managed to hold an arm aloft.

'Resist ... my forest, my trees ... cast them down ... cast them down!'

The armies of the Free and the Fey stood outside of the Citadel of Kor. Earlier that day they had approached it, expecting to face a siege and a struggle to take the gateway into the Witchking's realm. But the citadel was left unguarded and they had ventured within unopposed.

From its high walls they could see the Citadel of Ushgarak several leagues northwards. By contrast, it was clear there was great activity within. Hordes of Doomguard warriors swarmed about it. The army formed up behind the citadel, ready to ride north.

Dreams walked within the halls of Kor, lamenting its filthy and ruined state.

'This was built by the Free, long moons ago,' he said. 'I would see it restored if I could, in memory of the lost folk of this realm.'

'The Witchking has retreated within his own walls at Ushgarak,' Gard said, frowning as he stared out into the snowy landscape, trying to determine what was going on. 'Is he truly that perturbed by our arrival and the loss of the Crown?'

'Perhaps,' Luxor said. 'I perceive that the Ice Crown is everything to our foe. If it fails, he fails. Yet Morkin remains in peril. We must press on.'

'Morkin can withstand the ice-fear well enough,' Corleth said. 'But we would be wise to do what we can to keep the Doomguard occupied.'

Luxor turned to Rorthron, who was standing alongside, also gazing north.

'Your counsel?'

Rorthron sighed. 'There is but one course left now, Moonprince. We confront the foe.'

Blasted, desolate and windswept were these parts, a grim and desolate valley that was choked with fractured ice and jagged rock, gateway into the Witchking's realm.

The Plains of Despair.

And nestled at the very centre, the abode of the Witchking himself, the Citadel of Ushgarak.

'Should we require respite my home is not more than a few days march to the east,' Dreams said.

'I hope we will not need it,' Luxor replied. 'Though I would give much to know what goes on within the Witchking's mind.'

'I sense little enough of anything,' Dreams said. 'He does

indeed seem preoccupied with other matters. To allow us to reach this point unchallenged.'

'His citadel is secure enough,' Gard said. 'Perhaps he feels he has nothing to fear.'

'We have the element of surprise,' Luxor said. 'He cannot have expected us to arrive in this fashion or so soon. Let us see what we might make of that!'

With that Luxor spurred his horse. The armies marched onwards into the Plains of Despair, Ushgarak before them.

A day's march saw them camped a league south of the gates of Ushgarak. Luxor and the Lords saw to the organisation of the army, ensuring it was arrayed in a suitable fashion. Such weapons as they had brought with them were assembled and readied for battle. All the while there was no response from the Citadel of Ushgarak. The armies seemed to have retreated within. A few Doomguard warriors had been spied upon the walls of the Citadel, but that was all.

With the army prepared to his satisfaction Luxor assembled the seniority of Midnight.

'My friends,' he said. 'We have come through great trials to reach this point, and our sorest test yet lies ahead. In all the history of the Free and the Fey, we have never come to stand before the gates of the Witchking together in such strength. Such a force is testament to wrongs forgiven and the bonds of friendship and trust that have been forged between us. Those bonds are our salvation. Look to those around you and take heart, together we have already achieved the impossible and thrown back the Witchking's might. Now we must cast him down for once and for all, lest he rises once more. Arise Midnight!'

The chant was taken up around him, fanning out across the army. Spears and swords were rattled and thumped against shields in a rhythmic beat that echoed out across the plains.

Luxor led the Lords of Midnight forwards, riding under

the shadow of the Citadel. There he planted his standard and moved his horse forward a few steps. He could spy the guards upon the towers and battlements.

Luxor raised his voice.

'We would have your surrender, Witchking!' he called. 'You have laid waste to our lands, pillaged our realms and put our people to the sword. Your crimes are many and you are answerable to us for your kingship long ago gone awry. Open unto us and put yourself at the mercy of the Lords of Midnight!'

The cavern was a relief to Morkin's mind after the haunting chill of the Witchking's realm, but the Ice Crown itself throbbed with a power all of its own. Morkin could hear it crying in his mind, seeking to call its master, seeking to give his location away. Whether the Witchking could sense it he knew not, but it seemed that at any moment that ghastly sepulchral figure would begin to take form nearby.

If it did, Morkin knew he would be lost, he could not face that terror again.

Around him the ghostly lights of the rocks flinched and backed away whenever the Ice Crown came close to them. Morkin found he had to switch it from one hand to the other lest his fingers grew too numb to hold it. When he touched his chilled fingers against the stones their light flickered and faded. He left blank hand prints behind him as he moved through the dimly lit spaces.

Each time it took longer for the chill to fade from his fingers. It seemed to matter not whether he carried it with gloves or not, the chill pervaded anything.

It's cursing me … chilling my body and my soul. If I carry it too long, then what?

Cold was suffusing him when he staggered out into the

cavern. Fawkrin was huddled by a small fire, his face white with terror as Morkin approached. Farflame's snout was wedged in the entrance.

'Young squire, your face …'

Fawkrin looked ashen. Whatever the Ice Crown was doing to him, Morkin knew its fell influence was working quickly.

'There's no time …'

WE FELT YOU DRAWING NEAR, THE ICE-FEAR …

Morkin held forth the Ice Crown. Fawkrin screeched in dismay. Whispering ghastly voices issued from the Ice Crown, shrieking torment and woe.

'You must blast it with your fire,' Morkin managed to say, through half frozen lips.

The dragon withdrew, the enormous muzzle disappearing outside.

'Farflame… do not delay, I cannot hold it much longer…'

But the dragon roared out a warning.

DOOMGUARD! DOOMGUARD ARE UPON US, WE MUST FLEE!

Crying with fear and terror Fawkrin grabbed the insensible Morkin and dragged him forward. Outside the cavern the snow was falling gently, but both could hear the cries of the Foul. Clearly the Witchking had been looking for them, scouting out possible avenues of escape.

So soon … the Ice Crown screams to its master …

Fire blossomed in the whiteness as the dragon's wrath struck forth. Morkin felt himself pulled a-dragonback. A mighty waft of air blasted past and the ground fell away below. Snow stung his face, but it was mild next to the throbbing cold that now lanced up his arm and shoulders, seeking a way across his torso and down into his heart.

The Ice Crown pulsed with malice. Despair clutched at his mind.

'Lake Mirrow!' he gasped. 'We must reach the lake!'

The wind blew around the Citadel of Ushgarak, but its great gates remained locked and motionless. Luxor, flanked by the Lords of Midnight, stood beneath their banners as they fluttered in the air above them.

Luxor's declaration had echoed off the steep mountain sides that flanked the citadel, loud and clear despite the wind. It could not have gone unheard.

'Where is his foulness?' Blood demanded. 'Here we stand at his very gate …'

'He knows we are here,' Corleth replied. 'He toys with us … hold fast.'

Snow swirled before them and a chill blast of air swept through them, causing them to step back and shield their eyes from its fury. Gasps were drawn from them as they turned back.

A figure formed before them, cloaked and cowled. It was barely more substantial than the snow flurries about it, but they sensed its chill and the fear it wrapped about itself.

SO THIS IS THE FABLED MOONPRINCE OF MIDNIGHT? A MINOR LORD OF LITTLE NOTE AND THE FEEBLEST OF THE WISE, LEADING A RABBLE TO MY DOORSTEP?

The voice was inaudible, sepulchral, yet somehow rang in their ears. Many cringed at the words, clasping at their heads at the sheer horror the voice induced. It clutched at the heart, numbing it, sending fingers of ice creeping into the soul.

DISBAND AND BEGONE, I WILL SPARE THOSE WHO CAPITULATE. RAISE NOT YOUR FURY AGAINST ME, BLAME THE ONE WHO HAS LED YOU CLOSE TO RUIN! TURN BACK!

Rorthron's voice sounded beside him.

'Resist, do not quail before him!'

About him Luxor sensed the ice-fear growing, the fortitude dissolving amidst the Witchking's hypnotic powers. He raised his hand, unclenching his fist, turning his hand palm outwards towards the ephemeral figure.

SO, THE MOONPRINCE BEARS A PRETTY BAUBLE! THAT WILL AVAIL YOU NOT. GO BEFORE MY WRATH DESCENDS ...

Beside him, Lord Blood gave a yell and drew his sword. Before anyone could stop him he swung the great blade down upon the figure.

A flash of whiteness, a crash of splintering ice. Blood himself lay upon the snow, thrown backwards by the force of the blow, his sword shattered by the impact. The figure had raised a skeletal arm, but was otherwise unaffected.

SEEK NOT TO IMPINGE UPON MY REALM. NONE WILL PREVAIL.

The figure raised its arm higher. Ice crackled around it, spikes erupted through the ground around them, striking upwards like daggers thrust from beneath the snow. From upon high the ice-fear descended, terrifying, cold and brutal, crushing the spirit and saturating the mind.

The group buckled under its onslaught, collapsing to their knees before the fell power, screaming out their terror as the unreasoning dread clutched at their hearts.

All save one.

A burning fire surrounded their leader. Luxor stood firm amidst the frightful assault, his own arm raised in challenge.

The Moon Ring burst forth in splendour, radiating an intense heat that bathed the area about them with ruddy light. The ice softened and melted about him.

Ice-fear fought the fire of the Free.

The Witchking's form crumpled inwards and faded into the swirling snow.

And then even the wind faded away. The snow ceased and the mist withdrew. The citadel lay before them once more, stark and austere.

With a grinding crash the gates before them started to open.

Luxor recovered first.

'To arms!' he called. 'To arms! This is our battle, today we decide the fate of Midnight once and for all!'

Around the Citadel of Dreams the forest burned, whipped to a frenzy by wind and the fell arts of the Witchking. The foliage was consumed, trees fell in great crashes of sparks accompanied every time by a rending scream of torment from the high pinnacles of the Citadel.

Tarithel, almost crazed by the pain, stood, supported by the ailing Lord Whispers, trying to oversee the unearthly battle between the warriors of the Foul and the trees of the forest.

Branches writhed and twisted, battering the invading warriors to pulp and casting their torn and broken bodies into the depths, but more followed, spraying their horrendous liquid fire before them, immolating the vegetation around them.

They were almost at the city gates. Lord Whispers felt Tarithel go limp in his arms.

'I can do no more,' she gasped, her voice barely audible above the tumult of the fire. 'It is lost, all is despair ...'

Whispers tried to hold her upright, but he could not and the pair sank to the cobbled stone paving of the battlements.

'Nothing but fire and smoke,' Tarithel muttered. 'We are consumed. All is at an end. All hope is lost. I was too late ...'

Her eyes reflected the fire all about them. Dull thuds echoed through Whisper's mind, the Doomguard at the gates. Within minutes the Citadel would be overrun. None remained to defend it now.

'Night has fallen,' she said, tears dripping down her cheeks. 'Night has fallen and it will ever be thus. Victory goes to the Foul!'

The armies of the Free and the Fey were quickly put in ordered array. Warriors stood with halberds and shields, archers behind them, flanked with the riders. Before them the armies of the Doomguard were arranged in a similar fashion. The bright gold of the Free and the Green of the Fey stood in sharp contrast to the darkness of the Foul.

Behind the Free and the Fey lay the vastness of the Plains of Despair and the route to the south. Behind the Foul lay the Citadel of Ushgarak itself, the dwelling of the Witchking.

And the army of the Witchking was the greater.

From the gates more continued to issue, rank after rank of the loathsome minions of the Witchking.

Luxor sat upon his horse, surveying the scene, Rorthron at his side. The Lords of Midnight rode up alongside him. Marakith, Xajorkith, Shimeril, Kumar, Ithrorn, Blood, Morning and Silence of the Free to his right. To his left came the Fey; Dreams, Dregrim, Thimrath, Thrall and Corleth.

All drew their swords and knives simultaneously. Even Rorthron held forth his staff and Luxor could see it was wreathed in a strange red fire.

Horns sounded and they began to walk towards the foe, slowly gaining pace until the whole army was on the move.

In moments battle cries were hurled into the air and the trot became a charge.

The bloody sword of battle brought death in the domain of Despair and of Ushgarak.

It was a battle of desperation. Great deeds were done and undone. Thousands were slain upon either side as the mightiest armies ever to be assembled in the long history of Midnight clashed and then clashed again. Arrows smote the air, swords were notched, shields cracked and thrown aside.

The unbridled power of the Wise was brought forth too. Luxor saw Rorthron drive the Foul before him, somehow setting them ablaze with the power of his staff.

The sun westered in the sky and still the battle raged. Free, Fey and Foul alike fell headlong into the bloodstained snow, the air was rent by the rage of the embattled and the screams of the dying.

The press of the engagement was extreme, all fought in close quarters, exhaustion being the end of many rather than a lack of prowess in battle. The Foul pressed hard against those who held the banners of the Free and the Fey, seeking to bring them down and embolden their own. The Free and the Fey pushed back, attempting to wrest a path into the Citadel.

The ebb and flow of the conflict swept one way and then another, neither willing to give up. The Free and the Fey motivated by a righteous cause, the Foul by fear of failure before their dark master.

But the Free and the Fey were outnumbered as they had always been. Minute by minute their numbers grew less, and though they made good account of themselves, the immutable laws of conflict were inexorably tilting against them.

The darkness grew about them. Ice and mist rose and the ice-fear began to choke the hope of all those who dared to defy it.

Cloud whipped past him, but the cold and biting wind was as nothing compared to the cold seeping into him. The dragon's wings heaved through the thick air. He was shivering uncontrollably now, he could no longer feel the fist which was clenched around the Ice Crown. Only by looking could he confirm it was still there.

Blue sky above and the sun shone brightly through the gloom. Below Morkin could just make out a forest, a huge ring of it with a tower at the centre …

Lothoril …

Fawkrin's squeak of alarm made him look over to his right. Smoke was drifting upwards in the still frosty air.

Morkin squinted, seeing marks upon the ground, faint flashes of red and gold, blue and green, but the dragon was too high for him to see more.

People?

The dragon's throat rumbled between his legs.

AN ARMY, ALL SLAIN …

'Whose?' Morkin muttered, between the chattering of his teeth.

I SEE BANNERS OF RED LIONS AND MAGENTA EAGLES …

Morkin knew those devices well.

No … Gloom and Lothoril …

THEY KNEW THEIR DUTY, THEY KNEW WHAT THEY RISKED. HONOUR WAS THEIRS IN LIFE, AS IT IS NOW … IN DEATH.

Cloud enveloped them once more. Morkin would have cried, but his tears froze on his cheeks, crackling away and were lost to the wind.

Morkin could sense the mighty dragon was tiring. His breaths were coming in huge heaving gasps and they were losing altitude.

I CAN FLY NO FURTHER, YOUNG SQUIRE …

'You have done enough!' Morkin shouted, above the rushing wind. 'We cannot be far now.'

'There,' Fawkrin yelled, stretching out his hand and pointing. 'The lake! Khlee! The lake!'

The clouds thinned and were left behind them as Farflame sank lower. The lake was before them, perhaps a league or so.

'Glide us, Farflame!' Morkin called. 'You can reach it.'

Morkin sensed the dragon's muscles tense against the air and the wings stretch that little further.

'Good, that's it …'

Morkin squinted. There was a dark mark on the ground, no a cluster of black dots … moving, swarming …

'Doomguard!' Fawkrin yelled. 'They must have defeated Gloom and Lothoril. They knew where we were bound. The cursed ones …'

Arrows flashed through the air about them.

Before Morkin could yell another command, Farflame gave a deafening howl and lurched to one side, his right wing crunching back in the airflow. Morkin saw the ground tilt and spin about him as the dragon spiralled out of the sky.

'Farflame … Farflame!'

Morkin could barely see, the world was a spinning whiteness all about him, a dizzying blur of motion and confusion. He heard Fawkrin scream from before him. His ears popped with the sudden descent.

With a lurch that almost threw him from the dragon's neck the world stopped spinning, but now Morkin could see that they were in a vertiginous dive, falling from the sky. Below him he could see the upturned helmets of the Doomguard warriors, still firing. They were going to crash into the ice and be dashed to eternity.

The baleful cold of the Ice Crown throbbed in his hand.

'No …'

With a screeching agonising cry, Farflame managed to

unfurl his wings. Morkin was crushed down on to the dragon's scales, the breath knocked from him as the beast tried to arrest the downward plummet.

The Doomguard were left behind as the dragon soared above them.

But only for a moment.

The impact was brutal. Morkin was crushed down still further, hearing Farflame's roar of pain. Snow blustered up all around them. Morkin lost his hold and was cast through the air to lie prone upon the surface, stunned.

For a moment all was white and drifting snowflakes. A high-pitched note sounded in his ears. He couldn't move, but lay there as the snow drifted down around him. A distant bellow reached his ears. He clenched his eyes against the pain that streaked through his body. The bellow sounded again.

MORKIN!

He rolled on to his side, propping himself up to see. He blinked, wiping the snow from his eyes.

The great dragon lay on its side, wings twisted at an unnatural angle, flapping feebly. As Morkin's vision cleared he could see the delicate membranes were torn and shredded, the dragon's chest festooned with arrows.

Morkin's heart clenched within him, horror and despair clawed at him.

Farflame!

NO TIME! THE ICE CROWN BOY, LAY IT BEFORE ME!

Morkin stumbled forwards. All about him the cries of the Doomguard rose. They were running towards the fallen dragon, perhaps three or four hundred yards beyond.

The Ice Crown was clenched in his hand, a hand that was now ice-white and numb. His fingers wouldn't release it, he had to prise it away with his other hand before he could drop it before the great beasts snout.

Farflame coiled backwards, crying out in anguish as he did so. Smoke billowed from his nostrils.

STAND BACK!

Morkin staggered away. A furious burst of flames engulfed the Ice Crown. Morkin could see it was unharmed, whilst the snow about it sprang into steam and spray. Then it sank, drowned in a puddle of melted ice.

The fire faded. Morkin stared in horror as Farflame body convulsed and then fell upon the snow.

'No … Farflame … no …'

THE LAKE, YOU MUST REACH …

A blast of snow threw him backwards, a whirling torrent of ice-flecked hail lancing across. He heard a roar and a long drawn out howl of pain.

'No …'

The yells of the Doomguard reached his ears. Then something pulled him, he could not see Farflame …

'Master! They come, we must be swift! The lake, it is not far …'

Morkin collapsed by the puddle of water, plunging his hand in it and grabbing the Ice Crown from within its depths. The water was already cooling, the Ice Crown attempting to freeze it and lock itself safely within.

Morkin wrestled it back to the surface, seeing the surface of the puddle freezing. He punched at the ice and grappled the Ice Crown away.

Fawkrin pulled him to his feet and they ran, slipping and sliding towards the lake. Behind they could hear the Doom-guard charging after them, their heavy footfalls thumping through the snow. More than once they stumbled, crashing down into snow drifts and hidden drops.

They staggered on as arrows flew about them. One tore through the clothing on Morkin's arm.

Before them lay the lake, they raced on to the shoreline, the rocky beach crunching under their boots.

'Now, Fawkrin … the sleep-frost!'

The little skulkrin withdrew a pouch from his tunic, fumbled with the drawstrings and then doused the Ice Crown with the contents. Icy blue light flashed from the Ice Crown as the skulkrin's magic laced it and was absorbed.

'Now master, into the lake with it …'

The Ice Crown was freezing to the touch. Morkin grasped it again and swung back his arm. More arrows sliced the air about him. He yelled out one last time and threw forward with all his might.

'For Yanathel, for Luxor … for Midnight!'

Before the gates of Ushgarak the battle raged. The armies of the Free and the Fey were hemmed in, assailed on all sides by the overwhelming numbers of the Foul. They rallied many times, fighting to keep their banners aloft.

As they struggled the Doomguard abruptly broke ranks, making a clear way between their ranks. Luxor could see a figure striding up in their midst. This time it was no illusion, no ephemeral vision.

'The Witchking!' someone yelled. 'The Witchking cometh!'

A palpable wall of terror seemed to surround the figure. Even the Foul retreated from it, dropping back and away, leaving the figure striding up straight towards the beleaguered armies of the Free and the Fey.

'Hold fast!'

Then the figure was before them, an animated black cowl and cloak, framing skeletal limbs of purest white. Hands were outstretched and an icy sword formed in the air before it, which it grasped and then held poised.

Rorthron stood before him.

YOU CANNOT DEFY ME, YOUNG ONE …

504

Rorthron struck his staff out before him and a stream of red fire issued from it, enveloping the hated figure of the Witchking in immolating fury.

Yet, in moments, ice and frost cut through the flames and a stinging torrent of icy shards issued forth in return. Rorthron cried out and was cast back upon the snow, his staff wrenched from his grasp.

The Free and the Fey rushed forward to attack, but a sweep of the Witchking's sword left them slain, writhing on the ground in their death throes as their bodies turned to ice. The sword cut anything; weapons, armour and flesh, rending them down into its own composition of implacable cold and ice. Warriors fell, their bodies freezing in mid air and shattering into fragments as they hit the ground.

The figure advanced, cutting down all before it. Behind, the Foul roared in approval, goading their leader on to greater wrath.

Luxor himself was next in line. He brought up his own sword, ready to face his nemesis when another stepped in his way.

The Witchking watched and turned to deal with the interloper. Corleth had swung around before him, still astride his charger, galloping down upon the Witchking, sword raised high.

'Fall back!' Luxor yelled. 'You cannot face him!'

A blast of ice unseated the Fey, crashing him down into the snow to lie unmoving. Luxor's own horse, terrified beyond measure, bucked and unseated him. Luxor rolled aside, struggling to get to his knees.

He looked up. Rorthron and Corleth were cast upon the snow unmoving.

Another stood before the dark cloaked figure, cloaked herself, knives in both hands.

'You will not assail my liege!'

The cry of Silence was sharp and clear.

505

'No!' Luxor cried, struggling forward through the snow. But he was too far away.

Silence leapt forward as the Witchking's sword fell in a sweeping arc. She feinted and moved aside, avoiding the killing blow, striking her own in return. The Witchking, possessed by his own fell energy, slipped aside out of reach.

'I have slain your minions,' she cried. 'Now you will fall by my blades!'

DEATH AWAITS YOU, WEAK AND FOOLISH WOMAN!

The sword came down again, flashing faster than the eye could see. Silence ducked it this time, throwing herself upon the snow and rolling aside. She was on her feet again to jump the sword as it came around to slice her in twain on the third stroke.

That was the opportunity she had been waiting for. As the sword swung back in its upstroke, she lunged forward, stabbing both knives deep into the hated figure before her, driving the deadly blades into the Witchking's chest, aiming for the source of his icy heart.

For a moment all was still.

Silence screamed as ice frosted up the handles of the knives, crackling over her fingers, hands and halfway up her arms.

The Witchking laughed as he shook off the blow and then struck down with the sword.

To the horror of all who watched, the blow shattered Silence's hands into splinters of ice, her long drawn out cry of torment abruptly ended by the fifth and final downstroke of the Witchking's blade. Her body fell to one side and broke in two.

NONE MAY CHALLENGE ME, MOONPRINCE. NONE! DEATH AWAITS YOU NOW. YOU HAVE BEEN MY PUPPET THROUGHOUT ALL YOUR TRIALS. IT WAS THE MOON RING I HAVE LONG SOUGHT AND YOU HAVE BOUGHT IT DIRECT TO ME. FOOL!

The Witchking kicked through the shattered remnants of

Silence's body and strode towards him, the sword poised, glinting with fierce cold.

Luxor raised his own sword and stood firm.

The Witchking raised his own weapon, the unearthly cold sword shining in the pale light. Luxor blocked the blow that followed. His own sword shattered in his hands, leaving him with just the pommel clenched in his fist, the force of the impact throwing him back upon the snow.

He could hear yells and screams about him as others sought to reach him, but it was too late.

The Witchking's sword began another fatal downstroke. Luxor watched in horrified fascination as the icy blade descended.

Morkin watched as the Ice Crown tumbled through the air, describing an arc across the water. About it the snow ceased its motion, the air thickening as if the Crown were trying to freeze the very wind. Morkin cried out and clamped his hands across his ears as a terrifying howl of pain split the air.

The Ice Crown itself shrieked and screamed as it dropped towards the water. Below, the surface of the lake bubbled and frothed. The Crown seemed to slow in mid-air and Morkin watched in horrified fascination as time crackled to an icy halt about him, snowflakes dancing lazily in the air.

It will never reach the lake! All this for nought …

Yet, in excruciating hesitation, it fell.

The Ice Crown touched the surface of the lake.

And shattered …

A great gust of steam exploded out of the surface, water blasting in all directions from the point of impact, as if some great source of heat had been released. Lightning crackled and thunder smashed, throwing Morkin back to lie upon the shoreline, the blast ripping at his clothing and hair.

For long moments he assumed it was the end, that death was upon him. The breath was torn from his lungs, and darkness swirled about him.

But the tumult ceased.

When he looked up, the waters had settled. The Ice Crown was no more. The steam evaporated away and there was nothing but a keening wail that faded away upon the wind.

'Master ...'

Morkin turned to see Fawkrin crawling towards him. Beyond, the Doomguard stood stock still, their weapons falling from their hands before, one by one, they collapsed and lay still upon the snow.

'Fawkrin?'

The skulkrin rolled over and Morkin could see a crossbow bolt embedded in his back, his tunic bloodstained. Morkin crawled forward and grasped his hand.

'Think well of us skulkrin kind boy, think well.'

Morkin blinked back tears. 'This cannot be ...'

'Sing songs of the part we played,' Fawkrin's voice cracked. 'No more shame for us.'

'You will be honoured amongst the mighty of Midnight,' Morkin managed. 'I promise ...'

Fawkrin smiled. 'You are a good boy, kind boy, strong squire. Lord Morkin someday, sure of it ... Khlee ...'

'Fawkrin ...'

'Farewell master.'

The skulkrin's body went limp. Morkin pulled it to him, sobbing into the matted hair, clutching the tiny form to him, shuddering and weeping.

A wrenching scream sounded in his ears, high-pitched and agonised. He looked up to see the Fey-girl of his visions falling to her knees before him, her arms outstretched, flames surrounding her.

'Victory goes to the Foul!'

Before he could even think to reach out her image was obscured by smoke and lost to his sight. Despair flooded his mind before the bliss of unconsciousness stole him away.

Luxor cringed as the terrifying sword of the Witchking loomed over him.

Yet the Witchking's blow did not fall.

The air was rent by an ear-splitting scream of pain and anguish. A cry so cold and desolate it cracked the ice underfoot. Spikes of ice erupted and shattered about the Witchking as he thrashed in some torment of his own, his body writhing this way and that, turning and grasping at the air.

The ice-fear writhed with him, washing across Luxor in waves of horror, pulsing and unsteady.

IT CANNOT BE! THE ICE CROWN …

Luxor watched, frozen to the spot, as the sword sagged. It was melting, as if some burning hot ray of bright sunshine had fallen upon it. It fell from the Witchking's grasp, turning to water and splashing across the snow. All about the Witchking's thrashing form the snow was melting, sinking inwards. Luxor scrambled backwards as a gout of steam burst upwards, consuming what was left of the Witchking's form.

The fury of the steam was short lived, evaporating into a fine mist that drifted upwards. Beyond, Luxor could see the hordes of the Foul were no longer attacking, but retreating away from the battle, swords dropping from their hands before they themselves collapsed full length upon the ground.

Luxor peered over the rim of a depression in the ground. Below, the ice had been carved away revealing dirt and soil some four or five feet down. Lying prone in the hollow lay a wizened figure, a man of great age, naked save for the cowled cloak. Impossibly thin almost transparent flesh coated a skeletal frame, eyes sunk in eye sockets, the merest trace of hair upon the head.

About her the flames crackled and died. Tarithel blinked, seeing smoke rising into the air. At the same moment the crashing noise from the gates of the citadel stopped. She propped herself up, feeling the rough stones beneath her palms. The stench of burning was in her nostrils; she coughed, trying to clear her lungs.

Ash was falling through the air. Beside her, Whispers was stirring. Guards were staggering back to their positions.

'The forest.'

She got to her feet and limped across the cobbled stones, peering over the edge of the Citadel's battlements down into the courtyards below.

The forest still smouldered, but the fires were already gone. In the ruin of the burnt and twisted branches lay the corpses of the Doomguard, all struck down in a moment.

Tarithel looked about her, bewildered.

Luxor watched for a moment. There was no movement. Others gathered around him. He looked aside into the fearful eyes of the remaining Lords of Midnight.

'What happened?' Shimeril rasped.

'Give me a sword,' Luxor replied. Shimeril handed his weapon and Luxor made his way down into the hollow, the sword poised before him.

The ground was slippery underfoot, but it took him only moments to make the descent. He stood over the wretched body of his foe. He lowered the sword.

Nothing moved. Luxor stepped closer. The silence was palpable. After the noise and tumult of the battle it was as if the world held its breath …

The figure convulsed, reaching out towards Luxor with a sudden move, arms outstretched, the skull like face twisted in hatred.

AVENGE ME, SHARETH! AVENGE ME!

Luxor swung the sword he held, a decisive blow straight through the midriff. The figure collapsed, shattering into a tangled heap of broken bones which crackled and broke into dust as he watched leaving only the black cloak as scant final evidence of an ancient evil.

And upon his finger, the Moon Ring cooled, its fires and potency waning as they were no longer needed.

Chapter Twenty

She stands in the fortress of Kahangrorn, looking south.

The Fortress echoed to her screams, an unearthly howling interspersed with an animal-like screech of fury. The very rocks that formed the foundations rang and shook with her passing. Stone flew before her as her elegant fingers clawed and ripped at the walls surrounding her.

Before her a guard stood, rooted to the spot in fear and awe. As he watched she spun around, her tormented gaze falling upon him.

'Such tidings! How dare he? How dare he usurp me!'

Before he could think to move aside, the guard found her fingers at his throat. He was hoist bodily into the air, desperately struggling him to free himself.

Yet, to be the bearer of ill tidings before the Heartstealer ...

Her fingers, now claw like and possessed of some fell strength beyond the limits of humanity crushed his neck, her other hand swept across his torso. Blood flew as she ripped his body to shreds with her bare hands, luxuriating in the strangled screams that, all too briefly, emerged as his flesh flew.

Moments later, careless of the blood and gore, she threw his body aside, her bloodstained dark robes somehow cleansing themselves as she strode forward, her eyes glittering with hatred and thoughts of revenge.

'I will bathe in his blood! I will feast on his very flesh!'

The heavy oak doors of the hall flew back with an echoing clang as she gestured to them, crashing back on their hinges and ringing with the impact. Her form moved through the darkened fortress faster than any could see, a darkness, almost without shape until she came to a halt on the battlements.

There, on the southern walls of the Fortress of Kahangrorn, Shareth shrieked her hatred and summoned to her all the shattered remnants of the power her father had commanded. Cloud and wind shrieked about her as she gathered her inheritance to her.

Below vast armies stood ready at her beck and call. There would be time enough for their application in the days and moons to come. For now a greater wrath consumed her.

She trembled with apoplexy.

Luxor has slain my father, freed the lands of Midnight from his grasp. His death was to be mine!

Shareth had long watched the arts of the Witchking from afar. The offspring of his brief union with a cold queen of the Icemark, Shareth possessed the body and mind of a beautiful temptress, but was imbued with a heart and soul of ice, colder, if possible, than her own father's frozen corpse. The Witchking had tutored her in his Foul ways, and tutored her too well.

He had loved her, but she had no feelings in return.

No grief. Shareth did not feel such things. Her heart channelled only anger, rage and fury.

Luxor has stolen my right to subdue Midnight, taking it from my father as I had long planned. Very well, moon-princeling! Steal from me and face my wrath …

She had heard the Witchking's dying words, if death was the right word for his end. A cry cold and penetrating, that shocked northwards through the Frozen Wastes, across the Kingdom of the Giants and onwards to the Frozen Empire in which her fortress lay.

AVENGE ME, SHARETH, AVENGE ME!

My wrath will be my own, but it will be no less terrible!

The battlements of Kahangrorn darkened as the storm clouds gathered, summoned from the ice-barriers of the North by Shareth's incantations. Lightning crackled and thunder rolled as she raised her arms to focus her powers on the subject of her thoughts.

She cried into the wind, uttering words no man could understand. The storm leapt and swirled as her strident voice pierced the air. Across the Frozen Empire, from Fangrorn to Imiriel, the tortured sky erupted into boiling turmoil. Ferocious storms, twisting billows of cloud and angry squalls focussed their fury at her beck and call.

It took but a single gesture. Shareth had learnt her father's fell arts well.

She stretched out her arm and pointed south.

A violent wind arose and the clouds moved, mightier than any army of Free, Fey, Dwarf or Giant, it flung itself across the sky, rolling and boiling, lashing down with snow, sleet and rain, pounding all before it in a howling gale.

Trees fell, boulders were strewn and even the mountainsides cracked before the fury as the maelstrom moved away, leaving storm damaged wreckage in its wake.

Night fell swiftly upon the Icemark, far to the north east of Midnight. Within the great city of Varangrim, the giants of that realm gathered and watched as the storm broke across them. Likewise from Carudrium to Carorthay, the Dwarves redoubled the watch upon their lands, fearing trouble from Shareth's own loyal Iceguard.

To the south of the Icemark, the great forests of the Fey bent under the onslaught. In the city of Imorthorn, the Fey of Icemark met in council to discuss the import of the great tumult in the sky. Some claimed the dwarves had betrayed them to the Heartstealer, others counselled patience and observation, reasoning that even if that were so, it would be better to fight the Iceguard in the midst of the forests rather than march forth upon the open plains.

Lord Imorthorn though, was wiser still.

'You will have heard by now, surely my Lords, rumours of the war that has been raging in the lost land of Midnight, far to the south west of Icemark. If it be true, a revealed Moonprince has won victory over the Heartstealer's very own father, the Witchking. His name? Luxor.'

The Lords hung on his words, waiting for further revelations, muttering together in consternation.

Imorthorn continued. 'Rumours of secret traffic between the Heartstealer and the Witchking have often come to our ears. She supplied armies to him on many occasions. On the eve of the Solstice mere moons ago, did we not waylay a band of dark and foul warriors riding north from the Gate of Varenorn? I know it is many, many moons since any of our number have dared its terrors, but that is the only passage we know of that still leads to Midnight.'

Muted mumbles of agreement greeted this statement and a few of the old Fey Lords nodded vigorously.

'I am sure,' Imorthorn said, raising his voice. 'The Heartstealer sends the storm not against us, but against this Luxor, this legendary Moonprince of Midnight. Even now, the storm turns south west!'

The assembled council could attest to his words. The dark, flying clouds were indeed headed in that direction. They argued back and forth about what to do about the matter. At length, they agreed that their brothers in the land of Midnight, the Fey of the Forest of Dreams and other realms long sundered from them, must be warned of the peril of the Heartstealer. They too should make ready for war, for there was no doubt that Shareth's plans would threaten their own safety too. If she desired to attack Midnight, her passage across the Icemark would not be peaceable.

It began in the south, but slowly proceeded northwards. All about the ice was fading, everywhere was the sound of melt water. The ground, frozen so hard for so long was becoming sodden under foot. Rivers, locked solid for longer than most could remember, began to move and then to surge. Ice cracked across their surfaces, until, with a grumbling roar, it broke away, the might of the water sweeping it asunder.

The Foul were cast down where they had stood, dying on their feet, as if their lifeforce had been wrenched away in an instant of time. Their bodies were pulled high in pyres that were set ablaze across Midnight wherever they might be found, blazing long into the night.

Throughout the land the mountains echoed to sudden avalanches as Midnight shook itself free from the deadlock grip of the ice. Each day the ice retreated further, the greenery of the forest realms shone forth. Each morning and evening the realm was bathed in mists that silently swirled like wraiths searching for some long lost purpose.

In the Citadels and Keeps, the villages and dwellings, those that had survived the ravages of war looked out as their land began the long months of healing that lay before it, hardly daring to believe that the fearsome power of the Witchking had been broken. All looked in amazement as first plants sprung forth in the warming spring sunlight, and then insects and animals, most only stories out of the ancient past, began to roam the softening plains where once only a desolate icescape had been.

Even on the edges of the realm, at least to the east, west

and south, the utter barrier of the Frozen Wastes themselves was softening. Mist plumed upwards in great clouds of thick gloom, but even these could not stand against the ever brightening might of the sun. Each day their razor sharp edges were dulled still further until with a great tumult of noise and shattering ice, they too began to fall in ruin and were thus consumed by the landscape beneath. To the north, some vestige of the fell magic seemed to keep the icy wastes intact.

Rain fell, the sun blazed brighter every day and rainbows split the sky, bringing gasps of wonder from all who saw them. Spring was in the air in every way, pointing to a summer of plenty that none had ever known before. Historians were in much demand everywhere, as the lost arts of farming and husbandry were called upon for the first time in living memory. A generation would have to refamiliarise themselves with these forgotten skills. Folks felt the sun upon their faces and for the first time thought of more than just raw survival, that they might prosper and even increase their lot.

Laughter and song followed, borne upon whispers and tidings. Hearts were gladdened that had too long been hardened by despair. In its wake, many of the warriors of the Free and the Fey made their weary way home; some to Keeps and Citadels ravaged by the war, others to forests and homesteads. Each was welcomed as hero or heroine by the places they stopped at upon their journeys, yet all longed for the welcome of their own hearth fires and the glad faces of their kin. Some returns were bittersweet, for the ravages of the Witchking's hordes had been many and brutal.

Of Luxor's victorious army, less than half of those who marched forth from Xajorkith with brittle hope kindled in their hearts had survived that final overwhelming struggle against the ice and fear. Luxor knew grief enough. Those that had died fighting under his banner. He brought all their faces to mind. He tried to imprint their visages in his thoughts so that they would never be forgotten. Dawn who had died to defend his own people, facing down the terrifying Utarg. Shadows of the Fey, proving after all the false starts that the Fey would always stand with the Free when the time required it.

And the Lady of Silence, a brave soul who had never retreated from any conflict, and might have saved them in their first adversity after the Plains of Blood. Gard, once so dismissive, had arranged for the few shards of her body to be given full honours, to be entombed in the halls of the mighty in the catacombs of Gard, an honour none had received in several generations of his people. Of her people only a few remained, but Gard had already arranged for her articles of incorporation to be published in the western realms. The stewardship of Silence would pass to another, once a line of succession was established.

Others still. Herath, fallen in the warning of Kumar and Marakith. Brith, Mitharg and Rorath in the defence of Blood. Trorn in the defence of Xajorkith and Korinel, first to fall.

The army turned south west and plunged into the Forest of Dreams. No signposts marked their way but the Fey, gathering out of the gloom of the trees bearing lanterns and firesticks, lit a deep road into the darkening forest to their hidden capital, the fabled Citadel of Dreams.

The victorious army made camp beneath its shimmering walls, wreathed with the pulsing life of the forest itself. The great city was in turmoil as it set about to prepare for a vast feast of celebration, unprecedented even in its long history. Children ran here and there, festooning the halls, walkways, houses, avenues and newly planted flowerbeds with garlands and ribbons.

And there at last, the Lords of Free and Fey were fully reconciled. Tributes were given, speeches made and promises forged.

The horse bore Morkin onwards, lost, confused and bereft. He knew little of his whereabouts, only that the slimmest possibility of salvation lay to the east. He could not even recall how he had come across the horse, only that it had come to his salvation, somewhere, somehow. He vaguely recalled crossing a vast plain, littered with the detritus of battle. A forest had appeared and he had staggered into its eaves. The boughs closed about him, shielding him from the cold and ice, but they could do little for the horror and the evil that still pervaded his mind.

Moonlight struck down through the trees, coldly lighting his face with its cold brilliance. His eyes were as a cold as death, his mouth a thin scar on a face of stone.

Death had stalked him all the way. Of Free and Fey, his friends willingly giving their lives so that he might complete his mission. Farflame, Fawkrin, Lothoril and Balor, Lord of Gloom. All gone now, all sacrificed to end an evil so potent that its undoing shook the very earth upon which he stood. His mind was just a wilderness now, bleaker than the Plains of Despair across which he had ridden. His soul frozen by the horror and the desolation. Only some distant part of his will kept going, his horse plodding onwards, keeping him moving.

He had destroyed it, what else now? Was it a cold and unhappy victory? Were any left alive to benefit, or was Midnight now bereft of life, all slaughtered in the final struggle to resist the Witchking?

Fawkrin died in my arms ... Farflame ... what became of Farflame? He was gone when I walked back ...

A whisper reached his ears. He stopped, thinking that a final madness was now overtaking him. The trees themselves seemed to be bending close in the twilight. The sun had set and stars were springing into a clear cloudless sky, something he had not seen for days. He looked up in wonder as those distant lights twinkled above him, cold and stark, yet somehow comforting in their familiarity.

Just a little further …

It must have been his imagination; a sweet voice in his head, almost singing, its tone a caress and a salve upon his tortured thoughts and feelings.

The horse walked into a glade, somehow lit by a brighter green than the forest that bordered it. The horse whinnied and came to a halt, its breath floating up in a faint mist about it. It stepped aside, unsure which way to go. Morkin raised his head, seeing only a green blur about him. He blinked and the world swam into focus. Green towers of tall plants, draped in dew drops, glistening in a wholesome glow that was not moonlight or starlight, but something else entirely.

A figure stood on the opposite side of the glade, small and wraithlike, draped in a long gown of grey. From its neck hung a jewel, also glowing green, so bright that it might be the source of the illumination in the glade. He stared, unable to comprehend.

The figure raised its hand and Morkin heard snatches of a wordless song, swift of rhythm yet slow at heart. It spoke of days in the sun, of summer, the bright water of a fresh stream and the bracing wind on a warm spring day. His horse cantered towards the figure as if greeting an old friend, nuzzling into its cloak. Morkin had no time to even think to stop it. If the figure meant him harm it was already too late.

He blinked.

The figure dropped its cowl. Morkin gasped.

Before him stood a girl, a young woman of such perfect beauty he could do nothing but stare, captivated, into her deep green eyes. Such a depth of compassion lay there, and such longing and love shone back from her face that he could do nothing but hold her gaze, lost in rapture and fierce tenderness.

'You …' he managed to utter.

She reached out, placing a finger upon his lips.

'I know you …'

She smiled and he saw images of times before. Her, standing on a the walls of a citadel, looking out into the gloom, her again, locked in a tower room battering at the doors, and once more, standing in the snow, tears glistening on her cheeks. Dreams flowed into him and he knew.

I have watched you for a long time. Now you are here.

'Where is here?' Morkin asked.

'I bid you welcome,' she said. 'To the Forest of Dreams.'

'Dreams!' Morkin said. 'Fortune has been kind to me then. I thought never to travel so far.'

The girl turned and pointed. 'Yonder is the citadel of my people. You must come, there is food and shelter. The celebration has already begun …'

'Celebration?' Morkin said, his muscles stiffening and his body trembling. 'How can they?'

The girl paused and looked up at him.

'How can they do what?' she asked.

'How can they rejoice in such despair?'

The girl frowned. 'We play host to the victorious armies of Midnight. This is Imlath Quiriniel, stronghold of the Fey. Within our walls lie the armies of Luxor the Moonprince, bearer of the Moon Ring, the War Ring of the House of the Moon. They have journeyed here from the gates of Ushgarak itself. Surely you know? The Witchking is defeated, slain by the sword of Moonprince Luxor himself!'

Morkin was thunderstruck. His grip on the reins of his horse slackened and he felt himself slip from the saddle, the world about him spinning in confusion. He felt arms about him. The girl had caught him and borne him safely to the ground. He lay on his back, looking up at her beauty, seeing her face contract in a worried frown.

'Sir, what ails you?'

Her voice was high with worry. He felt her pull him close, wrapping her arms about him and hugging him tightly. The comfort melted something in his heart, tears erupted into uncontrolled sobs that racked his body. He heard her gentle questions and words of solace, but he could not speak.

Only after long minutes did the touch of her hand upon his register in his mind. His sobbing ebbed away.

'I thought he was dead,' he said. 'I thought the war was lost and Midnight ruined. I thought this was the Witchking's final victory, after all our woes.'

'The Witchking is defeated ...'

'Defeated? But I heard you cry out that victory had gone to the Foul! I thought I'd found it and destroyed it all in vain. Too late to help, too late for anything.'

'Destroyed it?' the girl asked. 'Destroyed what? You talk in riddles ...'

Morkin shivered, the horror still echoing in his mind. 'When I cast it into the lake, it shrieked and screamed as if a thousand souls burnt in an everlasting fire. It dropped into the water, even the air about it seemed to thicken, as though the thing was trying to save itself by freezing the very wind. It fell so slowly, like a knife dropped in syrup. I despaired it might never complete its fall. But then, it touched the water and broke apart, shattering into uncounted fragments that boiled away in a tumult of steam and spray.'

He jolted in her arms.

'It was gone. Gone forever. And yet, I heard his voice, mocking me. Telling me it was too late, that Luxor was slain, Xajorkith and the cities of the Free were all aflame and the forests of the Fey hewn into ruin.'

His eyes glazed over and he shivered.

'What did you destroy?' she insisted, her voice clear and sharp.

Her question caught him off guard.

'Why, the Ice Crown of course.'

She didn't respond for a long moment, but then her arms tightened further about him and he felt her head come down, her warm breath on his neck, nuzzling in close. She too was trembling, but not from fear or dread.

She was laughing.

Her humour was intoxicating, lifting his spirits and raising joy in his heart. He sat up and looked at her.

'Why, the Ice Crown of course,' she mimicked, gasping from her mirth. 'Such a sweet answer. A mere bauble, a trifle, a deed of no more consequence than casting away an old cloak …'

She pulled back in sudden realisation.

'That was the quest of which Rorthron spoke! It is you who have saved us!' Tears welled up in her eyes. 'You saved the forest, you saved me. The Doomguard were poised to slay us all … You are Morkin! Morkin, son of the Moonprince himself! The half-Fey.'

'Yes, I am Morkin,' he said. 'But your name I know not.'

She smiled. 'You know me already in your heart. We have been together these long moons. But my name?'

He nodded. 'I would know it, as I know you!'

'I am Tarithel, the daughter of the Lord of Dreams, Lady of the Forest.'

Shareth had returned to her private sanctuary, a room set high in the central Tower of her fortress, her fury spent for now. Few had seen the inside and none had lived to tell the tale. It was told that men she took a fancy to were invited within, but none had ever emerged, not even their bodies.

No ceilings or walls, yet the room had a strange substance to it. Everywhere was mirrored, leaving her abode a shifting collection of images all focussed on her. It was how she saw herself, and how she intended the world to see her.

She lay, lithe and voluptuous, upon the silken sheets of the bed that lay in the very centre of her boudoir. Men would see her as she wished when the mood took her. A young and heartstoppingly beautiful young woman, mature in her desires and lusts, ready and willing to share the delights her body advertised with little concealment.

Her cheeks were flushed, her sculpted face a perfect and irresistible glory. The strongest wills crumpled at the sight of her when she wished it. No man had ever been able to turn her down. Her curves strained enticingly against the satin of her gown.

'I am so beautiful.' She smiled, appraising herself in the mirror above. 'The whole world will love me, or they will perish ...'

She laughed at her own conceit, knowing it to be true nonetheless.

Her father had loved only one thing. Shareth followed his example faithfully. As he had loved her, she loved herself too. She fell asleep each night marvelling in her own perfection and beauty, waking each morning more irresistible than ever.

She cast her thoughts out in the lee of the storm, reaching with her vision as her father had taught her. Seeking knowledge of the adversary that had stolen away her inheritance.

In her mind's eye she could see the lofty spires of a great Citadel. Her father had spoken of the cursed Fey often enough for her to know it as the Citadel of Dreams. She looked closer, seeing Fey and Free dancing in the clearings and the court-yards as snow and ice melted from the trees about them. The sun was bright and strong, the green of spring already sprouting about them.

She spied the hated Moonprince himself, standing shoulder to shoulder with the Lords of Free and Fey, drinking in celebration at her father's demise. Rage took her again and her screams of fury rang out once more.

How long he gazed into her eyes he could not recall. For minutes or hours, perhaps days or years he found himself lost in the tranquillity of her gaze. The longer he tarried, the more the ice in his soul retreated. He felt warmth swell in his heart as dawn broke about them.

Somehow he had known her, known her for far longer than he could recall. She had been with him from the very start, looking after him, watching over him. She had always been there; how he did not know, but every curve of her face, the line of her cheeks and the colour of her hair – he knew them as if he'd always known them.

'How can this ...?'

She touched a finger to his lips, silencing him.

Her eyes ... Tarithel ...

Golden light cascaded about him, the forest seemed aglow with the light and warmth of summer, but for him there was nothing but the gaze of the green eyes before him. Green like the vanished spring of yore, green like the warmest glade of the forgotten summer; enveloping him and caressing him.

Feelings and experiences flowed between them, absent of the tawdry necessity of words, faster flowing and more meaningful than any conversation could describe. Morkin knew not how it took place, only that it did and his heart sang with the realisation that his desire for the young woman before him was matched by her own feelings for him.

Around them the forest burst into bud, heralding a spring too long denied to the land of Midnight. New life, new possibilities and new chances.

He blinked, a measure of awareness of his surroundings coming back to him.

The question was upon his lips, but he dared not utter it.

She smiled and nodded.

It was enough.

'Your father awaits you,' she said. 'We should tarry no longer.'

Tarithel led him to her horse and they mounted it together, Morkin at the fore. Morkin's own horse plodded wearily behind. They rode out through the Gate of Dreams towards the pavilions of Luxor and his Lords. The crowds of soldiers and townsfolk parted, with a flurry of whispers and questions, and closed in again behind them, staring in wonderment. But when they dismounted at the doorway of Luxor's pavilion, Morkin found the way barred by a sentry.

'You cannot pass. Lord Luxor is in council and will not be disturbed by commoners.'

Morkin looked down at himself. His clothing was torn, muddied and stained. His face unshaven and encrusted with dirt. A laugh, the first in many moons, crackled up his throat and shook his body.

Tarithel faced the sentry.

'I fear Lord Luxor will be very disturbed indeed,' she said, 'if you bar the way to his son, good soldier. Pray let us pass.'

'My Lady ...' the sentry said. 'I did not see you, but ...'

'This is Morkin, son and squire of Lord Luxor,' she said. 'Make way!'

The sentry snapped back. Tarithel led him into the pavilion.

The whole assembly turned as they entered. Conversation dropped and the Moonprince leapt to his feet at the unasked for intrusion. At first he looked puzzled, not expecting to see such slight and slender figures approach.

'Who is this you bring before me?' Luxor demanded.

Morkin had his head lowered, but raised it upon hearing his father's voice.

A cup of wine crashed down from Luxor's grasp.

'Morkin?' he gasped, his voice barely above a whisper. 'You live? I thought you surely slain! The Moon Ring's vision no longer strives ...'

'He lives,' Tarithel exclaimed, her eyes shining in the dim light. 'And he has done all that was demanded of him ...'

Luxor stared for a moment, unable to take in the revelation. Then he recovered.

'Rise! Rise all of you!' he shouted. 'My son has returned!'

Shining with pride, Luxor cast aside his chair at the high table and rushed to greet the boy as he climbed the steps to the dais, hand-in-hand with Tarithel. He stared into Morkin's face for long minutes, seeing the weariness, pain and suffering etched upon his visage. Then he pulled him close, unashamed tears of joy streaking his face.

'Morkin, my son.'

'Father ...'

Luxor stood back and gazed upon him once more. 'But you are exhausted! The Ice Crown ...'

'Destroyed,' Morkin said, unable to conceal a shudder. 'Gone and finished ...'

Luxor nodded. 'I felt it die, its fell power evaporating like mist in spring sunshine. Sore relief to me it was! I knew at that moment you had succeeded. But to see you again ...'

Words failed him for a moment and he clenched his jaw before recovering his composure.

'Then all of Midnight owes you a great debt,' Luxor said, raising his voice. 'Let it be known here and now. My son, Morkin, is the true saviour of Midnight. By his hand was the

Ice Crown destroyed, gifting us the chance to slay the Witchking …'

Morkin shook his head. 'But it is you that have won the great victory …'

But his words were lost in the hubbub. At Luxor's proclamation there was a murmur of approval from the gathered Lords. Luxor turned to them and raised Morkin's arm up high.

'This is the boy who saved us at Ushgarak, who, as we fought our bloody way through hordes of Foul creatures to the gates of the Witchking's palace and felt his cold breath clawing at our strength and our courage, smashed the heart of his dread power and lifted the burden of the Ice Crown's terror from us! Salute him, my Lords. Though mine was the sword which plunged into the foul one's heart, this is truly the hand that slew him!'

The assembled warriors lifted their swords high into the air and cheered loud and long.

Not alone. Fawkrin, Farflame, Lothoril and Gloom too, Free, Fey, Wise, dragonkind and skulkrin …

Morkin tried to tug his hand down, but Luxor kept a firm grip until the applause had dwindled. Then the Moonprince turned back to the boy.

'My son, I would thank thee for simply being still alive, but now we all have cause to give you our thanks. If there is a gift that lies in my power to grant, name it and it shall be yours.'

'Father, I played my part … but to my shame it was disobedience to you that led me there …'

'And I was wrong,' Luxor replied. 'Wrong to have doubted your fortitude and wrong to have been blind to your potential.'

'Yet it was you who slew the Witchking, these worthy Lords aided you in breaking the gates of Ushgarak, your skill and vigour brought evil to its knees,' Morkin said.

'Your part was as much,' Luxor insisted. 'More! Do you imagine we could have succeeded without you? I speak not now as your father, Morkin, but as Moonprince of Midnight; name your wish. The Lords of Midnight will not countenance your refusal. Make your request!'

Around him the Lords were nodding, Free and Fey alike.

Morkin swallowed, feeling Tarithel's grip upon his hand tighten.

'I fear it is not yours to grant, my Lord,' he said.

'How so?' asked Luxor. 'Come now! Tell me your desire!'

Morkin looked away and then back again, made to speak and then coughed before being able to say the words that scrambled out of him.

'The hand, tomorrow, of this fair maiden who stands beside me: Tarithel, Lady of the Forest of Dreams.'

A gasp from the assembled crowd. Before him, Luxor blinked in surprise. Alongside him, Corleth stifled a laugh.

'That is my wish, Father,' Morkin replied, breaking the sudden silence.

'I ...' Luxor began.

Amongst the assembled Lords, there were more than a few swiftly stifled guffaws and the company was suddenly beset by an outbreak of coughing and clearing of throats. Luxor stayed impassive, as if he had not heard the words his son had uttered. Then Morkin turned to Tarithel and Tarithel turned to him. The smiles that passed between them left no doubt as to the candour of the boy's resolve.

The Lord of Dreams got to his feet and stood beside the Moonprince.

'Shall I come to your aid?' Dreams said, with a faint chuckle. 'It seems you need my help in battle once more ...'

Luxor looked at him. 'I would indeed value your counsel, my Lord!'

Dreams looked across to Morkin and Tarithel.

'My Lord Moonprince,' he began, 'This is my only daughter who stands before you. Her hand is not yours to give, but I fear it is not mine either. Once she has set her heart upon a course of action there is little her father might do or say to change its course.'

'Then we are at an impasse!' Luxor said.

'Indeed,' Dreams replied. 'I can only suggest we ask her if this be her wish also … trust my words, the Lady of the Forest knows her own mind …'

Luxor smiled.

'Then Tarithel, Lady of the Forest,' Luxor said. 'Would you give your hand to my son as he requests?'

'I would!' Tarithel cried.

'Then let this be a token then,' said the Lord of Dreams. 'That the Fey and the Free are now as one under the protection of the House of the Moon. My consent, if it means anything, is given!'

With that, the Lord of Dreams sat down again. There was turmoil, then, amongst the gathered company. Loud cheers and congratulations filled the long pavilion. The Moonprince smiled and waited till the tumult died away.

'Your wish seems granted! A fairer daughter I could not hope for. Yet you are both so young. Think upon it, both of you, before you tie a knot that all of time cannot undo.'

His words were hardly from his mouth before they both answered, almost in unison, 'We have, my Lord!'

The Moonprince turned to his council and laughed, as if in appeal to them.

'What can I do, my Lords? I have given my word,' he said. Then turning back to face Morkin and Tarithel, 'So it shall be. On the morrow you shall wed. All that remains now is to celebrate this happy, unlooked-for moment. Come, sit with me, and we will talk of the things that have passed before the new feast begins – a feast this night of love, not war!'

'Well said, my Lord Luxor!' Corleth said, raising a toast.

Many tales were told that day, many battles retold, each growing more legendary in the telling. Luxor's high council, summoned to decide the fate of Doomdark's old dominions, put aside its purpose and fell to reminiscing. The mead flowed, brave deeds grew braver, terrors waxed more terrible yet and the day drew slowly on. Morkin, exhausted though he was, had taken a bath and returned, clean and dressed the part, but those about could tell he only had eyes for Tarithel.

Epilogue

They stand in the Citadel of Dreams,
looking north to the Forest of Dreams.

Hours passed. Twilight fell upon the grounds. The lights of candles illuminated the grand arches of the pavilion. As the company was thinking of retiring there came a fluttering of wings.

A white falcon flew in through the open doorway of the pavilion, circled thrice above the high table, then came to rest on the shoulder of the Lord of Dreams. As the company stared in amazement at the bird, Tarithel reached a gentle hand towards it and nimbly untied its jesses. Then, at a soft word from her, it took flight again and disappeared beyond.

'It is a message …' she exclaimed, unwrapping a leather thong and presenting it to her father.

He took it, puzzling over the seal for a moment, then broke it apart to unravel the parchment.

The ancient Fey runes he found there surprised him; his skill in them had not been lost but it was many moons since he had needed to use it. He read the message slowly and carefully before turning to Luxor. His expression was a mixture of astonishment and concern.

'My Lord Moonprince,' he began. 'This message hails from lands beyond our ken, from the distant lands of the Icemark, far to the north east.'

The end

*The Chronicles of Midnight continue in book 2,
'Doomdark's Revenge'.*

About the Author

Drew Wagar is a science fiction and fantasy author. He lives in Kent with his wife, two sons, one girlfriend (not his) a dog and a cat. His favourite colour is dark green. He drives a small convertible car which occasionally works. He doesn't require a conservatory or any double glazing.

You can reach Drew as follows:

Drew's Website: http://www.drewwagar.com
Facebook: http://www.facebook.com/drewwagarwriter
Twitter: http://www.twitter.com/drewwagar

If you have enjoyed this book, please consider leaving a review for Drew to let him know what you thought of his work.

You can find out more about Drew on his author page on the Fantastic Books Store. While you're there, why not browse our delightful tales and wonderfully woven prose?

www.fantasticbooksstore.com